The First Genesis

Kipjo K. Ewers

EvoUNIVERSE

Copyright © 2018 by Kipjo K. Ewers
THIS IS A EVO UNIVERSE BOOK

PUBLISHED BY EVO UNIVERSE, L.L.C.

All rights reserved under International and Pan-American Copyright Conventions. Published in the United States by EVO. Universe, L.L.C., New Jersey, and distributed by EVO. Universe, L.L.C., New Jersey.
www.evouniverse.com
All rights reserved.

ASIN: B09KN65YH6
ISBN- 979-8495247550
Copyright © 2018 Kipjo K. Ewers
All rights reserved.

Genesis

Genesis
Copyright © 2018 by EVO Universe

All rights reserved. All rights reserved under International and Pan-American Copyright Conventions. Published in the United States by EVO Universe, LLC, New Jersey, and distributed by EVO Universe, LLC, New Jersey. No part of this book may be reproduced or transmitted in any form or by any means without written permission from the author.

ASIN: B09KN65YH6

Printed in the USA by EVO Universe
Email: info@evouniverse.com
On-Line Chat: go to our website, www.evouniverse.com.

Genesis

Dedication

I would like to thank everyone who has been a fan and supported the EVO Universe over these past years. As a fan of this beautiful genre myself, I know it would not be possible without all of you.

So, from the bottom of my heart to everyone around the globe who has taken the time to pick up one of my books. Thank you.

Genesis
OTHER WORKS

THE FIRST: (THE FIRST SERIES BOOK 1)

EVO UPRISING: (THE FIRST SERIES BOOK 2)

EYE OF RA

FRED & MARY

"HELP! I'M A SUPERHERO!": BOOK ONE

THE ELF AND THE LARP: BOOK ONE

WAR OF MORTAL GODS: BOOK ONE

Genesis

Foreword

There is none …sit back and enjoy the story!

Genesis
PROLOGUE

April 4, 1945. Ohrdruf concentration camp, located south of Gotha, in Thuringia, Germany. Part of the Buchenwald concentration camp network and the first Nazi concentration camp.

It was the first camp liberated by the United States 4th Armored Division and the 89th Infantry Division.

On that day, good men, sons, brothers, and fathers who traveled halfway around the world to join the fight against a tyrannical dictator and his murderous regime happened upon sights that would haunt them until their final days.

Brave soldiers lost their lunch upon seeing the stacked piles of bodies, some covered with lime, others partially incinerated on pyres.

Standing amid the gruesome and deplorable scene, First Sergeant Bradley Jackson forced his eyes to be forever stained. On one side of the camp, emancipated prisoners in their own filth, more dead than alive, were treated by military medics. On the other side were their captors sitting on their rears in the dirt with their hands behind their heads, nervously wondering their fate. He wanted the image burnt into his skull so that if he returned to the States, Jackson could tell the world what he saw to ensure this would never happen again.

As he contemplated dragging out a couple of high-ranking camp commanders, shoving them face down in the dirt, and placing several rounds from his sidearm into the back of their skull, a Private First Class trotted over to him with an unnerved countenance.

"First Sergeant, sir," he swallowed. "I think you need to come with me. We found something that you need to see to believe."

"Peterson, whatever you found can't be more fucked up than what I've already seen," returned the irritated First Sergeant. "Suck it up, and get Private …"

"Sir," Peterson nervously cut him off, whispering. "We found a

Genesis

secret facility under this camp. You really need to come with me and see this."

~~~~~~~~~~~~~~~~~~~~~~~~~~~~~~~~~~

First Sergeant Jackson followed Private First Class Peterson to something resembling a fallout bunker entrance. Its location was way off from the actual camp itself. A detail of four soldiers stood guard. Lying dead on the ground were three Nazi soldiers, one Obersturmbannführer, which stood for "SS-Senior storm unit leader," and what appeared to be two scientists in white lab coats.

"What the hell happened here?" scowled the First Sergeant.

"We caught the sons of bitches while they were coming out," explained Peterson. "The two in white coats were carrying those two cases over there. Looks like they were trying to run with whatever they could escape with. Corporal Higgins is down there. I got to warn you, First Sergeant … downstairs is like you've descended into the sixth level of hell."

First Sergeant Jackson nodded as he descended the steps of the bunker into the unknown. Halfway down, he stopped and shuddered. He turned and hocked a spit to prevent puking from the foul odor that invaded his nostrils.

Overcoming the horrid scent, he continued down the steps and reached the bottom, where he continued down a narrow hallway. The smell grew more pungent as he walked through two steel swinging doors into a room that appeared out of the pages of a mad scientist horror comic book.

He covered his mouth, finding trouble keeping down the rations he had eaten early that morning as he was smacked and choked by the strangling odor of death, human waste, and other putrid scents. Around him were bodies in cages and on examination tables. Some appeared to have died from whatever inhuman experimentations they were subjected to, while others were clearly shot, so they could never tell the tale of the horrors they had to endure. He shook his head in disbelief, and for the first time in his life, he questioned the rationale of a God he had prayed to since

Genesis

he was a child in Sunday school for making a race that could do such nightmarish things to one another.

"Jesus, Mary, and Joseph," he uttered.

"That's not who's down here, sir," answered a voice to his left.

Jackson kept his rock-solid visage even though Corporal Higgins's voice scared him out of his skin. He turned and faced the Corporal and Chief Medical Doctor, who had the glasses and face of the typical poindexter he used to pants in grade school atop a six-foot-one linebacker's frame that demanded respect.

What disturbed him even more was the euphoric smile plastered all over his face. In his mind, it was highly inappropriate, given their surroundings.

"What the hell is this, Higgins?" Jackson demanded to know. "Some type of experimentation in germ warfare?

"No, sir," Higgins looked around with a near-dazed look. "I believe what we're standing in is the Third Reich's attempt to push the boundaries of human evolution, and they almost cracked the seal."

"I'm not an egghead, Higgins," snapped the First Sergeant.

"Neither am I, sir," respectfully answered Higgins.

He opened a thin black leather ledger with the Nazi emblem in gold on the front that Jackson was unaware he was holding.

"From what I can tell from my subpar German," Higgins explained. "This is the Nazis' superhuman program."

"You're pulling my short and curlies, right?" The First Sergeant asked in disbelief.

"Not in a million years, sir," responded the Corporal. "We're going to need someone with a more advanced degree than me to decipher this, but

Genesis

from what I can make out, they found a way to introduce a type of virus that, if the subject survived the effects of the infection, would change them from the inside out. Make them stronger, faster, more durable, and able to heal quicker. Probably even improve their mental capabilities."

He quickly glanced around the room before meeting the eyes of the baffled First Sergeant again.

"As you can see, there were a lot of failed tries," he gulped.

"Where the hell did they get such a thing?" The First Sergeant furrowed his brows. "They just cook it up?"

"No, sir," Higgins nervously shook his head. "They got it from Egypt."

"Egypt?" Jackson screwed up his face.

The Corporal turned and walked away, knowing the First Sergeant would follow him. They walked further into the lab, passing more corpses on slabs or in cages that had endured more horrific ordeals. Finally, they reached two more steel doors and entered a near-sterile room colder than the first. It was a miniature lab purposely kept sanitary for its current residents. The First Sergeant's eyes appeared briefly as if they would pop from their sockets as they gazed upon what Higgins wanted him to see.

Against the lab's wall stood a giant glass cylinder tank on a metallic base with instruments around it that ran the floor's length to the ceiling. A naked young woman with long raven hair was floating inside the tank with wires attached to different body parts in a solution that clearly was not water. Her features, from what he could make out, were either Middle Eastern or African, while her blank expression and near-emaciated physique told Jackson that she was deceased, or he at least hoped it did.

"Apparently, the rumors of Hitler dabbling into the occult and supernatural were true," sighed Higgins.

"Higgins, remind yourself that I only finished high school and make some damn sense," snapped Jackson. "Who the hell is she?

Genesis

"She is an over two-thousand-year-old Egyptian woman," answered the Corporal. "Maybe even older."

"Ain't she supposed to be more shriveled up than that?" A perplexed Jackson pointed, raising an eyebrow.

"You are correct on that, sir," Higgins nodded. "What I'm going to tell you next is going to sound insane, but apparently, the Nazis sent an expedition to Egypt. They were looking for the supposed tomb of the Egyptian god Horus."

"Tell me you're reading that wrong," he slowly turned to him.

"My German isn't that bad, First Sergeant," Higgins shook his head. "Horus is supposed to be the god of the sky and kingship."

"So what … **she's** Horus?" The First Sergeant turned, looking at her again.

"No, the supposed tomb of Horus that they found was not his tomb at all," Higgins answered. "It was actually the location of the tomb that housed her. Her name is supposed to be Sekhmet, the same as the Egyptian goddess of fire, war, vengeance, and healing. She's who they were taking the samples from to create the virus."

Jackson's heart felt as if it was close to bursting out of his chest at the rate it was beating. He took several steps forward to get a closer look at her.

"You said earlier that they were close to 'breaking the seal,'" Jackson asked without looking at him. "How close?"

"Again, we need someone with an extremely advanced degree in genetics to decipher all of this," Higgins swallowed. "But from what I can make out, whatever they were extracting from her if properly synthesized, is capable of turning regular humans …into gods."

A cold sweat washed over the First Sergeant as the wheels began to turn in his skull.

Genesis

"Aside from you and the detail upstairs," Jackson glanced his way. "Does anyone else know about this?"

"Sir, no sir," Higgins answered.

"Keep it that way," the First Sergeant commanded. "Two questions, is she dead, and do you think this can be moved?"

"If you look closer, you can see that her head is actually severed from the rest of her body, so I believe so," he responded. "Which is crazy because the readings here say that there's no sign of brain activity or heart rate, but the cell samples I've examined show very little deterioration and are very much alive, and I don't have the slightest idea how that is possible. As far as moving it, it appears to be designed for transport."

"Get upstairs and tell the detail to remain where they are, guard the front entrance with their life, and to keep their mouths shut about this," ordered the First Sergeant. "Get an encrypted message to the brass. Tell them what we found. Tell them we need three large inconspicuous transports that can move without detection from both enemy and allied forces. Then get back here and help me gather all of this data; we're going to take the written stuff and burn all pictures and images. No one must see what we're hauling back to the States …ever."

"Sir, yes, sir," Higgins acknowledged.

"Higgins," Jackson asked him one final time, "Do you think anyone else knows about this?"

Higgins hesitantly paused before answering, understanding what he was referring to.

"I'm not one hundred percent sure about the grunts, but those in high command that we captured probably know."

"We can't take any chances; there were no prisoners of war on this base," the First Sergeant gave his final order. "Can you make it happen, Corporal?"

Genesis

"If I can pick the right guys," fumbled Higgins. "We can make it look like an attempted escape during the dead of night."

"Get to it then," authorized the First Sergeant.

"Sir, yes, sir," the Corporal nodded.

As Higgins turned on his heel, heading back upstairs to carry out the First Sergeant's orders, Jackson walked closer to the containment tank to look at Sekhmet.

"With your help, we're going to make America a country not to be fucked with, our **Holy Grail**," swallowed First Sergeant Jackson. "God help us if we're not ready for this."

Unbeknownst to the First Sergeant and even the Corporal, the monitors of that era, though primitive, were picking up activity. It was the most minuscule activity that the human eye or ear could not detect, but that activity was slowly increasing.

Genesis

CHAPTER 1

October 2015, The Grand Canyon National Park, midafternoon Colorado time.

At the very bottom of the old dried-up riverbed, made out of red rock and first established on February 26, 1919, was a part of the canyon wall that was not actually a wall. Although it mimicked its environment's features, it was created of reinforced metal with a hidden door that slid open once a hidden camera and surveillance system confirmed facial and retinal recognition of the individual or individuals wishing to enter.

Once the person entered through the hidden faux stone wall door, they went down a sizable elevator shaft one mile underneath the canyon, where they were met by heavily armed superhuman-enhanced guards with high-tech body armor and additional security protocol checks.

Once the individual reached that checkpoint, they entered a sterile silver hallway with a moving escalator floor, which took them to their next destination. During the ride, X-ray, thermal, and behavioral scans are taken. The door at the end of the trip does not open unless the person clears those last scans.

Finally, if the person clears the last security scans, the enormous circular silver door splits apart, allowing entrance into the facility, which houses the next phase of project EVOlution.

Around the facility, enhanced guards were strategically placed. At the same time, scientists, geneticists, and lab technicians moved about or were at their stations working to further push human evolution boundaries on behalf of the United States Government.

Genesis

In the center of the facility was the primary reason the lab base was created. Four cylindrical metal chambers lined up next to one another, labeled from right to left with numbers one to four. A team of forty lab technicians and geneticists broke into mandatory eight-person crews. It provided round-the-clock observation of the four fetuses submerged within a thick, clear nutrient fluid in each chamber.

Standing in front of the four chambers with his arms casually clasped behind his back was the new Director of Project Evolution, the soon-to-be former Secretary of Defense Robert Graves, and Dr. Egan Alexander, the Chief Head Scientist of the Colorado facility.

"This batch appears to be progressing very nicely," Graves nodded.

"Yes, considering that we have passed the five-month incubation period without any fatalities," Dr. Alexander nodded. "I am quite confident these latest specimens will make it to full maturity."

"Let us hope so," Graves sighed. "This project has already been delayed due to previous setbacks."

"You'll have to understand that this is still new and uncharted territory." Dr. Alexander explained. "Cloning is one thing, but accelerated growth is a whole new field onto itself. Forcing an embryo to bypass its natural growth process is not the same as changing its eye or hair color. Based on calculations, we still have until the eighteenth month period until we can determine if our efforts are a success."

"I am fully aware that Rome was not built in a day, doctor," Graves acknowledged. "However, it is imperative that we minimize the delay of this project as much as we possibly can. It took many persuasions to have the anonymity of this organization restored with both administrative and bipartisan support. Our secrecy, regardless of who takes the Oval next year, is conditional on the success of this program."

Graves finished his sentence and noticed that Dr. Alexander neither complied nor responded to what he had just said. He turned to see the doctor looking at him with an extra pale white face riddled with fear.

Genesis

Before he could ask what had the doctor in such a frightened state, he noticed that Alexander's eyes weren't on him but looking at someone or something over his left shoulder.

Now sensing the presence next to him, a frigid chill ran down Grave's spine as he slowly turned to his left and shuddered.

Standing next to him was a barefooted, towering, muscular young man in his mid-twenties with dark brown skin and thick, curly raven hair wearing nothing more than a tattered, multi-colored skirt.

His arms were casually folded behind his back as he observed the creation chambers as if he had been there all along.

"Your calculations are incorrect, doctor," the young man relayed in perfect English. "They won't last no more than twelve months give or take. None of these specimens have inherited their mother's regenerative capability, which is key to ensuring they survive the accelerated growth process. A simple fix, except your current technology, is incapable of pinpointing what that gene is in such a complex DNA matrix."

Graves stepped backward, falling into the catatonic doctor as the young man turned, revealing his faint white glowing eyes.

"Security!"

"Are all loyal to me now," the young man informed.

Graves choked as the enhanced guards within the vicinity snapped to attention, remaining where they stood.

"I simply erased all their memories. All they know is that they were born to serve and kill for me. I also removed their existence from the memories of their loved ones and anyone they have ever encountered, just a tiny fraction of my infinite power. I have also broken the mental tether you have with your 'agent' who is protecting your mind," he smirked. "She still thinks she is guarding it. I could have killed her, but that would have drawn attention to me, and I am not ready to be revealed. You know who I am, don't you, boy?"

Genesis

Graves swallowed deeply to the point of gagging as Dr. Alexander stood behind him, clutching his tablet with a mixture of fear and fascination on his face. The young man stepped closer, examining Graves.

"Oh, yes," he nodded. "You know very well who I am, and I know what you and those before you have done."

He walked around Graves and began to examine Dr. Alexander, tapping one of the lenses on his glasses and feeling his lab jacket's texture. With a finger, he made the doctor extend his arm to look at the computer tablet he held while pulling out one of his pens from the front pocket of his lab coat.

"It took me a while after I recovered from my imprisonment and regained some strength to read mind after mind across the planet and follow the trail leading me here. It started with a former soldier or two from a defeated regime; they knew nothing. I was then able to locate one of your last surviving soldiers of the Second World War who laid eyes on my beloved. I found it hidden in the deep recesses of his failed mind. That narrowed my search to this part of the world, where I searched for those who had knowledge of my 'Holy Grail.'

Step by step, I followed the trail, reading mind after mind after mind, until I found you, boy.

You, in turn, upon my command, brought me here, unbeknownst to you.

Here, where you have the desecrated remains of my beloved Sekhmet, my Eye. Here, you mutilated her body with your experimentations to learn the secret of the gods and duplicated them for your own means. Yes, child …I have been down to the lowest level of this facility and seen what you have done."

The Ancient now stood toe to toe with a terrified Graves drenched in sweat. He leaned in, getting face-to-face with him.

"What is my name,…boy?"

Genesis

"Horus …your name …is Horus." Graves answered with a swallow while edging his bottom jaw.

The Ancient slowly nodded as a sinister smirk formed on his visage.

"As I stood gazing upon the remains of my beloved that you picked apart, the first thing that came to mind to punish you for your insolence was to shatter every one of your brittle bones with just a thought and to watch you die a slow and agonizing death."

He leaned in to whisper into a quaking Graves's ear.

"But there are worse things than death, boy. Fates far worse than physical pain, for men like yourself who have spent your entire life obtaining power. The greatest pain I can inflict upon you …is just to take it away. And that is what I shall do. You shall be the one to bear witness as I wipe your ruling governments from the face of this planet and bring this world to heel under my rule."

"I have news for you, someone went down that road," Graves found a sliver of defiance to utter his words. "And they failed."

"Although I already knew what you were about to say," the Ancient smirked, "I am curious to know why you would say this to me when you know I can kill you for it?"

"Guess it's the old Army war dog in me," Graves swallowed. "It tends to come out from time to time. And you can't be all that powerful if you were locked up somewhere this whole time …Horus."

A menacing smile formed on Horus's lips as if he found Graves's retort amusing. It quickly disappeared as a dull, ominous stare took its place.

"Remove your clothes and bow before me. All of you."

The words were a loud echo within each of their skulls. A shocked Graves, Dr. Alexander, and his terrified lab staff found themselves stripping

Genesis

off their clothing until they were all stark naked. They all collapsed to their knees, scraping and bowing before a sinister grinning Horus. The ancient immortal standing over a humiliated Graves lifted his dusty barefoot, bringing it in front of his nostrils.

"Now... kiss my foot ...slave."

A powerless Graves found himself grasping Horus's foot and kissing it.

"Maddening, isn't it, to be in control of your mind, but not your body? To see, feel, hear, and know all that you do while I command your body with just the words from my lips. The first of many lessons, you shall learn, boy," Horus snarled while glaring down at him. "Your experimentations only bore you at best demi-gods who pale in comparison to the god that stands before you. When the time is right, I shall claim this world with a whisper ...not a roar."

Horus turned his attention back to the incubation chambers.

"But for now, I must first resurrect my Sekhmet and bear more children. You there, rise and come forth."

Dr. Alexander found his body reaching its feet and moving on its own, bringing him to stand before Horus.

"Kill the children growing within these chambers."

Dr. Alexander's face bore an expression of horror as his body did as commanded, moving to one of the computer terminals and typing in the termination code, which shut off life support, drained the nutrient bath, and then flooded the chambers with a solution that dissolved the fetuses until there was nothing left of them. Horus nodded with approval as he turned to Graves.

"The first lesson in creating a god boy is to select from superior stock."

Horus then palmed Dr. Alexander's face, causing him to gasp and collapse onto his knees, convulsing. His eyes widened in shock as tears ran from them.

"Oh …oh god …I see …I see it now." He shuddered.

"Good, you will have three days to rebuild these chambers to my specifications," Horus instructed him. "Also, dispose of the inferior male seed you have stored; you will be using my seed for this birthing process."

"I …I will require the help of my staff to complete your task Lord Horus," Dr. Alexander said as he willingly bowed before him.

"Very well," Horus agreed. "All others rise, except for you, boy."

Dr. Alexander rose to his feet along with his staff, who regained control of their bodies; he quickly glanced at Graves, still down at his knees, then back at Horus.

"These two will also remain with me...."

Dr. Alexander looked to whom Horus was pointing; the first was a female lab technician who wore square spectacles and long brunette hair in a ponytail. Tears streamed from her eyes as she meekly tried to cover herself; the second woman who also burst into tears was a junior biochemist with short, thick, curly hair and tan skin.

"These two will remain to clean me, escort me to proper chambers, feed, service, and collect my seed," Horus commanded, "Afterwards, I shall summon you to fashion proper clothing for me. And then accompany me down to the lower levels of this place to tend to the remains of my beloved Sekhmet. Be sure to complete your instruction to your staff before then."

"Yes, Lord Horus," Dr. Alexander bowed. "May we please …get dressed?"

"Why?" Horus coldly asked.

"We …are not comfortable working this way," he swallowed. "I think we would be more productive if we …"

Genesis

Before Dr. Alexander could finish, his words were choked out of him as one of the mind-reprogrammed enhanced guards walked up, pulled out his sidearm, and shot the nearest female lab technician, causing screams to erupt throughout the remaining living. Her lifeless body slammed savagely onto the floor, causing everyone to jump.

More screams erupted as another male lab technician let out a blood-curdling scream as he was hoisted into the air by Horus via his powerful telekinesis. A painful shriek came from him as the ancient, with just a thought, began to pluck out both his eyes, every one of his teeth followed by his tongue and then the nails from his fingers and toes. Mortified wails and hollers came from Dr. Alexander's staff as they helplessly watched as Horus crushed every bone within his body one by one.

A near-catatonic Dr. Alexander, battered with trauma, fell to his knees as Horus calmly strolled up, looking down at him with his hands clasped behind his back.

"Let us have understanding," Horus calmly sighed. "You are a slave, while I am a god. Your comfort means nothing to me. Your very lives mean nothing to me. All that matters to me is your service to me. Do we have understanding, slave?"

"Yes, Lord Horus," Dr. Alexander whimpered. "Yes."

With a thought, Horus slammed the young man's corpse against a wall and pulled out three construction rivets from an opposite wall, which he used to crucify the body as an omen to those who would defy him.

"If I am pleased, then maybe I shall allow you to clothe yourselves. You have greatly reduced the time to instruct your staff and get them to work. Focus on that instead of trivial things. And remember that I see and hear all, slave, now be gone."

"Yes, Lord Horus."

Dr. Alexander fought past his current trauma to get to his feet. He began to herd and usher his remaining staff away to get their minds right

Genesis

and start the work Horus instructed him to do. Horus, the women he selected, and Graves, still down on his hands and knees, strolled over to the powerless and humiliated Director, looking down on him.

"My how the tide of power so quickly shifts, today you awoke the commander of this facility, with every living soul here subordinate to you. And now you are reduced to nothing more than a gnat at my feet. Yet I sense that you still have some defiance left that I must squeeze from out of you."

With a thought, Horus forced a groan out of Graves as he made him raise his chin to look him in the eyes.

"You're lucky I don't fancy myself a boy lover, or my cock would be the tool I would use to remove the last scrap of insolence from you. Perhaps some time on your hands and knees grinding into the unforgiving floor will teach you to show honor and humility to your better."

Horus turned his attention to the two terrified women whose bodies began to rattle with fear.

"Know that I can hear your thoughts. Your fear, I can understand, but your reluctance to be in my company troubles me. Did I mistakenly pick the wrong concubines?"

The lab technician, realizing what was at stake by his words, got her head in the game, quickly wiping her eyes and forcing a smile on her face while grabbing the hand of the junior biochemist, gently squeezing it, relaying to her to get her mind right if they both hoped to survive.

"No, Lord Horus," the lab technician said with a chirpy voice, quickly shaking her head. "We are both very honored to serve you and look forward to tending to your needs."

"We shall see," an unconvinced Horus scoffed, "To the bath ...or what you call showers, I wish to be properly scrubbed free of the stench that reminds me of the centuries of captivity I had to endure."

The technician nodded with a nervous smile while mustering every

Genesis

ounce of strength she could find to elude some form of sensuality. Still holding the hand of the junior biochemist mentally teetering near-catatonic, she turned to put a little more movement in her hips as she led her and a skeptical Egyptian god to the women's shower, leaving Graves trapped in his mentally controlled body rooted to the floor where he knelt.

Genesis

CHAPTER 2

September 2016, San Diego, California.

On her way to the mall in her mother's SUV, sixteen-year-old Rachael Stein lowered the music so that she could break the law. She picked up her Smartphone and swiped it open with her finger while concentrating on the road. She speed-dialed a saved number with two taps and activated the speaker function as it began to ring until someone picked up.

"Sup, girl!" Came a chirpy young female voice on the other end of the phone.

"Sup with you? Where you at?"

"Home picking out an outfit for the party tonight; where you at?"

"Heading to the mall to get an outfit for tonight's party."

"You bitch! Why didn't you come get me?"

"Because I'm using my mom's car due to still being semi-grounded," Rachael rolled her eyes in disgust. "She wants me there and back in an hour and a half, or I won't get to go tonight."

"Ouch."

"My parents are acting like real A-Holes," She scoffed. "I ran a stop sign; I didn't murder the friggin pope."

"While texting and driving," her friend reminded her.

Genesis

"Whose side are you on?" Rachael snapped.

"I'm just saying, girl, in this day and age, it's a real dumbass reason to get a ticket; you forgot what happened to Samantha Bear?" Her friend continued to lecture. "Wait a minute …have you been driving and talking to me this whole time?"

"Uh …duh yeah, what did you think I was doing?"

"I thought your dad put on that app that won't allow you to use your phone while you're driving?"

"He did," Rachael deviously smirked. "But they don't know about the pre-paid phone. Ricky bought it for me for my birthday last year."

"Shit, I forgot about that …I got both numbers under your contact," Her friend sighed. "I'm hanging up before I become an accessory to a crime. Stay off your phone bitch!"

"Whateva, I'll call you when I get home. Lata."

"Lata."

Rachael reluctantly exhaled as she set her phone down, heeding her friend's advice. She hesitated due to the phone vibrating in her hand. Being a creature of habit, she turned the phone over to see what the screen read.

"Ricky!" She beamed. "He sent a video!"

While swiping and clicking to see a video where cats go through brain freeze after licking ice cream cones, Rachael neglected to see seven-year-old Michael Henderson walking next to his mother as they entered the crosswalk on a red light.

"Oh my god!"

With less than three feet between the vehicle and Michael, Rachael's attempt to hit the brakes on her mother's SUV was futile.

Genesis

~~~~~~~~~~~~~~~~~~~~~~~~~~~~~~~~

The Next Day, Early Morning:

Channel 8 San Diego Morning News Team:

"Another near-fatal accident occurred due to texting and driving yesterday," news anchor Nichelle Medina announced.

"Around 4 P.M. yesterday, a teenage driver struck a young boy, age seven." Her fellow anchor Dan Cohen reported. "The teenager who was driving her parents' car at the time, totaled it on impact against the young child a registered superhuman. The young woman was taken to the hospital, where she was treated for her injuries. The young boy and his mother, who was walking with him, were unharmed from the incident."

"Just another lesson for people to stop texting and driving," reinforced Medina. "You really don't know who you are going to run into these days."

"You got that right, Nichelle," agreed Henderson. "In other news, the body of the young woman that fell out of the Chicago sky yesterday was identified as Patricia Samson, also known as Flaming Jay, one of the last living members of the Chicago superhero team known as the Defenders of Justice."

"Patrica Samson, a.k.a Flaming Jay, took heavy scrutiny for abandoning her team during their battle with the female superhuman terrorist known as Peace. All of her team members were killed during the confrontation, while Ms. Samson was reported to have fled to safety," Nichelle Medina continued to say. "Ms. Samson also reportedly had her own brush with the law for alcohol and drug abuse and was said to have checked into a rehabilitation center for treatment. Authorities are ruling her death a suicide. Ms. Samson is survived by her parents and a younger brother."

"In International news, it is now almost four months since the superhuman terrorist attack on British Parliament, leaving thirty dead," Dan Cohen began jumping into his following report. "The attack, which took

Genesis

place one week after the United Kingdom's intended withdrawal from the European Union, was carried out by ten superhuman citizens of the United Kingdom. The attack, which was the most massive causality of government officials of the United Kingdom, was thwarted by the UK's superhuman military unit known as the Lions of Elizabeth, aided by Sophia Dennison, also known as Freedom. Of the ten terrorists that initiated the attack, six were captured, while four were killed.

Those captured were recorded chanting, 'We are the future, evolve or die.' The motto of the superhuman supremacy group known worldwide as Vitruvian Absolute, the organization continues to express that they neither condoned nor sanctioned the terrorist assault on Parliament. This brings us to our special report later tonight."

"Tonight's special report is the rise of genetic prejudice," Nichelle Medina announced, "An issue that is not only plaguing minorities prone to prejudice but other racist and supremacy groups as well. Groups like the KKK, Neo-Nazi, and White Nationalists have reported assaults, along with businesses, homes, and meeting places either vandalized or destroyed by alleged superhumans. Our report will also discuss genetic self-hatred and superhuman boosting, rapidly becoming the largest drug epidemic worldwide. Join us tonight at 6 P.M. for our special report, and now the weather."

~~~~~~~~~~~~~~~~~~~~~~~~~~~~~~~~~~~

Ryongsong Residence, located in the Ryongsong district in northern Pyongyang, is the official presidential palace in North Korea and the Supreme Leader's principal residence.

Freedom sat calmly in one of the many elegant chairs within the presidential office with her legs adequately crossed. Her hood was down, allowing her long-braided mane to hang over her shoulders. Fresh battle burns and scuff marks covered parts of her hero attire.

"First of all, thank you so much for having this meeting with me. I know you're very busy so let me just get to the point. I get that you have a country to run and an image to uphold, but your latest actions have become completely unacceptable. If you don't want to take a page from Iran, that is

Genesis

your business. You are the Supreme Leader of your country."

She leaned forward a bit, narrowing her eyes.

"But when your ships begin to edge toward borders, they have no business being near, and when you start doing "missile tests" in areas that make people nervous, you become my problem and don't want to be my problem. So, it's simple: you either keep your ships on your side of the fence, or I will beach your entire fleet in Pyongyang. And if you fire one more rocket too close to South Korea or any other allied border, I will return it and park it in your bedroom.

Are we clear?"

She said her entire statement in Korean as she sat across from the Chairman of the Workers' Party of Korea and Supreme Leader of the Democratic People's Republic of Korea, who wore a visage of a mixture of sulking, anger, and frustration.

Behind him, standing guard for his protection, was the Guards of the Republic, North Korea's six-person super-soldier program adorned with their leader's same visage with a sprinkle of humiliation. Two of the six had a more intense look of rage as they stood more disheveled than their other comrades.

"One more thing," she continued while leaning forward. "You ever make any more threats towards my island, and I will personally come back here and show your people how powerful their 'Supreme Leader' actually is. The five thousand North Korean defectors that I walked out of China are under my protection, and you will never get them back. So, deal with it. Are we also clear on that?"

She watched as he glared at her, shifting in his seat, unable to deal with being powerless.

"I'm going to take this current state of silence as a yes," Freedom beamed a pleasant smile. "Now, as I said, I understand that you're a busy man, and I have someplace to get to as well, so if you don't mind, I will show myself out."

Genesis

Freedom rose from her seat, wagging a finger at the Guards of the Republic.

"Next time, be more courteous when a lady comes and says she wants to sit down and talk."

She purposely turned her back to them as she exited the palace. A smirk formed on her face as her ears picked up the sound of a fist violently hammering expensive wood and a slew of profanity and racial remarks spewing from an enraged and embarrassed Supreme Leader. As his voice faded away, she took her time admiring the halls of the Ryongsong Residence. Slight sadness washed over her as she pondered how her species could build such beautiful structures yet be so monstrous toward one another.

She shook away a depressing thought as she neared the palace doors, quickly held open by the palace guards, who scrambled as they saw her coming. As she exited, Freedom inhaled the fresh outdoor air as the sun shined high above, which brought a smile back to her face as she descended the sea of steps.

"Well, that wasn't too bad," she sighed. "What do you think, Vincent?"

"Aside from the minor confrontation," Vincent calculated. "I believed the conversation was as productive as it could be considering his behavioral pattern."

"Well, hopefully, he won't make me have to come back here again. How are we on time?"

"You will be thirty minutes early for your interview with Ms. Winfrey if you depart now."

"Perfect, the sooner we get this over with my e-mail and phone won't be hijacked by her publicist, and everyone on the island, including my mother, will stop hounding me to do this."

"You do not care for Ms. Winfrey?" Vincent asked.

Genesis

"That's not it," Freedom shook her head with a huff. "I avoided interviews for a reason; you accept one, then everyone will be at my door requesting a sit-down. Then I go from being a political target to a tabloid whore."

"May I ask the difference considering both are negative labels?" inquired Vincent.

"Political target means the focus is on me," Freedom answered. "Tabloid whore means it's open season on my family and friends. I prefer all guns on me."

"I shall make a note of that."

"Play me some uplifting travel music Vincent," Freedom requested while looking around. "This place is depressing me."

"How about 'Larger than Life,' an oldie but goodie?"

"Tempting," she smirked. "But I was thinking of something that we could broadcast to encourage both civility and a little culture sharing if you know what I mean."

"I believe I understand and know how to achieve both goals."

Freedom took her time slowly hovering off the ground as North Koreans exited their homes and workplaces to sound the South Korean boy band BTS's Steve Aoki remixed song "Mic Drop" booming from the audio speakers strategically stationed around the country to deliver their leader's message. Some covered their ears in irritation, while others inconspicuously nodded their heads, attempting to find the beat, all including a furious dictator and his superhuman unit who came out onto the balcony of his palace to look up at the most powerful superhuman on the planet looking down at them with a smile on her face.

With a mid-level sonic boom, she rocketed off to her next destination.

~ ~

Genesis

Saturday 11:30 P.M., Sanctuary Island Time

Sophia sat curled up on her sofa in her bedclothes consisting of a simple white tank top and green boy shorts, watching the replay of the latest episode of Bill Maher on HBO on her flatscreen television with the aid of her A.I. Vincent. She wasn't a faithful fan of his show, mostly because she did not see Eye to Eye with some of his ideologies, but she had a keen interest in tonight's show.

She patiently waited to listen to his jokes intermingled with the news of the week and sharp comedic jabs at the Republican candidate and the Party itself for selecting him. He then announced his first guest of the night before his panel discussion. As his show's theme music played, he walked off to his interview stage and greeted a tall, lean, chocolate-skinned, clean-shaven man with a shiny, hairless dome wearing a well-tailored navy-blue suit with a crisp white shirt and an onyx-colored tie.

They shook hands before taking their respective seats.

"You have to forgive me," Mr. Maher began the interview. "I have talked a lot of shit about superhero movies in the past, so to actually have one of you on here is freaking me the fuck out. I am now rethinking every single religious joke I ever made."

His guest chuckled while the crowd erupted in laughter.

"So, is it safe to call you Deacon Absolute or Xavier Lamonster?" Bill Maher inquired.

"I prefer Deacon Absolute," Xavier Lamonster nodded.

"This is also the first time I have ever had a founding member of a supremacy group on my show," Bill Maher got serious, "But you're a little different from the rest because instead of race or religion, your organization promotes genetic superiority."

"Well, I am your genetic superior," Deacon Absolute unapologetically answered. "I am stronger and more durable than ordinary humans. Wounds and injuries that would kill an average person or hospitalize them for months I can survive or heal from in a matter of seconds or minutes. I am immune to diseases that would kill a regular human. I can run from here to New York City in forty-five minutes without tiring while my senses and reflexes are several times faster than a regular human."

The audience made a sound of uneasiness as Bill Maher paused to carefully deliver his next question.

"Okay, so you've just proven that your dick is bigger than mine and a lot of people in the world, but you were once a normal human being like everyone else; you weren't born with these abilities."

"No, that's true," Deacon Absolute agreed.

"So why the hatred toward your own species?" Bill Maher asked, getting to the point.

"Our organization is not about hatred toward regular humans," Deacon Absolute calmly answered. "It's about promoting the evolution of the human race, which has proven to be possible and is, in our opinion, drastically needed."

"So, your views do fall in line with the female terrorist known as Peace?"

"We don't believe in the extreme actions our mother took ..."

"Wait ...hold on," Bill Maher stopped him, "Your mother?"

"Yes, her and Ms. Dennison's genetic code flows within me and is the reason for my evolution," Deacon Absolute proudly answered. "So, she and Ms. Dennison are our evolutionary mothers."

His answer made Sophia shift uncomfortably in her seat as if eyes were on her.

"We don't condone the violent acts that Mother Peace chose to take to further the evolution of humankind, but we do understand and

Genesis

believe in her cause. Regular humans, such as yourself, are flawed on both a mental and physical level. You don't have to look any further than the state of the world and the antics of the Republican candidate, which is being grossly overlooked by his own Party to prove that point."

"I'm flawed?" Bill Maher asked, leaning back with a sardonic look of shock.

"Yes, you are," Deacon Absolute retorted, leaning forward. "Because liberals like you, right-wingers, and everyone else who chose to label themselves as anything else other than human beings are the main reason why the world is failing. You continue to remain divided, and choose sides thinking of only your personal self-interests when there should only be one side and one interest, that of humankind."

"All this talk of mothers and one side, you sound like a Borg collective," Bill Maher smirked.

"A Borg collective does not have their own thoughts and identity; we still do," Deacon Absolute said with a smile. "The difference between you and us is our ability to see both sides of the coin; for example, unlike you, we believe in God, Allah, El Shaddai, and we believe in science."

"Which is impossible," Bill Maher answered, getting serious again.

"By definition, God is a being that is of omniscience, omnipotence, and omnipresence," Deacon Absolute said. "The first means He is a Being of infinite intelligence, and if I am created of Him, that means I was made with a microscopic fraction of His knowledge, which allows me to understand and perceive the world around me, and this was all before my upgrade.

The jump start of human evolution seven years ago reveals the untapped potential we were created with but failed to master because we were obsessed with trivial things that have done nothing more than stunt our growth. We have already proven that we can create life in a Petri dish and alter its genetic code before it is given shape and takes its first breath. It's not hard to believe that we inherited the ability to do these things from the Being that created us, not for me or like-minded people anyway."

Genesis

"Let save that for another long discussion," Bill Maher said, deciding to change the subject. "If you believe that superhumans are superior in every way to regular humans, how do you explain things like the attack on Parliament which claimed a lot of innocent lives, the vandalism, and bigotous actions of some superhumans against regular people? From my and many other viewpoints, we don't see evolution, but the same ideology and tactics implemented by individuals with destructive abilities."

"Well, as my organization has expressed, we don't condone the actions of these individuals," Deacon Absolute answered while clearing his throat. "And being evolved does not mean that we are perfect, just better."

"Better at causing death and destruction?"

"Now that's not fair, Bill."

"Is it?" Bill Maher said, going on the attack. "Because from what I can see, being evolved has allowed certain individuals to do or hurt anyone they want on a massive scale without the fear of repercussions until they are stopped by a stronger person like say Freedom. It appears as if organizations like Vitruvian Absolute are fanning the flames of a new form of hatred."

"We're not fanning any flames of hatred, Bill."

"'We are the future, evolve or die,' is the Vitruvian Absolute motto. It is what those terrorists were screaming after they were captured. That motto and your organization's symbol has been spray-painted over churches, mosques, synagogue, cemeteries, schools, and public statues all over the world."

"You forgot to add that they've been found on Neo-Nazi, KKK, White Nationalist, Black Panther, and other supremacist organizations." Deacon Absolute retorted. "And while we state again that we don't condone the actions of these individuals, nor do we promote violence of any kind, we can understand their actions."

"You understand their actions?"

Genesis

"For centuries, this has always been a world where the powerful has always ruled over and oppressed the weak. Where the only option given to the weak was to peacefully march or organize a sit-in, which most likely came with you either being arrested, getting maced in the face, your head getting beaten in with a baton, blasted by a water hose, or chewed to bits by a dog. What did you people expect to happen when the balance of power has now been significantly shifted? That is why you may hate to admit it, but you actually need an organization like Vitruvian Absolute."

"We need Vitruvian Absolute?" Bill Maher asked, leaning back with a look of genuine shock.

"Vitruvian Absolute is the only organization where anyone can join and become a part of," Deacon Absolute explained, confidently leaning forward. "If you believe that there is only one race and one species and we must do everything in our power to reach our maximum potential, you have a place in Vitruvian Absolute. The birth rates for superhumans are increasing yearly, regular people are taking drugs and treatments to activate their dormant abilities, and our organization has expanded, where we will soon surpass the NRA. We estimate we'll be more prominent within a year or two than Islam itself.

So, this is happening, Mr. Maher, no matter how many jokes you make.

Vitruvian Absolute is the only organization able to lead and guide this new generation and the world to a better, peaceful way of life. So yes, our motto says, 'We are the future, evolve or die,' because we are the future, and we chose to evolve into the species we were destined to be, into the species God intended us to be, instead of dying. We invite everyone to become a part of that future."

"Very tempting offer, but the only superpower I need is the ability to get high," smiled Bill Maher. "Thank you again, Deacon Absolute; please come back anytime, and now to our panel discussion!"

Having little interest in listening to Bill Maher spar with Rick Santorum and Anne Coulter, Sophia lowered the volume as her countenance became grim and solemn from what she heard.

Genesis

~~~~~~~~~~~~~~~~~~~~~~~~~~~~~~~~~~~~

Her mind wandered back to that horrible day of the attack. In Hawaii, she assisted with bringing a stalled cruise liner to port when Vincent informed her of the assault. She broke the speed barrier several times and went orbital to cut her travel time down as much as possible, but it was not enough.

The Palace of Westminster was again in smoking ruins, while the Lions of Elizabeth were in a fierce, bloody battle in the middle of Westminster. An enraged Sophia went into action doing what she now did best: busting heads. One by one, she made short work of the heavy hitters, dropping them with either one-shot blows or draining their energy from them depending on the situation. The rest quickly surrendered, realizing that the battle was lost.

As they rounded up the remaining living terrorists, placing them in restraints, Sophia shifted her attention to assist with locating the injured and dead within the Palace of Westminster when the Lions of Elizabeth's team leader approached her.

"Dr. Dennison, thank you for your help," the photon energy wielder said, extending his hand.

"Not necessary, Major," she answered, returning the handshake. "I'm going in to see …"

"But I think it's best that you leave…right now."

His stern words took her off guard as they locked eyes.

"First, let me say I'm not some dumb twat," Sir Knight Light whispered to her. "I know none of this is your fault; you didn't ask for this, none of us did, and if it wasn't for you, this could have turned out far worse than it already has. But we both know the world ain't reasonable, and that little speech you had played for the UN has muddied up your reputation, at least around here.

Some people are afraid of you and unsure of what you stand for."

Genesis

Freedom felt what he was talking about as she looked around at some of the injured looking at her, witnessing the hatred and fear in their eyes. Her eyes returned to Sir Knight Light's glowing white eyes.

"Don't take it personally, love; I know your one of the good ones. People just don't like the taste of the truth, especially when it's served by someone who doesn't look like them."

"How do you know I'm one of the good ones?" Freedom softly asked.

"You wouldn't have given the world seven years to get their houses in order," he said flatly. "You would have done what Peace was going to do, maybe not as brutal as her, but you would have done it just the same."

"I'm not going to let people's opinion of me because I spoke the truth scare me away."

"I'm not saying you do that," Sir Knight Light pressed. "Despite what anyone might say, this world does need you, probably more than ever. I'm saying till things cool down, don't linger. Let your actions speak for you, then get the hell out of dodge."

She pulled the hood to her suit further over her head, hiding the saddened smile on her face, reluctantly agreeing with his reasoning.

"You're going to be telling us really soon, 'I told you so.' Forgive me if I'm on the side, praying that you're wrong. Now get out of here, and don't worry about this mess; England will always prevail."

"I wish that too, Major," Freedom said to him. "Even more than you do. Good luck."

Reluctantly, she took a step back and rocketed off into the sky. She flew home to be alone with her thoughts until her daughter came home.

Although it was reported that she was the effective aid that stopped the terrorist attack, her critics still found a way to have a field day and hurl

Genesis

their stones.

~~~~~~~~~~~~~~~~~~~~~~~~~~~~~~~~~~~~

    Out of nowhere, Sophia was shaken out of her trance by the sound of a loud boom and screaming. On reflex, she sprang out of her loveseat and made a beeline up the stairs to her daughter's room. Flinging open the door, she gazed upon Kimberly, sitting in her bed, drenched in sweat, trembling with tears as she tried to catch her breath.

    Without a word, she strolled over to her, sitting down and embracing her. Sophia kissed her forehead and soothingly rubbed her back as her child clung to her tank top.

    "I'm sorry …I'm sorry," Kimberly got out between sobs.

    "It's okay, baby," she whispered while wiping some excess sweat from her forehead.

    "I tried to control it," she groaned, "I tried to block it out."

    "I know you did," she kissed her head again, "don't worry, I'm here."

Genesis

CHAPTER 3

Six hundred hours military time early morning, Ninawa, Iraq, September 2016.

One of the two newly rebuilt Tornados cruised in silent cloak mode forty-five thousand feet above sea level as Maxine piloted the craft to its destination. Old school hip hop pumped throughout the cabin as the newly expanded Regulator team prepared for their mission in their own way.

Rosann Esposito, who went by the call sign Merge, sat silently with her legs and arms folded, staring into space. Before that, she had checked her gear and sidearms three times while in transit to their destination. Across from her sat her teammate and current boyfriend, Oliver Brandon, whose call sign was Blitz. He also sat with his arms and legs folded, looking at her sternly.

It was due to the thousand-yard stare that had taken residence in her eyes and the ice water pumping through her veins. The boisterous girl from Staten Island had been savagely murdered and replaced by a hardened soldier and efficient killer.

Her record-long sessions within the Hurt Locker allowed her to master her organic elemental abilities to the point that she could access previous transformations with concentrated thought.

However, the hardened super soldier she had become severely strained her and Oliver's relationship. The love born from a secret crush and Oliver's "death" and "resurrection" were strangled by their opposing views of being members of the Regulator team. Merge believed Oliver was still playing hero when he should be a soldier, especially after his near death. At the same time, Blitz felt her assessment of him was inaccurate and that she was taking her warrior role too seriously to the point that it was infecting her and their personal lives. It also didn't help that her twin brother, who accidentally walked into it in their latest spat, weighed in, taking Blitz's side.

"What?" Merge asked while not looking in Blitz's direction.

"I didn't say anything," he said gruffly.

"Then stop giving me that look." She fluttered her eyes.

"What look?" Blitz asked with a put-off tone.

"The one like you think I'm fucking someone else." She snarled. "This is why I prefer doing separate missions. I don't need you in my head."

A pleasant, sarcastic smile fell over his face as he nodded.

"I'm gonna remove myself before I say something I can't and wouldn't want to take back."

He sprung to his feet, walking off. He wasn't fast enough not to hear Rosann's last words.

"Fine, go somewhere."

His body began to spark from the anger building within as he continued to walk, getting some distance from her. It caught the attention of the two newest members of the team.

A wide-eyed Teuila Kalani, who went by the call sign Cyclone, jumped a bit as she watched a sparking Blitz walk past her. She turned to Agnes Shareef, who went by the call sign Sister Sledge, adorned in a red, black, and gray version of Cyclone's light blue and black Impact suit. She sat in a relaxed position with her eyes closed, head down, legs crossed, and arms folded under her chest in what appeared to be sleep.

"Don't ask me; I don't know what that's all about," Sister Sledge said with her head still down.

Genesis

Cyclone nodded, averting her eyes forward and minding her own business.

The third and final addition to the team, Aashif Salek, also known by his call sign Nitro, sat wearing an orange and black version of the Regulator Impact combat suit. He quickly moved his feet out of Blitz's path as he barreled through and plopped down next to Rosann's twin brother Adrian, who went by the call sign Heavy Element, playing a game on his Smartphone. He continued to spark as he sat there, grinding his teeth to dust.

"Bitch mode?" Heavy Element nonchalantly asked while focusing on his game.

"Yep," Blitz nodded.

"Please don't zap my phone, like last time."

Sitting quietly alone, watching everything underneath his black beanie, was the Regulator leader himself, Sergeant Abraham Rogers, who went by the call sign Sarge. Slight head movements revealed he was very much awake and not sleeping with his rifle in his grip as he silently observed each new and old team member.

"Sergeant Rogers," called out Maxine over the Tornado's audio system. "We will be in the strike zone in approximately ten minutes. Hostile forces are unaware of our approach."

"Roger that."

The Sarge balled his sledgehammer-sized fist, lightly hammering the metal hull of the Tornado to get everyone's attention. Sister Sledge raised her head, looking in his direction along with the rest of her teammates.

"Heavy Element, begin church," he ordered.

The male Esposito nodded, shutting off his phone and sliding it back into a slim, hidden compartment in the leg of his suit. He stood up,

Genesis

making eye contact with each team member.

"Alright, boys and girls, you have already been debriefed; this is just the short version. Once again, we have been called upon to be the cleaner, more efficient alternative to drone strikes. Because this is an ISIS base we will be hitting, we can and will go all out, but we will also be taking prisoners, more specifically key leaders to the ISIS extremist regime, which our Eye in the sky has reported are down there. So, don't go crazy, and do not get sloppy; the objective is to hit em hard and keep the cockroaches from scattering."

"Does everyone understand the words coming out of Heavy Element's mouth?" The Sarge roared his question.

"Yes, sir!" Everyone else roared back.

Rogers nodded his approval while giving his sidearm a final check. Merge did that same, checking her sidearms on her hip holsters one last time while her brother plopped back down in his seat next to a still-brooding Blitz. Nitro leaned over and waved inconspicuously to get Heavy Element's attention.

"Sup?"

"Why does the Sarge use guns when he clearly possesses superhuman strength, regeneration, and durability?" Nitro whispered to him.

"Why don't you ask him yourself?" Heavy Element smirked. "Yo Sarge, Nitro over here is asking how come you prefer guns to knocking people's heads off with your bare hands."

Rogers calmly locked eyes with Nitro, who was slightly flustered and irritated that Heavy Element dimed him out. The Sarge finished checking his sidearm, placing it back in its leg holster before he answered.

"Don't like touching people, and I don't like people touching me …that answer your question?"

Genesis

"Yes, sir," Nitro answered with a nervous nod.

Heavy Element chuckled while Nitro cut him a dirty look with his red glowing retinas.

Sister Sledge, out of her seat, strolled past the two of them, sauntering to Rogers and sitting beside him.

"So …you don't like people touching you?"

"Certain people," he answered.

"Good to know," she smiled.

"Can I help you with something?"

"Requesting permission for a ten-minute window to have an all-female strike force to hit the camp first."

"Reason?"

"Couple of ladies raining down unholy hell on the camp is a bigger impact," she shrugged, "considering Jihadists are terrified of being killed by a woman."

"But I'm all locked and loaded," he shrugged. "I came to have me some fun."

She answered back in a soft whisper.

"Check your phone."

The Sarge pulled out his smartphone from one of the compartment pouches in his battle harness and activated it with a tap. He gave the message she sent him a quick read and then grunted while lowering his beanie.

"Get your team ready …you get a ten-minute head start from the second you hit the ground."

Genesis

"Thank you, sir."

"Aight ladies, on your feet!" She barked while jumping up. "We're on the field first!"

Upon Sister Sledge's announcement, Merge shot to her feet, getting in a good stretch before heading to the aircraft's exit point. Now, on her third mission, a jittery Cyclone waited for her to pass before getting up and following her. As the Sarge continued to check his primary weapon, Heavy Element inconspicuously glanced at him while attempting to hide the smirk forming on his face.

"You got something to say to me tin can?" the Sarge growled.

"No, sir," he answered while clearing his throat.

Heavy Element mockingly began to make silent whipping gestures.

"You're five seconds from getting shot in the face, boy." the Sarge warned.

"We are now over the strike zone," Maxine announced, "Switching to VTOL mode and opening side hatch."

The Tornado came to a quiet stop, hovering several thousand miles up from the drop zone while the side door hatch slid open, bringing in the ice-cold air of the high altitude. Sister Sledge poked her head out, narrowing her eyes to focus her vision through the chilly winds generated by the VTOL thrusters so that she could find her target.

Merge turned, glancing in Blitz's direction. Slight sadness fell over her as she noticed he did not look up at her when she walked by him and wasn't looking in her direction before she prepared to exit the plane. She closed her eyes, concentrating as her skin matched her boyfriend's color while her straight black hair turned bright white and curled into a kinky afro. Her eyes blazed white as she charged up, mimicking Blitz's abilities to harness and manipulate electricity.

Genesis

Merge turned her direction to the door, focusing on the mission, unaware Oliver's eyes lifted and were focused on her. Her brother was the only one to notice. He also saw that Sarge's eyes were fixed on Sister Sledge as she prepared to bail out.

"Glad I don't shit where I eat," he grunted to himself.

"You say something, Heavy Element?" Nitro raised his voice for everyone to hear.

His face read that he was paying him back for putting him on the Sarge's radar earlier. Heavy Element's face read for him not to try it.

"I didn't say anything."

"No, I think you just said you're glad you don't eat where …"

Heavy Element touched the metal part of his seat, transforming into its metal property, and went to stomp on his foot. A quicker Nitro moved his foot out of the way, jumping into another chair with a massive grin.

The lock and loading of Rogers's rifle and the evil glare he gave them were a warning to knock off the shenanigans. Heavy Element threw Nitro a dirty look and the "I'm watching you" hand gesture, promising to get him back.

Sister Sledge ignored the antics and focused on preparing to dive out of an aircraft without a parachute. Despite doing simulation training, actual real-life exercise, and executing it on three past missions, a tiny sliver of fear crept up on her as she gripped the sides of the exit. Sister Sledge remembered attempting two false running starts the first time on her first mission and then screaming her lungs all the way down, giving off the team's location before they hit the ground. Despite the success, Rogers tore Sister Shareef, a new one almost turning into a brawl between them in front of the entire team.

"Fifty-something years old, and I'm jumping out of a perfect airplane to take out a terrorist cell," Sister Sledge whispered. "What a life."

Genesis

She leaped out, going into a dive bomb; Merge followed without a thought, mimicking Blitz's ability of electrical propulsion chasing after her. Cyclone slapped both sides of her face and broke into a running start, diving out. She waited ten seconds after clearing the ship to channel the air around her with the force of a mini-tornado, granting her flight. Sister Sledge began to hum as she tore through the air, descending at speeds that would make a regular human blackout.

As the camp came into view, the rest of her team with flight capability hung back, giving her the honor to strike first. Sister Sledge pulled herself out of her dive past the point of no return and began to position herself to make a devastating impact.

Down below, murderers, rapists, and defilers of a beautiful religion stopped whatever they were doing or whence they were going within their camp as their ears popped up to the sound of a bomb dropping. Seconds before impacting the ground, she roared her battle cry for all to hear.

"Allah Akbar!"

Sister Sledge obliterated a jeep in the middle of the ISIS camp, sending debris and bodies flying everywhere. The grandmother rose to her feet, standing in the center of the destruction she caused only to be pelted by the assault of automatic gunfire that bounced off her skin and suit.

The feeble offensive would not last long as a hovering Cyclone unleashed gale-force wind blasts from her hands, blinding and sweeping away terrorists near her attack. Those out of range were struck down by Merge's concentrated electrical bolts.

More massive gunfire filled the air as an Old Russian GAZ-66 truck with an operated heavy machine gun mounted on top barreled toward Sister Sledge, laying down salvos of rounds that just bounced off her. The driver roared as he slammed his foot on the gas pedal, determined to run her over.

She stood her ground cocking back her right fist. The female Titan laid waste to the truck with one shot, caving in the front end with one powerful shot; the punch's force was enough to send the driver through the

Genesis

driver-side window and the gunner over the top of the truck, taking a nasty spill on the sand.

"Oh damn ... she Hancocked the truck!" beamed Cyclone.

"Don't worry about what Sister Sledge is doing," Merge barked into Cyclone's earpiece. "Keep your head in the game. You got a party of five coming on your six."

"Roger that," Cyclone apologetically coughed.

She spun mid-air with her right arm extended as concentrated air twisted around her hand. She unleashed a furious tornado blast, slamming incoming assailants off their feet.

Merge darted across the sky, unleashing tanking melting bolts of electrical heat, striking down everyone and everything that appeared to be a hostile threat.

"Careful girls," Sister Sledge advised. "Be on the lookout for human shields and, more importantly, snipers."

"Roger that." Both of her teammates confirmed.

She fell under the attack of her own precaution as a sniper armed with an M-60 machine gun from a reinforced watchtower fired upon her, hoping to bring her down with armor-piercing rounds. She retaliated by reaching into the truck's torn open grill. Sister Sledge ripped out the entire engine block with one hand, and shot put it in his direction. The machine gunner bailed out of his nest, slamming painfully into the ground as the engine cannonballed through the Watchtower, bringing it down.

"Those that can boost, boost now," screamed an ISIS terrorist in Arabic over his dual-band military radio, "Boost now!"

Upon receiving his command, several ISIS soldiers reached into tactical pouches on their person, pulled out a syringe filled with a red liquid, and injected the needles into their arms, legs, or chest areas.

Genesis

"Oh shit, we got boosters!" Cyclone announced. "We got boosters on the ground!"

"Calm down, rook," Merge barked. "It's going to take a while before their …"

Her advice was interrupted as she barely evaded a powerful head-removing photon blast from an ISIS-boosted terrorist. She mouthed the words "What the fuck?" and got her head back into the game, strafing away as she came under fire from two other boosted soldiers employing thermal and solar energy attacks.

"These are not regular boosters!" Merge yelled. "I repeat, these are not regular boosters! Whatever the hell they're on is boosting them instantly!"

Before Sister Shareef could respond, she turned around to see what was left of the truck, which she totaled, levitating into the air.

"Oh shit."

An ISIS soldier powering magnetic fields slammed the truck right into her, taking her off her feet and plowing her into a nearby compound. Cyclone came to her teammate's aide, flattening the terrorist with the force of a hurricane. She was forced to stop her assault as another boosted with similar abilities focused his power on the ground, creating a sandstorm and blinding her.

"Son of a bitch!" She screamed, covering her eyes.

The soldier armed himself with a machete while channeling the air around his legs, similar to Cyclone, granting him flight ability. He took to the air to remove her head from her body. He was stopped by a hole punched through his chest from an electrical blast delivered by Merge, which left her open for a deadly two-on-one assault from her thermal and solar-powered assailants, now airborne and flanking her for a shot.

They were blasted to cinder out of the sky by earth-shaking electrical blasts from the Regulator team's original electricity wielder. Blitz

Genesis

hovered beside her, covering his entire body in light blue plasma.

"The Sarge thought you ladies had enough fun time."

"The air is yours," she turned, looking away. "I'm going hunting."

With a thought, she canceled Blitz's abilities, returning to her regular form and dropping out of the sky. Halfway down, Merge focused again, transforming into her were-lioness form, landing on her hands and feet. She rose to bellow a deafening roar as she charged, mauled, and clawed to death any unlikely ISIS soldier within her path.

Blitz sadly shook his head only to realize he was spacing out. At the same time, bullets from terrorist soldiers still brave enough to fight made a splatter sound as they melted on impact from the electrical field he generated around himself.

"Get your head in the game Blitz!" Nitro yelled, whizzing past him.

The thermo-kinetic energy wielder used his super-heated plasma energy to slow his descent. Coming in at an angle, he tucked into a tumble roll as he hit the ground. Staying in a crouched position, he unleashed an incendiary plasma blast, turning ISIS terrorists within his vicinity to ash, except for one with Titan abilities who covered up taking his onslaught. Nitro halted his assault and shook his head as the Titan-boosted soldier tore off the remains of his scorched military jacket and shirt while his regenerative healing repaired the fatal burn marks he was able to inflict on his skin.

The soldier pulled out a sizeable razor-sharp bowie knife with the intention of fish-gutting him.

"Fucking Titans," he sneered.

Nitro powered up again as the soldier advanced, blindsided by a Russian army jeep, knocking him off his feet. It was delivered by a recovered Sister Sledge, who used a super leap to close the distance, pouncing on top of the soldier. Using her new military training and strength,

Genesis

which dwarfed the boosted soldier's, she trapped his attempted knife lunge, executed a textbook judo throw, slamming him into the ground, and then hit a sitting armbar, hyperextending and snapping his arm. The soldier screamed, dropping his knife, and then fought through the pain, getting to a kneeling position.

Knowing he would attempt to lift her even with a broken arm, Sister Shareef transitioned into a gogoplata submission hold. As she cut off his air supply with her sturdy legs, she used her free hand to open up a hidden compartment on the sleeve of her suit. She pulled out and activated an ion body damper, slapping it on the side of his skull, overloading his nervous system with several thousand volts of electricity.

She released him, getting to her feet as his eyes rolled into the back of his head while he fish-flopped on the sand.

"You got a problem with Titans?" Sister Sledge asked as her eyes stayed fixed on the terrorist soldier she had just downed.

"No, ma'am," Nitro quickly shook his head. "No problem at all."

High above, Heavy Element, back in his human form, leaned up casually against the Tornado's opened exit door, waiting for the Sarge.

"What the hell are you waiting for?" He asked while looking Heavy Element up and down with a scowl on his face.

"Nothing," he smirked. "Was just hoping you'd say something motivational like 'Regulators, regula …'"

"Get your ass out of this plane and go destroy something!" He snapped at him.

"Yes, sir!" Heavy Element beamed, snapping a salute.

With a slap on the Tornado's outer hull, Heavy Element changed his entire body composition into dark metal as he dived out of the aircraft, making his descent to Earth even faster. His target was a barrack, which he dead-leveled on impact, sending debris and bodies flying in different

Genesis

directions. Merge's inorganic elemental twin walked out of the destroyed structure, dusting dirt and sand off of himself.

"Allah Akbar! Allah Akbar!"

Was the sound of a battle cry from advancing soldiers converging on him; Heavy Element drew his Desert Walter 01 sidearm, took the SUL position, squeezing off high-velocity rounds to dispatch several regular ISIS soldiers opening fire on him with their AK-47s only to see their bullets bounce off his suit and hardened skin. In the heat of the gun battle, another boosted Titan charged him in an attempt to take him down. Executing a textbook sidestep at the last second, he used his legs to wrap his charging opponent's legs into a scissor hold, dropping him face-first into the sand. Heavy Element, rolling to one knee, took aim with his firearm, triple-tapping him in the back of the skull at point-blank range, blowing his head clean off.

"Regenerate from that."

As he rose back to his feet, securing the area, his ears picked up the sound of a tank turret firing before feeling the shell striking him dead center in the chest, sending him flying. Heavy Element cursed and groaned as he bounced violently off the sand before coming to a rest. Now, on his back, he continued spewing a slew of profanity, mainly Italian, as he clutched his chest.

"Heavy Element, you dead?" Nitro yelled his question over his commlink.

"I'ma kill someone …," he groaned as shell fire smoke billowed from his mouth, "When I get up, I'ma kill someone!"

Before Nitro let off a sarcastic joke, he turned to see the assailing culprit rolling into the camp.

"Guys, these idiots got a Soviet T-62M," Nitro snarled over his commlink while powering up.

"Nice that you know your tanks!" Heavy Element spat back. "Now

Genesis

turn that damn thing into an ashtray!"

Before Nitro could unleash a super-heated plasma blast, his attack was interrupted by the Sarge touching down several yards before him with a thunderous thud, shaking the Earth while spraying sand everywhere.

He calmly raised his M2-X Ballistics rifle without a word, a modified, shorter version of the M1. He unleashed a sheering blue and white energy volley that cut through the air and obliterated the heavily armored Russian battled tank with one shot with one trigger squeeze. Everyone froze in their tracks just from the loud blast from the Sarge's rifle.

"In case you didn't figure it out, taking prisoners is optional!" He howled, "So if you are allergic to getting killed, I suggest…!"

"Allah Akbar!"

The Sarge's order to surrender was interrupted by a lone terrorist sprinting towards him. Rogers turned to take aim and fire, only to stop and lower his rifle after realizing he wore a vest full of explosives strapped to his chest and a dead man's detonator trigger in his right hand.

"Rogers!" Sister Sledge yelled in disbelief.

"What the hell is he doing?" Heavy Element asked with a contorted face.

The Sarge stood his ground and closed his eyes as the terrorist, now within a foot of his space, released the trigger, detonating the explosive vest and engulfing him in flames.

"Oh my god!" screamed Cyclone.

"Rogers!" Sister Sledge shrilled while clutching both sides of her head.

Without thought, she broke into a run heading towards him. She slowed down less than a yard from the detonation zone as the thick smoke began to clear.

Genesis

Standing tall and alive in the center of the chunky dissipating smolder was the Sarge, covered in blood and small body parts from the now-deceased suicide assassin. He opened his eyes and sighed, billowing smoke from his nostrils and mouth as he pulled one of the dead ISIS terrorist's fingers from his left ear, flicking it away. It broke the remaining extremists' will, still standing as they tossed down their weapons, dropping to their knees to surrender.

As minor wounds and burn marks around his face quickly healed, Rogers saw that the fighting was officially over and nonchalantly reached into one of the pouch compartments on his tactical gear, pulling out a freshly cut Cuban cigar along with a lighter to have a victory smoke. Heavy Element smirked, shaking his head, while a furious Sister Sledge glared at him with her fists clenched.

The Sarge responded with a semi-innocent shrug, wondering what he did wrong as she cut her eyes at him and stormed away to assist in the roundup of the terrorists they captured. Puffing on his cigar, the Sarge quickly scanned the perimeter, taking a quick headcount of all the Regulators present.

"Where's Merge?"

His question was answered by a deafening roar that came from one of the barracks.

"Sir, I got her," Blitz answered while strafing toward the roar.

~ ~

Within one of the still-standing barracks, Merge cornered a young ISIS terrorist trembling like a leaf as he held a machete out to defend himself. He was the last of the living after she savagely stormed it, mauling everyone in her path.

She paced the floor, staring at her mouse with her fangs reared. She released a booming roar, which caused the young man to almost drop his weapon.

Genesis

"Please…don't kill me…" He choked in his Arabic tongue. "Please…I surrender…I surrender…"

"Drop your weapon; get on your knees with your hands behind your head."

Merge's ears propped against Blitz's voice, but her eyes remained trained on her kill.

Blitz used the translator on his suit to let the boy understand what he was saying.

"Drop your weapon now, and get down like I told you, or she will kill you."

The young man quickly obeyed, dropping the weapon, and assumed the surrender position Blitz instructed him to take.

However, Merge bellowed another roar as she prepared to pounce on him.

"Merge, he has surrendered," Blitz said with a forceful tone. "The combatant is no longer a threat. Take him into custody. Merge!"

She turned back to her human form without a word, looking down at the ISIS fighter with disgust before turning to Blitz.

"You can take him into custody."

She walked out of the bunker, not giving him a second look as he turned to watch her leave, wondering what was going on between the two of them and how long he'd be able to endure this side of her he had not seen before. Questioning if it was always there.

Outside, a recovered Heavy Element and Sister Sledge began patting down, removing weapons, and applying plastic restraints while Nitro and Cyclone marched in stragglers. The quiet descending Tornado started a scan, securing the perimeter from above. With his rifle in safety, the Sarge stood like a granite sentinel covering his team against the

Genesis

unexpected.

"You demons!"

The howl came from a defiant terrorist sitting on the ground with his comrades.

"You think you won! Allah is on our side, and he will strike you all down!"

Every member of the Regulator team paused and slowly looked up at the sky, waiting to be struck down.

"You infidels!" He screamed. "You dare mock Allah!"

"No, they mock you," Nitro answered while approaching him. "They are waiting to see if Allah will answer the prayers of a murderer and rapist."

"Don't forget to add hypocrite," Heavy Element said as he held up a red vial of the unknown substance some terrorists used to gain superhuman abilities. "Considering you're roiding your soldiers up on this shit to obtain the power of 'demons.'"

"We do it in the name of Allah!" the terrorist howled. "We do it in the name of Islam!"

"Spoken like a true religious extremist," Nitro scoffed. "There's a special place in hell for people like you who twist the words of Allah for their own ends."

"Fuck you, you traitor!" the terrorist spat in his direction," I Agharr Salaam spit in your mother's pussy!"

The verbal offense was enough to cause Nitro to charge up and advance to incinerate the ISIS soldier where he sat.

"What the fuck did you say about my mother, you piece of shit?"

Genesis

Heavy Element jumped in Nitro's path, placing a firm metallic hand on his chest, stopping him.

"Private, remember who you are."

Nitro reluctantly powered down and stormed off, getting some needed distance to calm down, while Sister Sledge strolled over to the vocally radical terrorist.

"Unless you want me to grab you by your scrawny legs and slam you around like a rag doll until it rips off, shut up."

"I don't take orders from a fucking woman!" Agharr howled from his seated position. "I heard you as you fell from the sky, demon! It is bad enough that you invade our lands! How dare an infidel like you yell Allah Akbar?"

"I dare because I am Muslim," she glared back at him.

"Then you are worse than an infidel," Agharr spat on the ground, "You too are a traitor! A traitor to Allah! A traitor to Islam! You are nothing more than a filthy traitorous…"

His foul words choked out of him as Sister Sledge reached down, wrapping her hand around his throat, and effortlessly hoisted him.

"You are the traitor!" She spat back in perfect Arabic. "All of you have betrayed Allah and Islam! The way of Allah is not spilling the blood of the innocent! It is not murder, rape, or subjugation! Allah is all-powerful! He is omnipotent! He is the Creator of all! He does not need you to fight wars for Him!"

She violently released him, dropping him back into the group of captured prisoners.

"That is why Allah has blessed me with this strength!" She pointed at him. "This is my jihad! I will fight the likes of you forever to restore the true honor of Islam! The difference between you and I is that I can do it forever, and I will win!"

Genesis

"Sister Sledge."

She turned at Rogers's voice as he gave her a look, requesting to keep it professional. She fired him a dirty look, still remembering the stunt he pulled before walking off.

Amid the roundup, Merge returned and was greeted by her twin brother, stepping in her path, observing her suit and skin's large blood pattern.

"What happened to you?"

"Mauled a couple of insurgents in their barracks," She flatly answered while observing the blast pattern on his chest. "What happened to you?"

"Tank shell to the chest."

"Again?"

"Where's Oliver?"

"Bringing in a lone survivor," she pointed back with her thumb, "Is this everyone?"

"Maxine's doing a thermal scan from the Tornado as we speak; so far, she took out two snipers. The pat-down is almost complete, and I need to take a tally of this red shit; you should go report to the Sarge."

She nodded as he walked away; she turned to see Oliver walking with the young insurgent from the barracks in restraints, setting him down with the rest of the terrorists they captured.

Preoccupied by her thoughts, she barely noticed Cyclone walking up to her.

"Thanks for having my back today ... I ..."

"You ever get distracted in a combat situation again," Merge addressed her with a thick bass tone and zero eye contact. "You will be done. Do you hear me rook?"

Before Cyclone could acknowledge, she walked off to report to the Sarge. Cyclone sighed while shaking her head as Nitro walked up behind her.

"Don't take it personally; her bark is worse than her bite."

Cyclone turned to him, giving him a dull, sarcastic look.

"Yeah, that's a lie," he slightly lowered his head. "Both her bark and bite are horrible."

The Sarge stood calmly, spewing smoke from his nose and mouth as his cigar remained fixed within his jaw while his eyes stayed locked on the prisoners his team and him captured with a dull gaze. They moved slightly as Merge walked up to him to report in.

"Reporting in, sir," she responded with a stiff salute.

"You alright?" He asked with a gruff.

"Yes, sir."

He acknowledged her with a head nod and additional smoke.

"Take over babysitting duty; I want to check out this red shit Heavy Element is rounding up. Don't eat anyone."

"Yes, sir."

As he walked off, Merge transformed into her were-version of a timber wolf. Her savage growl had several of the captured insurgents yelp where they sat.

The Sarge strolled up to Heavy Element on one knee, tallying the number of pouches, each housing red vials to boost the ISIS insurgents.

Genesis

"Every last one of these sons of bitches had a pouch on them, Sarge," Heavy Element said while extending a pouch to him. "Considering the numbers and how fast this stuff apparently works, this should have been a lot harder."

The Sarge took the black pouch, opened it, and examined its contents. He began to slowly scan the dead and the living huddled together.

"Less than half their number boosted."

"Yep."

"There's more of this shit lying around here."

"Yep."

"Run a sweep of the entire camp," he ordered. "And don't forget to use the Doozers."

"You're never going to let me live that down," Heavy Element shook his head.

"You're just lucky your sorry ass was in metal form, and all you suffered was smoke inhalation."

"You do realize you just let ..."

The Sarge narrowed his eyes at Heavy Element, pulling rank as he blew thick white Cuban smoke from his nostrils and mouth. He took the hint, straightening up a bit.

"Yes, sir," he cleared his throat before activating his commlink. "Maxine, we're going to need some Doozers to do some ground sweeps."

"Sending them down," she acknowledged.

"And contact Lieutenant Colonel Stantz so he can send in his team and the transports." The Sarge interjected.

Genesis

"Affirmative."

~~~~~~~~~~~~~~~~~~~~~~~~~~~~~~~~~

As suspected, the base sweep unveiled more crates of the unknown red serum. On Roger's orders, the containers were loaded onto the Tornado before members of the 3rd Battalion, 25th Marines, showed up to retrieve the prisoners they captured. The prisoners were then split into two different transport vehicles.

The Regulators took those who boosted into custody and transported them via a prison shuttle commanded by Replicators backed by two black hulking Quad Doozers taking them to the newly constructed Purgatory. They were to be held until their powers went dormant. After a quick verbal debriefing where the Sarge left out and finding the red booster serum the ISIS soldiers used during the battle, the team departed, returning stateside to the Ranch.

The flight back was primarily silent, with thick molasses tension within the cabin as individual members chose to sit far away. In contrast, others sat in the middle of the ship, making no subtle movements as they prayed for the hypersonic craft to fly faster and land so that they could get off. The only unaffected, Adrian leaned back in his chair with his headphones on, cracking up as he watched the latest Foamy the Squirrel episode on YouTube.

He looked up from his screen and saw a frustrated Aashif with his head down, running his hand through his partially dyed fire orange and black hair. With a huff, he paused the video, removed his headset, and sat up, leaning forward into his junior teammate's space.

"Aashif, you alright?"

Aashif lifted his head from his thoughts, answering him with a nod.

"You know, I remember I got into this huge fight at school because this punk said something about my mother," Adrian jumped into his story. "Busted his nose, closed his eye, I got suspended for two weeks. When I got

Genesis

home, my mother almost killed me, which was a shock because my dad was usually trying to murder me when I screwed up. When she calmed down, she told me she was hurt because I of all people who she gave birth to and raised should know what type of lady she is in the streets, the type of wife she is to my father, and the type of mother she is to my sister and me. She said my fists are only to be thrown at people who try to physically hurt my family, not for punks who throw out lies with their mouth and don't know jack about her."

Adrian gave Aashif's leg a sharp brotherly smack as he looked him dead in the eyes.

"Your mom was a proud soldier who served her country, a hero, and no insult from some insurgent bitch who's now off to a black site changes that. You got that?"

"Thanks," Aashif nodded with a smirk.

He changed the subject, glancing at the tension coming from opposite sides of the ship.

"So, what do we do about this?" Aashif whispered.

"Well, I can transform into the properties of metal," Adrian shrugged. "As for you, I'd strongly advise not making any sudden movements until this bird lands, then find your way to the exit as quickly as possible."

Both Teuila, listening to the conversation, and Aashif cut him a sardonic dirty look as Adrian leaned back in his seat with a bright grin, repositioning his headset back over his ears to listen to the rest of the video on his phone.

~~~~~~~~~~~~~~~~~~~~~~~~~~~~~~~~~~~

Finally, arriving at the Ranch, the roof of the massive hanger slid open. Maxine performed a VTOL landing inside of it. The platform locks engaged, securing the Tornado as the top closed, while the floor underneath the ship disengaged, slanting downward into the newly reconstructed

Genesis

Regulator base.

Waiting at the bottom was Erica Champion, who went by the call sign Lady Tech, accompanied by Maxine's younger android sisters, Jennifer and Angie, and two human-sized Quad Doozers.

She stuck her hands in her white lab coat, dressed in simple jeans, a black Wu-Tang t-shirt, and Converse sneakers. As the floor stopped locking next to the second Tornado, Erica strolled closer to the opening side hatch.

Teuila and Aashif were the first to exit the ship with faces of relief.

"Welcome ...back?" She greeted them with a face of confusion.

Both wore mirrored visages as if they were too scared to speak.

"What happened?" Erica asked with narrowed eyes.

"Not a thing," Teuila answered, shaking her head.

"Not a damn thing," Aashif firmly reiterated, shaking his head.

Erica fluttered her eyes with irritated disgust as Rosann, followed by Sister Shareef, exited the ship next. Her eyes first locked onto the thick, dried-up blood on Rosann's leotard bodysuit, bare legs, and one side of her face.

"Uh ...welcome back."

Rosann greeted Erica with a half-smirk while Sister Shareef walked up to her with a pleasant smile, giving her a pat on the shoulder.

"Maxine reported that the mission was a success."

"It was," Shareef nodded.

"So why does everyone look like we're in an episode of the Walking Dead?"

Genesis

Shareef's pleasant expression changed to displeasure as more boots came down the ship's boarding steps. Adrian was the first to come down with a big yawn and stretch, followed by Oliver, who made zero eye contact with Rosann as he walked up to Erica, throwing a fake smile on. She then realized what was actually going on.

"I stand corrected," Erica muttered to herself. "We're in an episode of Friends."

A granite face Rogers was second to last to exit the ship, followed by Maxine. Sister Shareef rolled her eyes, not even looking in his direction, and walked away to keep the distance between them. Erica sighed and mentally willed herself out of her teammates' personal affairs as Rogers approached her.

"Any problems with the M2?"

"A slight kickback," Rogers answered, shaking his head, "But nothing too serious, far better than the M1."

"So, what's this new booster you uncovered that you decided to both hide and secretly rush back here with?"

Rogers handed her one of the pouches they removed from an ISIS insurgent. She opened it up, took out the vial of red liquid, and looked it over.

"We uncovered twelve additional crates of this stuff," Rogers frowned. "It apparently works the second it's injected, every insurgent had a similar pouch on their person, but for some reason, not all of them boosted."

"I'll run some tests."

Erica's face formed a scowl as she leaned in, giving Rogers a whiff.

"Why do you smell like blood and burnt meat?" She asked while coiling back.

Genesis

"Because he's a dumbass."

They both turned to Sister Shareef's voice as she glared at him from where she stood.

"You don't need to know the gory details, child."

"Fine with me," Erica shrugged while wafting the scent away.

She uncomfortably stood in the middle of the two as Sister Shareef continued to look at Rogers with dagger eyes.

"Something you want to say to me?" Rogers asked with a gruff.

Sister Shareef sucked her teeth before answering.

"Nope …I'm off to the showers and will be in my room afterward …and I don't wish to be disturbed."

Lady Tech took over as she sauntered off, giving him a disapproving glare.

"What did you do?"

Rogers looked down at her with a dull expression she knew all too well.

"The day you furnish a birth certificate that says I came from your womb, I might tell you."

He then spun on his heel, walking away.

"You make me think about getting my tubes tied!" She shot back.

"Rosann and Oliver, a word," Rogers waved them over with a hand gesture.

They glanced at one another before walking over to Rogers standing before him.

Genesis

"What did I say about keeping your personal shit out of my missions?" he whispered.

Oliver embarrassingly looked away while Rosann shamefully lowered her head.

"Normally I deliver, one warning, but you two have enough salt in you that I can extend you this one-time courtesy and deliver one …final …warning. Break up, stay together, I don't give a damn. Figure it out on your own time and keep it the hell out of my missions. Is that understood?"

"Yes, sir," they both acknowledged.

"There won't be a strike three. That's all, go get cleaned up and some food in you."

Rosann turned to march off with a scowl on her face as Oliver sucked in and exhaled all of the air into his lungs in frustration following behind at a safe distance.

"Ms. Kalani and Mr. Salek, step into my presence," Rogers barked.

Both nervously glanced at each other as they approached him and stood at the stiffest attention. Rogers took a minute as he folded his arms, using his eyes to look them up and down.

"Ms. Kalani, I don't have to reiterate Ms. Esposito's warning to you…do I?"

"No, sir," she shook her head.

"Good, because her warning…is my warning… which also goes for you, Mr. Salek."

Aashif semi-choked on his swallow as Rogers stared right through him.

"Unless it's a recon mission, I don't ever want to hear in the middle of a fight what the enemy has unless it's something you can't turn into slag, in which case you will then need back up. And the last I checked, tank armor is a cakewalk for you. The time you took to call out the name of the damn thing, you could have scorched it from the damn Earth. Do not ever make me have to come over and do your job again."

"Sir…it won't ever happen again," Aashif apologetically answered while clearing his throat.

"You're damn right, it won't," Rogers slightly raised his voice. "There is a reason why this team only has two additional members out of hundreds of applicants. On paper, four of you beat out the rest, and only you two survived your six months under me. Whether you continue to keep the spots you've earned is entirely up to you and how you perform during missions, is that understood?"

"Yes, sir!" They both yelled.

"Aside from that, you both did some good work out there today," Rogers nodded. "So, get rid of the other shit, and keep impressing me. Go, get cleaned up and some food in you."

"Yes, sir!"

As they quickly turned and hurried off to get out of the Sergeant's sight, Adrian strolled up to Rogers with a mischievous smile, who greeted him with his trademark dull look.

"Any assessment of me today, Sarge?"

"Yeah, stop getting shot by tanks."

"That's all you got for me?" Adrian asked as his face switched to one of perplexed.

"It's been a weird day," Rogers answered with narrowed eyes. "Do I need to tell you what to do next?"

"Shit, shower, and food."

Genesis

Rogers put on his "Out of my face" visage, which was Adrian's hint to take his leave.

~ ~

As the day turned into night,

Rogers leaned back in the chair in his quarters, reviewing the debriefing on his tablet that he dictated to Maxine about the Regulator's latest mission.

"Sergeant Rogers, Ms. Shareef, is at your door waiting to enter."

Rogers lowered his head, kneading his brow.

He knew if he opened the door, Abe was in for a colossal argument he did not wish to have. However, if he did not open the door, he would be in for a massive disagreement the following day if she didn't decide to kick it down.

"Let her in."

As the door slid open, she strolled in with her long silver braids tied back, wearing a simple green tank top and black tights. Shareef's face still had a disapproving scowl as she walked up to him. Rogers looked up from his chair, returning fire with a visage of irritation.

She deflected his gaze as she took the tablet from his hand, placed it on his desk, sat in his lap, straddled, cupped his face, and kissed him deeply.

The reinforced chair groaned and creaked from the two Titans' weight as Rogers returned the kiss, sliding his hands down her back to cup her rear. He lifted her into the air, carrying her over to his bed while she wrapped her legs around him, pulled off her top, and tossed it away.

Shareef continued to kiss him as he laid her down. He removed his shirt, chucking it away as she undid his belt buckle and pulled down his pants. She leaned back, arching her back, panting as he kissed her belly

Genesis

while pulling off her tights.

~ ~

Inside the Ranch's recreation room, Erica and Aashif teamed up in a tag team battle against Adrian and Teuila in the latest Battlefield Wrestling Industries fighting game "Legacy Twelve." The stage was the "Legacy Twelve" Pay-Per-View, with their teams competing in a championship ladder match with the BWI World Tag Team Championship belts hanging over the ring as the prize. Adrian controlled Abe Rogers in his BWI persona, while Teuila commanded BWI female wrestler Kira Bristow. Their opponents were Erica, manning the first female BWI World Champion, Yuku Shiro, while Aashif operated one of Rogers's arch-rivals, Sammy Nyte.

In the middle of the trash-talking and button-tapping, Adrian managed to hurl Erica's character out of the ring for a nasty spill. Teuila's character ducked at the last moment, pulling the ropes as Aashif's wrestler came in for a clothesline, only to spill over the top rope onto the ring floor.

"Dammit!" Aashif cursed.

"And here we go!" Teuila grinned.

Teuila's character, Kira Bristow, broke into the run on her command, hitting the opposite ropes, and dashed across the ring, gaining momentum. With a sequence of taps, her character dived over the top ropes, hitting a flying cross body and crashing down on Aashif's character.

"Booyah bitch!" She yelled.

"Nice one," Adrian nodded. "Going for the belts!"

Adrian scrambled up the ladder toward the hanging BWI World Tag Championship belts.

"No, you're not," Erica smirked.

Her Yuku Shiro character gripped the ropes, pulling them back.

Genesis

"Oh shit! Teuila, get your ass in the ring now!"

"I'm trying!"

"Over my dead body!" Aashif roared.

His Sammy Nyte character attacked her character, Kira Bristow, from behind, grabbing her legs and yanking her off the apron; he then bounced her skull off the ring apron, preventing her from entering the ring.

Erica's character leaped onto the top rope and then springboarded off, dropkicking the ladder, causing it to fall and for Rogers to fly off it, crashing hard to the mat.

"Son of a bitch!" Adrian stomped.

"That's what happens when you mess with the Queen of Queens," Erica taunted.

"Miss, Sergeant Rogers, and Sister Shareef will be unavailable for the rest of the evening," Maxine announced over the audio system.

"Oye, Dios Mio," she palmed her face.

"I feel like a choir boy compared to those two," Adrian said. "When the hell are they going to come out and just say they're seeing each other? They gotta know by now they ain't fooling anyone."

"I thought they didn't like each other?" Aashif interjected.

"In the beginning, they didn't," Teuila answered with a smirk.

"You guys got to understand this is awkward and uncomfortable for the both of them," Erica said. "She is a mature woman in her sexual prime with Titan physiology, taking her literally back to her physical twenties, and Rogers is a mature man who's been around the block and also knocked back to his sexual prime when he became a Titan. It is the perfect chemistry for boot-knocking. I'm surprised they find the restraint to leave their room. Acting like hormone-fueled teenagers can be a bit embarrassing

Genesis

for people their age, especially for Rogers, who's also our team leader."

"Well, I think it's cute," Teuila said with a shrug. "I grew up seeing my parents like that, and they still paw at each other even to this day."

"I'm surprised she's giving him the business considering what he did," Erica scoffed while leaning back in her seat.

Awkwardness stepped into the room as all three looked at each other, wondering who tattled on Rogers. They then leered at her with narrowed eyes, wondering if she had read their minds.

"You three forgot Maxine was surveying the mission via the Tornado?" Erica leered back at them in disbelief, asking. "What I got to ask is how all of you could stand there and let it happen."

"No one let anything happen; no one expected him to do what he did," Adrian answered, looking her dead in the eyes. "We've all seen the Sarge clip a moving target with your rifles from four miles away. An ISIS terrorist from less than a yard should have been like taking a piss for him. Even Sister Shareef was shocked when it happened."

"That's why she was so pissed at him," Aashif interjected, shaking his head. "I saw her face when the bomb went off. She was scared …really scared. She took off running before all of us and didn't stop until the smoke cleared."

Aashif's revelation blanketed the room with an uncomfortability that damaged the gameplay.

"Maxine, schedule a mandatory psych evaluation for Sergeant Rogers on both of our calendars," Erica commanded. "Make sure to put it in bold and in red with several annoying alarm reminders."

"Yes, Miss."

~ ~

Genesis

Several hours later,

Shareef and Abe panted and laughed as they lay entangled in one another, drenched in sweat, with just a thin sheet covering the lower half of their bodies. Shareef nuzzled against his chest as Rogers wrapped an arm around her, holding her close while attempting to catch his breath.

"I think … we broke our record … again," he choked.

"At least … it wasn't the bed … again," she chuckled.

"Yeah, I don't think I could handle Erica looking at me with those eyes of disgust while I'm lying to her face," he said.

"'I tripped and fell' is a stupid excuse," she giggled, "Especially when you couldn't explain what you tripped on."

"My mind went blank, especially when I saw you running out of the room wrapped in my sheets."

"Everyone was coming!"

"But you just threw me off of you and left me sitting there on a broken bed butt ass naked trying to figure out how I was going to explain myself. And all I could think of was you running through the halls of a base that has cameras everywhere."

She paused for a second, thinking about it. She blushed as her forehead fell on Rogers's chest.

"Yeah, that was stupid too."

The two of them burst into more boisterous laughter over the memory. Sister Shareef quickly wiped her eyes as it brought her close to tears.

"Why do you think anyone hasn't said anything yet?" She asked while clearing her throat.

Genesis

"Probably too scared to ask," He shrugged, saying.

"Speaking of scared."

She raised her head a bit, making eye contact with him, as the humor fell from her face. He slowly removed his own, respecting her new demeanor that was still unhappy with him.

"You need to explain to me what happened out there today," she demanded to know with a stern tone. "And I swear to Allah if you don't answer or deflect with some off-color joke, I will …"

Rogers took her hand into his own, holding it as he kept eye contact with her. The simple act made her eyes glassy as she finally revealed how much he had frightened her that morning.

"I have been shot by almost every known armament that has ever been created to kill," he explained. "I lost count of how many bullets have hit me. I survived one of Oliver's supernova blasts. I've totaled cars that slammed into me and stopped a truck attempting to run me over with my bare hands. I jump out of planes from high velocities, like jumping into a pool. And last week …I got a call from my daughter-in-law that my eldest son accidentally broke his arm after falling off a ladder from cleaning his gutters. His birthday is a month from now, and he's two years from forty."

Shareef bowed her head, now understanding what had happened.

"A parent is not supposed to bury their children. Being like this …barring an insane event like Peace or a group like the Zombie Nation has sealed my fate for what is most likely in store for me." Rogers said as his lower jaw shifted while he attempted to cage his emotions. "Erica's analysis says the virus has added a hundred …maybe even two hundred years to my lifespan. I already had to bury my wife; I don't think I can handle burying all of my kids …and possibly my grandkids."

"You're not feeling suicidal …are you?" She asked with concern.

"No!" He snapped at her while sitting up and wearing his angry face. "That was me using a psychological tactic to end a damn conflict! I've

Genesis

been hit by far worse than the rig that son of a bitch was wearing today. No one wants to continue fighting someone you can't kill."

"There are far better ways to get that point across than getting blown up, Abe," she retorted while sitting on her knees on the bed.

Shareef grabbed the sheet, wrapping it around her body before she took a seat next to him. She took one of his textured cinderblock hands, caressing the back and the knuckles while gazing into his eyes.

"As you very well know, I have a son and daughter who I am estranged from because of what I did. I have been gone for so long; my daughter, who was a borderline infant when I went in, has problems both being around me and relating to me, especially now that I am superhuman." Shareef exhaled. "While my son wants nothing to do with me because I killed his father, I don't know what is worse …him telling me I should have been the one to die or the fact that he is a dedicated Republican."

Shareef threw on a bright smile as her tears began to run.

"Allah has been merciful to me," she continued scratchily. "Because despite me, my son went on to make something of himself: a House Rep for Austin, a beautiful wife who I want to desperately believe has a brain-rattling around that skull of hers, and three lovely grandchildren that I still have not seen. And I, too, have to realize, just like you, that one day …I may be the one burying them."

Rogers reached out with his other hand, wiping away the tears from her cheeks with his thumb.

"But the future is not written in stone," Shareef sternly pressed while placing a hand on the left cheek of his face, "If someone like Captain Omega can bite the farm, there's a headstone in the future for both you and me. Being who I am now affords me two advantages …time to fix what I broke all those years ago and a chance to create a safe world for them to live in. If it is my lot in life to bury my children, let it be of natural causes where they are surrounded by their children, and hopefully their grandchildren … I can live with that."

Genesis

She leaned in closer, nuzzling her nose against his.

"Your children don't want you thinking about their possible deaths; they want you in the moment with them enjoying life for however long it carries. Not to mention, there are far more productive things you could be doing than getting yourself blown up."

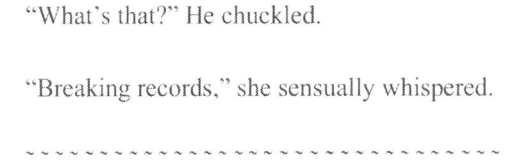

"What's that?" He chuckled.

"Breaking records," she sensually whispered.

~ ~

On the other side of the base, Oliver and Rosann sat in his living quarters, half staring at one another. They had not spoken since their return; they did not even bother eating with one another after cleaning up.

After dinner, Oliver went to his quarters while Rosann retired to the shooting range.

Two hours later, she was at his door. She said no word to him as she barged in wearing his tank top and boxers. She went to his bed, plopping down on it, and grabbed his game controller, picking up from her spot on the video game Overwatch. He went back to the comic books on his tablet that he downloaded.

An ominous silence choked the room until Rosann became frustrated over a level she could not clear, and Oliver ran out of books to read. He decided to be the one to break it first.

"So, is the honeymoon over, or is this something else?"

"I told you when we're on missions just to leave me be," she said dryly. "I can't afford you to be in my head, and you don't need to think about me either."

"All I was doing was sitting across from you, and I saving your ass today proved my head is always in the game."

Genesis

Rosann glared at him as he folded his arms, wearing a Teflon demeanor to deflect her dagger-like stares.

"What are we doing, Rose?" He softened a bit while rubbing the bridge of his nose. "Do you not want to be with me anymore?"

"That's not it," she said while lowering her head.

"Then, what is it?"

Rosann raised her head, locking eyes with him.

"Eight months ago, I stood over your body, and there was no heartbeat. You were dead cold. And you walk around and act like it didn't happen."

A sliver of irritation appeared on Oliver's face, but he held his peace, wanting her to finish.

"That image is forever carved into my skull," She said with a scowl. "It wakes me up out of my sleep. And when I lay next to you, I sometimes check if you're still breathing. I don't ever want to see that image again. So, every time we go out there and face people whose sole intention is to kill us by any means necessary, I turn into a callous, cold-hearted bitch before each of our missions to make sure that I can do everything within my power to ensure we all make it home. And I'm sorry, but sometimes it feels like you're still playing hero instead of being a soldier, and it pisses me the fuck off."

"Are you finished?" He asked with a low growl in his voice.

Oliver paused a minute to ensure that his anger remained in check.

"First of all, ...how dare you. You don't think I don't know I was dead? I was the one with that bitch's hand around my throat. I was the one who felt his life slipping away while she was taking it away from me. You're checking to see if I'm breathing? How many countless nights have I jumped out of my sleep-in cold sweats screaming my head off, clutching my chest, searching for a heartbeat? But I refuse to let what Peace did cripple me. I get up every day on a mission to make sure she did not beat me by being just me. And I don't need my girlfriend treating me like shit because I'm not some dark brooding anti-hero!"

Her composure and expression switched to one of confusion.

"What the hell does that mean?"

"It means I love you, Rose, but my patience is running thin. Death is an occupational hazard of being on this team, there is no avoiding it, and I have no intention of quitting. If I can stand here and deal with the fact that there is a possibility I could end up permanently on a slab again, you need to come to terms with it too. Or at least show me more of this side instead of the person I feel like I want to be as far away from as possible. If not …I don't think we can continue this."

Her eyes became glassy as tears began to trickle down them. The weight of her tears caused her head to lower a bit.

"I don't want that …"

His head dropped as a painful sigh came out of him.

"I don't want that either …"

"I wanna try; I don't want to be like this …it's just getting harder and harder to turn it off when we come back."

Oliver stepped toward her, but Rosann held a hand up, stopping him.

"I don't need you to come over here and comfort me."

A turned off, Oliver fell back against the wall, folding his arms. She quickly raised her head so he could see her.

"I need you to come over here," Rosann whispered. "And make me scream."

Genesis

~~~~~~~~~~~~~~~~~~~~~~~~~~~~~~~~~~~

Coahuila, Mexico, sometime after midnight,

Miguel Ángel Castillo, an alleged former lieutenant under El Chapo, now head of his own cartel, sat disheveled and battered with a swollen right eye on the opposite side of his desk within his mini-mansion. With his healthy left eye, he timidly looked at the inhuman damage done to his office and the dead bodies of his men that littered the floor.

He clutched his broken right arm, whimpering as his working eye finally returned to the man sitting in his chair on his side of the desk, looking back at him.

He knew it was a man based on his build, but that was where the identification ended. The man sat adorned in a jet-black hooded jumpsuit made from some unknown material with a dull shine. The hood covered the top of his head, while a red and black shiny metallic kabuki mask covered his visage. Two of his henchmen flanking Miguel's left and right wore similar outfits, except their masks were pure jet black. His third, a woman wearing similar attire, stood off to the side, holding up a little camcorder recording the ominous event as their boss clasped his gloved hands while sadly shaking his head at Castillo.

"Ángel ... Ángel," the man spoke with a synthesized distorted voice in Spanish, "I gave you and everyone who agreed to purchase Rebirth from me two distinct and unbreakable rules that were non-negotiable. Number one, do not get caught using Rebirth. I gave you and your men clear instructions and a schedule for when to boost up, and as long as you followed it to the letter, you would have had the most powerful cartel in all of Mexico.

The second rule, even more critical than the first, is that Rebirth is not resalable under any circumstances. The sole purpose of selling Rebirth to organizations like yours was to put you back on equal footing with all the do-good heroes and super-powered government units. You, like everyone else, agreed to these terms. We shook on it."

The masked man extended his right hand out.

Genesis

"This hand, you shook this hand and agreed to my terms and rules. And then, you went behind my back and blatantly broke my rule selling it to the one organization I would never in a million years sell Rebirth to, religious fanatics. Do you want to know why I don't sell to groups like ISIS Ángel? Do you?"

"I …I …I didn't," a terrified Ángel attempted to escape, pleading his case.

"Because survey says, they don't follow the rules aside from their own, they're irrational, and they could potentially lead a paper trail back to me," the man continued. "Which is what I don't want, I am a man of privacy, and I cannot maintain my privacy if my product is in the hands of terrorists. And now, because of you, my product is in the hands of the United States Government."

"I swear, man, it wasn't me!" Ángel screamed. "I swear!"

"Stop it, Angel, you're embarrassing yourself," He waved him off, scolding him. "I have surveillance on all of my customers twenty-four hours a day. I know all of your conversations, even from the burner phones that you used. Oh, by the way, that nice ten million you made off of my product sitting in your offshore account, which is a fucking insult, is now mine. I could have made them pay ten times that amount if I chose to do business with them. I also emptied out your other accounts as compensation for placing me in this most uncomfortable predicament."

"Take it, take it all," He begged. "Just please, don't kill me."

"My initial plan was to let you complete the transaction, kill every last one of your customers that you sold to. Cleaning up the mess you made for me, and then come back here, dropping their heads at your feet before I killed you. Unfortunately, due to miscalculations, the United States Super Soldier Unit, known as the Regulators, raided the compound one hour before we were going to strike and now has my product, further complicating my life."

He leaned forward, wagging a finger at Castillo.

Genesis

"All because you took one look at me and figured that I was a sweet tight wet pussy you could fuck."

"No man …no."

"I'm going to tell you one last time, Ángel, stop embarrassing yourself," he furiously pointed. "You looked at me in my outfit and my shiny mask and said, 'This idiot looks like he came straight out of a comic book; he ain't going to do shit to me. I'm going to do what I want to do because I'm Miguel Ángel Castillo, the Angel of Death; I ran with El Chapo, I'm a boss! No one can tell me shit what to do.' That is what you thought; you grossly underestimated my power, which is why all of your men and your family are dead, your empire obliterated, and I am now sitting in your chair."

The masked man extended his right hand, gesturing as if gripping something. At the same time, Angel clutched his throat with his working arm gurgling from some unknown force choking him. As the masked man rose from his seat, lifting his arm higher, Castillo, with a face that turned beet red, was raised out of the chair he sat in and suspended three feet off the ground. His legs flailed violently from being strangled in mid-air.

"I actually abhor violence," he exhaled under his mask, "I do my best to explore all other avenues and channels to avoid it. But at the end of the day, examples must be made when laws are broken and rules are violated. Do you have any idea what this world would be like without public order, the chaos and insanity that would ensue? You had rules and consequences for breaking the rules within your own organization Ángel. You knew better. Now, as you can probably tell, I'm a huge Star Wars fan. Guess who my favorite character is. Come on, guess. Give you a hint, he used to be a Jedi."

"Please, man …please…," Castillo spat out as his face became purple.

"One of my favorite force moves, which you only read about in the novels and see in the video games, is called the force crush. As you're about to find out, it's pretty self-explanatory."

Genesis

The hi-tech kabuki-masked man in black used both his hands, gesturing as if he was about to squash a soda can. A still suspended Castillo, no longer asphyxiated, now felt as if he was within the crushing force of a trash compactor.

"Now, just to let you know, the last time I tried this move, I got a guy down to the size of a medicine ball. With you, I'd like to shoot for a soccer ball. What do you say, Angel?"

"No, man! No! No!"

Castillo screamed as the two henchmen backed up so as not to get blood splatter on them while the female with the camcorder moved closer, adjusting the view and zooming in on the soon-to-be gruesome scene.

That night, Miguel Ángel Castillo's screams were more horrifying and bloodcurdling than the rest of the dead throughout the compound, mixed in with the crunching of bones.

When it all ended, the man in black walked out the front door of Miguel Ángel Castillo's mini-mansion, taking in a good stretch, followed by the rest of his crew. Their boss spun on his heel, turning to them to give them instructions.

"Turn all of the bodies to ash and then burn this place to the ground to cover your tracks."

His men nodded as he turned to the woman.

"Finish the video with the burning of the mansion. Make copies and have them couriered to all of our clients. Be sure to add some dramatic horror background music of some kind, liven it up."

The woman nodded as he turned his back to them and propelled himself into the air using the unknown power he wielded.

Genesis

CHAPTER 4

September 2016, Sunday 8:45 PM, Sanctuary Island time,

Sophia walked around her kitchen, preparing breakfast. It became her routine because her daughter still attended regular school in Washington, DC.

"Kimberly, breakfast is ready!" She called out, "You're going to be late!"

"Coming!" Her daughter yelled back from her room upstairs.

She shook her head as she peeled a banana and handed it to Sir George, the family spider monkey who stretched out his hands, taking it from her. She gave him a light pat on his head as he glanced up at her while munching away on his breakfast. She glanced at the digital clock on the wall and prepared to yell another forceful command when she heard feet coming down the steps.

"You keep cutting it close, young lady."

"Mom, it takes me less than fifteen minutes tops to get to school from here," Kimberly answered with fluttered eyes.

"That's only when you go orbital, which ends up ruining the lunch that I make for you."

"I don't know why you keep making lunch for me when I can just buy cafeteria food," Kimberly said, shrugging while sitting at the table.

"Because you don't eat lunch unless I make it for you," Sophia answered with narrowed eyes.

Genesis

She sat at the head of the table next to her daughter and waited as Kimberly sighed, forking some pancakes and turkey sausage onto her plate. She then took her spoon, scooping up some scrambled eggs.

"I really don't need to eat food or drink water, so I don't know what the big deal is."

"For the umpteenth time, yes, you do," Sophia pressed softly, steely, "You cannot function on just your bioenergy alone. If that were the case, your digestive system would shut down altogether. Let's not have this conversation again …eat …please."

Kimberly huffed as she scooped up some sliced banana and strawberries from a bowl, putting it on her plate, and then grabbed the bottle of maple syrup, drizzling it on top of the pancakes. Holding her knife, she set up a slice of pancake and some fruit, putting it in her mouth. A gentle smile grew on her mother's face as the opinionated, headstrong child began to dig into the food.

Sophia's eyes slowly examined her from head to toe, starting with her neatly braided hair tied back with a red scrunchy to the blue and black matching skintight long-sleeve Nike workout shirt and tights she wore. Kimberly, feeling the extra intensity of her mother's eyes on her, slowly looked up in the middle of chewing her food.

"What?"

"You actually have school clothes in your bookbag, right? Because you are not wearing that all day."

"Yes, mom, they're in my bag."

Kimberly rolled her eyes as she continued to eat. While chewing on a sausage, she muttered something she thought her mother wouldn't hear.

"If I had my flight suit …"

"You know why you don't have it anymore."

Genesis

Sophia folded her arms, waiting for her to say something smart. Kimberly decided not to tempt fate and kept her head down while finishing the fruit on her plate. Her mother softened her demeanor as she prepared to ask a subtle question.

"So … do you want to talk about it?"

"Talk about what, mom?"

"Saturday night."

"What's there to talk about? I had a bad dream," Kimberly said, shrugging as she ate. "It was a slip."

"You know it's okay, right?" Sophia gingerly urged.

"I know, mom," Kimberly said, fluttering her eyes again with an added voice of irritation. "It was just a dream … the Draugr is not coming back ever. I sent him into space myself, remember?"

"Don't do that," Sophia sternly warned her. "Do not bring some tough, cocky persona to me because I am going to see right through it. And do not shut me out either. Now, if it was just a slip, we will leave it as a slip. But if it was something else …"

"Mom …it was just a slip."

She looked into her daughter's eyes, which pleaded for her to drop it. With a nod, she let it go.

"I'm full; can I go to school now?"

"Yes," Sophia nodded again. "Don't forget to take your lunch, do not go orbital, and remember to text me when you get there."

"Yes, mom."

Kimberly got up from her seat and walked over to the table, grabbing the paper bag with her lunch and placing it in her book bag. She

Genesis

closed the bag, secured it onto her shoulders, and headed for the door.

"I don't get a kiss now?" Sophia asked with folded arms.

With another huff, her daughter spun on her heel, running back, and kissed her. She then gave Sir George a quick kiss on his head before darting out of the house through the main door. Sophia was already on her feet, moving to the large central pane window to watch her child leap off the porch, landing on the sand. She trotted a few steps before exploding into the air and taking flight. The crackling of a thunderous sonic boom erupted across the sky as she went hypersonic, heading to her school in Washington, DC.

A sad sigh came from Sophia's lips. She only had seven sweet months of escorting her to school.

~ ~

After the battle with Peace and the Zombie Nation, Kimberly officially became the second powerful EVO on the planet; though nowhere near her mother's planetary strength range, her power was comfortably in the upper echelon continental level, indicated by Lady Tech's tests. As she continued to age, it would quickly reach and possibly surpass Sophia's and her other abilities.

Having a child fueled with bioenergy came with a new set of challenges.

Like her mother, Kimberly did not need to sleep or eat to sustain herself anymore. Nonetheless, Sophia had to forcefully reinforce both a diet and a strict sleeping pattern for her, which caused some conflicts.

Kimberly would forget to eat for almost an entire day, not understanding the need for organic sustenance if she was self-sustaining. It was quickly remedied by a stern tone and the second she got a whiff of her mother's cooking. Keeping her on a sleeping schedule proved to be more difficult. Sophia explained in detail that sleep was still essential for them to stay mentally sound. Even though it would no longer harm her physically, lack of sleep would cause the days and nights to blur together. She would

Genesis

soon lose track of time itself and reality, which happened to Sophia the first couple of months after returning.

Kimberly put up a much stronger fight when it came to sleep due to her night terrors, which began to manifest days after the battle with the Draugr. Based on Erica's analysis, which Sophia bitterly agreed with, Kimberly's eidetic memory was causing her nightmares while she slept. The dreams usually involved her alone or surrounded by a sea of dead bodies. Eventually, the Draugr would come for her, and no matter how hard she fought, he would overpower her, drag her away, and do unspeakable things that haunted Sophia just from hearing them.

Sophia and Erica began to teach Kimberly mental techniques to suppress stressful memories during sleep, triggering night terrors. The training sessions' focal point was to focus and stay positive to bury the memory.

Kimberly could control her memories and dreams in time, stopping the nightmares. However, there were still times when slips would occur, most notably when she was in a bad mood.

These slips forced Sophia to reconstruct and reinforce Kimberly's bed and bedroom, which sometimes took the full brunt of her waking up in terrified screaming fits.

This produced another challenge as Kimberly became obsessed with surpassing her limits and getting stronger. Like her mother, she started watching every video she could find on hand-to-hand combat, both on a human and superhuman level.

If she could physically duplicate it, she watched it. Regular human hand-to-hand was terrible enough due to Kimberly's shockwaves when using her super speed. Her attempt to copy superhuman abilities proved problematic on a dangerous level.

Sophia's mind wandered back to one of the more recent incidents that strained their new and fresh relationship.

Like her mother, Kimberly could produce energy attacks with the

Genesis

bioenergy stored within her. Knowing the negative aspect of forbidding her to use this ability, Sophia begrudgingly helped her hone it, agreeing that she only used it in her presence. Kimberly kept her promise mostly, but her age explored other boundaries to cross like all children.

One Saturday afternoon, while sitting in her office attempting to get some personal work done, she felt all the hairs on her body stand on end. It was followed by the tensing of her muscles and a ball of knots forming in her stomach. She got up from her seat to peer out her office window and witnessed a surging white light growing brighter on the other side of the beach.

"Oh no ..."

Sophia went on instinct as she rushed out of the house, damaging the main door. She leaped off the porch, launching into the sky, heading toward the glowing surge of energy. Her heart boomed within her chest while she prayed to get there on time. Sophia violently touched the beach, spraying sand everywhere as her daughter assumed a cliché stance from many video game and anime shows. In the middle of her hands was a ball of white energy savagely crackling and growing as the power poured from the pores of her skin to form it.

Witnessing the spectacle from a supposed safe distance were her friends Kyle and Akram and other children from the island.

"Kimberly! What the hell are you doing?!"

"I got it, mom! I got it!"

She trembled as she tried to control the surging ball of energy aggressively expanding between her hands.

"You're giving it too much power! Shut it down now!"

"Mom, I said I got this!"

A furious Sophia bolted over, grabbed her daughter's hands, and focused on draining the energy. Her eyes blazed bright blue as she absorbed

Genesis

the power into herself until the ball dissipated. She swayed a bit due to the lightheadedness of coming into contact with Awakening energy for the first time. An infuriated Kimberly wrenched her hands away from her mother.

"I said I had it, mom!"

"You foolish child," Sophia bared her teeth. "Do you have any idea what you could have done?!"

"Nothing was going to happen!" She yelled and stomped. "I wasn't going to fire it! I was in control …"

"You were in control of nothing!" Sophia roared at her. "You had no control of the bioenergy you were producing! If it continued to expand and accidentally detonated in your hands, you could have killed everyone on the island! You also don't have to extend your arms to release it! The slightest movement and that sphere can fire from the same stance you were in, and energy continues to move until it disperses! Did you think about the ship you could have hit or the damage it could do to the mainland it reached? California is that way!"

"I …I would have…"

"What?! Fired it into the air?!" Sophia got into Kimberly's face, admonishing her. "Where there are airplanes?! You know we have satellites that orbit our planet and a damn space station! Not to mention what could have happened if the blast was on a supernova level; best case, you destroy the Earth's ozone layer, which would slowly kill off all life, worse case, you ignite the oxygen in the atmosphere and turn the entire planet into a friggin fireball!"

"Mom!" Kimberly coiled back, whimpering.

"Do not …!"

Sophia caught herself, realizing they were not alone as the other children present stood there with scared looks on their faces, watching her lay into her daughter. She lowered her head and forced her body to stop shaking.

Genesis

"Go to the house ...now," she sternly whispered.

A thoroughly embarrassed Kimberly, with streaming tears, turned on her heel and rocketed off back to the house.

"The rest of you go back home to your parents," she ordered the children. "Kyle and Akram ...come here, please."

Both boys nervously shuffled over to stand within arm's reach of her.

"We didn't ..." They began to say in unison.

"Do not lie to me," she stopped them with a steel-toned voice. "You three are as thick as thieves. Do you have any idea what could have happened today?"

They both sadly nodded.

"A lot of people could have gotten hurt," she swallowed. "You could have gotten hurt, or worse. If you are her friends, you will never encourage her to do this ever again. Are we clear?"

"Yes, ma'am," they meekly nodded.

"Go home."

As they shamefully walked away, Sophia turned to look out into the bright blue ocean as a wave of emotion washed over her, followed by blinding tears. She muffled her mouth as her body began to rattle.

Guilt was beating her about how she treated Kimberly, and fear was punching her in the gut, realizing what would have happened if she was a second too late or away on a mission, saving the day.

She cursed out her frustration to the sea and then sat in the sand for twenty minutes, taking in her tropical scenery to calm down.

She finally got up and returned to the house to further settle her

Genesis

nerves. As she entered the house, she called Kimberly downstairs, sat her down, and apologized for embarrassing her in front of her friends. She explained to her why she was angry.

"I was afraid, for you ...and what would have happened if you lost control."

"But I wasn't ...," Kimberly raised her voice.

She stopped mid-sentence as her mother's eyes told her she wasn't going to take her, both interrupting and speaking to her as if she was one of their friends. She sat quietly and gave her both the respect and attention she demanded.

"You were not in control of it. Firing a stream is not the same as building a charge." Sophia exhaled while explaining. "Discharging energy is like cutting an artery. Once you release it, the flow of energy increases until you tie it off. Like I taught you, I count between one to ten seconds in my head every time I fire a stream; anything higher than ten, and I can wipe out half a city. And that's just using my eye beams ...I count to eight when I use my hands, and I never hold a charge while I'm on the planet."

"But I saw you do it twice at the mountain," Kimberly pouted. "When I was little ..."

"I know you did," Sophia agreed, nodding. "But I was not as powerful as I am now, and you are more powerful than I was back then. Also, on that day, I was both angry and reckless. If I had actually released that enormous charge, I could have killed countless people, including you. I was lucky to focus it into a stream with the second charge, and it didn't take much to obliterate that mountain. This power within us ...it's not something that can be easily controlled, honey. One false slip and the consequences are devastating."

"But how was I supposed to know that?" Kimberly asked while sadly lowering her head.

"You weren't," Sophia said with a shameful huff.

Genesis

She moved closer, holding her hand.

"I should have taught you; that was my mistake. I was scared. I have been scared. A lot of what I have done at this point was through a lot of trial and error. And so, I have been dragging my feet when it comes to teaching you because if I teach you, I can't take this weapon away once we're done and lock it up for another time. Do you understand what I am trying to say?"

"I think so."

"I don't know what I am doing," Sophia admittedly shook her head. "If I make a mistake, it is on me, and I have to live with it. If you make a mistake …it is still on me because you are my responsibility, and I have to live with it."

Sophia took another deep breath as she decided what to do.

"I need for you to promise me that you will not use any type of energy attacks …for now. I am asking you to do this for two reasons. One, I need to get my act together and figure out the proper way to guide you in using your abilities. Trial and error are not acceptable. The second reason is unless you're going to use it to start a fire or weld metal …you don't need to master an ability like that right now."

"But what if …?" Kimberly began to protest.

Sophia stopped her with a smile and a gentle hand placed on the left side of her face.

"You already know you can do it; you don't need to master it right now."

A teary-eyed Kimberly finally gave in to her mother's request with a nod. Sophia pulled her in, wrapping her arms around her. She softly kissed her forehead and whispered into her daughter's ear.

"You are safe. I will always keep you safe."

Genesis

Sophia pulled herself out of her stroll down memory lane, walking back to the dinner table. She took a seat, staring at the food. Dread and resentment began as Sophia remembered what she was cheated out of. She would never feel the joys of Kimberly's infancy or times as a toddler. Even her terrible twos were ripped away from her. Soon, it would be pre- and teenage years when she wouldn't want to be around her as much. Time was moving way too fast for her, and she did not have the power to slow it down.

Sophia gave each side of her face a jolting light slap to keep from falling into depression. She began to dish out her food.

"Vincent, are you there?"

"Always Ms. Dennison," her personal A.I. announced itself through the audio speakers within her home. "How may I assist you?"

"Is my scheduled appointment with Dr. Champion still on for later today?"

"Yes, Ms. Dennison, I have confirmed with Maxine, the appointment is still on for later today."

"Thank you."

As the audio system went silent, Sophia sat alone, preparing to eat until Sir George approached her, eyeing the fruit slices on her plate. It brought forth a smile from her as she picked up a piece of banana and handed it to him.

"Doesn't matter how old you get, as long as I have a banana, you won't leave me, will you, boy?"

She gave him a two-finger rub on the top of his head as he took a perched seat at the end of the table next to her, becoming her breakfast companion for another night.

Genesis

Genesis

CHAPTER 5

September 2016, seven hundred hours military time early morning, Bridgeport, California,

All seven Regulator team members sat in the team debriefing room, waiting patiently for Rogers to arrive. Each sat wearing either the team sweatsuit or tracksuit set, which came in tactical blue. The tracksuit had an added white piping on the side. Each outfit had the silver Regulator emblem embroidered on the right breast of the tops.

There was minimal small talk between the team as each person appeared to be still waking up or in their own world. Adrian was the most energetic as he typed away on his iPhone with a broad smile. His sister leaned over to take a look at his screen.

"Who you texting so feverishly this early in the morning, that chick you met at Barney NY, Ms. Barbara Moretti?"

"The same one, now quit fogging up my screen with your halitosis breath," Adrian answered.

With a snarl, she went to smack her twin upside the back of his head until he grabbed a part of the chair he sat in, turning into its metal composition. She then grabbed her chair, mimicking his ability, and still smacked him, causing him to lurch forward.

"Stop, Rose, you're going to make me drop my phone!"

"How long you've been seeing each other again?" Oliver asked.

"We're going on almost four months now." He answered while still texting.

Genesis

"The longest relationship he's had without tapping it," his sister shook her head, "You sure she's a female, Adrian?"

"Yeah, I'm sure she's a female," Adrian answered sarcastically. "I checked. We've done other things besides that. We're just taking it slow and getting to know each other."

Rosann leaned back in her chair with a stunned look on her face.

"Adrian Esposito taking it slow; who the hell are you, and whatchu do with my brother?"

"I'm just surprised your other girl has been taking this so well," Oliver said with a smirk.

"She was never my girl," Adrian turned, replying, cutting him a dirty look. "And Erica fixed her."

"What other girl?" Aashif asked, jumping into the conversation.

"Angie," Oliver answered, filling him in.

"Stop playing man, she was never my girl!"

"Oh, you don't know about my brother and Angie, Aashif?" Rosann asked with a devious grin on her face. "They were hot and heavy for a minute. I thought I was gonna be an aunt to some T-1000s."

"Kiss my ass, Rose."

"Orange haired bubbly robot Angie?" Teuila asked with a coy grin on her face.

"She's an android, who made me late on my third date by hijacking the Tornado and flying me to Hawaii!" Adrian pointed the finger at everyone, correcting them with a growl. "And she was not, nor has she ever been my girlfriend! Erica fixed her!"

"I didn't fix Jack," Erica answered with her eyes closed, sitting back in her chair beside Sister Shareef. "She's a highly advanced cybernetic android with state-of-the-art artificial intelligence. She just got bored with your tired ass and moved on."

Erica's response caused all four, minus Adrian, to laugh while he gave her dagger eyes. Her comment even forced a smirk out of Sister Shareef, who shook her head.

Before Adrian could come up with a proper retort, Rogers, wearing a Regulator navy-blue t-shirt with the emblem on the right breast and standard marine fatigue pants and boots, walked in, bringing a semi-serious atmosphere back into the room. Adrian put his phone away while Erica and Sister Shareef sat up and opened their eyes, giving the Sergeant their full attention.

"Let's get down to business," Rogers said, entering Sergeant Mode. "The Vitruvian Absolute Rally in New York, which has been on our calendar, is today at 2 P.M. Eastern Standard time. The rally will be held in Union Square; based on the schematics we worked out for coverage, Oliver and Teuila will take strategic rooftop locations along with myself for air support and sniper duty. Shareef and Aashif will be in uniform, covering opposite sides of the stage to let the crowd know a military presence is watching the event. Rosann and Adrian will be in the crowd in their civvies, keeping their eyes peeled for anything suspicious.

Maxine will also be manning the Tornado, outfitted with maximum-capacity Nerve Hammers and Energy Dampeners. We'll even be bringing Sam for extra firepower. The military and police presence at Union Square will be limited because half of the NYPD's resources are routed to Trump Towers and the Secret Service to protect the Republican candidate and his family should this event go south."

"Sir, are we expecting it to go south?" Adrian asked with a raised hand.

"Honestly, no," Rogers shook his head. "Aside from the Houston incident, most of the rallies that have taken place around the world and state-wise have been fairly peaceful."

Genesis

"That's because, in Houston, a couple of dumbass militiamen thought they could bring their guns to a nuke fight," Rosann scoffed and fluttered her eyes in disgust while folding her arms.

"Yeah, that was some dumb shit," Teuila nodded in agreement, "Who they think they were going to intimidate when half the attendees are superhuman?"

"Are we done commenting about the dumbass militiamen?" Rogers asked, wishing to move along the debriefing. "As I stated, the likelihood of an incident is low because no acts of violence have taken place at past rallies. However, Vitruvian Absolute is still categorized as a hate group because their core ideology comes from a terrorist that damn near took over the entire planet, and their names are linked to genetic hate crimes occurring right here in the States and abroad.

Not to mention, we believe they have been bullying their way to get their 'peaceful rallies,' we're pretty sure they've been sending Prometheans to courthouses to mentally persuade officials into getting their permits to assemble. And then, when they figured out we were catching on, they sent in their lawyers with underlined threats of unlawful assembly.

You know what the scenarios we've run look like; even with our entire tech and crowd suppression tactics, the collateral and property damage shattered our stress test every time. So, states have been painfully allowing them to assemble and peacefully spewing their poison, which seems to be their primary tactic because their numbers have been steadily growing with each rally."

Everyone, including Sister Shareef and Erica, straightened up, taking Rogers's orders much more seriously.

"We will not have a London incident here on my watch," Rogers reinforced to the team. "Everyone bring their A-plus game today, is that understood."

"Yes, sir!" They all yelled, minus Erica.

"Moving onto our last mission," Rogers continued. "The good

Genesis

news is that this marked our fifteenth successful mission. As stated, these missions reduce the causality count and help weaken ISL forces within the region, so good work out there."

Rogers's report caused his team to nod with approval.

"And now the bad news, this latest mission has also uncovered a possible new threat on a global level. Erica will now explain what we are dealing with."

Rogers stepped away from the podium as Erica slowly opened her eyes and shot up from her seat, making her way to the podium.

"Time for a recap, boys, and girls," she began. "Maxine."

Upon command, the giant video screen behind her lit up with news reports and lab data.

"As we all know, one of the aftermaths of Peace's global terrorist actions is superhuman boosting," Erica huffed, "Now that the entire world knows that basically every single human on the planet possesses the EVO gene within them. Those who can are racing to research ways to activate the dormant gene to acquire abilities. This has led to either the recruitment or abduction of any geneticist who has half a decent Master's degree. The latest most addictive narcotics to sweep the planet are those designed to manifest superhuman abilities. And it's proving to be deadlier than any other drug ever manufactured."

Erica paused a minute to project other findings onto the massive theatre screen.

"As you already know, we're facing two epidemics," she explained, motioning to the split-screen. "The first is what I have categorized as 'temps.' These are drugs that, when injected, agitate the EVO gene, causing abilities to temporarily manifest. Depending on the type of serum and the dosage, abilities usually last from an hour to several hours. The two most potent drugs currently on the black market are 'Human Boost' and 'Ascension.' Major drug cartels worldwide have spearheaded the manufacturing and selling of these two narcotics. They are sold cheap,

Genesis

going for sixty to seventy dollars a dose.

Our other problem is those attempting to become perms. For half a million and up, people are paying for treatments to make the activation of the EVO gene within them permanent."

"Excuse me," Aashif said, raising his hand and getting her attention. "From what we know of the failings of the original 'drug war,' what makes this any different? Aside from the abductions, if ordinary people want abilities like us, who are we to stop them from acquiring them?"

With a dry smile, Erica projected her answer on the screen.

"Kara Martin, age twenty-three, somehow snuck her way up to the 423 Park Avenue building in New York City, intending to leap off. Lucky for her, a local hero named Sky Blast swooped in, snatching her up before she jumped. Ms. Martin was cursing, punching, and kicking him on the way down. After she was arrested, she was asked if she was suicidal. She said no, she was attempting to activate her powers, and she was pissed that Sky Blast interrupted her.

Peter Murdock, age nineteen, was arrested near the Yucca Mountain Nuclear Waste Repository for trespassing. In his bag, they found a giant tarantula. He explained that he wanted a little bit of radiation to infect the tarantula with so that when it bit him, it would activate and tailor his powers to his liking."

Oliver shook his head in disbelief while Adrian cupped his mouth, choking down his laughter, as images of the people Erica was speaking about appeared on the screen.

"And those are the minor cases, Jonathan Snyder, age forty-two, and an engineer at the Nine Mile Point Nuclear Generating Station literally walked into the reactor chamber and died of extreme radiation poisoning. His home revealed he was a huge fan of Freedom."

The humor was wiped from everyone's faces as she continued.

Genesis

"And then, we have incidents like this."

Erica switched the screen to a video camera feed taken within a Starbucks.

"This was taken four days ago," she explained.

As everyone watched, a young man surfing the web on his tablet while indulging in a caramel macchiato began to display symptoms of shivers while swaying in his seat. He finally fell out of his chair, going into convulsions. Fellow patrons came to his aid as his eyes lit up, emitting a bright red color matching the veins bulging underneath his skin. Smoke began to spew from his orifices, causing some people to back up as he appeared to be screaming. Everyone witnessed as his back arched before he detonated, obliterating everyone and everything within his vicinity, killing the camera feed.

"The kid's name was Bart Williams," Erica turned to address Aashif. "He was twenty-two years old. That blast took out four stores and killed thirty-eight people while injuring almost eighty others. This is the third incident to happen in the past two months on U.S. soil. Similar incidents have occurred in different parts of Europe, Asia, Latin America, and Africa."

Aashif swallowed and nodded, now understanding how dire the situation was. Erica switched to a 3D diagram of the male human anatomy. The figure injected itself with a syringe, displaying what happened to the body when a booster entered the system.

"Regular humans are only infected with less than ten percent of the EVO virus, which stays dormant. Most of the percentile that is not dormant has found its way to the human reproductive system in both men and women, which is why regular humans can give birth to EVO children. 'Human Boost' and 'Ascension' are agitating agents created to target the EVO virus, forcing it to activate temporarily, granting human beings abilities. The problem is that normal human cells cannot withstand the genetic information transmitted by the virus and the energy output of specific abilities.

Genesis

This is why so many people died when the EVO virus first spread. By my hypothesis, there were three types of virus infection in the population: Active, dormant, and defective.

Active spreads throughout our bodies, killing our normal human cells one by one while taking over their functions and becoming our new cellular structure.

Dormant is what's within the majority of the population; it does nothing and is only transmitted through sexual intercourse, which in turn produces EVO children."

Erica briefly glanced Rogers's way before continuing.

"Defective is the EVO Virus that did not complete the replication process for some reason and continued to transmit. Those infected with the defective virus eventually died because their bodies could not withstand the genetic information the virus shared or, as I stated earlier, the energy output their abilities generated.

This explains why there are more infected Titans and Mercurian classes than Apollos. Most people who died from the Judgment Virus had Apollo abilities."

From the corner of her eye, she could see Rogers drop his chin into his chest as his eyes went to the briefing room floor. Sister Shareef subtly looked at him with eyes of concern.

"So even though these boosters are producing temporary abilities," Erica concluded. "They are also causing the same effect of a defective EVO Virus, but at an aggravated rate. Constant use of these boosters either causes the subject to burn out all of their cells and die or for a person's body to become unstable and eventually spontaneously combust."

"So how does this tie into the red booster we captured during our raid yesterday?" Oliver asked.

"Because this is not just a booster," Erica answered flatly. "This is a serum capable of turning regular humans into EVOs permanently."

Genesis

The expression on everyone's face was an ice-cold concern; even Adrian didn't have a quick wit for the bombshell she dropped.

"How is that possible?" Teuila asked while shaking her head.

"Maxine, pull up the specs on the serum, please." Erica requested.

The screen switched, displaying the chemical breakdown of the red booster serum. Everyone aside from Erica, Rogers, and Sister Shareef leaned back in their seats, stunned at the results.

"I identified twenty new chemical elements created to make up this serum," she answered with a flat stern voice. "Five of these elements which make up the twenty is nowhere on the periodical table; we will get to that later. I then ran several simulations; basically, what it does is get the dormant virus to gradually do what the virus has done for each of us."

"Gradually?" asked Shareef.

Erica projected her simulation on the screen for all to see.

"Each time an injection is administered, the virus not only activates, but it also kills normal cells and multiplies before going dormant again. With each injection, the virus spreads and remains more active, until finally it no longer goes into a dormant mode. The person becomes a fully blown EVO with continued full access to their abilities."

"But why gradually?" Sister Shareef asked, "Why not with one injection? Why not a steady dosage?"

Erica projected the results.

"A steady dosage results in certain, painful fatality. Each vial contains the right amount of serum that must only be taken within forty-eight hours of the last dosage. That's why all of them had the vials on them, but only a certain number boosted; the rest did not complete the cool-down cycle to take another injection. By my simulation, it took at least sixty vials for the process to stay permanent, which means a regular human can become a full-powered EVO in three months."

Genesis

"Three months?" Adrian choked.

"That sucks in so many ways," Oliver muttered, kneading his brow.

"Do we have an idea of who could have manufactured this?" Rogers asked.

"Aside from me," Erica shrugs, answering, "Another Promethean with either the same, or a higher IQ than me, or someone off-planet."

"Off-planet," Aashif asked with a twisted face of confusion. "Surely, you're not talking …?"

"Yes, I'm talking extra-terrestrials," Erica replied, looking dead at him, "As I said before, this serum was created by someone who created twenty new elements, and five of the original properties that created these new elements are nowhere on our periodical table at all."

Everyone's expression varied after Erica's answer. The new recruits still had a prominent concern on their faces, while the original core team put on disgust and irritation.

"So, you're saying we might have aliens, arming ISIS terrorists?" Oliver asked with a visage of disbelief.

"That sounds so messed up just hearing it," Adrian murmured, shaking his head.

"Knowing what we know now," Erica sighed. "There is a high probability."

Adrian displayed an annoying smirk before asking his next question.

"Any chance you can call your golden boy …"

Before he could finish, his seat was telekinetically ripped from underneath him, causing him to hit the floor hard."

Genesis

"Son of a …!" He gasped.

"He's not my boyfriend, asshole," Erica said with a scowl.

"Oh, damn!" Teuila yelled under her covered mouth.

"She warned you to stop f'n with her," his sister sighed.

Adrian used one of the other chairs to help himself as he glared at Erica, throwing dagger eyes back at him.

"If everyone is done dicking around," Rogers elevated his authoritative voice. "Erica, what is the probability that the first scenario is more possible than the second?"

"It's also highly probable," Erica said, fluttering her eyes. "All you would need is either a nuclear reactor or particle accelerator and someone with intelligence on a superhuman level with knowledge of chemistry and genetics, which would narrow our search down considerably because that would mean we'd be looking for a government-backed facility or someone with a shit ton of money."

"Considering who their clientele is, we can narrow the number of governments willing to risk sanctions and going to war," Sister Shareef interjected.

"What about Iran?" Aashif asked with a raised hand. "The deal promised that they would not begin a nuclear weapons program; it said nothing of a superhuman program. Considering their track record with supplying known terrorist organizations, they would be the obvious choice."

"That's a good point," Rogers answered while nodding. "But before we start pointing fingers, we're going to rule out everyone else, including ET. We have to be balls to the wall, damn sure about this. With what is going on with this election, I'm not giving either side any free talking points. Are we clear?"

"I've already compiled a list of possible suspects," Erica confirmed.

Genesis

"Alright, this gets put on the backburner for now," Rogers ordered." Our main priority for today is getting ready for the Vitruvian Absolute rally, so let's get it done, folks."

"Sarge, can I get five minutes?" Adrian asked.

"Yeah, wait for me outside," he nodded. "Erica, stay behind, please."

She rolled her eyes and walked over to him as everyone exited the briefing room.

"Care to explain that little outburst?" Rogers asked with narrowed eyes.

"He's acting like a dick!" She snapped. "The Eye of Ra looks borderline my father's age and probably older than Moses!"

"Not a justifiable reason," he lectured. "Especially when I hear the barbs you throw at each other in the Rec room when you're playing your little video games. Something you want to talk about?"

"No, sir," she answered while cutting her eyes.

"You don't seem like you've been getting a lot of sleep."

"I got a lot of work on my plate between people creating serums that actually create superhumans, and someone draining a nuclear power plant and then disappearing into thin air without a trace."

"It's been almost a year since that happened," Rogers nodded. "Still, no leads?"

"None," she answered, lowering her frustrated and weary eyes to the floor.

He looked at her for a minute, preparing to say something else, but chose to change the subject. Rogers made a face, not believing he was asking his next question.

Genesis

"Can you contact the Eye of Ra to confirm if the serum was made by an alien race?"

"Based on the energy frequency he's allowed me to track him with, he's off-planet," she shrugged, answering. "And considering he could be anywhere in the universe, I have no way of connecting with him until he returns to Earth."

"Keep me updated," Rogers nodded, exhaling. "And I never want to see that shit in my briefing room again. Are we clear?"

"Yes, sir," she said, snapping a sarcastic salute.

"Miss, Dr. Dennison is here for her final checkup," Maxine announced over the audio system.

Rogers fluttered his eyes in disgust at the announcement.

"Someone needs to follow their own advice," Erica whistled, "Especially when their …"

Rogers gave her a warning glare that she was pushing her luck. She turned to skip out the door as he watched her leave with fatherly concern written on his face.

"One more thing," he raised his voice so she could hear him. "Do not tell Dennison anything about this briefing."

Erica halted in her tracks and turned to him with a perplexed look.

"Why not?"

"Because she is not a part of this team and does not need to know this information," he said authoritatively. "This is still a government facility, and she is a civilian. The information about the serum is officially classified; is that understood?"

"Yes, sir," Erica said, giving him a sharp, disapproving gaze before walking away.

Genesis

"And get some sleep!"

"Alright!" She howled.

Adrian re-entered the briefing room, walking up to him.

"If you came to whine about her being mean to you, I already …"

"Forgotten the second I walked out the door Sarge, although I shall have my revenge …"

"Esposito …"

"Why the hell are we doing detective work when we have the answers to our questions either sitting in black sites or Gitmo?" Adrian asked, getting serious and to the point. "We captured over two hundred and eighty insurgents last week, with five high ranking ISIS officers. One, if not all, of them has to know where those boosters came from. Erica can figure that out just by …"

"I know," Rogers acknowledged, nodding in agreement. "But we're not going that route. I'm not going to force her to dive into the mind of those animals, especially after what she's been through. And we can't go interrogating captured prisoners without divulging what we are interrogating them for."

"And why are we not divulging this information?" Adrian asked.

"With what's going on with this election," Rogers said with a lowered voice. "Do you really want it to get out that there is a serum that can turn regular humans into superhumans in less than three months? Can you imagine what would happen if something like this got out?"

Adrian nodded while swallowing deeply as he began to see the predicted bleak future in store for the world that Rogers saw should such information be revealed.

"For now, we have to take the long road to figure this out," Rogers reaffirmed. "So, get your running shoes on."

Genesis

Adrian gave Rogers his game face.

"Yes, sir."

~~~~~~~~~~~~~~~~~~~~~~~~~~~~~~~~~

Erica waited in the Ranch's hanger area as one of the facility's lifts brought Sophia down. She stepped out wearing a simple blue and white Fabletics workout set with a Yankees baseball cap and blue flip-flops.

"You look so suburban MILF right now," Erica declared.

"You look tired," Sophia proclaimed.

"Well, we all can't have limitless stamina like you," Erica said with a Cheshire sneer. "Come on, let's get this over with."

"Is that crank a symptom of fatigue, or are you not happy to see me?"

"Crank comes with the fatigue," Erica dryly answered while fighting to soften up. "I also got a lot on my mind. Come on; let's get you checked out for an official clean bill of health."

~~~~~~~~~~~~~~~~~~~~~~~~~~~~~~~~~

Minutes later, Sophia stood still in just her underwear within one of Erica's medical tubes as she completed her final scan of her.

"All done," Erica announced.

As the long cylinder tube rose back into the ceiling, she stepped out while Erica pulled up the last test results on the screen for Sophia to see.

"So, the good news is, after almost a year, you've completely healed," Erica exhaled while examining her scans. "Energy levels are still under ninety percent when compared to the first initial scan I took from you almost a year ago, but they are steadily rising. I'd say another six months,

Genesis

and you will be back to full power. You're still the most powerful EVO on the planet at these levels."

"Bad news is, I have a limit," Sophia said, standing next to her, examining the yearlong progression of scans. "There's been no physical change to my cellular structure to prevent the damage I caused to myself when I tapped my reserves during my battle with Peace."

"None," Erica said, shaking her head.

In the historical record of scans, Erica expanded three in particular.

The first one was when she fitted Sophia for her first outfit, the second was a couple of months after her battle with Peace, and the final scan Erica took several minutes ago.

"As you can see from the second scan," Erica pointed. "You literally burnt yourself from the inside out when you went into "World Buster mode."

"You've given it a name now?"

"You shook the entire damn planet just by moving," Erica glared at her, snapping. "Hell yeah, I am giving it a name. Unfortunately, the law of equivalent exchange pertains to even you. Your cells started to burn out one by one; the longer you tapped your reserves, you destroyed over forty percent of the cells within your body. I'm shocked you're still alive and functioning after that."

"I finally fainted a month after officially becoming Freedom remember?"

~ ~

To be more accurate, as Sophia remembered it, everything went black while flying from the States back to her island. When she finally woke up, she was being fished out of the ocean by the Regulators. Vincent, her A.I., had alerted them to her predicament and location.

Genesis

She remembered going into severe distress after seeing the second scan, believing it to be some form of incurable cancer until Erica calmed her down, revealing that her cells were slowly replicating new ones to replace the dead, burnt-out cells within her. The replicated ones also absorbed the dead ones, no doubt attempting to use whatever materials could be salvaged.

Sophia's nervous breakdown was ignited by the fear that something could separate her from her daughter again, that by saving the world again, she almost cheated herself out of the life she wanted. She did not deny that Peace had to be stopped, and she did not regret putting her own life on the line to stop her, but when the dust settled, and order was once again somewhat restored, Sophia claimed her prize, the only thing she wanted.

Time.

It was her time to be a mother, and she did not want anyone or anything to take that away from her.

After the initial shock and fear had passed and her rationale returned, Sophia asked Erica to keep her diagnosis between them. She even held it from Kimberly. She made sure she did not overstrain herself, limited her flying or anything else that would cause her to overexert herself, and scheduled monthly scans with Erica to examine her recovery progress. After a month and a half, the dizzy spells disappeared altogether.

~~~~~~~~~~~~~~~~~~~~~~~~~~~~~~~~~~

"I wish I could research the difference between the time I was in … 'World Buster mode' for a straight twenty-four hours until I figured out how to power down and what had to be a five-minute final battle with Peace."

"I have a theory." Erica said, turning to her, "You weren't in a fight for your life."

She pulled up a simulation of her final fight with Peace, focusing on Sophia's body and its effect on the planet.

Genesis

"As we previously discussed, your energy reserves, when independently regulated by your body, serves to grant you an additional boost of strength and power when needed. This is usually triggered in two ways, by overexertion or long periods of physical activity. The first regulates additional energy to you in massive boosts in cases where the weight you are lifting exceeds your base strength; the second is slow and gradual based on, for example, physical combat. This means the longer you exert yourself, your body begins to increase the amount of energy circulating through your system until it rests. You would have eventually surpassed Peace in strength, but based on her massive power levels, you two would have to been fighting non-stop for hours for that to have happened. We both know the planet would not have been able to withstand such a drawn-out battle."

"Obviously," Sophia said, nodding in agreement.

"By you mentally or physically tapping into those reserves, you shut off whatever governor your body has put on this stored energy supply. That's why it was building at such an exponential rate; it's not the type of power you can control yourself. By the time you left Earth's atmosphere with Peace, you were generating three-quarters of this planet's gravitational force within you. In a near-dormant state, you kill a couple of cells, no harm, no foul, but one punch was like setting off several megaton nukes within you. At best guess you had three, maybe two more minutes before you went supernova."

Sophia swallowed deeply as she watched the worst-case scenario appear in a holographic image. Erica froze the image with a tap and left it up so that it would sink in.

"Basically, your body is like a race car Dennison," Erica huffed, "it's built for speed, and if you treat it right, it will take you to the finish line. If you don't, well …this happens."

Erica pointed to the holographic image.

"The diagnosis is quite simple; if you want to continue to live and watch Kimberly grow up …Don't ever do this again."

Genesis

Sophia huffed as her eyes remained fixed on the image of her simulated death.

"So, how are you doing?" Sophia cautiously slid her question in.

"You want the lie or the truth?" Erica turned to her with a direct stare, asking.

"What do you think?"

"I think I'm the last person you want to use the Jedi Mind Trick on," Erica sarcastically smirked.

She rolled her eyes as Sophia narrowed hers, indicating she didn't appreciate the sassing she was giving her.

"What do you want me to say?" Erica asked with a shrug. "That I'm alright? That I don't space out in the middle of a conversation or work? That I don't wake up from night terrors? I do, and it sucks. Even after I decided to hang up my cape, I'm not the first, nor will I be the last person to suffer from PTSD."

Sadness fell over Sophia's face as her mind replayed the events that brought on Erica's grim mental state and demeanor.

~ ~

Eight months ago, the Regulators were involved in a joint investigation with the FBI that started with encrypted chatter that Lady Tech intercepted about a massive human trafficking shipment coming in through Miami's ports to be delivered by the Chinese Triad.

From what Eric picked up, the shipment was to be divided between the Russian Mob and the Brazilian Cartel. Each organization was bringing its own form of superhuman muscle for backup.

Seeing how human trafficking and white slavery interest Freedom, she was invited to participate in the raid.

Genesis

It was an intense battle that was luckily centralized to the seaport with minimal damage and casualties; most human and superhuman criminals were captured and arrested, while at least three EVOs fled. Three containers were opened as frightened teenagers and children as young as seven huddled together, unsure of their fate. Freedom, Rogers, and other agents with experience with this situation went to work, coaxing the children out of the containers and assuring them they were safe.

Lady Tech exited her SAM armor, heading toward a mini trailer. With a wave of her hand, she ripped away the heavy-duty lock that kept it secure.

"Lady Tech, what are you doing?" inquired Rogers, who got Freedom's attention.

"Maxine just told me there are two Rottweilers and three pitbulls in here," Lady Tech said, turning to him.

A frigid chill shot through Freedom's spine as she locked eyes with Rogers.

"Erica, do not open that trailer," he commanded.

"I can handle a couple of rabid dogs, Rogers," she retorted, glaring at him. "Maxine detected something else in there with them but could not make it out."

The squeals of the children who saw what Lady Tech was doing made the horrible feeling in Freedom's belly even worse.

"Erica, do not open that trailer!" She roared her own order.

"I thought I only had one set of parents?" Lady Tech scoffed at them.

Her telekinesis at that range was faster than Freedom's speed as she turned the latch and flew the heavy steel door up to look at what was inside. She was prepared to mentally put the dogs to sleep; however, what she saw inside shattered her concentration.

Genesis

She gripped her heart as if she was about to have a stroke while blood-thick tears fell from her eyes, filling up her goggles as she went into an autistic shock.

The blood on the trailer's floor was molasses-thick, which matted the animals' fur.

At their feet were torn, chewed up, mutilated body parts, and ripped clothing, explaining why Maxine could not determine what else was inside with the dogs.

All four animals savagely growled with mixed blood and saliva dripping from their jaws as they rushed to turn Lady Tech into their next meal.

They would not make it out of the trailer as Freedom got to her first and unleashed a salvo of highly concentrated atomic eyebeam blasts, turning them into cinder.

Lady Tech collapsed to her knees, repeatedly screaming the same word.

"Blood! Blood! Blood!"

Rogers was already by her side, picking her up and cradling her in his arms.

"Dammit, girl," He groaned, pressing her head against his own. "It's going to be alright. Someone secure this goddamn trailer!"

As Rogers walked away with the SAM armor following him to take a hysterical Lady Tech back to the Tornado, Freedom's ears picked up, chuckling from a couple of the gang members sitting on their rears. It ended as she made a beeline in their direction with eyes ablaze to do what she did to the dogs.

They were saved by an intercepting Sister Sledge and Heavy Element jumping in her path.

Genesis

"Hey girl, whatcha doin?" Sledge asked, holding up a hand.

"Get out of my way Shareef."

"You know I can't do that."

"I said, move!"

Her angry voice rattled a taller Sister Sledge endowed with Titan strength even though she stood her ground.

"Miss Dennison, please don't do this," Heavy Element in metallic form pleaded. "Don't sink to these sons of bitches' level. Think about the kids watching."

Freedom slowly turned to lock eyes with some of the traumatized children looking in her direction and forced herself to power down as she wiped away the tears that did not evaporate from the heat she generated.

"Get them out of my sight … now!"

Heavy Element coordinated the prisoners' movement into transports while Sister Shareef stayed by her friend's side.

By the account of the children who could talk despite the horrors they endured, the trailer was a sadistic warning implemented by their captors. Before loading into their containers, they were forced to watch as they pulled a random child, tossing them into the trailer. The traffickers then brought in the dogs and forced the children to watch what would happen to them if they made a sound while within the containers.

Sophia made her way to the Tornado to see Rogers with a face of impotent rage, attempting to rock and soothe Erica, still in a near-catatonic regressive state.

She had pulled off her goggles, throwing them to the floor, and was either repeating "Blood" or screaming incoherently as she gripped the straps on Roger's combat harness.

Genesis

"Give her to me," Sophia requested, motioning to Abe. "Rogers, give her to me."

"What are you going to do?"

"There's a song her mother sung to her when she's in this state," Freedom whispered.

As she took her in her arms, Erica, still screaming, grabbed a handful of her braids. An unfazed Sophia held her close, singing a lullaby in Spanish while mimicking Erica's mother's voice, which caused her to wail louder before eventually calming her down. Erica emerged from her episode after a couple rounds of singing, soft kisses to the forehead, and rocking her like an infant.

"Put me down …please," Erica requested.

As Freedom set her back on her feet, Erica sat on one of the chairs, affixing her eyes to the floor of the Tornado. Rogers walked over, kneeling in front of her.

"You don't have to tell me," Lady Tech whispered. "I screwed up."

"That was the last thing coming out of my mouth," Rogers gruffed. "But you're done for the night. Is that clear?"

With tear-filled eyes, she nodded in agreement. Rogers gave her a pat on the shoulder before heading back out to help supervise with clean up. Sophia walked over, taking a seat next to her.

"I'm not going to say a word," She whispered.

"Thank you," Erica's voice cracked.

It didn't take long for her to burst into tears.

"I saw it all," she whimpered. "I saw it all. Through each of their eyes …I heard their screams and cries …tearing of flesh and snapping of

Genesis

her little bones... her brother ...was forced to watch ...and those fuckers out there ...they just laughed ...they just watched and laughed ..."

Erica lost her voice to the sobs and wails flowing from her lips. Sophia spun her chair around so that she faced her.

"I don't need a hug ...I'm fine ...I'm fine."

Freedom ignored her as she took her in her arms again and held her tight, while Erica's little body trembled as she buried her head in Sophia's chest, bawling hysterically, gripping her bodysuit.

"What's wrong with us? What is wrong with us?"

"I don't know," Freedom said as her tears fell. "I don't know."

~~~~~~~~~~~~~~~~~~~~~~~~~~~~~~~

After that night, Erica removed herself from active duty. Maxine became the designated pilot for the Tornado, taking the Regulators on their missions. Simultaneously, she expanded the SAM's Artificial Intelligence, removed its cockpit, and converted its body into a fully functional automaton, providing the team extra strength and firepower during missions. She focused on her research, R&D, maintenance, and upgrading the base.

It was a partial relief to Sophia, and especially Rogers, except on that night, the light within Erica was dimmed, giving birth to a type of cynicism that came out in irritation and ice-cold sarcasm.

~~~~~~~~~~~~~~~~~~~~~~~~~~~~~~~

"So, how's that kid of yours?" Erica asked, wishing to end the subject about her.

"Growing too fast," Sophia sighed.

"She still trying to be the strongest there is?"

Genesis

Sophia answered her with fluttered eyes of disgust.

"Well, at least she's not still shattering asteroids with one punch," Erica said, shaking her head.

"I still remember your voice when you called me on that day," Sophia said before mimicking her vocals, repeating the message. "Dennison, go get your kid! She's out there, busting asteroids, and some of them are getting too close to Earth!"

"Yeah, that was crazy," Erica chuckled with another headshake.

"I have a kid who attempted to go to Mars," Sophia replied, giving a hurt look. "Not Disney Land, Mars! And she would have made it if I didn't stop her before she got there!"

~ ~

The Mars incident strained her and Kimberly's relationship, changing her from the cool mom with superpowers to the strict, stern mother who was stronger than her daughter and not afraid to show it.

A regular outing to the International Space Station turned into Kimberly taking it upon herself to go on an interstellar trip to Mars.

It was not the first time her daughter had gone orbital; it cut down much travel time from continent to continent. The "minor" incidents that Sophia overlooked, like fly-bys over military bases or visits to the International Space Station, initially startled the astronauts and scientists until they discovered who her mother was.

Sophia handled them with sit-downs and compromising productive talks. Kimberly promised not to fly by military bases. After speaking with NASA representatives, she was allowed to visit the station once a week for half the day and even help with repairs and projects.

Smashing asteroids was deemed a no-no; the punishment was two weeks of supervised flights, no video games, and no phone.

Genesis

Sophia understood the burden of having a child with an array of powers and abilities that were nearly limitless. It would have been insane to expect her not to attempt to test her potential. She also knew Kimberly, like any other child, was pushing the boundaries of what she could get away with.

So, she used textbook parenting and reasoning skills to rear her, balancing between being a responsible parent and allowing her to cut loose.

Until Mars.

Kimberly's visits to the space station gave her a free education on Mar's orbital trajectory from Earth. She believed she had a ballpark idea with her superhuman eidetic memory where it was; all she had to do was look for a red planet.

It was a perfect plan, except she miscalculated the Earth's distance to mask the power she generated to obtain near-light speed flight. The force of her thrust lit up every energy and radar detection system around the globe, including Vincent.

Sophia didn't answer Erica's calls as she suited up and went after her daughter. It wasn't that difficult to track her flight pattern. Although Kimberly had a head start, it wasn't that hard to close the distance. Rage and betrayal bolstered her speed as she tore through the solar system to catch up with her daughter. She was on her after two hundred sixty-five million kilometers of straight flight time.

Seeing her daughter strafing through space without a care in the world pissed her off to no end, melting away the calmly reasonable doctor with a Ph.D. and Master's degree, revealing the fury of a half Central American, half Caribbean mother.

Kimberly looked over her shoulder on instinct. Her eyes widened to the size of silver dollars as her face displayed fear, shock, and surprise to see her mother upon her. Sophia slammed into her daughter, sending them spiraling violently through space. Eventually, Sophia managed to stabilize their out-of-control spiral within the harsh environment.

Genesis

Sophia's eyes blazed brighter than any other star as she held Kimberly by the front of the flight suit given to her by Erica. She felt her daughter shaking like a leaf in sheer fear of her mother. Her first inclination was to shake her senseless in the deep void of space.

She chose instead to calm herself.

Without a word, she pointed back toward Earth, which Kimberly quickly propelled herself back to after her mother released her. The return flight felt longer because Sophia wasn't pumped with maternal anger. As she looked at the infinite universe around her that she was flying through, having traveled distances no human had visited before, Sophia understood why Kimberly did what she did.

However, she could not stomach nor condone the lies and deception used to embark on her little voyage.

As much as she hated to do it, some strict law and order had to be enforced when they returned home.

The second they landed back onto Sanctuary's soil, and Sophia chased her daughter back into their house, a nervous Kimberly already had her hands up, attempting to reason with her angry mother.

"Mom ... mom, let me explain!" She began with a jittery voice." You see ...what had happened was ..."

"You say one more word, young lady, and I'm going to literally knock you into Africa!" Sophia roared. "Go upstairs, take off the suit, the bracers, and boots, and bring them downstairs to me right now!"

"No ..." whispered a defiant Kimberly.

Sophia paused with a stuck look, attempting to register what her child just said to her.

"What did you just say to me?"

"I said ...no," Kimberly said with a louder voice. "Erica gave this

Genesis

to me! I didn't do anything wrong, mom! I get straight A's in school! I don't get into any trouble! All I wanted to do was go to Mars! I wasn't hurting anyone!"

"Are you done?" Sophia asked with blazing eyes, "You lied and deceived me! We've been to the moon; how hard would it have been to ask me to take a trip to Mars?"

"I ...I didn't think ..."

"No, you didn't think!" Sophia snapped while advancing toward her. "Did you think what being in that prolonged atmosphere would do to you, or what would happen if you got in trouble out there? Did you think about what would happen if you did make it to Mars, and you got in trouble there, who would come to your aide Kimberly, who?"

"I ... I ...."

"No one, no one would have been there to help you! You are not an adult, and you are not invincible young lady!" Sophia roared at her. "You are a child! My child! Now I'm going to tell you again. Go upstairs, take off the suit and gear and bring it down to me ...right ...now."

A trembling Kimberly folded her arms and stood her ground, refusing to budge. It caused a sinister chuckle from her mother as she looked up to the heavens in disbelief.

"Dis rawtid pickney aw really try fee test me today?"

Sophia took several steps, now towering over her daughter with clenched fists. A rattled and intimidated Kimberly slowly unfolded her arms, looking up at her.

"Me ah go say dis one time," Sophia growled. "I am not your friend, and you are not going to be one of dem likle disrespectful brats who tink dem can say anyting dem want to dem parents. Ah me ah yah madda, whatever happened in the past happened, and you chose to come home, which means until you turn eighteen, your little ass belongs to me, and in this house ...there is only one woman ...and one child. Now, I have tried to be diplomatic, and I have tried reasoning, but you seem to be picking and choosing what you want to respond to, and that does not fly with me. This will be the final time I will tell you to go upstairs and do what I told you to do. And I'm only giving you to the count of two …one."

A dejected and pouting Kimberly turned and stomped away, heading upstairs.

"Keep it up, and let me find one crack or splinter on these floors or steps, young lady!" Sophia warned. "And God help you if you slam that door!"

She heard the attempted door slam before it stopped and was quietly closed. A mentally exhausted Sophia sat at the foot of her bedroom steps, saddened by what just happened, as a realization washed over her.

"Great …I just became my mother."

After confiscating Kimberly's suit, she grounded her for three months, including supervised flights to school and back. Limited solo flights were monitored by Vincent tracking her flight pattern via her smartphone. She was given limited phone usage, additional chores, a set curfew to hang out with a friend on and off the island, and her video games were also taken for three months. Computer time was only limited to doing homework.

The aftermath of the Mars incident set their relationship backward by several steps. Sophia assumed a stricter mother's role, while Kimberly took the angry child role and did what she was told with visible reluctance. The playful mother-daughter closeness they began to forge had disappeared, which was heartbreaking for Sophia, and she knew not how to get it back after that day or find the balance.

All she knew was that "strict mom Sophia" kept her daughter and the world in check and safe. A necessary sacrifice she would have to endure for now.

~ ~

Genesis

Returning from her memories, a defeated Sophia fell against one of the lab tables with her shoulders slumped.

"She's changing, and I don't know how to slow it down. School bores her; children her own age are beginning to bore her. She figured out how to fly without overexerting the bioenergy within her. She then taught me. The two things she loves to do are pushing the upper limits of her powers and visiting her grandparents. In a few years, she's not going to need me anymore …I don't even think she needs me now."

"Someone once told me, as powerful as they are, they can't hug themselves even when they are at their lowest." Erica lectured.

Sophia lifted her head, displaying a slight smirk.

"There isn't a kid out there that doesn't need their parents," Erica said with an eye roll, "especially their mothers. Just give her time."

"What she needs is mental stimulation on a highly advanced and complex level and a way to push her abilities to their upper limits until she's content," Sophia formulated. "But with my current responsibilities, which now entail being a superhero, I don't have a clue how to accomplish that."

"Why don't you let her hang out with me?" Erica shrugged, inquiring.

Sophia stood there with an awkward deer-in-headlights expression on her face.

"Are you seriously looking at me like I'd be a bad influence on your daughter?" Erica scowled, asking.

"I did not say that," Sophia squealed defensively, holding her hands.

"Then, you're looking at me like I'd have her up in here like a lab rat!"

Genesis

"I didn't say that, either!" She squeaked while attempting to inconspicuously shift her eyes.

Erica narrowed her eyes as she strolled up to stand closer to her friend and elder for a heart-to-heart.

"Let's converse as two people who have their degrees in psychiatry, and not as one who dropped a kid, and one who didn't. Kimberly and I may not be the same age-wise," Erica said while folding her arms. "But I've been where she is and still feel it from time to time, out of place. Most current EVOs are in their late teens and older, while the new generation is still among infants to early grade school. With me, she'd be hanging out with someone who looks her age, can mentally get her, and be a big sister to her. Not to mention, she can come here and cut loose in a place where she can learn to properly control her abilities."

"Allow my kid to hang out on a government base," Sophia said sarcastically, smirking while folding her arms. "Yeah, I'm really going to win Mother of the Year."

"We both know instilling fear is A) not very productive, and B) has an age limit. Right now, she's compliant and brooding; eventually, as she gets older, she will resort back to acting out again," Erica said with narrowed eyes. "And as she keeps getting older and stronger, she's neither going to be afraid nor is she going to want to listen to you anymore."

Erica's grim outlook made Sophia nervously shift her stance a bit.

"I would try all peaceful avenues before it gets to that point."

"Mom! Mommy! Mom! Mom!" A deep, growling cybernetic voice echoed from the outside hanger.

It was followed by thunderous foot-stomping, which caused Erica to palm her face and turn her hand into a claw as she wished she could rip her forehead off.

"I think that's for you,… 'mom,'" Sophia said, pointing.

Genesis

Erica stormed out of the lab with her following into the massive hangar of the Ranch.

"Oh! Oh my god!" A startled Sophia squeaked.

Erica gave her an irritated side-eye.

"Seriously? You've fought cannibalistic superhumans, but this makes you jump?"

"Sorry, he's just a little bit jarring to look at," Sophia said sheepishly. "Especially when he looks like that."

Standing before them was Sam, Erica's former battle armor, now a fully functional cybernetic automaton like his sisters. Except for this time, Sam was walking around without his armored shell. His black and slate grey synthetic skin, massive muscular body, four-digit fingers, digitigrade legs and feet, blank face, and slant glowing yellow eyes made him look like an alien life form from another planet than a hulking android.

"Sam!" Erica yelled at him. "What did I tell you about walking around here with no clothes or armor plating?"

"Not to do it," he groaned out his answer.

"Why?"

"Because it looks like I am naked, and it's indecent."

"Where's the jumpsuit I fabricated for you?"

"Stupid Buster ripped it," he answered, pointing.

"El cielo me ayude, no necesito quedarme embarazada," she muttered. "Buster, get over here!"

"Buster?" Sophia scowled her face, asking.

Her eyes widened to the heavy metallic thumping sound she felt

Genesis

through the floor and grew louder the closer it got. As she looked up, her eyes expanded to the point that they might fall out.

It was four-legged and massive, twice the size of SAM. Its long, thick, metallic tail hovered in the air as it swung back and forth while its glowing yellow eyes curiously locked onto Sophia as it tilted its humongous horned head. In its mouth hung a large piece of silver and blue torn fabric.

"A dragon … you built … a dragon."

"Yep," Erica said, proudly nodding.

"Why?"

"I was bored," she huffed, answering. "And they're in. Buster, did you rip Sam's jumpsuit?"

The metallic behemoth purred while bashfully nodding its head.

"Roughhousing, right?"

It gave another shameful nod.

She stuck a finger in its face.

"I'm going to repeat; if you two can't play nice, then you won't play at all. You want me to put you in time out?"

It quickly shook its head no.

"Then do not rip your brother's clothes again," she warned, pulling the torn cloth from its mouth. "Jennifer!"

The purple and black-haired female android strolled out of the lab with a teenage angst expression on her face.

"What?"

"Don't 'what' me." Erica scolded her, scowling, "Go take your

Genesis

brother and get another jumpsuit made for him!"

"Why can't he do it his damn self!?" She yelled.

"¡Chica, estás seriamente probar mi paciencia, y dos segundos de un tiempo fuera!" She screamed. "¡Toma tu culo irrespetuoso, e ir a poner ropa a tu hermano! ¡Ahora!"

"Vamos, gran bebé!" Jennifer stormed off, pouting and snapping at Sam.

"Jennifer is a stupid head," Sam muttered as it stomped off, following her.

"You're a stupid head," she spat back.

"You both are two seconds from a time out!" Erica screamed at them.

Buster stomped to Sophia during the family spat, curiously scanning and analyzing her. She leaned back a bit, holding a hand up to it with her palm outward like one would do a real animal.

"Easy boy," she swallowed. "Easy."

"Its A.I. is only two weeks old, so it's still learning. Go ahead, give him a touch." Erica brightly gestured. "He won't bite."

Sophia cautiously extended her hand, placing her palm on the side of its long serpent neck. Her eyebrows knitted together in bewilderment as she felt something funny about its "metal scale skin." With a bit of force, she realized that her hand could push inward, making a slight imprint. Upon release, the metal skin snapped back into place.

"Flex metal, similar to Sam's inner skin," Eric smirked. "Greatly minimizes blunt force impact."

It began wagging its tail while nuzzling its face against her hand.

Genesis

"Let me guess, not your brain pattern," Sophia said, observing.

"It belonged to my dog Akuma," Erica answered. "A beautiful black and white Pitbull, he passed away at the age of sixteen. Had to do a bit of modifying so that it understood it was in the body of a mechanized dragon and not a dog."

"Question of all your children, why does Maxine show the least emotion?"

"She didn't see the need for it," Erica shrugged, answering. "She can explore emotions like her brothers and sisters, but she decided that emotions were only useful for intimate and sexual interactions. And since she can't feel pleasure or reproduce, she had no need for it. It pops out from time to time whenever her siblings do something they're not supposed to be doing."

"On another matter, how's your investigation on the Tarapur Atomic Power Station incident?"

The question brought back Erica's brooding scowl.

~~~~~~~~~~~~~~~~~~~~~~~~~~~~~~~~~

Almost eleven months ago, Sophia and the Regulators were alerted to the Tarapur Atomic Power Station in India losing absolute power in minutes. Upon arriving, they discovered that someone or something had put a massive hole in the main reactor's side and drained all of the energy. However, all cameras went down at the time of the breach, and none of the facility's alarms went off. None of the twenty-five employees present that night, including security, engineers, technicians, operators, and janitors, knew or saw anyone until the station was drained.

Erica ran a spectrum of scans from DNA to fingerprint and could not find any trace of who caused the drain.

The return of Peace was instantly ruled out due to Erica's new sensor system attuned to her energy frequency capable of detecting her the second she got past the distance of Jupiter.

Genesis

The consensus was that a superhuman was the culprit. The EVO responsible had both eluded, confounded, and frustrated Erica to no end.

~ ~

Sophia was not shocked by Erica's demeanor, knowing that it was a sensitive topic that would set her off, nor her cold response.

"Still nada."

Sophia decided to quickly change the topic to prevent awkwardness from sneaking in.

"So, how are our former Zombie Nation members?"

"Still locked up in the psychiatric section of the new Purgatory," Erica sighed.

Thanks to a boost in their budget, the Regulators moved the superhuman prison facility underneath the Ranch. They took a page out of comic books, planting it in the middle of the Pacific Ocean. It was the first fully automated federal prison for EVOs, run by a Replicator staff along with Erica's revamped security of Doozers, providing extra muscle and firepower.

"Angela Waters, formerly known as Wendigo, is responding very well to weekly sessions. She has her episodes occasionally, but I finally got her to verbally communicate with me last week. Angela's very soft and intelligent; when alone, she attempts to draw out her power from the little sound wave of music we play in her room. It's not enough to do any damage; she usually uses it to create sonic constructs of spheres or discs to fly around her room. She's completely different from the individual we fought almost a year ago.

I haven't heard it from her lips yet, but I think it's kinda apparent her state of mind was altered after her abduction at the hands of other members of the Zombie Nation."

"Have her parents come to see her yet?"

Genesis

"No," Erica exhaled.

"What about Mr. Westgate?"

Erica's face changed to disgust and borderline hatred at the mention of his name.

"Michael Westgate, formerly known as Anchimayen, who will only answer to Anchimayen, is a textbook sociopath with psychopathic tendencies, and no argument you put forth is going to change my findings on that."

An uncomfortable tension spewed out of nowhere between the two as Sophia narrowed her eyes at an unintimidated Erica staring back at her.

"Erica ..."

"He enjoys murdering, and he's only seven." Erica cut her off. "You've seen the sessions and heard them with your own ears. His pleasure of choice is using his telekinesis to rack people and then slowly tear their limbs off one by one. His youngest victims were three years old, and he enjoys it so much that he pleasures himself to the act. He has a complete and total understanding of what he's done and no remorse for any kind. That is not a child that is a monster in the making, whose abilities will only increase as he ages. If it weren't for our current laws, I'd have him executed after three sessions."

"What about exile?" Sophia suggested. "It worked for the other members."

"You guys decided on exile," Erica steely reminded her. "I wanted the ax man for all of them, not to send them off to be someone else's problem in the universe."

Sophia sadly shook her head.

"Erica ...you don't want this on your conscience."

She took a bold step forward toward Sophia, locking eyes with her.

Genesis

"He said the second he finds a way to get free, he will kill millions …billions with just a thought, and in the most excruciating way possible. Make them all believe they are drowning until their hearts stop. His second option is to do what he did in Manhattan to escape the first time but on a global scale.

His greatest pleasure is to project all those deaths onto me so I can see every last one and know that I did not do what was necessary to stop him.

I am constantly monitoring his inhibitors and either boosting or upgrading them to suppress his abilities, which grow yearly at a monstrous rate.

I understand this is a major sore spot for you, but my conscience will be clear once that little shit gets the needle the second he turns eighteen."

Erica's words brought considerable tension between them to a fever pitch, with Sophia shouldering most of the discomfort.

Walking over to see her friend, Sister Shareef felt the heat instantly.

"Uh, you two aight?" She asked, shifting her eyes between the two of them.

"We're fine," Sophia cleared her throat. "Thank you for a clean bill of health, Dr. Champion."

"You're welcome, Dr. Dennison," Erica said as her head lowered.

"We'll talk later."

Was Sophia's final words as she walked off.

A bewildered Sister Shareef glanced at Erica with a "What the hell?" expression before following her. Erica cursed under her breath while stomping the hangar floor in frustration, morbidly regretting what she

Genesis

allowed out of her mouth.

"Soph, slow up," Sister Shareef urged, grabbing her arm. "Seriously, slow up! Stop! What happened?"

"Nothing," Sophia said as she finally stopped. "We just had a touchy conversation that is a political sore spot for the both of us."

"So, you're officially in tip-top shape?" Sister Shareef asked, taking the hint not to pry any further.

"Back to full optimal fighting capacity and will apparently stay that way as long as I don't overdo it."

Sophia changed the questioning from herself with a coy look on her face.

"So, how are you and the Sergeant these days?"

"We're okay."

Sister Shareef's meek response took her back a bit.

"Ew, don't tell me there's trouble in paradise."

"No, it's nothing serious," she waved Sophia off. "Both of us are just going through some things together."

"Oh my god," Sophia beamed, cupping her mouth. "You really …"

"Child …" Sister Shareef held up a stern warning finger. "Don't you dare say it …I'm not ready to admit that yet."

"Well, I'm happy for you anyway," she quickly said.

"So, what about you?" Sister Shareef redirected the question.

"What about me?" Sophia gave her an authentic, confused look, inquiring.

Genesis

"When are you going to pry those superhuman legs of yours apart and let someone in?" Sister Shareef sternly asked while folding her arms.

Her question caused Sophia to erupt into hysterical laughter. She abruptly stopped when she realized she wasn't laughing with her.

"Oh, you were serious."

Her serious demeanor brought an irritated scowl to Sophia's face.

"First, my mother, now you, why the hell is everyone up in my love life as of late?"

"Because you're driving certain people a bit crazy," Sister Shareef snorted. "And quite frankly, I'm starting to see it."

Irritation turned to anger as Sophia narrowed her eyes at Sister Shareef, knowing who she was referring to.

"And when did she come to you with this revelation?"

Sister Shareef immediately raised her hands, not wishing to start an argument.

"She called me a couple of days ago; I told her she should sit down and talk to you face to face."

"Really?" Sophia asked as her right eye began to twitch.

"She said she feels a bit suffocated, and I told her all parents who care about their children are like that," Shareef continued. "And she's mad because it's been months, and you refuse to give back her suit and gear."

"That little …she's not getting any of it back because she tried to go to Mars!" Sophia snarled.

"I told her that, but she is right; she only tried to go to Mars; she didn't try to blow up the planet."

Genesis

"She almost did that too, but that's another story …"

"Look, that is your child; I am not, nor would I ever tell you how to raise her," Sister Shareef stopped her before she accused her of it. "I'm just saying that it's not just with her; you've been moody and borderline tyrannical, even with me."

"When?" A bewildered Sophia asked.

"Two weeks ago, when I stayed over at your place, you almost tore my head off after you had said it was okay to raid your closet for bedclothes after I forgot mine."

"You didn't forget; ever since you got out of prison, you refused to wear any!" Sophia corrected her. "And I thought you were going to put on one of my pajamas sets, not my favorite sky-blue Thistle and Spire cami and short set, which you ended up stretching out because you're two sizes bigger than me!"

"First of all, I don't know how in tarnation you expected me to wear a pajama set on that hot ass tropical island of yours, and secondly, there was spandex in the lining; it was made to stretch!"

"For a regular woman, maybe, not for a Titan! And let's not forget that you went commando when you put them on, and the only reason you did it was because Earl was at the door!"

"No! No …I did not!" Shareef answered back as her voice went up several octaves.

"Yeah, you did, because that was the week you came over because you and your man got into an argument," Sophia reminded her. "So here you come, standing at the top of my steps with a doe-eyed look, half-naked in one of my favorite outfits looking like it's painted on her, channeling Tina Turner 1985. Attempting to give one of my good friends a stroke, only for your man to show up three days later at my doorstep looking for you!"

Shareef, visibly embarrassed, looked everywhere but her friend's face, attempting to come up with an answer.

Genesis

"We had a new mission to prepare for …"

"Don't lie, you damn flirt, and let me get this straight. Your solution for my, and let's call it what you and everyone else is calling it, 'bitchiness' is to become like you, a textbook cliché from a friggin relationship movie."

Sophia waited for her confirmation with sternly folded arms.

"First of all, even superheroes get laid so you wouldn't be a cliché," Shareef said while regaining her steel, "Secondly, as a progressive Muslim; there is nothing wrong with a little sexual release. It is why Allah created sex, so we don't kill each other. Maybe if you popped your cherry once in a while, you'd release all that tension and moodiness you got built up … Maybe you can ask a certain Egyptian god to ..."

"He's not an Egyptian god!" Sophia let out an irritated groan. "He's an alien from a highly advanced race! I'm pretty sure he's the age of Moses."

"Which means he probably has tons of experience," Shareef retorted with her hands on her hips.

Sophia took a deep breath through her nose and slowly released it through her lips.

"Agnes, seriously, my complicated life has no place for a relationship of any kind."

"Don't tell me you're going to be one of those moms," Shareef coiled back with a disturbed look.

"No, you ass, I am not going to be another Norma Bates," She glared at her, retorting. "It's not like I haven't thought about having a relationship. I honestly don't have the time for someone either feeling that they're in my massive shadow, or I'm not spending enough time with them, questioning if they're adequate enough, or whatever other stupid insecurities they might bring.

Genesis

With great power comes great responsibility. I don't have any more room for additional responsibilities …especially if the reward is thirty minutes of possibly sub-par or lousy intimacy with an optional orgasm."

"Dear Lord, who the hell have you been sleeping with?" Shareef asked with a sneer.

Sophia's face telegraphed that she wanted to end the uncomfortable conversation about getting herself a love life. Sister Shareef complied for now.

"So, are you going to the rally today?" Shareef innocently whistled.

"Yeah, I'm going to the rally Agnes," Sophia sneered at her.

"Okay, uh …do you really need to go?"

"Did Rogers put you up to this?"

"Rogers didn't put me up to anything," Shareef answered with bass. "With what's been happening in the world and right here in our country, you being at the rally might not be the smart move."

"It was the smart move in Houston," Sophia retorted with her bass-filled voice.

"We had that covered in Houston. You diving down from the heavens turned it into a media circus with many believing you're siding with Vitruvian Absolute."

Sophia's face displayed an "Are you serious?" while Sister Shareef's look answered back with an "I am dead serious."

"Well, look at you," Sophia snorted, "an official dog of the military."

"I don't know what that means, and I ain't anyone's dog. You are the one who coaxed me to join this unit, 'A perfect opportunity to once

Genesis

again make a real change from the inside,' remember? Well, you are right, it may be the military, but we are doing really good work here."

"That might change depending on who wins in November," Sophia muttered.

"You just want to make smart ass comments, or do you want to have an adult conversation?" Shareef snarled at her. "As your friend, I am advising you not to go to this rally. You will do more harm than good if you show up, trust me."

Sophia shook her head and blew air through her nose before tactfully answering her friend.

"As your friend, I understand what you are saying and respect where you are coming from. But you should know by now that I don't care what anyone thinks of me, and there's no way in hell after London that I am not going to be at that rally. I will do you the professional courtesy of staying out of sight and hanging back until things get out of your team's control."

"Define out of our control."

"That is at my discretion."

Agnes nodded while holding her hands up, accepting the stalemate as Sophia stood her ground.

"For what it's worth," Sophia said while looking her up and down. "This does suit you. Tell your rude ass boyfriend, I said hi."

"Tell little Ms. Space Exploration I said hi, and don't be too hard on her for talking to me."

"Yeah …yeah …I won't."

Sophia entered the elevator and turned to her friend, waving goodbye with a fake smile plastered on her face before it closed, taking her back up to the surface. It was quickly removed the second the doors closed

Genesis

as her mind was filled with the rally and the uncomfortable conversation she and Kimberly would have once her daughter got home from school.

Genesis

CHAPTER 6

September 2016, 3:00 AM Sanctuary time,

Sophia sat silently in her bedroom, watching her wall-mounted flat-screen television as Vincent remotely patched in the televised coverage of the Vitruvian Absolute rally taking place in Union Square. She slowly turned to her Freedom uniform and gear within a cylinder glass casing Kimberly made for her in the corner of the room. Her chest expanded and then retracted as she turned back to the television while her thoughts had a quiet war within her mind as she contemplated what she should do.

~~~~~~~~~~~~~~~~~~~~~~~~~~~~~~~

2:00 PM Eastern Standard Time, Union Square, Manhattan, New York, Rogers stood on a rooftop staring down at a sea of people gathered by the thousands in minutes. It was a mixture of superhumans and humans, many of whom traveled from different parts of the globe—all unified with one chant.

"We are the future! Evolve or die! We are the future! Evolve or die!"

The Sarge tapped on his headset.

"Is everyone in position?"

"I'm in position," Blitz answered, standing on the roof of a building on the opposite side of the square.

"I'm in position, Sir," Cyclone also responded from a building roof on another side of the square.

Genesis

"I'm in position," Sister Sledge answered as she stood several yards from the main stage.

"Sir, in position," Nitro answered several yards on the opposite side of the stage.

Heavy Element was wearing regular civilian clothing in the chanting crowd.

"In position Sarge."

"In position, Sergeant."

Merge's final confirmation came as she inconspicuously stood amongst the crowd in civies closer to the main stage.

"Alright people, 'staying vigilant' is the phrase of the day," Rogers reinforced. "So, keep your eyes peeled, and this channel open."

Each team member acknowledged one by one with a clicking sound from their headset, which Rogers counted. He then switched channels to converse with his eye in the sky.

"Maxine, what's the view from up above?"

"Crowd capacity has reached an estimated ten thousand, forty percent being EVOs while the remainder is human."

"What is the outcome of containment should this go sideways?" Rogers asked.

"With the Tornado at full capacity with neutralizing armament, forty-five percent outcome within the first three-block radius, fifty-five percent within the first five-block radius."

"Where is Dennison?"

"Energy scans show she is still on her island."

Genesis

"Keep me posted on her location," Rogers commanded. "It looks like the shows about to start down below."

The band known as Imaginary Dragon's song "Radioactive" began to bellow from the audio speakers on the stage. It ended the vast crowd's chant as they all erupted into a volcanic sea of cheers as the five founding members of Vitruvian Absolute took to the stage.

Standing side by side as they waved to the adulating crowd from right to left was an Asian male with evident Apollo class abilities, emitted through his eyes via green glowing energy. Next to him was a very tall, lean, and muscular Latin woman with long, dark, silky hair braided into a long ponytail hanging down the middle of her back. Next to her stood Deacon Absolute adorned in a black and gold fitted t-shirt with the Vitruvian Absolute symbol on the shirt's right-left breast, which all five of them wore.

Next to him stood a Middle Eastern woman whose physical features did not display her superhuman abilities. Finally, next to her was a Caucasian man with a muscular physique, the trademark of Titan class EVOs. As the music lowered, the Middle Eastern woman stepped forward, taking the microphone in the middle of the stage to begin the rally.

"Welcome everyone to our NYC rally!" she screamed. "For those who are at our rally for the first time, allow me to introduce myself! I am one of the founding members of Vitruvian Absolute! My original human name used to be Aafreen Hannan, but now I go by my superhuman name, Saraswati Absolute! If you're happy to be here, let me hear a cheer so loud, they can hear it all the way in Midtown!"

Saraswati Absolute took the microphone off its stand, extending it to the crowd as they detonated into a near-deafening cheer that wiped out all the other sounds within the vicinity of Union Square. The other members of Vitruvian Absolute nodded and clapped with approval as Saraswati Absolute ran the length of the stage to capture the vibrating sound of the crowd through the microphone.

"That is what I want to hear!" She screamed as the crowd died down. "Now allow me to introduce you to the other four founding members

Genesis

of Vitruvian Absolute! From right to left, the devilishly handsome man, you see before you, who was our main speaker at our San Francisco rally, is called Ryu Absolute, the exotic beauty next to him, our main speaker at our Texas rally, is called Diana Absolute! Standing next to her is the man who needs no introduction; you saw and heard him on our podcast, and as a political commentator on CNN, you also saw him spar with Bill Maher, Deacon Absolute!"

The crowd roared with near-white noise cheers as Deacon Absolute took a grinning bow.

"And finally, our speaker for today," she turned, pointing to the Caucasian male. "If you watch our YouTube show and listen to our Podcast, this man also needs no introduction, the one, and only Maximus Absolute!"

Upon introduction, Maximus Absolute, a man in his early forties in a Vitruvian Absolute t-shirt, jeans, and boots with a brunette buzz cut, stepped forward wearing a headset. The crowd erupted with a fever pitch of cheers as he waved and bowed in appreciation.

"Thank you! Thank you all for coming to this glorious rally right here in Union Square," He began. "For those who came out of curiosity and did not know my story, before I became Maximus Absolute, my human name was Brian Greene. I was once a firefighter and one of the many first responders on 9/11. As many of you know, many like me went into those buildings looking for the trapped, buried, and the remains of the dead so that their families could adequately bury them.

Let me first note before I continue that at that time, I was a man in good health."

An image appeared of Maximus Absolute as Brian Greene in his former New York Fireman's uniform with fellow firefighters from his firehouse.

"And like so many, I ended up developing several illnesses such as sleep apnea, sinusitis, gastroesophageal reflux disease, restrictive lung disease, post-traumatic stress, rhinitis, asthma, and swelling of the liver so

Genesis

severe it began to interfere with my blood platelets, esophagus, diaphragm, stomach, and other digestive organs.

And like so many others, the United States government left me to die."

The crowd erupted in a chorus of boos as Maximus Absolute nodded as he paced the stage. The big screen split, showing a picture of him in a wheelchair in a thin, sickly state with an oxygen mask covering the lower half of his face.

"What should have been basic common sense, the treatment of heroes who took the call to action on one of the worst days in the history of this country, was not a priority for our government. Working was no longer an option; eventually, my savings were used for my medical bills, and I could no longer afford my medication.

While I was enduring my slow and painful death sentence, which I was told only gave me between six months to a year, I put seven of my brothers, who are in the picture behind me, into the ground. I settled all my affairs, made peace with my Creator, and waited like a good Catholic for the end to come.

That was until that fateful day on September 9th, 2008, what we all know as Judgment Day."

The crowd erupted in cheers and began to chant once again.

"We are the future! Evolve or die! We are the future! Evolve or die!"

"Yes, we are!" Maximus Absolute roared. "Three days after Judgment day, I, like many of you here today, was not only judged but had their lives changed forever! My breathing returned to normal, I could eat properly again, and my weight and strength returned, but it didn't stop there.

Like many of you, I was re-born again a better, more superior human being. I naturally thought it was a miracle, a blessing from God

Genesis

Himself, a second chance to live and do right by my fellow man.

So, I returned to being a firefighter, and on my off days, I became a superhero.

That was until the truth was revealed to me."

He paused a minute, holding up a hand.

"Correction, that was until the truth was revealed to all of us."

"Mother Peace! Mother Peace! Mother Peace!" became the new chant of the energetic crowd.

"Is everyone hearing this bullshit?" Merge snarled.

"Only in America can a psycho become a hero," Blitz huffed.

"What about Syria and North Korea?" Cyclone interjected.

"What about keeping the line open for important shit, do you all not understand?" Rogers barked. "We're dealing with fanatics, boo hoo; move on."

"Superhuman fanatics Sarge," Heavy Element corrected him, "A lot of them."

"You're gonna find out who's worse if you don't keep this damn line clear!"

"Alright! Alright!" Heavy Element shot back.

"That's right! Mother Peace revealed the truth to us!" Maximus Absolute continued his idiom. "In one speech, she exposed the lies and secrets our government had been hiding from us for decades and revealed our true purpose. We were not chosen to be heroes or soldiers! We were not chosen to be the protectors of our feeble counterparts! We were chosen to flourish and surpass them, to become the rightful rulers of planet Earth, while they wither and die returning to the dirt in which they came from!"

Genesis

The crowd returned to their original chant.

"We are the future! Evolve or die! We are the future! Evolve or die!"

"Sergeant Rogers, Dr. Dennison, has just left her island and is en route here based on her trajectory," Maxine announced within Rogers's earpiece. "Her estimated arrival time is three minutes."

"Shit," Rogers muttered, lowering his head.

He quickly raised it back up, focusing on watching the rally from his viewpoint while Maximus Absolute continued his speech below.

"Here is the truth! Hate groups like the KKK and Neo-Nazis will never see or understand that White privilege, White power, or White supremacy is nothing but a farce, an illusion!" Maximus Absolute turned to point to the picture of his past frail self. "Look what my so-called 'white privilege' got me in my greatest time of need! People like these will forever be the unwitting victims of an age-old ploy engineered by wealthy people to divide poor people!"

"Yes, they will!"

"Activist groups like the Black Panthers and Black Lives Matter will never see that not everything is about racism, and to take responsibility for situations going on in their own community before they point the finger at others! They are quick to march when a dirty cop kills an innocent, but slow to act when one of their own shoots up a neighborhood park full of children!"

"Yes, they are!"

"Religious extremist groups like ISIL and the Westboro Baptist Church will never see that there is no holy war! Because you cannot war with God! That God or Allah, if He exists, does not need them and has most likely abandoned them because they brazenly twist and defile His laws and words to suit their own means, not His, and that is why we were chosen, and they were not!"

Genesis

"We were chosen! We are the future! Evolve or die! We are the future! Evolve or die!"

"Listen to the truth!" Maximus Absolute howled, "The one percent will never stop breaking the backs of the poor, raping our ecosystem, or driving our wildlife into extinction, because greed is an incurable disease!"

"No, they won't!" The crowd roared again.

"The ninety-nine percent will never know their self-worth and will forever remain under the heel of the wealthy and their government because they are weak! They are forever looking up wishing to be in the castle with the one percent not understanding that they are the wealthy's foundation as well as the foundation of their government and that without them, they would both come crumbling down to nothing!"

"No, they won't!"

"And finally, ...our world leaders ..."

Maximus Absolute paused with a sinister grin as the boos and jeers became the loudest they had ever been during the rally.

"They dodged a huge bullet, didn't they?"

"Yes, they did! Yes, they did!"

"Our world leaders and our governments around this planet will never learn that they were each put into office to serve the will of the people, not the other way around! They are like everyone else who has not been chosen and evolved into what we are! All who I have mentioned are weak, inferior creatures forever enslaved in the circle of archaic ideologies that will destroy them all! And from their ashes, we shall rise!"

"Yes, we will! We are the future! Evolve or die! We are the future! Evolve or die!"

"Now, I want to make this part of our message clear to those who have not physically evolved, like many of us have." Maximus Absolute

Genesis

lowered his voice a bit while holding up a hand. "The fact that you are standing here with us today means that although your bodies have not changed, your minds have! You can see that better future! And you, along with us, have a part to play in sowing the seeds for the rise of a better humankind!"

Cheers erupted from the crowd once again, mostly from women. The loudest cheers in the front came from ordinary and superhuman women, either pregnant or holding infants or children who were also superhuman.

"By doing your part, you not only ensure a better world to come, but you also ensure your immortality! Your perfect offspring will live on like the rest of us to create a better world in your name, so, while others who return to dust will be long forgotten, you will be remembered forever!"

"Yes, we will! We are the future! Evolve or die! We are the future! Evolve or die!"

Rogers inhaled and slowly exhaled his native New York air as he shook his head, not knowing what to make of the anarchy-laced speech that the hungry crowd was gorging on below.

"Sergeant Rogers, Freedom is here," Maxine announced.

"Where?"

"Approximately five miles up from where I am hovering."

"Connect me to her, Maxine."

"Connecting."

High above Manhattan, Freedom calmly hovered out of the visual range of everyone on the ground. With her earpiece locked in, Vincent tapped into the stage audio system to hear everything going on down below while she watched from the visual display on her bracer.

Genesis

The face she wore that no one could see said she did not care for what she heard below, like Rogers.

"Dr. Dennison, Sergeant Rogers, wishes to speak with you."

"Patch him in."

"Didn't think you'd answer," Rogers's gruff voice came into her ear.

"I don't remember having an issue with you, Rogers," She said plainly, "So why wouldn't I pick up?"

"I see you decided not to heed Sister Sledge's advice," Rogers said, sidestepping her question.

"Maybe I would have been more responsive if you didn't send your girlfriend to do your dirty work for you," Freedom responded bluntly, "I'm responsible for this gathering. I need to be here."

"Your presence here could most likely do more damage than help. My team and I have this covered."

"There are a couple thousand EVOs from around the globe with various abilities on different levels, and you with one A.I. operated ship and a seven-person team."

"Ten," Rogers corrected her. "Sam is on board the Tornado, ready to deploy. You also missed the three National Guard units and the Strategic Response Group backing us up."

"I didn't miss them. They're all positioned one block away from the action. You couldn't deputize some additional heroes for this event?"

"With what's going on with this election, the last thing I'm doing is deputizing anyone who's not one of my people," Rogers answered.

"And your issue with me being here is ….?"

Genesis

Rogers kneaded his forehead, feeling an imaginary migraine coming on.

"Just extend me the professional courtesy of allowing my team to diffuse any situation that might occur first before you decide to step in," he requested.

"I will consider it," she returned flatly.

"Dennison."

"I said I will consider it," she said, countering the bass in his voice with more bass in her tone.

Rogers muttered a curse under his breath as he focused on the highly charged rally and prayed for it to remain peaceful.

Gunshots from the crowd let him know that God was not listening to him today.

"Die you fucking abominations! Die! Die!"

A shocked and terrified crowd of humans and superhumans dispersed where the sound of shots fired came from. A lone gunman brandishing a Steyr SPP let loose a series of semi-automatic rounds aimed at the women and children several feet from him.

Luck was on their side as two of the mothers, who happened to be Titans, turned their backs, covering their own children and deflecting the gunman's bullets with their thick skins. Unfortunately, the ricocheting bullets struck two regular humans in the chaos.

A roaring Merge in her transformed were-version of a Desert Lynx leaped over the crowd, pouncing on top of the assailant, slamming him into the ground before he emptied the clip from his gun.

"Move! Move! Out of the way! United States Military! Get out of the friggin way!" Heavy Element yelled after transforming into metallic form while attempting to move through the panicked crowd to get to his

Genesis

sister.

When that did not work, he physically lifted and moved people out of the way to get to her while Blitz and Cyclone descended from their location to where Merge took down the assailant. In the middle of the mayhem, Sister Sledge and Nitro made their way to the stage to secure the attempted mass shooting perimeter.

"Status report, people!" Rogers barked from his rooftop.

"Merge has taken down the assailant," Blitz answered. "We are currently securing the perimeter!"

The gunman squealed and sniveled as saliva dripped on his face from a feral Merge growling over him with what came off as an intention to bite his face off.

"Merge, secure the assailant!" Heavy Element ordered his sister. "Merge!"

Merge turned, snarling at her brother before going through the procedure of taking out tie restraints to secure the shooter. After several sniffs, she let out a growl and began to tear open his jacket with her claws. Merge ripped out a black tactical shoulder harness with two handguns and a couple clips of ammo.

Heavy Element, in his metal form covering his sister, felt the heat of hatred and rage around him. He slowly turned to see a startled crowd now out for blood.

"Women and children!" Someone howled from the crowd. "The fucking son of a bitch shot at women and children!"

"Fucking unevolved apes!"

"Fuck this! We need to send a message!"

"Kill him! Kill him now!"

Genesis

As Blitz, Cyclone, and Nitro powered up for a confrontation, Heavy Element's eyes slightly widened as he realized how vastly outnumbered his team was as those with Apollo class abilities began to power up. In contrast, those with powers similar to himself and his sister began to transform. Everything went into slow motion as he slowly held up both his hands with palms facing outward as if the gesture could magically hold the frenzied, super-charged mob back as he attempted to reason with them. It was all futility as his eyes barely caught several Mercurian EVOs exploding from the crowd.

Blitz fired an electrical warning shot faster, scorching a line into the ground and stopping them in their tracks. This only caused several Apollo class EVOs to take to the air, ready to square off with him.

Three things that ran through Heavy Element's mind as Union Square prepared to become a battleground were that the gunman was good as dead, movies were bullshit, and Brett Ratner could eat a bag of dicks.

As he contemplated between going for his shoulder-holstered sidearm or using hand-to-hand combat, everyone froze at the sound of a thunderous sonic boom that shook the heavens, forcing all heads to look up.

She stopped mid-dive several yards up from Union Square and slowly descended to the ground. The crowd slowly retreated as she became the wall between them and the Regulators with the captured assailant.

Freedom's narrowed, stern gaze was an omen to those considering resorting to violent retaliation. She stood with her hands partially clenched, waiting for those EVOs within the crowd brave enough to challenge her to step forward or for the boos to come, followed by objects being thrown.

She was not prepared for what happened next.

In one motion, the sea of superhumans and humans fell to one knee with lowered heads bowing before her.

Slowly, she turned to the stage to see the members of Vitruvian Absolute doing the same.

Genesis

The only eyes on her now were the speechless Regulators and major news cameras reporting on the rally.

"Oh shit …" She whispered.

Then, the chants began.

"Lead us. Lead us. Lead us."

Freedom ignored the nervous spasms vibrating her bones as she kept a firm stance and poker face while turning to Heavy Element.

"Get him out of here."

Heavy Element agreed with a nod as he radioed in.

"Maxine, we need a transport drone stat."

"Sending one now," she confirmed.

Within seconds, three times the size of a Frisbee, a metallic silver and blue disc dropped from the sky and came to a hover. Sister Sledge brought the gunman to his feet as it went vertical and attached itself to his back. Parts of it broke open, forming a harness around his upper chest.

"Get going," Heavy Element commanded the drone.

The only thing louder than the growing chants was the gunman's scream as the drone took him back into the sky toward the Tornado. As it brought him in through the rear hatch, Maxine stood waiting to receive him.

"You are currently in a government vehicle and are being held for brandishing and discharging a firearm in public," she informed him. "Please have a seat where you will be restrained until you are transported to the proper authorities."

Realizing the assassin was near-catatonic, Maxine gently helped him to his feet as the drone released him, flying back to its docking station. She escorted him to a chair, sitting him down as arm, chest, and leg

Genesis

restraints popped from the chair, locking him in.

Down below, Rogers lowered his beanie and exhaled defeated New York air through his nostrils as the chants became louder, echoing out of Union Square.

"Lead us! Lead us! Lead us!"

Freedom quickly glanced at Sister Sledge, who gave her a nod before she exploded into the sky of New York City without a word. The sounds of disappointment swept the entire rally as the crowd rose to their feet, searching for Freedom in the sky. None of them noticed the wicked smiles from the members of Vitruvian Absolute as they quickly glanced at one another.

"That's okay!" Maximus Absolute yelled while getting to his feet. "That's okay! Give her time; our mother heard us! Give her time! Let's give a round of applause to our military's finest for stepping in… on behalf of the assailant that is."

The Regulators turned, glaring at the members of Vitruvian Absolute on the stage. Although keeping it professional, Heavy Element looked like he wanted to leap onto the stage and go to blows with the Titan. Merge, still in her Lynx form, growled his sentiment.

"We're also going to ask that no one stoops to the level of the person that was just removed from here!" Maximus Absolute continued. "This is what they want, to portray us as monsters easily swayed to violence like they are. But we are not them. We are better than them in every single way, and we proved it once again today. They couldn't kill us, or intimidate us, they're the ones who are scared, because now they know …!"

"We are the future! Evolve or die! We are the future! Evolve or die!"

"Merge, Heavy Element, and Sister Sledge, coordinate with the National Guard and SRG unit to peacefully shut this down, and begin to disperse this crowd," Rogers began with his list of orders to his team. "Blitz, Cyclone, and Nitro head uptown to the Tower and provide additional

Genesis

protective detail to the Republican candidate. Maxine, start tracking the direction of the crowd, make sure none of them move towards the Tower."

~~~~~~~~~~~~~~~~~~~~~~~~~~~~~~~~~~~

After the rally, the Regulators handed over the assailant to the NYPD. Facial recognition from Maxine revealed him to be Mitch Rutherford from Columbia, South Carolina.

Mr. Rutherford, married, with two children with three priors for disorderly conduct, assault, battery, and drunk driving, was also a member of the Carolina Knights of the Ku Klux Klan.

Mr. Rutherford drove his 2014 Ram 1500 truck into Jersey City, New Jersey, a day before the rally and took a jitney bus into Port Authority Manhattan, where he walked to the rally. On his person was a Desert Eagle .50, a Steyr SPP (Special Purpose Pistol) semi-automatic pistol, a Walther P99 semi-automatic pistol, and several ammunition clips for each weapon.

It was a textbook shooter incident, but something in Rogers's gut did not feel right about it.

On the flight home, Rogers sat by himself, studying the shooting incident on a tablet. He repeatedly played the scene as Sister Shareef walked over, sitting beside him.

"What do you see?" She asked.

"Three children got hit, but their Titan and Mercurian physiology protected them from the rounds. Then two mothers moved in to block the remaining rounds," Rogers paused and pointed. "He keeps shooting in the same direction until Merge takes him down. One slight turn to his right and he could have hit several more targets. Nine times out of ten active shooters strive to hit as many targets as possible before going down, yet he stayed rooted and focused on the women and children."

"More proof that he's an evil …"

"We were here before the crowd formed, and Maxine was running

Genesis

scans for weapons using thermal and x-ray imaging. Yet this son of a bitch manages to evade her and stand next to one of the few Apollos in the crowd with electromagnetic capabilities to distort her scans."

Agnes leaned in, narrowing her eyes to take a closer look.

"That is odd."

"Once we get back," Rogers muttered. "I want to learn more about Mr. Rutherford, the EVO he was standing next to, and Vitruvian Absolute."

~ ~

May 2017, 10:20 PM Sanctuary time,

Sophia sat in the main Council Hall in a simple white blouse, pink linen pants, and a dazed look. Her thoughts were trapped in a loop as images of what occurred in Union Square nine months ago played repeatedly. A large part of her did not regret going. She believed her appearance defused an event that would have eclipsed every other riot in the United States. However, the wrenching knot in her stomach reminded her that every news station and device within the vicinity caught a sea of people bowing to her, asking for her leadership.

Social media had a field day with the footage drawing the lines visibly dividing those who still saw her as a champion and protector and those who verbally expressed their disdain for her, projecting her as the biggest threat to ordinary humankind.

The incident that saw no end to cooling down spilled into her personal life and Sanctuary; eight months later, twelve residents became former residents wishing to relocate. Sophia aided them using her resources with a smile and a broken heart, knowing that they no longer trusted her underneath their smiles, tears, and much appreciation for everything she had done for them.

Sophia's woes did not end as accusations from conspiracy theorists, the Alt-Right movement, and right-wing news outlets accused her of running an occult from her island. This, in turn, broke bonds and closed

Genesis

doors to her from specific organizations, including churches, barring her from speaking to those in need who would entertain coming to Sanctuary for a new start to rebuild their lives.

Not to be deterred, Sophia took her message to the streets where, at times, she was ambushed by either the media or protestors of the political, radical, or religious persuasion. At times, this sparked demonstrators to come to her defense, who either believed in her as a hero or worshipped her as a messiah, igniting at times into clashes that she had to put down herself, causing more turmoil in a world where things went viral.

These instances forced her to abandon specific states and regions she regularly frequented to help those in need to prevent violence in her name.

Many nights, Sophia broke her own rule, unable to sleep. Many nights, she'd quietly floated high enough so no one could hear her scream and cry her frustrations out as she gazed down at the Earth below, feeling powerless.

~~~~~~~~~~~~~~~~~~~~~~~~~~~~~~~~~~~~

Amid the chaos, she went to the only safe place that would allow her to think.

Sitting in her parent's dining room with a cup of peppermint tea in front of her, Sophia went home.

"I shouldn't have gone," she sighed.

"Is dat wut you believe?" Her father asked.

A bald-headed Mr. Dennison with a thick salt and peppered beard leaned forward in his chair at the head of the table with his hands clasped. His deep, soothing voice with her when she was learning to ride a bike without training wheels, was in the body of a slightly smaller older man in his early seventies who needed glasses to drive and read.

"I don't know, daddy."

Genesis

Sophia, feeling lost, dropped her eyes to her half-drunken cup.

"Memba when yu usta git sick an ah nastee cauf, yud hide becuz I'd feed yu honey, cod liva, an leman."

Sophia shuddered and gagged at the memory, which brought back the disgusting taste in her mouth.

"Gawd, I hated dat."

"But cha felt good aftawads, right?"

"Yeah, I did," she begrudgingly nodded, agreeing.

"Dem news reports all say if you wasn't dere nuff peeple wud ah died. Dem wud ah killed dat bwoy, an gawd knows wut wuda happened to New Yauk."

Mr. Dennison smirked as he reached over, placing his old, calloused hand over hers.

"Not everyting dat tis good will feel good, baby girl."

His words brought a soft smile back to her face as she picked up her father's hand and kissed it.

"Thank you, daddy."

Sophia narrowed her eyes as she saw a brighter smirk than usual on her father's face.

"Oh my god …dad, are you having a Jor-El moment?"

"Nah, mon!" Mr. Dennison snorted. "More like Mista Kent!"

Sophia's eyes became misty as she erupted into uncontrollable laughter, which became infectious to her dad, who let out his trademark chuckle.

Genesis
~~~~~~~~~~~~~~~~~~~~~~~~~~~~~~~~~

"Soph."

She snapped out of her trance, not from Earl's voice, but the soft touch of his hand on her shoulder. Slowly, she looked around the room at the concerned looks the other council members gave her as they bore witness to her spacing out.

"You okay?" Earl asked.

"I am so sorry," she swallowed. "What was the last thing that was said?"

"Um, it is becoming difficult to expand Sanctuary's infrastructure without damaging too much of the foliage," Hector Lopez, Sanctuary's Head of Construction, reiterated. "With the twenty-five hundred refugees we granted asylum from North Korea, we've gone from a large village to a sizeable town. I know you want to keep things 'green,' Sophia, but it's going to be challenging to get to people who might get sick or injured outside the main town's vicinity without proper roads, especially if you or Kimberly are not around. Our only two options to keep the town centralized are to move the preserve so we can expand in that area since it's closer to the village or start turning some houses in the central town into townhouses similar to the new constructions we're currently doing."

"That would take a lot of people out of their comfort zones; I don't want that." She huffed. "Any chance we can add a fifth addition to the newer houses?"

"Not advised after the last hurricane we had to endure," Hector said. "The taller the construction, the more likelihood of swaying, especially with those crazy winds we got. The trees, also being higher than the construction, helped cut down the wind force that hit us. If we go any higher, we're going to have some serious problems."

She leaned forward, placing her elbows on the table as her chin fell on her clasped hands. She sat there for a moment, focusing on her decision.

Genesis

"Hector, if you could evaluate for me how much of the wildlife preserve we could reasonably push back to get more space, I would appreciate that," she said, turning to him before addressing the rest of the council members. "As far as building up, I would like to quietly leave that up to each resident that has an old home. If you each can go from house to house within your sector and ask if they wouldn't mind having their homes converted into the new three-story townhouse-style to make additional space for new residents, we will consider the upgrades and how to proceed. Let them know it is strictly voluntary, and they are not obligated to upgrade if they do not want to."

She turned with a pleasant smile to the two newest members of the Council.

"Bong-Cha and Chung Ae, how are the people in your sectors adjusting to their new life here?"

Bong-Cha Yi was a twenty-five-year-old with long, beautiful jet-black hair and green eyes from Pukchin. Her father paid the ultimate price to slip her and her little sister across the North Korean border into China for a better life.

Twenty-seven-year-old Chung Ae Rey, with his newly grown hair and a soft smile that brought sunlight to the room, was from Sinhŭng County and a former soldier turned deserter. Chung Ae left after he savagely beat an old man for stealing food because he was hungry and then was ordered to execute him where he lay. The act haunted Chung Ae and opened his eyes to the cruelty of a regime under which he no longer wished to serve. So, like Bong-Cha, Chung Ae found an opportunity to escape to China.

Unlike Bong-Cha, Chung Ae had a bounty on his head for being a deserter. He counted the days until he would be caught and dragged back to North Korea for torture and execution. That day would never come due to Sophia.

On one visit with the Prime Minister of China, she was allowed to walk as many North Korean refugees out of China, giving them proper asylum from their former country.

Genesis

She took eight thousand North Korean refugees out of China with her own cargo planes and a couple she rented. Twenty-five hundred opted to come to her island and start a new life where they felt safe, while the remainder was divided between South Korea and Australia in a joint relocation effort.

Her actions shocked the world and brought both a mixture of praise and scrutiny to her.

It was not a decision she made on her own; she brought it to the feet of all the villagers of Sanctuary. The majority of residents were for it, while there was a sprinkle that had their reservations. In the end, it was put to a vote.

The cost was three other villagers requesting relocation.

From the first day, Bong-Cha stepped foot on the island with her little sister; she took charge, helping the rest of the refugees to get acclimated while stepping in to help break down language barriers. Chung Ae did the same, joining in with the construction workforce. When he was not helping to put up another structure, he was out on a boat fishing.

It took some time, but he eventually became one of her patients as he worked through his demons regarding his past life while finding forgiveness within himself for what he had done. As the months rolled by, she watched the stone-hardened, jittery soldier who walked off the plane melt away into a young man who loved rock music and sailing with an infectious laugh.

When invited to join the Council, Bong-Cha jumped at the opportunity. Chung Ae was more hesitant, believing he did not deserve the right to order or command anyone. In the end, Sophia coaxed him to join to show him that he had excellent leadership skills that could be utilized for good rather than evil. That he could be someone people looked up to, not feared.

Although they did their best to integrate the newly constructed houses with the homes already there to prevent any sense of separation, the North Korean defectors were now the largest population on the island. A

Genesis

tiny part of Sophia's mind whispered that she may have bitten off more than she could chew; a part of her heart told her what she did was right.

What she did know was she was at the point of no return. She had to work on the problem.

"Everyone is pleased to be here," Bong-Cha nervously smiled while looking around. "Many have said this feels like a dream come true, like paradise. It's just that …"

She paused, wondering how best to say what she wanted to say.

"I believe everyone wants to do more," Chung Ae jumped in. "To help …to become a part of the community."

"Which is awesome to hear and brings us to our next problem," Sanctuary's new Head of Finance jumped in. "This Island needs to start producing …"

He paused as he caught Sophia again fluttering her eyes in irritation, not wishing to hear his ominous projections for another month. She begrudgingly reigned it in, putting back on her adult hat.

"What are the projections, Indrajit?"

Indrajit cleared his throat before explaining while everyone followed along, reading the report on their respective computer tablets.

"With our next project coming up in a couple of weeks, our population is going to grow to that of a small city. Luckily, our treasury funds are equivalent to two New York States, so we will still be deep in the black. However, if we don't generate a viable income next year to maintain the treasury, we will run into some problems. Our issues are going to be general infrastructure maintenance, hospital and medical supplies, and future natural disasters, among other things."

Sophia kept her poker face while nodding as her inner voice unleashed every foul language she could imagine.

Genesis

"Set up some time for us to sit down and go over the numbers line by line."

Indrajit nodded as he checked her calendar on his tablet, setting up a time. Amid it, she noticed the other members of the Council glancing at each other, deciding who would speak.

"Out with it," Sophia rolled her eyes, sighing. "You guys know how much it irks me when you do that."

"We had a town hall meeting last week while you were away on one of your missions," a silver-haired Ms. Gertrude, the Head of Sanctuary's Agricultural department, said.

Sophia became a nervous child as she sat back in her chair.

"Okay."

"Everyone on the island agreed we want to start paying some form of tax to sustain the treasury and the island."

Her revelation brought on a slight scowl on Sophia's face.

"Why would you have that discussion without me?"

"Because we knew you wouldn't want to have that discussion in the first place," Ms. Gertrude calmly answered her back, speaking for everyone else. "Or, you would word it where people would not feel obligated to do it. For many of us, this is our home Sophia, and we're not children to be coddled. We have a good thing here, and we want to see it grow into something wonderful."

"It will be the first time in my life I'd be both happy and proud to pay taxes," Earl grunted. "I see firsthand where my money is going to."

Everyone except for Sophia laughed and nodded at Earl's joke in agreement. Sophia glanced at each of them with a look of injured betrayal.

"Stop with the pouting," Earl admonished her with a fatherly tone.

Genesis

"You cannot keep this place going by deep diving for gold and gems near the center of the Earth every couple of months. God knows what that is doing to our planet. This is positive progression."

Her inner toddler came out while she folded her arms.

"Not pouting," Sophia muttered.

She blushed, realizing who she was around, and sat up in her seat, becoming an adult again as light chuckles went around the room.

"So, I take it you all have ideas," Sophia asked with defeated clasped hands.

"Well, for one, we can start with our nonconflictual diamonds, the ones the size of footballs, I mean," Indrajit shrugged, suggesting.

This time, everyone, minus a confused Bong-Cha and Chung Ae, glared at him, making Indrajit feel like he was in a spotlight.

"What?"

"Spoken like a true Wall Street Broker," Hector scoffed with a headshake.

"I was also going to suggest Organic farming and seasonal fishing," Indrajit sneered at Hector, retorting. "We can also go into the natural energy manufacturing business; we've practically mastered producing environmental energy-efficient homes."

"Let's consider those options and put the diamond business on the back burner for now," Sophia said, mediating. "I would like everyone here to start the discussion around the island as to what export industry they would like the community to take on as a venture. We'll take the best four and then narrow it down to a community vote. I know I don't have to say anything illegal, but that also includes alcohol and tobacco, anything that needs FDA approval, or harmful to the environment."

"What about cannabis?" Indrajit asked with a raised hand.

Genesis

Once again, everyone, minus the new members sitting with confused faces, groaned and glared at him. Indrajit continued to stand his ground.

"Before you all take my head off, it's slowly becoming a billion-dollar industry. States like Colorado have been caking it in revenue ever since they made it legal, you can also make a vast number of products from it, like milk, paper, and oil, and as a doctor, you know better than anyone else its medicinal purposes Sophia."

Sophia's jaw slowly shifted from left to right as she searched for an answer to refute Indrajit's defense. The physician within her would not let her.

"I …will consider it."

"Thank you!"

Indrajit raised his hands in victory, doing a little dance in his seat while the seniors of the Council balled up wads of paper, throwing it at him.

"The time is now 10:30 PM," Vincent announced vocally, projecting from Sophia's tablet.

"And this meeting is officially adjourned," Sophia smiled at everyone, announcing while tapping the desk. "Next week, we'll be back to the noon meeting schedule."

Ms. Gertrude trotted over to kiss Sophia on the cheek before leaving.

"Taking myself home to get some rest, later, child."

"Have a good night, Ms. Gertrude, Bong-Cha, and Chung Ae. Could you both hang back a bit, please?" Sophia asked.

Both nodded and anxiously awaited as the other members said their goodbyes, minus Earl, and left to go home. Sophia got up, giving them a soft smile as she closed the gap between them. She began addressing them

Genesis

in their native tongue.

"I just want to make sure that you understand that you and all the new arrivals are included in this conversation. Even though you arrived in the middle of all this, this is your home as long as you are here. You are both on this Council because I see great leadership qualities in both of you, so don't be afraid to jump in and speak up."

They smiled and eagerly nodded back at her.

"Thank you again for giving us this opportunity," Bong-Cha replied.

"And for making us feel so welcome," Chung Ae interjected.

"Thank you both for being here, have a very good night," she smiled.

As they both walked away, Sophia turned to Earl, waiting to walk out with her.

"You know there was a tribal meeting concerning Indrajit," He coughed out while leaning against one of the chairs.

"We're not kicking him off the island Earl," she chuckled.

"The boy's too high strung and city savvy," Earl grunted. "In one meeting, he suggested us going from diamond selling into the weed business."

"The precious stones and gold in our reserves ensure the island's stability, especially during emergencies, so I just don't want to sell it off for cash, especially in this fluctuating market with the uncertainty of BREXIT and the state of the US and its new President and administration," Sophia sighed. "Not to mention word gets out we're in the diamond business, undesirables might attempt to grow a spine like the crew that came for Pop-Pop and our herd."

~ ~

Genesis

Earl gruffed a nervous chuckle as he remembered with her the day a group of poachers actually came via a small merchant ship. They intended to invade, kill, and take Sanctuary's horns of the steadily growing population of White and Black Rhinos, which was now at three hundred strong and building between the two species after almost eight years.

Most of the Rhinos were willingly given from other reserves worldwide who felt they could no longer defend the animals from poachers.

The television channel Animal Planet got wind of this and feverishly begged Sophia to do a special about how her reserve was protecting and steadily replenishing endangered species, with the rhinos being the feature of the interview.

Pop-Pop, named by Sophia, was the first male White Rhino successfully born in Sanctuary. He became an online social media sensation when the camera crew caught him squealing and running vigorously away from his own mother to nuzzle up to Sophia for attention.

Almost two weeks after the show aired, the poachers showed up the day Sophia handled a matter in the Middle East.

With Kimberly standing beside Earl, holding her computer tablet, she video recorded the invasion on the beach's shores. At the same time, he blared over a bullhorn, politely informing the poachers that they had exactly one minute to begin turning around and leaving their shores before they were brutally retaliated.

The poachers chose to show that they came with heavy armament and eight powerful superhumans for the extra muscle to get the job done.

With Kimberly still recording and unfazed, Earl, with Sophia on speakerphone, told her they chose not to comply.

Sophia flew from the Middle East in less than a minute without warning, tearing the poacher's ship in half with one hit. Although she pulled her punches, she ensured the EVOs that dared invade her shores felt her wrath for a lifetime.

Genesis

Kimberly, recording the entire beat down, uploaded it with some skillful editing and the brutal musical hook to Rob Bailey & The Hustle Standard's "Beast" minus the profanity as a warning to future poachers and superhumans brazen enough to approach their shores looking for fortune and glory.

The video went viral and almost shut down YouTube.

Sophia ordered Kimberly to take the video down and grounded her for a week for putting it up without her permission.

The video was copied, spoofed, analyzed, and memed to death, as with everything uploaded.

It further divided the world into a debate as it was the first recorded footage of her destructive power that was longer than three minutes.

~~~~~~~~~~~~~~~~~~~~~~~~~~~~~~~~~

"As far as selling cannabis," Sophia shrugged. "We do grow it here for medicinal purposes, and hemp can be used to create a variety of products. As long as we stay within those guidelines, it's not really an issue. You just don't care for his NYC Wall Street swagger."

"He's just loud and obnoxious sometimes," Earl growled.

"It's a defense mechanism Earl," Sophia softly defended Indrajit without diving too far into his life. "You had one too, remember? Underneath it all, he's trying to use the tools to prove that he can be a better person. It's a work in progress."

"The boy still irks me …sometimes."

Sophia gave Earl a smile, shaking her head, allowing him the final word on Indrajit.

"I know I practically see you every day," Earl said, changing the subject. "But how are things?"

Genesis

"I'm okay."

"Wanna talk about why you zoned out earlier?"

She slowly exhaled, knowing that was the next question out of his mouth.

"I have a superhuman eidetic memory; the reason I don't zone out more is that I have a handle on it. And no, I don't want to talk about it right now. Right now, I just want to go home, curl up on my couch, and binge on as many episodes of 'Outlander' I can watch before Kimberly comes home while praying Vincent doesn't alert me to some natural disaster or major crisis."

"Miss, I am receiving a call from the secretary at Kimberly's school; there has been an incident," Vincent announced through her computer tablet.

"What happened? Is she alright?" Sophia nervously asked.

"She is fine, but the secretary will only speak to you."

"Put her on."

Sophia picked up the earpiece from the table beside her tablet and put it on.

"Hello, Mrs. Beans, this is Ms. Dennison. Is everything alright?"

Sophia's eyes widened as if she had been tasered, which made Earl step forward in concern. Her expression quickly changed to one of anger.

"I see," she answered with a professional voice. "Thank you, Mrs. Bean, and please inform Principal Moe that I will be there shortly to see to the matter. Good day."

Sophia removed her earpiece, tossing it on the table next to her tablet as she took a deep breath, hoping it would extinguish the anger that had been stoked.

Genesis

It did not.

"No, Claire or Jaime for me tonight. I have to fly to Kimberly's school."

"Why?" Asked a concerned Earl.

She looked up, glaring at him before she answered.

"So, I can kill her."

Genesis

CHAPTER 7

An hour and a half later, a semi-calm Sophia stood before Kimberly's middle school, ready to enter.

She stopped at Michelle's house and changed into a two-piece tan business skirt suit with a white blouse underneath, nude stockings, and brown pumps. She then took an Uber car from the house to the school. She made sure to wear shades to hide her eyes to not unnerve her driver but ended up taking them off when he concentrated less on getting Sophia to her destination and more on hitting on her.

As she walked onto the grounds, all eyes were on her despite her civilian attire. Nearing the steps, she was greeted by two familiar faces. One she was glad to see, while the other belonged to Rogers.

"Dustin, what's going on? Why are you here?" She asked with a voice filled with concern.

Dustin Mercer descended the steps to meet her halfway with a placid smile, holding his hands up in a calming gesture.

"Everything is alright," he reassured her. "Unfortunately, this is just procedure."

"What happened?" She asked with a bass-filled voice not directed at him.

"Kimberly kind of scared the piss out of another kid …literally," Dustin coughed. "Some of her other classmates were shaken up too. Police were called, now they tried to restrain her."

"Someone put handcuffs on my child?" Her eyes blazed with rage, asking.

Genesis

"They took the hint after she busted a set!" Dustin gestured with his hands, begging her to calm down. "My office was called, and I came down here. Everything is calm; she's in the principal's office waiting for you."

"So why are you here, Rogers?" Sophia slowly turned with narrowed eyes towards him, inquiring.

"Do you really need to ask that?" Rogers glared, retorting, "All superhuman affairs now fall into my lap. The boy, your kid, threatened just so happened to be the son of a GOP whip, who wanted to press charges, but I have advised him not to go that route, especially since no physical assault took place. You're welcome."

A larger Dustin stood uncomfortably between the suffocating tensions of the two superhumans in his presence. Sophia finally backed down, softening her mannerisms.

"Thank you."

"You can thank me by taking your kid home and not further complicating my life. And then, when you have a minute, thank your friend for sending a virus to erase all of the videos and live feeds of the incident before it went viral. Nice talking to you, Assistant Director Mercer."

Rogers, getting in the last word, walked down the steps past her, and Dustin returning to his vehicle.

As Sophia sighed while watching Rogers leave, Dustin asked the obvious question.

"Did you two use to...?"

"No."

"Okay."

"Thank you, Dustin," Sophia said, turning to him with a face full of embarrassment. "I am so sorry ..."

Genesis

"Don't apologize," he cut her off. "I have my own."

"How are you doing?"

"I miss my friend every day," Dustin exhaled, lowering his head. "Other than that, I'm alright; how about you?"

"Wishing I was meeting you under better circumstances," Sophia huffed, shaking her head. "But I am glad to see you."

"We ended up becoming one crazy family, didn't we?" He chuckled with a smirk. "Wasn't oh so long-ago Mark and I were chasing you with a fleet of squad cars through Houston."

"And shooting at me," Sophia smiled, reminding him.

Light laughter ensued, putting them both a bit at ease.

"What am I to do, Dustin?" Sophia earnestly asked.

"Go in there stern, but wait until you hear the entire story, especially from her lips," he advised her. "After that, you'll know what to do."

"Kimberly might get suspended over this," Sophia said, shaking her head.

"Worst case scenario a week," he shrugged, reassuring her. "Best case, Kimberly gets a couple of Saturday or after school detentions. She's a great kid, but they will all test you at some point."

"Your kid doesn't try to fly to Mars behind your back," she pouted.

"No, mine gets caught at a house party where the kid's parents are out of town. So, he decides to pull a Project X inviting half the school, where refreshments like spiked fruit punch, a keg of beer, and a half-pound of weed are served," Dustin growled sternly, knitting his brows. "I wish my kid tried to go to Mars."

Genesis

Sophia covered her mouth to muffle her laughter as Dustin shook his head in disgust.

"Go see your kid; we'll catch up next time you're in town." He said with a smile.

"Yes, we will, and thank you again."

After they embraced, Sophia stood there with a saddened heart, watching Dustin walk down the steps to the parking lot toward his vehicle. Alone again, she turned, entered the school, and went to the principal's office.

~~~~~~~~~~~~~~~~~~~~~~~~~~~~~~~~~

Sophia took a deep breath before she opened the door and entered the office. Mrs. Beans, the school secretary, recognizing her on sight, shot up from her desk, welcoming her before announcing and escorting her into the principal's office.

Her eyes first locked with Kimberly, who looked up to see the disapproving glare within her eyes. Kimberly quickly turned her head back down to her lap, attempting to make herself as small as possible. Sophia then turned to Mrs. Moe, who stood behind her desk to greet her with a cracked, nervous smile.

"Ms. Dennison, thank you so much for coming in."

"Thank you for notifying me, Mrs. Moe," Sophia said, extending her hand with a nervous smile.

Mrs. Moe timidly shook it and then gestured for her to have a seat. Sophia gave her daughter another stern glare as she sat down, forcing Kimberly to straighten up.

"Now, what seems to be the problem?" Sophia asked while clearing her throat.

"First, let me begin by stating that Kimberly is an excellent

Genesis

student," Mrs. Moe motioned. "Who has never shown or gotten into trouble until now."

Sophia's brows knitted as she read between the lines of Mrs. Moe's sentence.

"Were there other problems that I do not know about?"

"Not serious ones," Mrs. Moe raised a hand, squeaking. "Of late, Kimberly appears to be distracted or bored with class, even though she continues to participate and get stellar grades."

"Mrs. Moe," Sophia stopped her. "Before I became superhuman, I was human, and a very reasonable one. The only person in this room who is in trouble is my daughter."

Mrs. Moe nodded while calming herself.

"This afternoon in Mrs. Greene's history class, Kimberly and a male classmate got into a heated verbal debate. From her teacher and classmates' accounts, the young man said some unkind things about you. Kimberly got up from her seat and proceeded to threaten him. Again, from her teacher and fellow classmates' statement, her eyes began to glow extra bright as if she was going to …well."

"I understand what you are eluding to, Mrs. Moe."

"Unfortunately, it terrified the boy to the point he ended up relieving himself in front of the entire classroom," Mrs. Moe sighed. "Some of her classmates and her teacher were also a bit scared."

Sophia slowly turned her attention to Kimberly, who slightly leaned away from her mother due to feeling her look.

"Is this true?" she asked calmly, authoritatively.

"Yes, but …" Kimberly meekly began her defense.

"Then you are wrong," her mother elevated her voice. "You are

Genesis

wrong for so many reasons."

"But mom ..."

"I asked you a question," Sophia silenced her. "I did not ask for an explanation."

Kimberly lowered her head, shrinking in her seat, while her principal sat jittery in her chair, watching the exchange. Sophia turned to her, putting on a semi-pleasant smile.

"Please, continue."

"Unfortunately, due to the severity of this incident, I have no choice but to suspend Kimberly for at least two weeks," Mrs. Moe said with a swallow.

"Two weeks?" Sophia asked with a concerned knit brow. "Is that not harsh for a child who just made a verbal threat? She's a straight 'A' student on the principal's list who has never been in trouble before."

"Believe me, Ms. Dennison, I know, Kimberly is a model student," Mrs. Moe agreed. "But this is, unfortunately, a time where even verbal threats are taken very seriously, especially with her very ...unique abilities. I am personally considering that this was Kimberly's very first offense ever. Two weeks should be enough time for things to calm down, and to defuse this situation to prevent expulsion, which is what the young man's father is asking for."

Sophia took in some air and blew out the frustration in her chest. She reluctantly nodded in agreement. She turned to her daughter, who raised her head, feeling her mother's look on her.

"Do you have anything to say to your principal?"

She made sure to turn directly to her principal as she gave her a humble apology.

"I'm very sorry for what I did. Mrs. Moe ...it won't ever happen

Genesis

again. I promise."

"I know it won't," Mrs. Moe smiled, reassuring her. "I also know this isn't like you, nor does it reflect the nice young lady that you are. People make mistakes. The important thing is to learn from them and do better next time."

"I assure you, Mrs. Moe," Sophia said while glaring at her daughter, "She will do better next time."

Awkward silence twirled back into the office as Kimberly timidly lowered her head again, staring at the floor while Mrs. Moe stared at her desk as if she was in trouble.

"Will her teachers be in touch with any assignments or reading she must complete during her suspension?" Sophia asked, breaking the discomfort.

"Of course, we will make sure of that," Mrs. Moe nodded, informing her.

"Thank you, Mrs. Moe; I am very sorry that we are meeting again under these circumstances."

Sophia rose from her seat, which made Kimberly and her principal jump out of their chairs. She gave Mrs. Moe a handshake goodbye and walked toward the door, knowing Kimberly would follow behind her. She waited until they were back in the school's hallways before she gave her daughter one order.

"Walk in front of me."

~ ~

Sophia held her brimming temper at bay as they walked out of the middle school. She waited until they were down the steps and halfway out of the quad.

"You are grounded, I mean literally grounded," Sophia snarled.

Genesis

"If I see you even hovering, I'm swatting you out of the sky. Phones, tablets, and computers are gone when we get back. Television and video games are all gone; you have no idea how much trouble you are in, young lady. Do you have any idea what a suspension like this on your record will do in getting you into a decent high school or college?!"

"I don't know what the big deal is," Kimberly muttered.

"What did you just say?!"

Kimberly's pace increased, building the gap between them, which ignited Sophia's rage, causing her to detonate three feet from the middle school's main gate.

"Do not take another step, or even think of flying off Kimberly Dennison! Get over here!"

Sophia's booming voice halted a reluctant Kimberly, forcing her to slowly turn and face her parent with a pre-teen angst visage. Sophia folded her arms, waiting as her eyes blazed, reflecting her face's rage and disappointment. Her daughter stomped back over to her, keeping a safe distance between them.

"What did you just say?"

"Look at me, mom!" Kimberly's eyes blazed, revealing her own anger. "I highly doubt I'm getting a cushy office job after college!"

"I'm going to pretend like you lost your sanity for a split second and forgot who you were talking to," her mother growled, getting in her face. "Dial it back to zero."

"I'm going to be a superhero, mom," Kimberly answered back with a softer voice. "That's what I want to be when I grow up, maybe even a super soldier like dad was. Sergeant Rogers said I would make a great addition to the Regulator team, Heavy Element said I could even lead it someday."

"Did they now?"

Genesis

Sophia made a mental note to have a serious chat with the Regulators very soon.

"So, I really don't see the need for high school, college, or school period. I have the ability to retain and duplicate everything I read and hear; I don't feel challenged."

"So then tell me, what was so challenging about you maintaining your composure when you had your disagreement with that young man in your classroom? What type of 'hero' do you expect to be if a mere mortal can provoke you to anger? Answer me."

"Bradley Perkins is a lying jerk!" Kimberly howled at her mother. "He kept saying that you weren't a hero! That you were responsible for deaths the Judgment virus-caused and for freaks walking the Earth! That you were evil!"

"He is right!" Sophia fired back. "I am responsible for the Judgment virus! By my actions, I inadvertently caused thousands of people to die and created superhumans, some of who have done some unspeakable things, which included the Zombie Nation. So, you attacked a kid for being right."

"But his dad said you were worse than ISIS!" Kimberly shot back at her.

"I don't give a damn if his father said I'm having an affair with Donald Trump!"

Sophia paused and shuddered at her last statement, wishing to return it.

"Not only did you disrupt your class, traumatize that young man and possibly other students in your class," she furiously lectured her daughter. "You missed the whole point of the lesson! That young man had the right to express how he felt! No mattered if you disliked or disagreed with whatever he had to say, that is what freedom is about. That is what the symbols on the shoulders of my outfit that you chose for me stand for, the right to say what you feel without reprisal from your government or some

Genesis

higher power."

Kimberly turned her head away to pout, but her mother forcefully turned it back via her chin to maintain eye contact.

"You don't think I could have systematically wiped out the KKK and every Neo-Nazi hate group on the planet? I could have done it on any given weekend. But that is not freedom that is not democracy …that is a dictatorship, a monarchy, and that is the definition of what groups like ISIS and Al Qaeda are all about, subjugating people by violence to bend them to their will and belief structure. That is what I fight against every day."

"Then why do some people hate you?" Kimberly's eyes welled up with frustration.

"Some hate me because they are misinformed of my intentions," Sophia answered with a softer tone. "They believe I intend to take over the world and rule or something foolish like that, which were never my intentions and is far from my mind. I give voice to those who do not have a voice, and I fight for those who do not have the power to fight, and some people, especially certain ones in power, don't like that. Some of them prefer things the way they are because it profits them either politically or financially, and I'm interfering with the status quo when I should be just rescuing a cat from a tree or stopping a bank robbery. So, they spread lies and rumors about me, hoping that people will fear or hate me. But you want to know something?"

"What?"

"I don't care what anyone has to say about me," Sophia wiped the tears from Kimberly's eyes while caressing her cheek. "I don't care about the opinions of people who have their freedom, nor worry about someone kicking their door in and pointing a gun in their or of their family's faces or worse. Their opinion means nothing to me when drowned out by the cries of those begging to have the same rights and privileges those people running their mouths off already have. Not to mention, I know who I am, and you should know who I am by now, too, and as long as you do, you should not allow mere words to rattle you so quickly, especially about me.

Genesis

That is also why going to school in its many levels is essential; it allows you to interact with your peers who may not see eye to eye with you, civilly debate them, and sometimes agree to disagree peacefully."

Sophia sighed, expelling the last bit of anger.

"Your job is not to defend me. That is my job. Your job is to be a kid. The respectable young lady that I know you are. Okay?"

"Yes," Kimberly nodded, relenting.

"You're still grounded for a month," Sophia brought back the sternness.

"A month?!" Kimberly squeaked, stomping the concrete in frustration, cracking it.

"Destruction to public property just landed you two. You want to go for three?"

"No," she groaned.

"And during your suspension, you're going to write a letter of apology to your class and teacher," Sophia continued her sentencing. "And you are going to give this Bradley Perkins a personal apology. Now let's go, we're stopping by Michelle, so I can change, and then we're flying straight home."

Genesis

CHAPTER 8

September 2016, eleven hundred hours of military time, Bridgeport, California, almost a week after the Vitruvian Absolute New York rally,

At the Ranch, Rogers stood within central command in the middle of a video chat with Blitz, Nitro, and Cyclone.

A way off were behind them, local Chicago SWAT, federal agents in tactical gear and body armor, and paramedics walking back and forth in a fierce battle zone that came to an end.

"The bust was a success, Sarge," Blitz reported. "Although our Intel was way off, the Ivankov family had more superhuman muscle than reported. We met with some heavy resistance. We took down four moderately powered EVOs. Three are in custody; the fourth went down to deadly force. We also took some casualties; a couple of agents were injured, three in critical condition, two killed in action."

"What of the shipment?" Rogers asked.

"An estimated fifty million in guns and narcotics in the containers," Blitz answered. "Including a large supply of boosters, "Human Boost" and "Ascension," nothing on the level of the stuff we confiscated in Iraq."

"Dammit," Rogers muttered.

"We've participated in two different raids coming up with the same results, Sergeant," Blitz concluded. "No one has heard of or seen this type of booster."

"How the hell is it possible with what it can do?" Rogers shook his head, dumbfounded.

Genesis

"Sir, maybe this was something that wasn't supposed to be sold," Cyclone said, jumping into the conversation.

"You think what we discovered in Iraq was stolen from possibly an experimental facility?"

"It's the only logical explanation as to why there's no word about this stuff on the streets or even the dark web," Cyclone answered. "Something in my gut is telling me those boosters weren't supposed to be sold, not to ISIL terrorists anyway."

"If this is what is going on, we've got two new problems," Rogers huffed. "The trail to the origin of these boosters have gotten colder, and there's a good chance ISIL took a small part of the shipment somewhere else and is reverse engineering it to replicate the formula to make more."

"But Erica said a nuclear reactor or particle accelerator was needed to create the unknown properties." Nitro reminded them.

"Iran, Russia, and North Korea all have nuclear reactors and particle accelerators, and have been known to consort with terrorists," Rogers reminded them. "And Iran's current treaty does not cover the development of super soldiers."

All three looked at one another with faces of dread and concern.

In the middle of the conversation, Erica walked into the command center.

"Keep me updated if you find anything else," Rogers instructed. "Help oversee clean up and detention, then hall ass back here."

"Yes, sir," Blitz nodded, acknowledging.

As the video chat ended, Rogers turned to Erica, patiently waiting for him.

"Vitruvian Absolute, which stands for 'Absolute Man' or 'Mortal God,' was started by Aafreen Hannan and Xavier Lamonster, also known as

Genesis

Saraswati and Deacon Absolute, as a YouTube video podcast that went viral on their first show. Their initial funds were made through Patreon donations. Three months later, they added Brian Greene, Jiro Nakajima, and Valeria Lopez, also known as Maximus, Ryu, and Diana Absolute.

On their twentieth podcast, they officially announced themselves as the founding members of Vitruvian Absolute along with their mission statement …"

"Can you skip the dance and tell me how they're making their money?" Rogers impatiently requested.

Erica answered Rogers's impatience with an eye roll.

"Membership donations, speaker engagements, website subscriptions, and merchandise; a lot of their social media sites were shut down after the terrorist assault on Parliament in which their rhetoric was used. They run their weekly video podcast directly from their website. Their members, however, continue to grow in record numbers. As long as you subscribe to their ideology, you can become a member."

"So, they're clean," Rogers concluded.

"I didn't say that," Erica said, shaking her head. "Although it is well disguised, their operational capital does not add up to the monthly donations they receive."

"Meaning there's a larger outside party funding them," Rogers said, filling in the gaps.

"Yep," she nodded, answering. "Someone is handing them cash under the table and doing a good job at hiding it. Because this is technically out of our jurisdiction, I notified my contacts in the FBI and the CIA. They'll be mounting their own investigation to see if there is anything illegal like money laundering."

Rogers nodded in agreement.

"Anything else on Mr. Rutherford?"

Genesis

"Aside from the fact that he gave a full detail confession of how and why he planned his attack at the Vitruvian Absolute rally," Erica said with a straight face. "I think he was put up to it, against his will."

Her answer brought a grim look on Rogers's face as his gut told him the same thing.

"You are certain of this."

"Yep, Maxine, bring it up, please."

The large screen came alive, showing footage of the shooting at the Vitruvian Absolute rally. Erica zoomed in on Mitch Rutherford as he wielded the Steyr SPP, firing rounds into the front row of women and children.

Erica then brought up video footage of Mr. Rutherford wearing a Mullet and full beard in green tactical gear, brandishing an AR-15 at a local shooting range in his hometown.

"The FBI sent me this footage taken off his phone for comparison," Erica explained while profiling him. "What's the first thing you see?"

"In the footage at the rally, he's not comfortable with the weapon at all," Rogers answered with narrowed eyes. "He also looks frustrated."

"That's because he wants to shoot more people but can't."

Rogers kept quiet, waiting for her to clarify.

"Mind-altering control works best when you find a subject that wants to do what you want them to do. To do that, you must dive into their memories and subconscious to see who you are dealing with. Mr. Rutherford fits the textbook active shooter profile with borderline homicidal anarchist characteristics based on his mental state and beliefs, backed up by videos and posts on his Facebook and Twitter pages.

However, Mr. Rutherford is a moron with a ninth-grade education.

Genesis

Yet Mr. Rutherford, who has never traveled to New York City, not for a school field trip or a vacation, knew to drive to Jersey City the day before the event, where he checked into a motel with a fake ID and stolen credit card.

He then heads to Macy's at the Newport Mall in New Jersey and purchases the outfit he had on paying cash. He then gets a haircut and shave at a barbershop named Clip Joint and then gets a facial, manicure, and pedicure at V & C Image, also paying cash at the two locations.

Before his trip, he made one online purchase, a black Enforcer jacket from a company named ScotteVest, known for creating travel clothing with multiple hidden compartments. This was made with a stolen credit card.

On the event day, he catches a jitney bus on Kennedy Boulevard to Port Authority in Manhattan and then walks to Union Square to avoid police checks in the subway.

During the crowd's gathering, he is a virtual ghost and manages to stand next to the only EVO that can hide him from our scanners until he is ready to strike.

Mr. Rutherford, who is on the FBI Terrorist watchlist, due to his affiliation with the Carolina Knights of the Ku Klux Klan, accomplished all of this, telling no one of what he had planned, leaving no declaration of his intent, and with no research of any kind.

His history browser on his computer and other devices were clean."

"He even chose the perfect weapon for the job," Rogers added.

"All three weapons are registered in his name," Erica confirmed. "The Steyr SPP and ammo was purchased at the C&E Gun show at the Crown Expo Center on July 28th of this year."

"What about the Apollo he hid next to?" Rogers asked.

Genesis

"Paula Barton, age twenty-nine, is as clean as a whistle," Erica answered. "She's a fifth-grade schoolteacher, who uses her powers for recreational means like posting tricks on the Fad Five."

"Fad Five?"

"Facebook, YouTube, Twitter, Instagram, and Snap Chat."

"Google and Tumblr didn't make the cut?"

"Google is the new Myspace, and Tumblr is where you go when you want to read blogs and watch porn."

"Good to know. So, Rutherford gets there, starts to shoot, and wants to do more damage," Rogers began to conclude. "But whoever is controlling him wants him to stick to the plan. Cause a violent scene to prove a point, with as little damage as possible."

"Enough to heighten fear and anger in the crowd, but not push them over the edge where they want to burn the city down," Erica said, agreeing with him.

"They were going to burn the city down," Rogers muttered. "Whoever planned this was counting on someone else showing up to prevent that. Is there any way to link Vitruvian Absolute to Rutherford?"

"You think it's them?" Erica asked.

"You don't?"

"No, I do. Saraswati Absolute is a class seven Promethean. She's capable of mind control and altering. The problem is, even if she did it, it's not something that can be proven. Clearly, she tracked down the Carolina Knights and picked Rutherford as the perfect candidate for the job. I've been busy attempting to place her and the other members of Vitruvian Absolute in the vicinity of North Carolina in the past four months and came up with nothing. She didn't drive, take a bus or train, nor did she fly, or was driven down there."

Genesis

"Maybe she traveled by unconventional means," Rogers suggested.

"That was my next assumption," Erica agreed.

"For now, we don't have the jurisdiction to do an extensive investigation," Rogers grumbled. "We're not the police, nor are we the FBI. Whatever we do uncover has to be turned over to them to mount a proper investigation. Continue to search for the extra money and who's funding them, and whatever else we can find to bury these people."

"That will have to wait until I get back from the Cook County Medical Examiner Office in Chicago."

"For?"

"I got an email from the coroner there examining Flaming Jay's body after her suicide; he's requesting my professional expertise on EVO physiology to confirm something for him."

"Would you care to elaborate?" Rogers gestured as if he was pulling teeth.

"He eluded to a large burn mark on her neck, which is clearly odd to find on someone who is supposed to be physically impervious to high degrees of heat. I believe he wants me to confirm if her death was foul play or not."

"Fine, take Rosann with you."

"I don't need a babysitter, Rogers," Erica said with an eye roll.

"That wasn't a request," Rogers shot back. "I want her off the base doing something other than target practice and racking up record combat simulation time in the Hurt Locker."

"If you're attempting to change her mood, taking her to a coroner's office to see a dead hero is not the smartest idea."

"Miss, I just received a call from Chief Inspector Hector Martinez

Genesis

of the Mexican Federal Police. He is requesting that you come to Mexico to give your insight on the Castillo Cartel mass homicide case."

"Which homicide was this again?" Rogers asked with a furrowed brow.

"Maxine, pull it up, please," Erica requested.

They turned to the holographic globe in the center of the command center, which projected an exclusive CNN news feed.

"Miguel Ángel Castillo, the alleged former lieutenant under El Chapo, formed his own cartel when his alleged former boss was incarcerated. It was reported almost a week ago that the mansion he resided in was burnt to the ground. The number of casualties has not yet been determined. Local authorities are already blaming the attack on rival cartels."

"Well, you're not going to that," Rogers shook his head.

Erica turned to him with a perplexed scowl on her face.

"Excuse you?"

"You've already committed to going to Chicago," Rogers declared. "Esposito, Shareef, and I will go to Mexico; we'll take Maxine to run whatever analysis you need to run."

"But ..."

He moved closer, giving her a stern fatherly look.

"One dead body is enough."

Erica dropped the feisty retort she had planned. Although he verbally ordered her, Rogers's expression read that he asked her to do what he requested.

"Maxine, please update Rosann," she said with a whisper. "We

Genesis

leave in thirty minutes."

"Yes, Miss."

"Maxine, do the same for Esposito and Shareef," Rogers commanded.

"I already notified them, Sergeant Rogers. I am currently preparing both Tornadoes for departure."

~~~~~~~~~~~~~~~~~~~~~~~~~~~~~~~~

A half-hour later, the Tornado piloted by Maxine carrying the Sarge, Heavy Element, and Sister Sledge touched down at Campo Military Number One Air Force base in Mexico City. The rear hatch to the Tornado opened up, creating a rampway for the Sarge and Sister Sledge to walk down, where they were greeted by a First Sergeant in the Mexican Army and a military escort of two Humvees.

"Sergeant Rogers, my name is First Sergeant Francisco Rodriguez; welcome to Mexico."

"Sergeant Abraham Rogers of the Regulator unit, thank you for having us."

Rogers shook the First Sergeant's hand and smirked as he felt a firm grip as Rodriguez smiled back at him.

"Just you, or everyone here?" Rogers asked, looking at his unit.

"Myself and three others in this unit," First Sergeant Francisco Rodriguez answered. "There was talk about creating a separate unit like other countries, but we decided it was best for moral to integrate superhuman soldiers with regular soldiers to show that there isn't any division. Also, it keeps the cartels from distinguishing which one of us is a superhuman, especially when we wear our headgear."

"This is a member of my unit, Sister Sledge," Rogers introduced her.

Genesis

"Pleasure to meet you, Sister Sledge," First Sergeant Rodriguez greeted with a grin, shaking her hand. "I take it whatever you hit; you break."

"Pretty much," she answered with a smile.

"Our other two members Maxine and Heavy Element, are rolling out our ride," Rogers gestured.

Everyone turned to the sound of a rumbling engine as a grey gunmetal black off-road vehicle that appeared to be the child of a Jeep Wrangler and a Humvee with the Regulator symbol on the hood rolled down the rampway with Heavy Element behind the wheel and Maxine in the rear passenger seat. The First Sergeant and his unit all nodded with impressed approval.

"Let's get you and your team to the crime scene, Sergeant."

~ ~

Twenty-five minutes later, the Regulators, with a military escort, arrived at the late Miguel Ángel Castillo's residence.

"Yeah, that's burnt to the ground," Heavy Element commented.

Rogers silently nodded in agreement at seeing what was left of the mini-mansion. It was scorched to the foundation, with barely anything left but a few walls still standing. Although the smoke was gone, the smell of burnt rubble and human flesh lingered.

The onsite Chief Inspector greeted them as they came to a halt and exited the vehicle.

"Sergeant Rogers, thank you for coming here with your team to assist us," Chief Inspector Hector Martinez said while shaking his hand.

"We're glad to help." Rogers nodded before beginning introductions. "This is Sister Sledge and Heavy Element, Maxine; our resident android will be doing the analysis on your investigation on behalf

Genesis

of Dr. Champion, who could not be here due to another assignment."

"I am proficient in all forms of forensic methodologies," Maxine announced. "I look forward to assisting you with your investigation."

Chief Inspector Martinez and First Sergeant Rodriguez, who finally got a good look at Maxine, both wore masks of amazement. The Chief Inspector looked Maxine up and down, searching for the appropriate words.

"Um, thank you ...Maxine."

"So, what are we looking at, Chief Inspector?" Rogers asked, getting down to business.

"At face value, a textbook Cartel massacre," Chief Inspector Martinez began the rundown. "The problem is, we can't find one body."

All three human members of the Regulators glanced at one another with concerned perplexity.

"When you say you can't find one body ...?" Sister Sledge asked, requesting more clarification.

"I mean, we haven't found one bone fragment, tooth, or even a fingernail, much less a severed finger," Chief Inspector Martinez said, giving a broader explanation. "Feuding cartel assassinations are usually done with brutal, violent methods to send a warning to both the locals and other cartels. So dead, sometimes mutilated bodies are purposely left to instill fear."

"You're not suggesting someone kidnapped an entire cartel and burnt the mansion down as a cover?" Heavy Element threw out.

"As crazy as that sounds, that did enter my mind," Chief Inspector Martinez nodded while addressing him. "Mainly because we also did not find one shell from a firearm that was discharged, whoever did this wiped them all out without a single shot being fired. It's also not uncommon for Cartels to kidnap rivals and do recorded scenes of torture and executions.

Genesis

And with the world the way it is now, high jacking an entire Cartel is not that insane."

"But you don't believe that's what happened," Rogers said, reading his tone.

"No, I don't; inside the crime scene is a ton of ash. Our forensics team is ninety-nine percent sure the majority of it is human. So now my gut is telling me this was done by a superhuman, which is disturbing because Castillo, from what we knew, recruited a massive number of superhuman muscle on his roster already, and it was steadily growing."

"So, you're suspecting they got slaughtered by a couple of heavy hitters," Rogers deduced.

Chief Inspector Martinez answered with another nod.

"The reason we contacted Dr. Champion was to both confirm and then tell us what type of superhuman could do something like this and why."

"Well, let's find out who the hell we're dealing with," Rogers said while turning to the female android. "Maxine, care to take the lead?"

Without a word, Erica's firstborn's eyes lit up as she walked toward the destroyed mansion with the team, the Chief Inspector, and the First Sergeant following her. As she entered, Maxine ignored the forensics team already present as they looked at her with the same expression the Chief Inspector and the First Sergeant had when they first saw her. Her head slightly moved while her eyes swirled around in her eye sockets as she scanned the entire area, digitally recreating the structure.

Maxine then approached one of the small mounds of burnt structure and ash. She knelt down, extending her right pointer finger, which cracked open at the tip, and vacuumed some debris. Her eyes began to glow brighter.

"Analyzing content, the Chief Inspector is correct; ninety–eight-point-eight percent of this debris is human ash, the remainder is structural.

Genesis

Based on my restructuring of the crime scene, I estimate a casualty rate of thirty to forty people. The EVO responsible for this is capable of generating heat above eighteen thousand degrees Fahrenheit."

"All killed within the house?" First Sergeant Rodriguez asked.

"Negative," Maxine answered. "The scans I took while approaching the mansion reveal fresh footprints and body impressions in the lawn. Deeper imprints within the lawn moving in the building's direction reveal the victims killed outside were carried into the mansion before it was destroyed. The two assailants moving the bodies were male and female, wearing Salomon Forces Toundra Pro CSWP boots. Size eleven for the male, and size eight for the female. It is my analysis that the two assailants were of the Titan or Mercurian class."

"Titan and Mercurian class?" First Sergeant Rodriguez inquired with a confused look.

"Titans are the classification of superhumans with great superhuman strength, durability, and the ability to regenerate from injury, like yourself First Sergeant," Sister Sledge clarified. "Mercurian are superhumans capable of immense speed and reflexes, but they also possess a level of superhuman strength and regenerative healing."

The First Sergeant nodded with an expression as if he liked his classification.

"So, three superhumans came and took out almost forty people?" Chief Inspector Martinez asked in disbelief.

"Negative; based on my analysis majority of the victims had firearms," Maxine answered him. "Your forensics team was accurate in their confirmation that no firearms were discharged. I suspect a powerful Promethean was the fourth assailant."

"Promethean?" Chief Inspector Martinez asked.

"Our classification for a superhuman with vast intelligence and mental abilities ranging from mind reading and control, telepathy, psychokinesis, extrasensory perception, and telekinesis, to name a few." Heavy Element answered.

The Chief Inspector glanced at an equally stunned First Sergeant, who mirrored his expression.

"You people have some fascinating names for us," First Sergeant Rodriguez scoffed.

"Why would someone go to great lengths to burn all of the bodies down to ash?" Chief Inspector Martinez asked while looking around.

"Someone looking to hide something," Sister Sledge inferred.

"Chief Inspector, you said that Castillo was heavily recruiting superhumans for his cartel?" Heavy Element asked.

"Yes, at a very alarming rate," Chief Inspector Martinez answered. "He was under investigation for the murders of two cartel families in a week. He was becoming virtually untouchable. We were concerned at the rate his forces were growing that he might lead a revolt and take over Mexico itself."

"Guess karma is a bitch," Heavy Element grunted. "Were there any foreigners in his crew?"

"Aside from his accountant," Chief Inspector Martinez said, "No, all of them were Mexican. He didn't trust Gringos, nor did he believe they deserved to share in his profit margin. No offense."

"None taken," Rogers nodded. "Maxine, what is the current EVO demographic in Mexico?"

"EVOs?" First Sergeant Rodriguez asked.

"The current official US government term for superhumans," Heavy Element answered.

"An estimated .01 percent of one hundred twenty-seven point five

Genesis

million people in Mexico are infected EVOs," Maxine answered. "Ninety-eight percent of that .01 percent are female, while the remainder is male. One percent of the population are newborn EVOs, which is steadily growing."

"Is it safe to say that number is divided between law enforcement, military, and other cartels?" Rogers asked.

"It is," Maxine confirmed.

"I think we're running a lot of numbers and missing the bigger picture," Sister Sledge stepped in to take control of the conversation. "Chief Inspector, do you know if any of Castillo's people were all here, or are some still on the streets?"

Both Rogers and Heavy Element looked at Sister Sledge and then each other, understanding what she meant.

"At this point, no, it's a possibility some have gone into hiding, especially after this; why?"

"If they're out there, then we have someone to interrogate," she answered. "If they're not, that means they're all here around us, which means the assassins completed their mission."

Chief Inspector Martinez looked at each of them suspiciously before glancing at First Sergeant Rodriguez to confirm his misgiving.

"You people know something that you're not telling us."

"Yeah, we do," Rogers nodded, answering. "Unfortunately, we can't divulge that information to you, and it's best you don't know."

"Why wouldn't I want to know if it will help my investigation?" the Chief Inspector asked with a stern tone and lump in his throat.

"If these individuals do have a Promethean among them, they might be listening to this conversation as we speak," Rogers answered. "Even if we take you to our ship, which can block against such abilities,

Genesis

you will still know what we tell you, which will put your life at risk. All we can say is, we think your case is linked to our own investigation, which means we've got a huge problem on our hands."

"Sergeant Rogers, Director Alfred Mansfield of MI6 wishes to speak with you on an urgent matter," Maxine announced.

"Patch him in."

Rogers stepped away from the group to take the call.

"Director Mansfield, how can I help you? Yes, this is a secure line."

The Sarge's back became slightly stiff as he listened to Director Mansfield on the other end.

"My team and I will be there in forty minutes," Rogers whispered.

As he turned to face the group, Sister Sledge, and Heavy Element could already tell by his expression that he received an ear full of bad news.

"First Sergeant and Chief Inspector, we, unfortunately, have to cut this short due to an urgent matter in London."

Genesis

CHAPTER 9

Three hours earlier Central Daylight Time, the second Tornado piloted by Erica landed at O'Hare International Airport.

Unlike the team in Mexico, Erica and Rosann rolled out of the airport in a sleek midnight blue ion engine-powered four-seater sports car that appeared like a fighter jet on wheels. The two had not spoken to each other during the flight, and the silence continued during the estimated fifty-one-minute drive to the coroner's office as the artificially intelligent vehicle took them to their destination.

In an "MC Lyte as Rock" white t-shirt, leather jacket, jeans, and black and blue Converse sneakers, Erica swiped through her mail and social media feed displayed in front of her via holographic images. Occasionally, she glanced at a silent Rosann dressed in dark blue military fatigues with her rank of Private First Class and the Regulator symbol on the jacket's shoulders. Her long raven mane was pulled back into a ponytail while her matching cap covered the top part of her face.

"So, how's that brooding anti-hero shtick working for you?" Erica sarcastically asked with a nonchalant tone.

"I'll tell you when you tell me how that 'teenage angst, the whole world sucks' is working for you," Rosann answered back, matching her tone.

"Are you really throwing shade my way Rosann?" Erica asked while lazily leering at her, "Because I don't remember us having any issues."

"We don't."

"So, then what the hell is your problem?"

Genesis

"My problem is people thinking that I have a problem when I know I have none, and if I were a dude, no one would be asking what my problem is."

"Chica, if you were a dude, I'd be asking what your problem is more colorfully."

Rosann turned to her with a feral glare in her eyes, which Erica deflected with a Teflon demeanor. Rosann ended the stalemate by looking out the window again.

"I don't want to argue with you, Erica."

"I'm not trying to start a fight with you either," Erica returned, swiping her screens away while swiveling her seat toward her.

"Then do me a favor and save the million and one questions for our next mandatory scheduled session," Rosann requested. "The job is not getting to me; I knew what I signed up for just like everyone else who enters the service."

"Everyone else does not transform into were-versions of animals," Erica reminded her.

"The transformations are not affecting my state of mind, Erica; it's still me, I'm still in control, and at times more focused than I've ever been."

Erica's face read that Rosann's statement worried her. She was about to say what she thought verbally but held her tongue as the vehicle pulled into the coroner's office's parking lot.

"Let's get this over with," Rosann flatly said, waiting for the doors to open so she could exit.

They entered the building with Erica leading and Rosann following closely behind like a sentinel. Waiting for them at the security check-in was the Chief Medical Examiner of the facility. A husky, slightly heavyset, light-skinned man in his early forties with a bald dome sporting square bifocals and green medical scrubs underneath his white lab coat.

Genesis

"Dr. Champion, thank you for coming at such short notice," the man gratefully greeted her with a slight nervousness in his tone.

"Thank you for calling me in, Dr. Barnes," Erica said, smiling while shaking his hand. "This is a member of my team Private First Class Rosann Esposito."

"Doctor."

Rosann professionally extended her hand, which the doctor shook.

"Pleasure to meet you, Private First-Class Esposito. Well, let me take you both to the examination room so you can see why I called you here."

They followed him down a long, bland hallway through a set of double doors, making two left turns followed by a right turn. They entered the examining room with harsh medical lights that exposed everything. Dr. Barnes walked over to the body of Flaming Jay, lying as if sleeping on the examination table with just a thin white sheet covering her body up to her chest.

Erica glanced at Rosann, whose demeanor did not change at the sight of Flaming Jay's body. She stood at the foot of the table in a relaxed state of attention while Erica reached Flaming Jay's head to examine the body.

"Yep, that is definitely a burn mark, not self-inflicted."

"Which based on her physiology would not be possible because of her immunity to heat." Dr. Barnes interjected for confirmation.

"Correct Dr. Barnes, Ms. Samson can generate and survive heat up to eight hundred eighty thousand degrees Fahrenheit."

Erica pulled a pair of glasses from her jacket and put them on. She touched the frame's right side, causing the lens to light up as she scanned the burn mark on the body's neck.

Genesis

"Well, that's a handprint, alright," she sighed. "The size of the handprint indicates a male assailant. However, the heat generated has burnt away any possible chance of taking a DNA sample. This is definitely not a suicide. I'd like to see the inside of her."

"As you can see," Dr. Barnes gestured. "We have not opened her up yet."

"Won't need to," Erica replied, pulling a small metal rod from her large smartwatch.

The rod became malleable and began to move like a living Earthworm.

"What in the world is that?" Dr. Barnes asked with raised eyebrows of amazed curiosity.

"It's a mini-medical drone of my creation," she explained. "It will enter through her nasal cavity and work its way through her body while transmitting a visual map that we can view."

She laid the medical drone on Ms. Samson's chest.

The drone went to work quickly, scurrying up to her face before slithering into her right nostril.

Erica used her telekinesis to turn off the lights in the room and pressed a button on her watch, projecting a holographic image of Flaming Jay's body from the inside.

"Well, this is not good," Erica swallowed.

"She appears to be completely burnt from the inside," a mystified Dr. Barnes observed.

"It's a lot worse than that, Dr. Barnes," Erica double-checked the data, clarifying. "By these readings …every single cell in her body …is dead."

Genesis

"That's not possible," Dr. Barnes shook his head in disbelief.

"Why is that not possible?" inquired Rosann.

"When a body dies, many cells continue to function after death," Erica explained. "White blood cells can last up to three days; stem cells can remain alive with a corpse for at least seventeen. Ms. Samson here has only been dead for two days, and I'm not picking up any activity, not even on an atomic level."

A baffled Dr. Barnes kneaded his forehead as he attempted to comprehend what he was seeing before him.

"What kind of superhuman can do such a thing?"

"I have no idea, Dr. Barnes."

"Erica, are you there?" Rogers came over her commlink.

"I'm here."

"You and Esposito need to wrap up what you're doing and meet us in the UK," He ordered.

"Why, what's going on?" She asked.

"Are you two alone?"

"No."

"Secure the room." He instructed.

Erica turned to the doctor, wearing a pleasant smile.

"Doctor Barnes."

"Say no more; I'll be outside," The doctor replied, complying.

Genesis

As Dr. Barnes exited the room, Rosann locked the door behind him.

"Jammer field has been activated within the room," informed Maxine.

"I was just contacted by Director Mansfield of MI6, Knight Light from the Lions of Elizabeth has been murdered," Roger bluntly informed them.

"Say what?!" she asked with a raised voice of concern, "How?!"

"I wasn't given the details," continued Rogers. "What I do know is that the government is keeping a tight lid on this and that they are requesting our assistance, mainly yours. We're en route as we speak."

"We'll be there in an hour," she swallowed.

"Roger that."

As the transmission ended, Erica looked up at Merge.

"Rosann, why did you touch the body?"

Merge's eyes widen at her direct accusation.

"What the hell are you talking about? I didn't ..."

"Don't lie to me; I saw you touch her foot during the examination."

A chill of disquiet filled the room as the two stared each other down.

"We have to go," Erica announced, breaking the tension while turning away from her. "Rogers is expecting us to meet him in London."

~~~~~~~~~~~~~~~~~~~~~~~~~~~~~~~~

Genesis

Twenty minutes later, the strain as thick as molasses came back during the drive back to the airport and stayed in the cockpit of the second Tornado, along with the painfully awkward silence as Erica flew the two to the United Kingdom.

"So, are we going to talk about this?" Rosann softly asked while not making eye contact.

"What's there to talk about?" Erica sarcastically snorted. "You just decided to jack a dead girl's powers during her autopsy."

"You know I didn't steal anything," Rosann glared at her. "I just can duplicate her powers."

"You stole her DNA, Rosann, that's f'd up."

"It's adding another weapon to my arsenal! She's not going to need them anymore!"

Erica turned to Rosann as if she had reached over and slapped her.

"Autopilot."

Upon command, the ship's A.I. took over piloting the Tornado as she turned to confront her teammate.

"Seriously, chica, what the hell is up with you?" Erica asked with a voice laced with concern. "Some lines just should not be crossed, and you are hurdling over them."

"She deserted her team," Rosann turned, answering her with a dull ice-cold glare. "She left them to die. You were right there with me as we watched it happen. She didn't even try to save them."

"She would have ended up like the rest of her team," Erica answered back in the dead's defense, "None of them was a match for Peace."

"Neither were we," Rosann scoffed, "But we still never left a man

Genesis

behind …at least I didn't."

Erica fell back in her seat from Rosann's verbal gut check. A sarcastic smirk slowly formed on her face as she shook her head.

"Now we get to the truth of the matter. I asked you time and time again during our sessions if you carried some ill will against people you've been fighting beside regarding what happened to Oliver, and you've been lying to my face."

"I'm not carrying ill will toward anyone, Erica," Rosann nonchalantly responded while falling back in her chair. "I get it; hard decisions were made; people did what they thought they had to do. I just plan to make it my business to do what I must to ensure it doesn't happen again."

Rosann extended her right hand, concentrating as her skin, eyes, and hair changed to match the deceased Flaming Jay. Her hand slowly began to glow as sparks of flames burst from her pores and swirled around her hand.

"Flaming Jay was a Class Nine Apollo; with practice, I can become at least a seven or eight."

She broke her concentration, causing the flames to disperse as her features returned to normal. Rosann locked eyes with Erica again.

"Should I expect you to rat me out, recommend that I get benched for a psyche evaluation? The courtesy of a heads up would be nice."

Erica made a long obnoxious sucking sound with her teeth before spinning her chair back around and assuming control of the Tornado again. She mentally activated her music playlist as the two flew to the UK in silence for the trip's remainder.

~~~~~~~~~~~~~~~~~~~~~~~~~~~~~~~~

United Kingdom, MI6 Headquarters,

Genesis

Erica landed the second Tornado at the Royal Air Force base in Lakenheath, Brandon, where the first Tornado was parked. It was a two-hour drive to the MI6 office in Embankment, London. Fortunately, the sports vehicle Erica built came equipped with a short-range vertical take-off and flight package, cutting their travel time to twenty minutes.

They entered the facility escorted by two MI6 agents, where they met the rest of the team along with Director Mansfield, who was accompanied by Jack the Giant and Lady of the Lake, the Titan, and water-wielding Apollo of the UK's Lions of Elizabeth super-soldier team.

After the initial professional introductions, the Director got straight to the point.

"Thank you all for coming here at such short notice, as I debriefed Sergeant Rogers and the other part of your team, seven days ago Major Henry Butcher's body was found at eleven A.M. in the morning within his flat after he failed to report in, or answer any of his communication devices. An autopsy report revealed that his neck was broken, his trachea crushed, while his organs, muscle tissue, and bones had severe burn marks. The assailant, who appears to be male, left a burn mark print of his hand around the front and side of the Major's throat. We were, unfortunately, unable to recover any DNA for identification. However, our team identified grains of sand on the Major's fingertips, which trace back to Egypt."

Erica and Rosann glanced at each other as they wore mirror visages of dread in the middle of the Director's run-down.

"What is it?" Rogers asked.

"I'll have to examine the body but based on the Director's report, we might have a serial killer or an assassin on our hands," Erica said while biting her bottom lip, "Whoever killed Knight Light used the same method on Flaming Jay."

"Are you certain?" asked Director Mansfield.

"About one hundred percent certain, may we see the body?"

Genesis

"We'll take you to it now," Director Mansfield nodded.

~ ~

The Regulators followed Director Mansfield and the two members of the Lions of Elizabeth, taking an elevator three levels down to a highly secured section of MI6. There, they entered a guarded room used for medical forensics and autopsies. The covered body of Sir Knight Light lay on one of the autopsy tables.

Eric sadly pulled back the sheet to examine Sir Knight Light, only to jump backward, startled at the sight of the body. The rest of the Regulators had similar expressions as they turned to the Director and his team.

"Director Mansfield, what is going on?" Erica nervously swallowed. "You said the Major was killed seven days ago; based on the rate of decomposition, this looks like a body that's been deceased for several months."

"I said that the Major's body was found in his apartment," Director Mansfield answered, stepping forward. "I did not divulge to you the exact time of his death because it was something that you had to see for yourself, and we were standing in an unsecured location."

"This doesn't make a lick of sense," Heavy Element spoke up. "We saw the Major alive on television two weeks ago. He was reportedly attending a youth charity event with the rest of his team."

"You are correct, Private First Class," The Director answered, turning to him. "This does not make, as you phrase it 'a lick of sense,' because I spoke with the Major face to face in my office the day of that event. Our own autopsy has confirmed that this is one hundred percent Major Butcher's body, which means there was an individual in our midst who killed a highly decorated Special Forces trained super-soldier, and then physically mimicked him down to his fingerprints, speech pattern, mannerisms, and even retina scan. They were able to recall things from his past in intricate detail that only he and those close to him would know, which means whoever this person is both compromised and violated this

Genesis

organization and possibly others within our government."

"I take it the day you found the body, this individual also disappeared without a trace," Rogers deduced.

"You are also correct with your assessment, Sergeant." Director Mansfield confirmed, turning to him. "Our investigation of the crime scene revealed no additional fingerprints or DNA aside from Major Butcher's, close friends and associates who visited which we already ruled out."

"Do you know if people visited his apartment during the months this person was impersonating him?" Erica asked.

"Many times," Lady of the Lake spoke up. "The team celebrated New Year's Eve there last year, and we threw the Lieutenant's surprise party there last month."

A silent Jack the Giant lowered his head, looking at the ground upon that revelation. Erica turned back to the body, giving it a look over.

"That means the body was stored in a different location. Whoever this is either completed their mission or was compromised, it's the only logical explanation for the return of the Major's body."

Erica moved closer, examining the damage around the neck.

"Aside from the crushed trachea and broken neck, this is the same MO done to Ms. Samson."

Erica took out her glasses, putting them on, and activated them, scanning his neck."

"An exact match to the handprint on Flaming Jay, our assailant is definitely male."

"Are you sure the assailant was a male?" Director Mansfield sternly stressed his question.

Genesis

Erica turned to him with a "What you are getting at?" expression.

"Uh …yeah, my scans are flawless."

"I was under the impression that only one superhuman currently on this planet had the ability and strength to get close enough to the Major to inflict this kind of wound."

"I can assure you, Director Mansfield," Erica said with a defensive tone, looking him dead in the eye. "Who you are thinking about has nothing to do with this; she also doesn't have man hands."

"Seeing as how you are all chummy with her, would you really tell us if it was her?" a hostile Jack the Giant asked, stepping forward.

"Alright, people," Rogers brought forth a tone of authority. "We're all on the same side; let's not do something cliché here. Erica, is there anything else you can tell us?"

Erica maintained her professionalism as she pulled out her medical drone for the second time. She activated it once again, causing it to become malleable. She placed it on his chest, making it a beeline for his nostril.

"Whoa! Whoa!" Jack, the Giant, scowled, yelling. "What the bloody hell is that?!"

"Calm down," Erica said, holding a hand up toward him. "It's a medical drone."

As it entered his nose, making its way into his body, she used telekinesis, cutting the lights to the room and tapping on her watch, projecting an interior holographic map of Knight Light's body through her watch.

"Although he's been dead longer, the damage done on a cellular level is the same as Flaming Jay; every single cell in his body was burnt out before he died," she said while slowly moving her head to scan his body. "The burn mark handprint shows no foreign DNA; may I see the sand you collected from his hands?"

Genesis

"It's over here," the Director gestured.

"Maxine."

Upon Erica's request, Maxine walked over to the table where the additional evidence was laid. She picked up the specimen container and opened it up.

Maxine cracked open her finger, vacuuming up some of the sand like she did the ash in Mexico. Her eyes glowed brighter as she analyzed the evidence.

"The exact location this sand derives from is Luxor, Egypt."

"Luxor?" Director Mansfield asked while stepping closer.

"Yes, within the vicinity of the Valley of the Kings."

"Could it be that Egyptian that fought in DC?" Jack, the Giant, asked with an interrogative tone.

"He's not Egyptian; he's Annunaki," Erica clarified calmly, stepping in and turning to him. "And his power set is different."

"You seem to have an excuse for all of your friends," he snapped at her.

"Look, I understand you're angry and for a good reason," She said, standing her ground with him. "But pointing fingers at the wrong people is not going to solve anything."

"Then use dat wonder brain of yours along wit your female Gobot over there and point us in the right fuckin direction," Jack the Giant erupted. "We brought you here to tell us who da fuck put our leader on a slab and been impersonating him all these months! Not tickle our assholes and tell us who didn't!"

"Lieutenant!" Director Mansfield stepped in, admonishing him.

Genesis

An enraged and emotional Jack, the Giant stormed out, leaving an awkward silence to blanket the room.

"Apologies for the Lieutenant's reaction," Lady of the Lake somberly spoke on her teammate's behalf. "The Major and he were really close."

Erica nodded as she read what she meant by her facial expression.

"Is there anything else you can tell us about this Egyptian male?" Director Mansfield inquired, focusing back on the investigation.

"Whoever he is, he's not a pure EVO; by the handprint alone, he's too old to be one," Erica concluded. "The fact that he drained both Sir Knight Light and Flaming Jay, who are clearly two different energy types, means we're dealing with a possible mutation, someone who developed a one and a million-power set from others that we have successfully recorded."

"Why not a booster?" Lady of the Lake asked.

Erica quickly glanced at the Sarge while answering.

"No boosting agent on the planet will get a regular human to that power level. Whoever this was physically overpowered a class nine Apollo EVO with the ability to channel and unleash massive amounts of photon energy backed with years of Special Forces training without a struggle. This individual has monstrous capabilities, especially if we're adding shapeshifting and mimicry to his arsenal."

"If this person can shapeshift, how do we know it's not a woman posing as a man?" Sister Sledge asked.

"That's an excellent point," Erica admitted, "We don't know, which further complicates this case. What we do know is that this person is extremely deadly and highly intelligent to pull this off. I take it you're reviewing all areas this person had access to as the Major."

"We are; we have been reviewing months of footage and security

Genesis

access, leaving no stone unturned," Director Mansfield nodded. "So far, we have not confirmed anything that has been either stolen or copied."

"As I said earlier, this person was either compromised or completed their mission," Erica concluded. "We need to pull our resources together and work to hunt them down as quickly as possible."

The Director looked at an unnerved Lady of the Lake before agreeing.

"Thank you for assisting us in our investigation, but for now, this will remain an MI6 matter. Although I disapprove of the Lieutenant's outburst, I am extending you the professional courtesy in knowing that we will be placing this Eye of Ra at the top of our list of suspects."

"Director Mansfield, I just told you there is no way he could have done this," Erica stepped forward, slightly elevating her voice.

"No, Doctor Champion, you said he had a different power set from the assassin," the Director said, stepping forward sternly. "Do you have evidence that you have full knowledge of all of his abilities?"

"No, I do not, however …"

"However, he is the third being recorded on this planet to display abilities that clearly surpass any other superhuman on this planet rivaling both the First and Second Source. By your own admission, there are very few who could have overpowered the Major so easily. So, unless you can provide evidence leading to someone else, we need to question this individual."

"The Eye of Ra, to my knowledge, went off-planet three months after the battle with Peace and the Zombie nation and has not returned since," Erica answered with steel to her tone. "So, there is no way he could have murdered the Major within the timeline he was killed."

"Apologies, Dr. Champion, but due to your closeness to this Eye of Ra, I cannot trust that you are providing objective proof of his innocence?"

Genesis

"Forgive me, Director, but what the hell are you implying?" Erica scowled, inquiring.

"I am implying that despite your genius-level intelligence and technological advances, you were unable to detect the Second Source while she was on this very planet carrying out her plans to take over the world. Can you honestly say you know the whereabouts of an alien with superior technology to your own?"

Sister Sledge ran her hands through her white dreads while the Sarge lowered his head. Erica's jaw shifted from left to right while her eyes narrowed at the Director, unable to refute his argument.

"The Major and his team have become a beacon of light for the country, especially during these rocky times." Director Mansfield pressed. "His death will come with an astronomical blow once it is officially announced, and people will want answers. Answers that we currently do not have. Our stake is much greater than yours in identifying the individual responsible for his murder. Do we have an understanding, Sergeant Rogers?"

"Yes, we do," Rogers acknowledged, nodding, looking at him and then Erica.

"Superhumans and aliens," Director Mansfield exhaled sadly, shaking his head. "I never thought I'd see the day."

~ ~

The Regulators left MI6, not saying a word to one another. They all departed in the identical respective vehicles they came in, heading to the same destination. They waited until they were a mile away from MI6 to speak on a secure video channel between the two cars.

"Rogers ...," Erica began the conversation.

"I know what you're going to say," he stopped her. "I don't believe he did this either. Are you certain this isn't Peace?"

Genesis

"Even if she somehow found a way out of that black hole, there's no way she could get anywhere near Earth without our early warning system detecting her." Erica pressed. "My system is designed to detect her energy signature without fail."

"Can you use this system to find this guy or gal?" Heavy Element asked.

"I've been trying to find this person since they drained the power plant in India," Erica answered, shaking her head. "All I've been detecting is Dennison, and her daughter, whoever this individual is, should have a massive energy output similar to theirs."

"You actually think it's the same person?" Rosann asked, turning to her.

"Oh yeah, I am a thousand percent certain," Erica nodded, answering. "Based on the deterioration of Sir Knight Light's body, his time of death lines up with the draining of the power plant; I just can't put Flaming Jay in the picture and the motive to kill her."

"Based on your autopsy and the reports, she was dead before she hit the ground, right?" Merge asked. "What if she saw this person dressed as Sir Knight Light flying in her vicinity and went to investigate? What if she saw this person's face?"

The rest of her team's facial expressions read that she was onto something.

"I know we didn't share this with the Director for obvious reasons," Sister Sledge said. "But isn't it possible this is a boosted using the serum we found? Not only is it fast-acting, but we're also unable to determine the maximum output this thing can produce once it turns a human into a full-blown EVO."

"Sister Sledge has a good point, Sarge," Erica agreed. "These cases could be linked, considering this also originated out of the Middle East."

"Maxine, is Blitz, Nitro, and Cyclone back at the Ranch?" Rogers asked

"Yes, they are, Sergeant Rogers."

"Tell them to keep their asses there. Lockdown the base and put security on high alert until we get there. If these cases are related, we might be next."

Genesis

CHAPTER 10

Several light-years from her homeworld, the banished and presumed dead stood in the middle of a bedroom on a planet of a race older than her own with her wrists bound with metallic alien restraints. Much to her frustration, she could not escape the deceptively thin, frail-looking shackles. Every now and then, she'd slightly turn her head to check out the two-armed male and female guards at the door's entrance, calmly watching her every move.

~ ~

Her mind wandered back to her imprisonment as she hung naked in the ship's cell that fished her out of a crushing black hole. Time stood still as she patiently waited to strategize her escape once they came for her. The second her alien shackles were removed, she planned to leave a trail of bodies and destruction during her flight to freedom.

She remembered bracing herself as her ears picked up the footsteps coming. Her muscles began to pulsate as the orange crystalline cell door broke apart and slid away into the cell walls. She narrowed her eyes, focusing as two female guards entered the room. She sized them up, noting their toned muscular build over their dark snake-patterned skin. She'd have to focus on head and torso shots as they wore light gold and silver armor over their crimson sheer thigh-high toga outfits.

The taller of the two, with blue-black skin and orange-colored braided hair, clutched her sword's hilt as she squeezed a metallic green circular pendant around her neck with alien etchings. It caused her cocoon restraints to light up and then crack open, releasing each of her appendages.

She barely got her feet underneath her as she employed her flight ability to stop her descent; she then charged the two female guards to remove their heads from their bodies.

All they did was calmly slide away from each other, making a path for a third who rushed into the cell with blurring speed, slamming Peace

Genesis

with a vicious shoulder charge, knocking her back into the wall she hung from. Her body made a slight dent in the wall as she bounced off it and smacked face-first into the floor.

Clutching the center of her chest, which took the brunt of the hit, she scrambled to see the third female in the room, much smaller than the two guards with pitch-black skin wearing a blood-red Mohawk styled into six braids. She wore a near-sheer pink toga with golden accents. She wore bracers and greaves with ancient alien etchings that emitted a dim red glow on her arms and legs. A harsh red light glowed from her eyes as she wore a face that could slaughter a million legions by itself.

"So …you're the head boss bitch," Peace deduced with a sneer on her face.

Without another word, she unleashed her second plan of attack, firing off a pair of planet-shattering eyebeam blasts at her.

It was brought to a screeching halt in two moves as the alien used her bracers to block an eyebeam attack that Peace used to obliterate one of Saturn's many small moons. She bridged the gap between them with the same godly speed she entered the room by knocking her into semi-unconsciousness with a left hook to the side of her skull.

She remembered her naked body slamming violently onto the floor of her cell before feeling the same female's foot on the back of her neck. Her body went into spasms. It felt like her skull split in two as blood poured from her nostrils. She groaned and gurgled as her world went fuzzy. She was dumbfounded by the fact that there was a being in the universe that was not only undisputedly faster than her and Dennison but also hit a trillion times harder. She made a note to rethink her universal conquest plans should she leave her predicament alive.

Adding insult to injury, she felt her grab her by her dreads, lifting her back to her knees as the smaller two guards came forward, removing the restraints hanging from the sword belt on her hips. They were two thin metallic circles held together by an equally small, malleable bar. She grabbed each of her trembling hands, inserting them through each of the rings. Once in, the bands constricted to fit tightly over her wrists.

Genesis

"Try to focus life milk sow, for I shall only say this once," the female warrior calmly whispered in perfect English. "Do as you are instructed, or I shall kill you. Now move."

The high-ranking warrior pulled tighter on her dreads, forcing her to her feet before releasing her. A groggy Peace stumbled a bit as her vision and equilibrium eventually came back to her. She turned, cutting the commanding alien a nasty, murderous glare that did not scratch her Teflon demeanor. She did as told, spinning on her heel and following the guards flanking her as the red-haired, onyx-skinned super alien brought up the rear.

They exited her holding cell, where they walked sixty paces to a large room with several clear tubes lined next to one another. One of the cylinders began to rise to the ceiling as they approached it.

"Get in," the female alien leader commanded.

"And what pray tell am I fucking getting into?" Peace defiantly shot back.

"I shall not have my sacred homeworld defiled by your filth Earth, sow," she flatly answered. "Step in and get properly cleaned."

Peace scoffed while fluttering her eyes. She found a way to squeeze out a nasty wet fart before going to the alien shower. Once the tube descended around her, sealing her in, Peace was doused from an opening in the top of the machine by an ice-cold, sticky red liquid that began to move to coat her entire body. As it ran, it became sheering red hot in seconds so that even she could feel it. It then hardened into a crusted form. Before she could react with a smart-aleck comment, the same opening released backbreaking clear blue water into the chamber, flooding it.

Immune to drowning, Peace held up two middle fingers as the hardened liquid dissolved from her body, turning the water blue to red. Vents at the bottom of the chamber opened, allowing the water to drain. The same vents blasted hot steaming air until she was thoroughly dry. The tube then ascended, allowing her to step out.

"So, where's my spit-shine?" Peace asked, making a lewd gesture

Genesis

with her private area.

A male alien with slated gray reptilian skin and black pearl eyes wearing a blue toga with thick metallic silver bracers adorned with alien etchings entered the room, holding a type of sheer white linen.

"Raise your arms to eye level," the alien commander ordered. "And know that the Thracian that is here to clothe you will willingly die even if you threaten his life. You will have no bargaining chip if you attempt anything foolish, nor will you make it out of this room alive."

"Whatever," Peace snorted while rolling her eyes.

As she lifted her arms as told, the male Thracian walked up to her and skillfully pulled out a length full of the linen he held. He quickly twisted the cloth and covered and bound her breasts, fashioning the fabric into a bikini top. Pulling a curved blade from a hilt on his right hip, he cut the linen and tied the back into a stylish knot, securing her bra.

"Spread your legs apart," he commanded.

She did as she was told while sticking her tongue out, fluttering it around in the direction of the female in charge. The male Thracian took the rest of the linen, crouching down, and began wrapping her bottom and nether region, creating a hybrid bikini bottom sarong wrap, which he cut and tied off at her right hip. Peace became slightly unnerved and impressed by the skill and sensuality he used to fashion her outfit.

Not giving her a second look, he wrapped up the rest of the linen, respectfully bowed to the female Thracian in charge, and left the room.

"He might be outside sniffing his fingers," Peace blurted out.

The red-eyed female Thracian slowly narrowed her eyes at her, clearly thinking evil thoughts. Peace answered with a defiant shrug.

"I'm just saying …he snuck a swipe on two occasions."

"Fall in, you dusty breeding sow," the Thracian commander

Genesis

responded.

Peace's face read that she would not take being referred to as their version of a female pig much longer as she did what she was told.

She was led out of the room and walked by her count two hundred footsteps to what she could make out was an elevator lift, which doors slid open as they neared it. They entered with the guards flanking her and the six-braided redhead standing behind her. She could feel her eyes burning the back of her neck with her glare while her bare feet told her the elevator was descending further into the ship's hull. She closed her eyes, feeling it finally slow down, coming to a complete stop as the doors opened, revealing a hanger that housed a sea of starships that varied between fighters, shuttles, and transports.

They marched to a royal shuttle that had the shape of a sleek boomerang hovering quietly due to some unknown propulsion system primed and ready for departure; as they neared the craft, parts of the floor in the hanger raised up, creating floating steps to the entrance of the ship. Peace followed the female guards as their commander brought the rear behind her.

As she entered the ship, looking around at the bare hull, she snorted, unimpressed at what she saw until the lower part of the walls on both sides of the craft slid out, creating seating. Peace didn't need instructions to take a seat as the two Thracian guards sat down, flanking her, while their commander sat across from them, casually folding her arms and legs lazily, staring back at her.

Without the thin window slits in the craft, she would not have known they left the ship's hangar; it was her chance to execute one final escape attempt.

"What the …?"

A stunning, perplexed look appeared on Peace's visage. She looked up, narrowing her eyes at the soft chuckling from the Thracian commander sitting across her.

Genesis

"The restraints on your wrists also emit a bio-frequency that targets your nervous system preventing you from increasing your adrenaline, which is what you need to activate your ability to channel and manipulate the feeble energy you possess."

Her answer produced a murderous scowl on Peace's face, making the Thracian commander lean forward to lock eyes with her.

"You may have been extraordinary compared to others from that backwater planet you hail from, but here you are, nothing more than a toothless mongrel. You breathe air at my brother's leisure, become use to the yoke of your reality."

Peace continued staring her down with murderous intent, contemplating lunging for her throat even though she might be beaten to death for the attempt. Her graphic thoughts of violence were suppressed as her eyes picked up sunlight beaming through the ship's shrill viewing ports.

Due to the craft's speed and the limited view the windows provided, she saw little of the alien world outside until the ship landed. Defiant to the end, she waited for the commander and her guards to rise before getting to her feet. As the door hatch opened, she walked out to a bright blue-green sky and a Thracian battalion of a thousand strong standing in column formation. Walking down a new set of floating steps, Peace determined by their attire: the grunts and higher-ranked officers.

At the sight of the female Thracian commander, they all violently clanged the thick metal bracers on their arms together, roaring the words "Thrace! Thrace! Thrace!" before dropping to one knee, resting one forearm over a knee while bowing their heads.

The act almost made her forget to take in her surroundings. From what she could tell, she was on a military base. All around her was an ocean of ships, just like on the command vessel she just left. Behind them were smooth, massive, red metallic buildings gleaming in the sunlight and matching the metal ground she stood on. The second the commander's foot touched the Thracian ground, the army rose. Peace observed as she waited while one of the higher-ranked officers stepped out to greet her personally.

Genesis

He was tall with a ripped, muscular frame covered with white ash snake-scaled skin and full hair of long, thick green dreadlocks that hung down to the middle of his back. His eyes glowed with a faint orange hue, revealing he had some power to him, although nowhere in the ballpark of his commander.

Instead of a full toga, he wore what appeared to be a black leather kilt that matched his shin-high Grecian sandals and thick black combat harness that formed an 'X' shape across his chest with the straps. Attached to the harness's left and right shoulder area were red metal epaulets fashioned in an animal's head that looked like a wolf or bear. Yellow glowing gems were set into each of its six eye sockets while four enormous upper fangs reached the top of his arms.

They matched the thick red metallic bracers and greaves on his arms and legs etched with deep Thracian markings. Attached to the wide belt on his hip that had the texture of leather was a red scabbard housing a sizeable two-handed sword with a pointy curved gunmetal grey cross guard, a red metallic grip, and a sphere-shaped pommel with intricate Thracian etchings carved into it. Peace choked on her laughter about coming up as she noticed his long, flowing black cape attached to his harness and dragged him to the floor.

"This …is … Sparta," she whispered under her breath.

She listened as he spoke to the commander in the Thracian dialect. She nodded, answering him while motioning to her. A bit of nervous sweat ran down her back as he turned to her with narrowed eyes filled with irritation and curiosity.

"Husso! Naticala!" He roared. "Emoc draworf!

Upon his command, a male and female Thracian came forward and executed the same bow the army performed when they first landed before rising to their feet. Their outfits were similar to the officer's, except the female wore a single-shoulder dress. Their animal-shaped epaulets were a dark metallic grey color with red gems for the eyes, which matched their bracers and greaves. Unlike the officers, they did not wear a cape. Each had a faint white glow in their eyes, which told her they were heavy hitters.

Genesis

The female Thracian commander got her attention by getting in her face.

"I take my leave of you," she said with relief. "Two of my elite guards shall escort you to my brother's domicile. They have been instructed to kill you the second they believe you are producing a thought of escape in that grain of sand rolling around in that skull of yours. And even if you manage to somehow best them, which I highly doubt, I shall be there before your eyelids can flick to do what I should have done within your cell. So, I would advise you to remain obedient, although I do pray that you ignore warning and step out of bounds."

A faint smile appeared on Peace's face as she gave her a slow nod.

"All this time together …I didn't catch your name."

The Thracian commander snorted lightly as she looked her up and down again with just her eyes.

"I am Attea, first daughter of the High Region Nelron, and High Commanding General of the Thracian military regime."

"Thank you," Peace nodded. "Just so you know. In the very near future, when your pointy little Gelfling ears hear me screaming out your name. I'll be coming to kill you. And by killing you, I mean taking my bare teeth, sinking them deep into that scrawny little neck of yours, and ripping your fucking throat out. Then I intend to take a squat and relieve myself into the gape I made in your neck … with my teeth, while you choke on your blood, and whatever happens to flow out of my two orifices at that time."

Peace's threat made Attea burst into a chuckle while the green-haired high-ranking officer went to grip his sword.

"You insolent little …" he seethed.

Attea casually held up a hand, stopping him from drawing it out to cut her down. She then leaned in, whispering in Peace's ear.

"The day you scream out my name, you knuckle-dragging sow

Genesis

...you will be beseeching me to kill you."

Attea slowly stepped away from her, adorned with a look of disgust on her face.

"Be sure to cover her face with a harem veil," Attea ordered. "No one else must know of the abomination we brought to our great and illustrious homeworld. One whose mere breathe brings a foul, putrid stench to our air."

Peace's right eye went into a violent spastic twitch as the High Commanding General turned, giving her back to her. She took a few steps and then rocketed off into flight, going about her business. Peace's eyes went from her watching her soaring away to the green-haired Thracian officer towering over her, still gripping the handle of his sword within its sheath as he looked down at her. Another female Thracian warrior with thick blue braided hair styled in a mohawk, blue-black skin, and eyes that emitted a green glow in similar attire to the female named Naticala walked up, flanking his right, giving her a disgusted sneer.

"Fetch a harem's veil and bring forth one of the royal transports," the officer ordered. "Get this disgusting creature off of my base."

"As you wish, Lieutenant High Command," the blue-haired female Thracian answered.

She did not see much between the ride from the base to her current location. The thick red veil placed on her head obstructed most of her view. The rest was due to her looking down at the floor within the royal transport with the futuristic design of a closed-top horse-drawn carriage without the horses, wheels, or driver as it floated and moved about via a self-driving propulsion system. During the ride, she retreated into her own head.

The veil allowed her to be what she felt, which started when she woke up in the Thracian command ship's cell and could not break free from her restraints with her superhuman strength.

She felt terrified and alone.

Genesis

Inconspicuously, she pretended to play with the veil, tugging when she used the cloth to wipe away, forming tears.

She hated being scared and defenseless.

After entering the gates of the Crown Prince's home, her veil was removed, allowing her eyes to view a humongous Citadel forged from a smooth blood-red metal and a gleaming blue crystal material and then embedded into the most massive mountain she had ever seen. The inside was built from a white pearl material that brought a soft shine to the interior. She was taken up long, wide, winding steps made of the same stone that forged the wall. It felt warm under her bare feet and appeared to ascend into the heavens.

They got off at the one hundred and tenth floor by her count and walked down a hallway with the length and width of two jumbo jet hangar bays to reach her final destination.

A thick, colossal stone door on a track rolled away into the wall as her armed escorts ushered her into the Prince's bedroom chamber.

~ ~

Earlier, when she stood in the room, her eyes expanded to the size of golf balls as she began scanning her environment to figure out a possible escape route. Her new guards, Husso and Naticala, stood flanking the bedroom entrance calmly, watching her as she looked about the room made of red and purple marble-like material with a crystal glimmer.

A massive oval bed appeared as if it was built out of the floor and walls and could fit twenty people. The milky white sheets and pill-shaped pillows had a silky shimmer and felt soft just by looking at them. Her eyes picked up a giant oval mirror embedded into a wall right next to the bed that went from floor to ceiling and a sizable veranda made of the same material as the room with what she could tell was either a sunk-in Jacuzzi or wading pool with the reddest water she had ever seen.

"This prince is a freak ..." she whispered under her breath.

Genesis

Twenty minutes later, boredom began to set in as she stood there waiting. Peace began to move about the place, testing the limits of the guards. Other than their eyes tracking her, they moved not an inch from where they stood, but if she attempted to reach for something, their eyes narrowed while the energy with them intensified. She noted that neither of them went for the swords on their hips, which meant they were instructed to only subdue her.

She took a couple of steps toward the open veranda, which caused their eyes to pulsate again. She ignored them as she saw a disturbingly beautiful blue, green sky. She cursed the heavens for only being granted keen enhanced eyesight. The ability to see miles away would have allowed her to view the lay of the land, how close the nearest city was, and the location of the military base she came from.

Before Peace generated scenarios in her head where she made a break for the balcony while evading both Husso and Naticala to dive off the veranda, falling from a high altitude into the unknown below, her ears propped up to the sound of the bedchamber door rolling back.

Peace shook off the chill that ran down her spine as she dawned back on her game face. It still did not prepare her for who entered the room.

He was half-naked, dressed in a red loincloth with an oversized metallic silver and gold belt one would see Roman gladiators wear, except this one was carved with Thracian markings along with a sculpture in the middle that appeared to be a cross between a big cat and a hawk with its massive mouth open. The only other attire on his body was the thick golden bracers on his forearms with Thracian etchings that glowed red.

He had a long, slender body similar to a swimmer but more ripped and defined through his pearl-white scaly skin. His long blue mane was fashioned into a Mohawk with three thick braids hung over his left shoulder. She observed the confident, carefree swagger in his walk and the power within his eyes that glowed deep blue.

Unlike every other Thracian who laid eyes on her, he greeted her with a bright and cheerful smile.

Genesis

"Apologies for keeping you waiting," were his first words to her. "I was summoned to court by my father, unfortunately, when the High Regent calls, even I must make myself available."

For the first time ever, she did not have a humorous quip or sarcastic remark to produce as she stood there looking him up and down with just her eyes.

"How rude of me for not introducing myself," he sighed. "I am Merc, crown prince and third son of Nelron the High Regent of Thrace, brother to Attea, my younger sister, the crown princess and High Commanding General of the Thracian military regime, who I heard gave you a good thrashing for attempting to escape my hospitality."

"I've been hit by worse," Peace snorted.

"No, you have not," Prince Merc scoffed. "But, you maintain your bluff very well."

Merc strolled over, towering over her, grasping her restraints.

"Now, I must advise you of two things before I remove your claspers," Merc said with a smile. "Like my sister, I am more than capable of defending myself against the elemental energy you wield within you, and I would prefer you not cause any structural damage to my room, which took me a painstakingly long time to construct to my liking. Bey Breath stone is costly and rare in the known universe, and I will not be too pleased if I have to have it repaired. Secondly, I am known to strike harder than my little sister. So, I ask that you maintain yourself as a respectable guest in my domicile."

Without hesitation, he rested a thumb on the claspers' bar, causing her restraints to expand. Peace maintained eye contact with him as she slowly pulled her wrists and hands out of the cuffs' loops and began to rub the circulation back into her wrists. He displayed a toothy black gleaming grin while tossing the manacles to Husso, who caught and attached them to his belt.

"You two may leave us now," he ordered while giving Peace a

Genesis

thorough up-and-down look. "Take position outside of my bedchamber, so we are not disturbed."

"My prince," both guards acknowledged, taking a bowing knee before returning to their feet and exiting the room.

She watched as they took their leave to stand guard outside the door.

As the door rolled back shut, Peace turned to watch Prince Merc walk toward a sculpture of a beast that matched the room with the appearance of a lion with tusks and fur similar to a wooly mammoth. Within its open mouth was a bar filled with what Peace could tell was exotic wine and more vital spirits. The Prince confidently turned his back to her, taking up a clear crystal container, the size and shape of a softball, removing the triangle top.

"Would you like some?" He asked, pouring the glowing blue liquid into a crystal goblet. "Star Shade has a sweet taste going down and would instantly kill someone of your species. But I think a fine specimen such as you can handle such aged and revered liquor."

"What I want is to know what the fuck you want from me."

He turned to her, holding two full goblets between the fingers of his left hand and the bottle of Star Shade in the other as she took a defiant arm-folded stance.

"You didn't fish me out of that black hole because you want a drinking buddy," she said with a tilted head and narrowed eyes. "So, tell me what you want, or what position you want me to assume so that I can get off of this dirtball planet of yours and be on my way. Side note … I don't do anal …I give it."

Her remark only brought a chuckle out of Merc as he walked back over to her.

"I retrieved you from that sink vortex, not for your bedding talents …Mildred."

Genesis

Her arms dropped while her eyes widened with shock and rage at the sound of the name.

"Oh dear, not a name you fancy?" Merc wore a sardonic apologetic visage, inquiring. "I suppose hearing such a name again would have some sting when it came with a fist to the face, or worse. Humans and their disgusting desire to inbreed …if it's any consolation you were right to snuff out that little abomination within you before it could breathe air, it would not have been of good stock."

His words were the match that ignited her desire to remove his head from his body. She no longer cared about fatal repercussions as she threw a punch that could bring down a skyscraper. The room violently trembled as the crowned Prince took the punch head-on. The stone cracked underneath his bare feet as he stood his ground with his arms stretched, ensuring no drop of the Star Shade spilled from either goblet.

With her fist still on his cheek, Prince Merc's eyes fell upon the damage done to his floor, which made his eyes blaze. They dimmed as quickly as they ignited as he took a small breath.

"I have offended thee because you offended my homeworld and hospitality," he calmly said, staring at her. "And for my offense, I give apologies and shall stay my hand …this …one …time."

"How did you …?" She asked with a quivering voice.

"We have serums that can make someone of your physiology speak," he smirked, answering. "Especially with a mind such as yours that remains in a state of flux preventing itself from being read. And you had much to speak about once you were put under."

"My name … is Peace. Do not …ever call me by that name again," she said with a trembling growl. "Ever."

"You have my word."

An unnerved Peace kept what was left of her poker face on as she slowly retracted her fist from the side of his face. Merc politely handed her

Genesis

a goblet, which she took. He clanged his cup against hers for a "cheer" before siping.

"Now that we have put aside childish spat," he said with a grin. "Let us discuss your other talents, which I do need."

"If we're going to talk business, let's be honest," Peace deduced while taking a small test sip.

She shuddered a bit but quickly recovered.

"You didn't just happen by me in that 'Sink Vortex,'" Peace scoffed. "You been watching my planet; I'm guessing for quite some time."

"We have been watching your planet," Prince Merc said with a slight nod, "But that is not how we became privy to your whereabouts."

His answer brought on a perplexed look to Peace's face.

"Someone else told you I was there. Who?"

"I am not at liberty to reveal my source," Merc flatly answered. "Neither should you concern yourself with the minor logistics. Your concern is that this meeting provides a great opportunity for you."

His answer unnerved her, which she skillfully concealed. Peace began to walk around, taking in the room, every now and then sipping on her drink, which made her grunt. She glanced out of the open terrace once again at the blue-green sky. She watched Merc out of her eye as he watched her with intrigue.

"So, let me guess. You want to take over my planet," Peace deduced. "But you either answer to someone more powerful than you preventing you from invading Earth, or you have some type of treaty with someone either equally or more powerful than you are, which prohibits you from invading Earth. And the fact that it's pretty obvious that your people detest my people, bringing me here to your planet means you're probably pretty desperate …or probably on a time frame."

Genesis

Merc let loose a toothy grin before taking another sip from his goblet.

"You are quite skilled at deductive reasoning."

"Yeah, I'm really good at reading shit," she said with a nod while knocking back the Star Shade.

Peace gasped as her legs became rubbery. She hunched over, clutching her chest as if she was having a heart attack while her eyes grew watery. Peace cricked her neck as her strength returned, allowing her to stand upright.

She slowly shuffled back over to him, extending her empty goblet.

"Hit me."

Prince Merc hesitated before pulling the top off the bottle and pouring more Star Shade into her goblet. She strolled away from him again, running her hand across everything in arm's reach.

"So, here's my first question," she asked. "Why me, someone of your 'position' can't spread some cheddar around and find a couple of able rats to do your dirty work?"

"If I am deciphering your question correctly," Merc said with a raised eyebrow. "The universe is filled with ample mercenaries that I could tap to carry out this task."

He strolled over, cutting off her walk to look her in the eyes.

"But none have the skill set that I require for this task. My dear, you possess abilities that only a hand full of species possess and are mostly held by those of higher station or royal blood. Add to the scale that only I, my sister, and those loyal to me know of your existence makes you the perfect tool for my cause."

Merc reached out, taking a handful of her blonde locks to examine them; she invaded his space, giving him passive kitten eyes while tracing

Genesis

her fingers across his well-defined abs. She maintained eye contact with him as her hand slowly descended his torso into uncharted territory.

"Well, this tool comes with a price," she whispered.

"And what price may that be?" he asked with a purr.

"My freedom and my neck intact still breathing after the job is done, and whatever is the universal currency to ensure that my white ass is set for life," Peace snarled, "and a map of all the planets I can spend my earnings in peace."

"No desire to return to Earth?" He inquisitively asked.

"Fuck no," she spat. "I never want to see that shithole again. So, what's the job?"

"Let us say, I will need to commit a series of acts that will ensure a vote in my favor." Prince Merc smiled, informing her. "For now, you shall remain in the shade as a guest at my home until the time I shall give you instruction."

"Fair enough, I always wanted a vacation."

Peace knocked back another goblet full of Star Shade, which brought violent coughs and shivers running down her spine.

"Okay," she gasped while shrugging it off. "Take off that stupid ass pro wrestling belt and diaper so we can get this party started."

Perplexity plastered over Merc's face as he watched her sashay over to the wading pool and get in.

"Come again?"

"I've never fucked a prince or an alien before," she said while turning to him waist-deep in the red water. "Now I get to do both in one shot. Well, what the fuck are you waiting for? I ain't going to get any wetter than this."

Genesis

Merc huffed as he finished his drink, setting the goblet and bottle of Star Shade on the floor before making his way into the pool with her.

"I'll have you know I have sampled one or two of your female species from Bencari Skin Traders. Despite your boasted bedding prowess, they proved to be both grossly subpar and easy to break."

"That's what happens when you pick mutts over a thoroughbred," Peace growled, placing her hand down his loincloth. "Oh …call that Nati chick back in here …I want to play with her too."

"Naticala!" Merc politely barked while using a finger to slowly pull down her bandage top. "Do come in here …your presence and talents are required."

~~~~~~~~~~~~~~~~~~~~~~~~~~~~~~~~~

The following late morning on Thracian time, the crown prince made his way down his winding steps in a purple loincloth and a broad black belt similar to the one he wore the day before getting off at the third level of his castle.

Waiting for him was a dark grey-skinned Thracian who appeared to be his senior with a full head of silver and black dreads and a Fu Manchu mustache and beard adorned in a regal emerald green double shoulder toga.

"Your majesty," the Thracian elder uttered in his homeworld dialect as he took the knee.

"Embaro," Merc acknowledged him with a toothy grin. "How is my favorite Manor Lord?"

"Very well, my Prince, your day meal has been prepared for you. Princess Attea is also in the meal hall, awaiting an audience with you."

"Thank you, Embaro, oh, regarding my domicile guest upstairs. Make sure she is properly fed, bathed, and then clothed. Also, there is an annoying crack in my floor, be sure to have it repaired before nightshade."

Genesis

"As you command my Prince," Embaro replied with a slight bow.

"Carry on, Embaro."

Prince Merc continued to the meal hall as a loyal Embaro fluttered his eyes while heading up the steps in disgust over the fact that he had to tend to a human. Prince Merc began to whistle and hum as he swaggered into the hall to find his sister sitting in one of the one hundred seats of the meal table. Her guarded folded arms and legs and disapproving glare did very little to dim his good mood.

"Greetings, dear sister, have you eaten yet?" He asked with a genuinely concerned look. "Do not tell me Embaro left you sitting without ensuring your favorite meal was prepared?"

"Embaro is a faithful servant who never wavers in his duty, including when it comes to rearing you," She coldly answered. "I have already fed and declined his offer."

"Apologies, then if we dine and converse, Star Shade is the only thing to fill my belly since last night. I wish to add a proper meal to it."

The second Prince Merc took his seat, a circular door in the side of a far wall rolled away as a male servant entered the room, pushing a hovering cart on a polarized propulsion system. He took a knee showing respect to his Prince and princess, rose back to his feet, and began skillfully placing closed trays and removing the lids, revealing warm Thracian-cooked food and fresh fruits before his Prince as if performing a dance. He dropped each cover on top of the other, creating a stack back on the cart without making a loud clanging sound.

When he completed his task, he retook a knee, waiting for further instruction.

"Are you sure you hunger for nothing?" Merc earnestly asked his sister. "Not even a little slice of Sweet Delight?"

She looked at him with a face of disbelief.

Genesis

"Do I look like a youngling to you?"

"You will always look like a youngling to me, dear sister."

"I require nothing."

"Very well," he said with a shrug. "Thank you, Argeto, that shall be all, but remain close …no telling when this one will change her mind."

"Yes, my Prince," Argeto acknowledged.

He rose to his feet and returned to the door that rolled away, housing the kitchen as Merc dug in, grabbing food with his hands from different plates and placing them within his octagon-shaped emerald crystal plate. He started by popping the freshly cut fruit into his mouth, occasionally taking an animalistic bite from the meat on his plate.

"So, are you done playing with your new human pet?" Attea snarled, getting to the point. "Shall I inform mother and father that you have possibly sired them another half-breed bastard?"

"Wouldn't do much good considering he adores all of his greatchildren," Prince Merc grinned while chewing his food. "The news of another would crack a smile on his ancient countenance."

"Not when he finds out it might be from an excrement slinging human," she scoffed.

"She is of superior stock," He said, wagging a cooked limb from a dead animal at her. "And savagely skilled in the art of bedding, she even withstood both rut positions and actually begged me to bite her harder. Poor Naticala gave out before she did. Would you believe that she hoisted me onto her shoulders to pleasure my spike with her mouth, and then stuck a finger in my …."

"I did not come here to hear sordid details of you slumming it with a beastly human brother," Attea declared, glaring at him.

"Beings who you have struck with a glancing blow have either

Genesis

died days later or were never physically the same," Merc pointed out to her. "This human was able to recover from one of your strikes with considerable ease. She will be perfect for the task at hand. Pity, she shall be leaving mortal coil soon, and not just by our hands."

"No one told the life milk sucking sow to absorb so much elemental energy in one sitting," Attea muttered.

"You can see it in her eyes," he said, shaking his head. "Her cells eventually will not be able to keep up with the rate of absorption. I suspect she will either dry out or go the way of uncle Othotol."

"Don't place that backwater life milk rag on the same pedestal as uncle Othotol," Attea warned her brother. "He met his end like a true Thracian warrior."

"Taking five legions of Razcargians with him while going supernova," Merc recounted his uncle's death.

"And he slaughtered a couple hundred more before he met his glorious end," his sister added to the legendary Thracian tale. "I should only be so blessed to meet such an end."

"Still having nightmares of dying an old maid in your bed surrounded by your offspring?" Merc chuckled.

"Tis a pathetic way to leave this plane of existence," Attea scowled, muttering.

"Not for me; I so abhor violence."

"Yet you excel at it so well," she said while side-eyeing him. "One of the main reasons we have so few siblings."

"I reasoned with each and every one of them who challenged me for father's throne," Merc defended himself with a pouting face.

"Even our eldest Morgor?

Genesis

"Especially he," Merc said, wagging a finger. "I respectfully took him aside and gave him a detailed explanation as to why he was unfit to rule after father and why he should succeed to me. I even swore to find him a comfortable secondary title should he relinquish his claim to the throne to me. Poor Morgor …it hurt my heart to dispatch him in the Embary …he was the first to take me down by the riverbanks to spy upon females bathing."

"I remember," his sister recounted. "I was down by those riverbanks, you lecherous mongrels."

"All of them stubborn, just like father," Merc sighed, shaking his head. "A plague on our family, I tell you."

"Blessing from the gods that you managed to acquire mother's cunning and father's strength," Attea said sarcastically.

"I'm quite curious why you never challenged me for father's throne," Merc said inquisitively. "If there was ever anyone that fair …"

"You know I was never a politician," Attea cut him off with narrowed eyes. "I was born to lead our regime, crush our enemies, see them driven before us, and hear the sweet lamentations of their kinfolk, nothing more."

"And you excel at your station most magnificently, dear sister," Prince Merc answered while raising a cup to her.

"But the day you become smitten with that flea-ridden human sow and think to put a crown on her head," Attea snarled while pointing at her brother, "Is that day I come for both your heads and father's throne."

Merc calmly held his hands up, submitting to his sister.

"Fair enough."

"So now that you have acquired your pawn," Attea huffed while folding her arms, getting down to business. "We are actually proceeding as planned."

Genesis

"Of course," he answered, grinning while chucking a piece of fruit in his mouth.

Attea began to nervously fidget in her seat.

"If father ever found out what we are plotting …"

"Be still, dear sister," Merc rolled his irritated eyes, cutting off her sentence of fear. "By the time we have completed said task, father will be none the wiser, nor will he care. Neither will the Dominion Council …"

"I care not of the opinion of the Dominion Council, except for the embarrassment and ramifications it will bring father if said plan is found out. You know all too well the two acts that will move father to violence with his own hands."

"Breaking the law and embarrassing him," Merc muttered while fluttering his eyes in disgust.

"I would like nothing more than to wipe out the filthy humans and appropriate their worlds as our own," Attea said while tapping her sharp fingernail on his meal table. "But what we do treads deep into those murky waters."

"You act as if it is the first time I ever acquired planets before," an offended Merc snorted at her while folding his arms.

"None of those planets were the homeworld of a half-breed Annunaki and the second Eye of Ra," she growled back at him. "Conflict with Anu is also the last thing we require."

"And I say to thee again," Merc snapped back sternly at his little sister. "It shall not come to that."

He leaned back in his seat, taking a slow breath to calm himself.

"This little physical evolutionary leap the humans have taken in the past seven of their years is the gift we needed to present them to the Council as the potential threat to the universe they were theorized by many to be. As much as you detest my guest upstairs, she has more power than several triads of Razcargians. Given the human species' barbaric and sadistic history, which is well documented, we will be able to paint a bleak and dark picture of a possible future where all humans are capable of reaching her potential and what it would mean for the universe if the Council does not act."

Merc extended his hands in a peaceful gesture as a smile returned to his face.

"The humans will be wiped out for the good of the universe, the Earth, as well as the six additional planets within that sector, will be awarded to us, we will probably be hailed as heroes, and none shall be the wiser. Laurence Danjuma and those abducted by skin traders over the years, if they're not contracted to be a special dish, will live out their end days as the last remaining members of their species. That is how we shall write our tale and the final chapter of the human species."

"Do you think you will be able to publish your tale before the deadline?" Attea asked with a raised eyebrow. "Our cycle of shepherding the Earth and the other planets within its quadrant will be coming to an end very soon."

"That is why the next act will not only be executed swiftly but etched into the memories of those who will bear witness to it for eons to come."

"We still have no knowledge of who lead us to her," Attea raised another issue. "Or their agenda, which could very well be our undoing."

"I already relayed to you my source," Merc answered sternly.

"Enuc, the filthy Tangerian," she recited, fluttering her eyes in disgust. "Who relayed information to him? How did he become privy to her status, especially in a quadrant he avoids at all costs due to bounty on his head?"

"Enuc is a skilled information master, whose data has always been reliable. He is oath sworn to the protection of his sources," Merc reminded

Genesis

her. "He has also never brought secrets to my feet that would injure me knowing how deep my purse is and how well I have compensated him for his loyalty."

"Or is it the fact that either you or I will slowly remove his head from his body with our bare hands should he betray us?"

"That and the fact of how much he fancies you," Merc said with a devious grin.

His comment forced a wriggle of disgust from his sister as he bit down and chewed on a piece of tender meat, allowing the juices to run down his mouth.

"So, this is what has become of the great Thrace," Attea sighed, throwing up her hands in disgust and defeat. "We now debase our hallowed and feared heritage by becoming merchants and profiteers?"

"I would hardly say securing prime real estate for the benefit of our species as debasing ourselves," Merc snorted. "Especially when it entails taking it from a species that clearly does not appreciate it. The universe has vastly changed over the eons, dear sister, to survive, we must assimilate to that change. Those who are equal in power with us are our allies now, and our enemies do not possess the power to oppose us. Such are the wages for securing great power. The glory days of combat are as ancient as our father. Our new charge that we shall be revered for ensures that we bring continuous wealth and prosperity to our people by expanding our territories. Thereby ensuring their love and loyalty for eternity."

"Is that not something we already have?"

"The love of the people is like fire," Merc said, locking his narrowed eyes with his sister. "If not repeatedly stoked, it will wane and die. Once we secured the support to wipe that parasitic species from mortal coil …the Earth and the other six planets within that quadrant will be enough to kindle our people's love for a couple more eons."

~~~~~~~~~~~~~~~~~~~~~~~~~~~~~~~~~~~

Genesis

Back upstairs in Prince Merc's bedroom, a naked Peace lay on his bed covered in sheets and entangled in the bodies of the elite guards assigned to protect her.

As they peacefully slept from their sordid affair with her and their Prince, silent tears fell from Peace's eyes as she turned, looking at the mirror on the wall, realizing that she had been reduced to once again several billion light-years from Earth.

Once again, she was someone's pawn …someone's whore.

Peace turned her head, looking back up at the ceiling as her lips softly moved to form words without a voice.

Her mouth made the same motions over and over again.

"You survived, daddy …you survived Rosen …you will survive this."

Genesis

CHAPTER 11

May 2017, 6:00 A.M Sanctuary time,

Kimberly was startled out of her sleep by her mother, dressed in her Freedom uniform, barging into her room. A flustered Kimberly, whose body was reconditioned to sleep, sat up on her bed, rubbing her eyes, which quickly refocused after being startled awake. What made it worse was the ear-popping hand claps that made her body vibrate.

"Rise and shine, young lady," Sophia's voice boomed. "Come on! Get up!"

"Wha …what, what did I do?" A confused and semi-awake Kimberly frustratingly mumbled.

"Grounded doesn't mean you get to sleep in or lounge around this house or island and do nothing," Sophia said with a steel tone. "I am leaving for a mission and will be gone until tomorrow morning."

"Tomorrow morning?"

"There are five medical books downstairs. I want you to read before I get back and a list of chores that I wrote down on a paper and expect you to complete. Earl has a copy and will tell me if you do not finish them or are slacking off." Sophia continued. "I expect you to complete all of your chores before 5 P.M. this evening. And if you happen to finish them before that time, I expect you to find yourself back inside this house, you are still grounded, which means no telephone, tablet, television, radio, computer, video games, or internet. I have shut down the cable and internet in the house, and Vincent will know if you turn it back on or go looking for your devices. He will also know if you borrow one of your friend's devices, so do not do it."

"Why will you be gone all day?" Kimberly nervously asked.

Genesis

"Make yourself dinner, and find yourself in bed by 9 P.M.," Sophia kept going while ignoring her questions. "I want you up at 5 A.M. the next day. You are then to go into my room and put on a uniform I have laid out for you on my bed."

"Uniform?"

"I will be back at approximately 6:22 A.M. the next morning. I expect you to be dressed and on the airport tarmac before that time. God help you if I land, and you are not standing there waiting."

"What about breakfast?" Kimberly sheepishly asked.

"Go take those two arms, legs, and superhuman memory of yours and make your own breakfast," her mother scoffed. "You think you're an adult, you plan to become a hero? You're going to find out what being both is about right now."

Sophia spun on her heel and prepared to walk out the door.

"Mommy, I said I was sorry!" Kimberly said with a squealing pout.

"I know you're sorry," Sophia said, turning back to her with narrowed eyes. "This is not about that. Please do what I ask you to do and be on that tarmac tomorrow."

As she walked away, a still pouting Kimberly made her cheeks bigger while roughly folding her arms in frustration.

"This sucks."

She waited for her mother to leave the house before she went downstairs and found the written list of chores she had to complete before 5 P.M. that afternoon.

Her eyes widened and blazed with shock and disbelief at the nearly five-page single-spaced list her mother had left her.

Genesis

"Is she serious?!" Kimberly howled.

She then turned to see the five-half cinderblock thick medical books lying on the table, waiting for her to read.

"I take it back," Kimberly scowled, snapping. "She sucks!"

Begrudgingly, she did as she was told first, making herself and Sir George breakfast. Her eidetic memory of all the YouTube videos she watched allowed her to make chocolate pancakes. As she ate a stack of them with a vegetable omelet and turkey sausages, she quickly read through the medical books her mother left for her.

The task took her longer than expected as she was forced to look up words she did not understand in a standard dictionary. Eventually, she was done with all five books around 11 A.M. Earl showed up twice to check on her, and she gave him a legitimate excuse for finishing the reading Sophia expected her to complete before starting her chores.

Before she departed to begin her responsibilities, she trotted upstairs into her mother's room, curious about the uniform she was expected to wear the following early morning. Her face contorted in confusion as she stood over it and slowly picked up the top, looking it over.

"A nurse's outfit?"

The top was the standard color green. Kimberly laid it down next to the matching pants and then stepped back, noticing the pair of white shoes at the foot of the bed that nurses also wore. A nervous feeling washed over her as she wondered what her mother was up to.

"Why does she want me to be a nurse?" Kimberly asked herself.

"Kimberly! Kimberly! Are you finished with your reading?!" Earl yelled from outside. "You know I have to stay on you and make sure you complete your chores!"

"Coming, Mr. Earl!" She yelled back.

Genesis

She huffed as she gave the outfit one final look before heading downstairs.

With her speed and strength, she began to knock out task after task on her list, from assisting with construction, painting, gardening, collecting all of the garbage and recyclables in the village, and ensuring that all the animals in the preserve were fed.

It did not stop her from complaining about the unfair treatment she believed her mother inflicted on her, especially to anyone who would listen. Akram and Nadiya Romanenko, the new junior wildlife Preserve Keeper of Sanctuary, stood attentively from a distance as she whined through the handkerchief covering her face while shoveling elephant excrement into a wheel barrel to be used later as fertilizer.

"You all are witnesses," Kimberly screamed. "This is child abuse!"

"It's called punishment!" Nadiya yelled back. "Where I come from, children get a lot worse than this for disobeying their parents."

"Well, you never had a mother like mine," Kimberly said in frustration.

"My mother died giving birth to me," Nadiya shrugged, answering. "And my stepmother sold me into sex slavery."

Kimberly turned to an unapologetic Nadiya, who refused to chime into her sob story.

"Did you really have to make the kid pee in his pants?" Akram asked.

"I didn't make him pee in his pants!" Kimberly said with frustration, laced her voice. "That is not one of my superpowers!"

"No, you just got up out of your chair, which translates into any language as 'Take back what you said, or I'm going to kick your ass.'"

Kimberly's eyes began to emit a brighter glow, reflecting her

Genesis

building anger, which did not appreciate Akram's sarcastic retort. Akram stood unfazed by his friend's little temper tantrum.

"He equated my mom to a terrorist."

"You're talking to the unofficial face of terrorism," Akram scoffed.

"That's not funny," Kimberly admonished her friend with a stern visage.

"No, what's not funny is watching your uncle dragged through the streets, beaten and stoned to death, and then his body burnt beyond recognition because the person he chose to love was not a woman," Akram coldly returned. "I would rather endure a million punkass white boys calling me a terrorist over that experience any day."

"I'd prefer to be called a terrorist than a mail order bride any given day," Nadiya interjected. "Friggin Melanie Trump forced me to close my Twitter account."

"The problem with this world is that everyone is in everyone else's business instead of dealing with the business that really matters," Akram lectured his friend. "And we're all too damn sensitive! You keep talking about how you want to be a hero like your mom someday. Well, here's a reality check, not everyone likes your mom, and not everyone will like you. Many will even hate you; that is the world we live in. You're going to need a thick skin against words as well as bullets if you're going to be the great hero you want to be."

An impressed Nadiya nodded at the words of wisdom from a young Akram. A stubborn Kimberly, glancing at the ground, responded with her most robust comeback.

"Whatever."

"Kimberly, when are you going to tell your mom what happened between you and Kyle's father?" Akram asked.

Genesis

Her eyes met her friend's eyes. She had a genuine concern for her. She answered him with sadness in her own eyes before turning her back to him and continuing to shovel so that she could finish and move on to her next chore.

Chore, after chore, chipped through the mountain of anger and frustration within her as she breezed through them. It also helped that Earl, though stern, was kinder than her mother currently was and kept her giggling with the off-key humor that he kept rated PG.

Kimberly stood with her arms folded and her eyes narrowed as he carefully inspected the framework she put up for one of the new houses.

"Mr. Earl, you do know I've done this like a bazillion times."

"Don't sass me, girl," Mr. Earl retorted while checking the sturdiness of the frame. "And even if you did it a bazillion times, which you haven't, it doesn't hurt to have a second set of eyes to make sure it's been done right."

Kimberly secretly responded with an irritated eye roll as a satisfied Earl nodded approval over her work.

"Another job well done. You want to start on the foundation for the next lot while I get some guys in here to do the walls?"

"I don't understand why you don't just let me do it all," Kimberly shrugged, replying. "I could …"

"I'm pretty sure you can," Mr. Earl cut her off. "You know who could also probably do this by herself?"

"My mom," Kimberly muttered.

"But she's not here doing it all by herself, even when she's here. She depends on us mere mortals to make all of this work, including looking after you."

"Mr. Earl, do you know where my mom went?" Kimberly

Genesis

cautiously asked.

Earl, who had a horrible poker face, fidgeted; it was a natural giveaway that he knew.

"Your mother made me swear not to tell you, honey," Earl half-smiled, answering. "And as much as I would love to tell you, I think one of us on your mother's bad side is enough."

"My mother doesn't want me on the web or any type of communication device because she does not want me to know what she is up to …right?"

"What do you think?" Earl, with a fatherly tone, asked with his arms folded.

"I think this sucks," Kimberly pouted with her head down.

"That's life," Earl said with a shrug. "Sometimes it tastes like barbecue, and sometimes it tastes like Buckley's cold medicine."

"I don't understand what that means," Kimberly confusedly answered.

"When your momma comes home, ask her to let you get a little taste of some Buckley's," Mr. Earl said with a smirk. "You'll figure it out after one sip. Ready to do some foundation work?"

"Yes, sir."

~~~~~~~~~~~~~~~~~~~~~~~~~~~~~~~~~

As the day ended and she completed all of her chores, Kimberly went home as instructed, cleaned herself up, made herself dinner, and found other ways to entertain herself that did not involve an electronic device. Bored between teaching Sir George how to execute a double backflip and breaking Joseph Odhiambo's four hour and fifteen-minute record for spinning a basketball on her finger, she got ready for bed and spent the rest of the night catching up on reading some manga novels she purchased

Genesis

during her many visits to Japan.

That night, Kimberly sat on her bed but could not force herself to sleep. She stared aimlessly out her window, wondering where her mother was and what she was doing. Kimberly stayed awake all through the night, watching the clock on her desk until 5:30 A.M. She slowly got out of bed and went to her mother's room, switching out of her bedclothes and putting on the nurse's outfit. Kimberly took her time walking to the airport. The second she stepped onto the tarmac, nervous jitters radiated through her frame as the sun softly rose over the ocean.

Earl, the other Council members, and other villagers who caused her stomach to swirl were already waiting on the tarmac. The swirling was created by the uneasiness she saw on their faces. Most wore medical clothing while standing next to gurneys and medical apparatuses. On the tarmac were several transport vehicles lined up next to one another.

Kimberly timidly walked up quietly, standing next to Earl and another villager, waiting for what would come next. Her heart began to flutter as she heard the sound of thunder. It sped up as her keen eyesight picked up, her mother soaring towards them in cruise mode. She was not going faster because she was escorting the two humongous jumbo jets following behind her.

She increased her speed, breaking away, barreling towards them. Kimberly's entire body began to spasm out as Sophia slowed up and descended. Her touchdown was soft and graceful as her eyes locked onto her daughter's eyes, causing the young girl to fidget in her spot.

Earl was the first to notice her outfit's battle damage and scuff marks.

"What happened to you?"

"Bastard sent an anti-aircraft vehicle and two fighters in an attempt to shoot the jets down."

"Are you serious?" Earl asked with a face of disbelief.

Genesis

"He will be attempting to send me a bill for those two jets. He'll also be busy rebuilding the west wing of his Presidential Palace after I sent his anti-aircraft vehicle back to him."

"Well, we're all set here," Earl motioned.

They all looked up as the first jet came in for a landing while the second went into a circling pattern.

"Mom ... what's happening?" Kimberly timorously asked.

Her mother did not answer her question as she turned to the jet powering down. As the cargo door came down and was locked and secured, gurneys were rolled out and down the ramp of the plane, two in a row with people on them. They had medical bag drips attached to each man, woman, and child on a gurney. Some of the stretchers had plastic covers protecting the patient from the outside elements to avoid infection, which depended on how detrimental their illness was. Some of the patient's family members were around them. They nervously surveyed their new surroundings as they descended the aircraft with their loved ones.

"Alright, people, let's get to work!" Earl yelled, clapping his hands.

Everyone scrambled, heading for the jet to assist, leaving Kimberly and her mother standing there. At the same time, the other plane came in for a landing.

"Those ...are ...Syrians," Kimberly fretfully uttered.

"Yes," her mother answered. "Victims of the current civil war, which includes the Russian Syrian Sarin attack; these are the ones that can be safely transported here for treatment. Did you read the medical books I instructed you to read?"

"Yes."

"Then get to work," Sophia commanded, motioning toward the jets.

Genesis

"I …I can't…" Kimberly stammered.

"You wanted to be a hero," her mother cut her off with a soft, stern voice. "This is where you begin. You will start by helping with the transport to the new medical facility and then assisting with the basic treatment of the patients assigned to you. And they're going to need a lot of care."

"No …I can't…I don't want to," a frightened Kimberly shook her head, stammering, "I don't want to!"

She turned to fly off, only to feel the powerful grip of her mother grabbing her wrist and spinning her around. She shrunk and coiled in fright at the scowl on her mother's face as her blue eyes blazed brightly.

"Oh no, you're not running away from this young lady. You don't choose to act like you're an adult and then switch to a little girl the second you get scared." Sophia snapped at her with a booming voice, "Now, if you read the books, then you know what to do. You're not doing brain or open-heart surgery. All of the patients, for now, are stabilized; all they need is your care. You will not be alone, and any help you need you will get if you ask for it."

"Why are you doing this to me?" Kimberly blubbered. "Why?"

"What's being done to you, Kimberly? Tell me, what is being done to you?"

Sophia released her, placing her hands on her hips, waiting for an answer. Kimberly stood with her head down, frozen, unsure what to say.

"The little girl, who likes to shoot her mouth off about how she sent the big bad Draugr into space, is afraid of tending to sick people who are terrified because they have no idea what is happening to them. People who are not sure if they're going to make it until the next day. And if they do, there is a ninety percent chance they will never lead a normal life ever again. So, help me to understand what I am doing to you, and why you are so afraid?"

Kimberly slowly lowered her head, filled with shame.

Genesis

"I don't know."

"Well, that is a shame because I know why I am doing this to you."

Sophia took a step toward her daughter and reached out, lifting her daughter's chin so that she could look her in the eyes.

"I'm doing this because you need to understand what the hardest part of being a hero is about," Sophia said while pointing to the aircraft still being unloaded with patients. "Anyone can throw a punch, shoot a gun, or topple a building. Violence is easy. Feeding a person that cannot feed themselves. Periodically turning them so that they do not get bedsores, and cleaning them when they soil themselves, showing love and compassion to a human being whose health might not improve after everything you've done …that is hard. That is the makings of a true hero."

Sophia removed her hand from her chin. Kimberly kept her eyes trained on her mother, who was back to being calm again.

"Having the power to stop evil is not enough," Sophia softly concluded. "Because no matter how strong you are, how fast you are, you will never be in two places at the same time. While you're stopping a robbery on one side of the world, someone is being beaten or worse on the other side. This is the other side of my watch, making people whole again. By bringing someone back from the brink of destruction and helping them show evil that it did not break them. That is the greatest victory you will ever achieve if you can accomplish it."

Kimberly wiped her eyes and then turned to the refugee patients and their families on the tarmac. She watched as Earl and the other villagers worked to quickly coordinate and transport them to the new medical facility based on the severity of their health. Luckily, they loaded the sickliest last so that they would be the first to be taken off the jet.

"What do I do?"

"Earl and the team seem to have it here," Sophia answered as she observed. "Head to the facility and help Head Nurse Adetokunbo with getting each patient to their assigned beds. Anything she tells you to do, you do, understood?"

"Yes, ma'am," Kimberly nodded.

She turned, walking away, heading toward the new hospital.

"Kimberly."

"Yes, mom?" She asked, diffidently turning around.

"You can fly there if you want."

Kimberly's eyes filled with glassy tears as she nodded and quickly wiped them away with the sleeve of her arm. She turned on her heel and took to the air, flying off.

Sophia let out a huff of air, watching her soar off before turning back to monitor and observe her newest responsibility.

Genesis

CHAPTER 12

May 2017, eleven hundred hours military time, Bridgeport, California

Most of the Regulator team sat at the Ranch while Rogers and Erica stood in the front of the debriefing room. They all stared aimlessly at the pictures and data on the widescreen in a brainstorming attempt to piece together nine months of puzzle pieces with no substantial clues.

~~~~~~~~~~~~~~~~~~~~~~~~~~~~~~~~~

Months before this, the backlash of Sir Knight Light's death was worse than expected. It ripple effect within the United Kingdom and Worldwide, especially within the superhuman community due to Major Henry Butcher being beloved on an equivalent level to Prince William and Harry.

His televised funeral was estimated to be comparable to the passing of Princess Diana.

As expected, his death sparked questions that the government could not answer. The state of the Major's body, time of death, and the theory of a shapeshifter impersonating him for months were kept from the public to prevent panic.

Captain Amanda Taylor, who went by the call-sign Lady of the Lake, was promoted to Major and became the team's new leader with an oath to hunt down and bring the Major's murderer to justice.

Surprisingly, the worldwide public, including Freedom's critics, demanded to know when she would find Sir Knight Light's killer.

Genesis

This brought on an uncomfortable conversation between Erica and the world's unofficial champion.

Erica slowly exhaled as she looked back at Freedom via a video chat from her lab while she stood not too far from the location of Sir Knight Light's new tomb.

"I was expecting and dreading this call."

"Me too," Freedom sadly answered back.

"Before you ask, there are a few things you should know," Erica sighed. "MI6 is not asking for our help on this investigation."

"Can I ask the reason why?"

"Conflict of interest, our mutual golden friend from the stars, is a primary suspect. You almost made the list until I cleared you."

"There's no way the Eye of Ra could have done this."

"You're preaching to the choir," Erica agreed. "But Director Mansfield is unfortunately not hearing it."

"You have a suspect already," Freedom deduced. "The individual that drained the nuclear reactor in India."

"Major Butcher was killed without putting up so much as a fight," Erica nervously informed her friend. "There are no EVOs currently on the planet besides you who could have killed him so quickly without a struggle. Even Kimberly would have had problems before she overcame him, mainly due to his experience. The only other likely suspect would be the Eye of Ra. The only evidence tying him to the Major's murder is the sand underneath the Major's fingernails, which came from Luxor around the Valley of the Kings.

And before you start talking about a road trip to Egypt, the team and I have already been there. We even went past the valley where we found sand and an empty unknown tomb that, for some strange reason,

Genesis

dates before the Egyptian dynasty."

"By the look on your face, something was different about this tomb."

"It was dug a mile and a half down from the surface in a slant, which is extremely unnatural for that period. It also looked as if it was carved by a powerful energy weapon. The problem is the person who could verify it for me is off-planet."

"Why didn't you call me?" Freedom asked with a furrowed brow. "I could have …"

"I'm not supposed to be speaking to you about this, Sophia," Erica swallowed.

Her answer brought a glare to Freedom's face that she knew was not directed at her.

"Rogers …"

"Is doing what he's trained to do," Erica verbally stopped her. "We're not some fictional organization funded by a rich billionaire that answers to no one. We work for and answer to the United States government, which means when it comes to matters of national security, I am not at liberty to divulge classified information to a civilian, which you are."

"But this was an international incident," Freedom said with narrowed eyes.

Erica's face became stern as an uneasy stalemate fell between her and her friend.

"Like I said, I'm not supposed to be speaking to you about this."

"Erica …"

"The base is on lockdown indefinitely," Erica informed her while glancing at the floor. "I advise you not to come here for a while, especially since you have a clean bill of health."

It was a painfully awkward silence similar to their last disagreement. Freedom could tell that it wasn't something Erica wanted to say this time. She had to say it.

"I understand," Freedom slowly nodded, acknowledging.

They didn't bother saying goodbye to one another. They did not have to. Freedom's face read that Erica knew where to find her if she needed her.

Erica's face read that she knew.

~~~~~~~~~~~~~~~~~~~~~~~~~~~~~~~~~

Next to follow was an impromptu visit from Secretary of Defense Robert Graves and his Executive Assistant Michael Mendes. They briefly toured the Ranch, viewing the new upgrades to the facility and meeting with the team's new and old members.

Erica kept her promise to Rogers, remaining cordial and respectful of the Secretary of Defense, reeling in her usual wit and sarcasm whenever he was in their vicinity.

After the tour and talk, Graves sat in his office for a private conversation with Rogers.

"I have it on good knowledge that you have been busy, Sergeant." Graves got to the point. "Mexico called you in for the Castillo case, then MI6 for the Major Butcher incident. Is there anything you need to fill me in about?"

"I believe my report outlined everything," Rogers gestured, answering. "Based on the analysis and evidence both were related to superhuman activity, both had decided to handle the cases in-house."

Graves nodded, accepting his answer. Rogers tilted his head,

Genesis

noticing something off about him.

"You okay, sir?" Rogers asked. "You don't seem like yourself today."

Graves quickly shook his head with a sad smile on his face.

"Haven't been getting much sleep, especially after the results of this damn election, which is also why I am here."

Rogers leaned back in his chair, bracing himself for what he was about to hear.

"I heard firsthand on the Hill that you and your team's jobs are secure," Graves informed him. "The five branches want you to stay on, and you have the support from the Senate and House, who will put a ton of pressure on the new Administration to keep hands off of you. I'm going to advise you for the sake of yourself and your team to stay out of the politics. I'd even go as far as to advise that you sever whatever affiliation you have with Dennison."

"Oh?" Rogers asked with narrowed eyes.

"I don't think I need to go into detail about what a sore topic she's been of late, especially with what went down in New York. You and I did not see eye to eye on many things, Rogers," Graves said bluntly. "In the end, I hope we can agree that we do what is best for our country. Those are the reasons I not only respect you and your team, but I know, despite it all, that I made the perfect choice when I picked you. So, I ask that you heed what I say next and take it to heart.

With what was speculated to have happened with this election and what is to come, your country will need you and your team more than ever. Whatever happens, keep your head down, and stay clear of the politics and shit storm that is coming. Freedom is a shit storm magnet. The difference between you and her is that she will survive it; you and your team won't if you continue to stand next to her."

Rogers nodded, respecting Graves's advice.

Genesis

"Since you're shooting straight with me. Is it safe to say that you'll be heading the EVOlution project once you leave office?"

Graves leaned back in his seat, narrowing his eyes at Rogers. A slight smirk on his face formed before he answered.

"It's safe to say that."

Rogers nodded before he asked his second question.

"Is it safe to ask what the 'Holy Grail' is?"

Graves's face showed no surprise over Rogers's question.

"The Holy Grail was the body of an almost five-thousand-year-old Egyptian woman found by the Nazi regime during World War II in an experimental base underneath the Ohrdruf concentration camp. They believed her to be the ancient goddess Sekhmet. Her DNA and cellular properties were both the key and building blocks that created Project EVOlution, the D.E.A.D, and, indirectly, Sophia Dennison, which caused the Big Bang II incident.

The body was eventually destroyed to bury the failings of the first project. Its genetic material had become too degraded over the years for further use. And if you're asking why I decided to outright tell you this, I would prefer not to have you snooping around my operation like you've been doing once I leave office and take full charge of it. You can pass that on to Dr. Champion unless she listens to this conversation."

Rogers remained silent, keeping his trademark poker face.

"As I said to you on the day you barged into my office and placed your gun on my table, prepared to shoot me in the face. There are greater forces behind the scenes ensuring the safety of the Republic, Sergeant. They've been in place as safeguards by our forefathers and some of our former Presidents to guarantee that this great country remains standing, even with our new Commander-in-Chief taking office next year.

Your job is to fight for freedom wherever there is trouble and let

Genesis

our country see you do it so that they have something to cheer for and know they are safe.

My job will be to let certain people know that the United States still holds the keys to the gates of hell and will not hesitate to set the beasts loose under their beds if they do not behave.

It all works best if we do not step on each other's toes."

Rogers remained silent as his eyes narrowed slightly while Graves stretched in his chair, preparing to get up.

"Enough of this cloak and dagger shit," Graves yawned. "We'll no doubt be seeing one another one or two more times before my replacement is announced by the new Administration, whenever that is. You'll also be getting a personal invite to the inauguration next year; attendance is mandatory. Happy Holidays, Rogers."

Rogers got to his feet, snapping a salute, and then extended his hand to Graves for a handshake, which the Secretary of Defense took.

"Try and get some rest, sir," Rogers respectfully said.

"I will if you heed your own advice, Sergeant," Graves smirked. "Superhuman does not mean invincible."

~ ~

On the flight back to Washington, Graves sat silently, staring out his private airplane window. Observing from the opposite side of him, Mendes dawned with a face of concern for his boss.

"Sir, is everything alright?" Mendes asked. "You seem a bit off."

"I'm fine, Michael," Graves answered while still looking out the window. "When we get back, I want to discuss your options once I leave office."

His answer floored Mendes, forcing him to fall back in his seat.

Genesis

"Sir, I thought …you were taking me with you to Project EVOlution?"

"I was; however, I was advised to cut all personal strings to Washington before I take this position full time, including you," Graves said bluntly. "You have served this Administration and me without fail, delivering stellar work from day one. I want to ensure that you are both taken care of and that your career continues to excel once we have parted ways. You are destined for great things, Michael, just not under me."

Michael lowered his head, swatting away the mist formed in his eyes, both saddened and appreciative of Graves's words.

"Thank you, sir," Mendes said, raising his head. "It has been an honor serving underneath your office and by your side."

Graves nodded while still looking out the window, keeping his composure.

He did not want Michael to see the terror in his eyes as his heart pounded due to the voice drubbing in his head.

"Very good slave," Horus cackled. "Very good."

Mendes would never know of the horrific fate Graves saved him from that was far worse than death itself. A fate that made Graves a powerless instrumental pawn in destroying not only the very country and Republic he swore on his life to protect but possibly the world.

~~~~~~~~~~~~~~~~~~~~~~~~~~~~~~~~

Rogers, pacing back and forth, began the rundown of the incidents that have taken place.

"So, to recap our current workload, on one side, we have two dead Apollo Class EVOs both murdered by the same individual, which may be related to an individual who drained the nuclear power plant in India last year. On the other side, we have someone supplying criminal and terrorist organizations with a booster that can turn a person into an actual EVO

Genesis

permanently within three months."

"And one Mexican Drug Cartel that was possibly wiped out by the same individual or individuals supplying the boosters," Adrian added.

"I think the first thing we need to figure out is whether these incidents are caused by the same individuals or not," Oliver advised. "Clearly, the draining of the power plant and the murders of Flaming Jay and Sir Knight Light could be related, but whoever is the suspect hasn't made a move in months. The boosters, however, might be run by someone else. The only thing that is relatable in all of these cases is that the suspect or suspects we're looking for operate like ghosts leaving very few traces or leads for us to follow."

"Oliver is correct in that," Erica said, jumping in. "As far as our energy drainer goes, I have every type of energy frequency tracker you can image scanning the entire planet for this person and have still come up with zilch. I've even been tracking Apollo Class EVOs with massive power readings in the likelihood that he or she will strike again. I am one hundred percent certain this person is a mutation."

"Someone with the ability to deflect your scans?" Sister Shareef asked.

"Considering that I have a scanning system to detect that, no," Erica answered, shaking her head. "Whoever this person is can suppress the massive power output they currently have or is literally physically apart of the energy spectrum itself. I am more inclined to lean toward the latter because the former is leaning more toward fiction."

"You're using the word fiction in the current world we live in?" Rosann asked with a scoffing tone.

"I'm basing it on my current research of EVOs and praying that I am not wrong." Erica narrowed her eyes, turning to her and answering. "Infected EVOs have physical limitations they cannot surpass, even ones with mutations. The ability to suppress energy means this person has total physical and mental control of it on a molecular level."

Genesis

"But we manipulate energy," Aashif said, motioning between himself, Oliver, and Teuila.

"You don't manipulate energy," Erica corrected him. "You store, channel, and release it, which is all activated by your muscle contractions, adrenal glands, and specific neural triggers."

"This isn't manipulation?"

Oliver asked his question while focusing electricity into his hand, creating a sphere.

"Now, try turning it into a sword."

Erica patiently waited as everyone watched Oliver attempting to shape the ball of electricity in his hand into an ion sword. He quickly dispersed the energy before it became unstable.

"Holding a charge and creating a sphere is physical manipulation activated by muscle contractions, shaped by how you hold your hand, controlled by the independent functions of your brain, and released by how you position your fingers. The protective shielding you create works the same way based on how you position your body and tense up your muscles," Erica explained. "Molecular manipulation is pure mind control. The ability to command the molecules within, for example, electricity or plasma, to compact, forming solid matter and creating any shape one can imagine with thought. Only six infected EVOs are capable of molecular control and manipulation, and only two-level ten; one is in Africa, and the second lives in the Midwest.

Their control is strongest with solid and liquid molecules and air in the gas category. Thermal, kinetic, and nuclear energy is not only gaseous; it is fast-moving particles that no human mind could keep up with, which is the key to manipulating energy. The ability to see, feel, and connect with molecules moving near or at the speed of light is impossible."

"For a human mind," Teuila respectfully retorted.

"That is why I am praying that I am right," Erica answered, turning

Genesis

toward her. "The problem is if this person can psionically shift the cells and tissues in their body to change their physical appearance becoming an identical match for anyone they impersonate, then my theory which I am praying to be fiction will not be, and we now have a massive problem on our hands. It means this person's abilities are almost limitless."

Erica's grim notion silenced the room and lowered heads.

"Let's switch gears for a minute and put this 'limitless killer' theory on the backburner for now," Rogers requested. "Any leads on who could be responsible for the red booster?"

"After nine months of hacking and surveillance that if ever found out could create several disastrous international incidents, and even land me a sizable amount of jail time," Erica sighed while turning to him. "I can tell you it's not the Russians, it's not the Chinese, and it's not the Iranians or North Korea. I even checked allied countries like the UK, South Korea, Japan, and private sector companies …everyone is working on their own version of a serum, but no one has come close to engineering something like this …except for one company."

"One?" Teuila asked while falling back in her seat in disbelief.

"One," Erica confirmed, nodding, "But even that doesn't make them our prime suspect."

Erica removed all of the data on the screen, posting an image of a clean-cut, well-dressed Asian man with spiky raven hair and a well-groomed goatee in his mid-forties in front of everyone.

"Hello, nurse," Teuila said with a bright smile.

"Ken Shiro," Erica introduced. "Born in Japan of Japanese-Irish descent, the second eldest of six siblings who took up the family business of professional wrestling; a former multi-time world champion who's performed around the world for various different companies including Battlefield Wrestling Industries."

Her statement made everyone glance at Rogers's way. Abe

maintained a granite exterior, deflecting all eyes looking in his direction as he focused on the screen.

"Unlike other wrestlers who either took up politics, Mixed Martial Arts, or acting," Erica continued. "Mr. Shiro invested his money and built a multi-billion-dollar conglomerate called Northstar International. He created Northstar Automotive improving Elon Musk's design, making cars and SUVs and motorcycles, boats, and aircraft. He then went on to build Northstar Armament, which successfully tested the first fully armored propulsion combat suit along with a mobile armored combat mech line to be released next year fall, and finally, Northstar Genetics, which has made breakthroughs in research to cure a multitude of deceases including AIDs and Cancer, as well as creating extremely affordable and safe medicine."

"Wow, part war profiteer part humanitarian," Rosann snorted.

"And now he's thrown his hat into the superhuman ring," Erica continued. "During an interview on Bloomberg, he stated his company had the first successful medical trials which safely activated the judgment virus within human beings. I reiterate again that this does not make him or his company a suspect. But it also does not hurt us to investigate and cover our bases. We also need to tread very lightly people, we're not cops or the FBI, and the last thing we want to do is to tip-off anyone of what we have in our possession."

"So, who's going to talk to Mr. Shiro?" Sister Shareef asked.

"I am," Erica smiled, answering. "Their main corporate headquarters is in New York. I already have an appointment scheduled for him at 2 PM today."

"Then I'm going with you," Rogers decided.

The room became awkwardly silent as eyes turned to Rogers. This time, he gave each of them an unappreciative glare.

"What?"

"I don't know about anyone else," Erica shrugged, replying. "But

Genesis
I'm just wondering if I should wear a business suit or a referee shirt."

Everyone looked down, muffling their laughter as Rogers turned to her.

"How about keeping your smartass comments to yourself," he warned her. "Everyone else is on duty, including male Esposito up until 6 PM today because he's got a date."

Rogers's comment turned everyone's attention to Adrian, who dropped his head blushing as the "Ooohs," and "Aaahs" rang out.

"Yeah …yeah," Adrian muttered. "Don't hate."

"I just can't believe how much you're gushing over this chick," Rosann said, shaking her head.

"What can I say," Adrian nervously grinned, replying, "She's special."

"Special? Did he just say special?" His sister asked, almost falling out of her seat.

"I heard special," Aashif confirmed.

"Does that mean I'm finally going to meet her?" Rosann jumped up, rustling his hair, asking. "Are we talking wedding bells?"

"Get off me, Rose!" He shot back, swatting her away. "You're messing up my good hair!"

"We're twins, you, idiot! You're not the only one with good hair!"

"Alright! Debriefing over! Everyone get the hell out of my face!" Rogers commanded.

The team got up, still ragging on Adrian while exiting. Erica sheepishly walked over to Rogers after her dig at him.

Genesis

"I got nothing to say to you," he said flatly," See you on the tarmac at twelve-thirty hundred hours. Don't be late."

"Dress to impress," she warned him before walking off.

Sister Shareef remained in the room, walking up to him with her arms folded.

"You okay?"

"Why wouldn't I be?" Rogers shrugged, asking.

"You seemed a bit agitated."

"I'm not 'agitated,' and there's no past history between Shiro and me. He was a funny guy and a hardworking ring general. We did a couple of feuds together; he worked the BWI for about two years and moved on to a better offer with another promotion, that's it."

"Okay," she shrugged, replying. "Then, don't be hanging out in New York sharing war stories."

She pecked him on the lips before he could retort, walking away. Rogers sighed, frustrated, before glancing again at Shiro's picture on the screen.

~~~~~~~~~~~~~~~~~~~~~~~~~~~~~~~~

1:15 PM New York Time,

Rogers manually drove the ion-powered vehicle through Manhattan's streets, now and then glancing at the GPS system mapping out the shortest route to the Northstar International building that Erica insisted be activated during the drive.

Like her journey with Rosann, they had no talk during the flight to New York or JFK's drive into the city.

Now and then, Rogers glanced at her, shifting uncomfortably in

Genesis

her two-piece navy blue business suit with a white blouse and caramel pantyhose stockings. She had kicked off her black high heels while in the car. Her blue and black dyed hair, which had grown with some length, was neatly tied back into a bun as she quietly went through her email and social media on her tablet.

Rogers was also uncomfortable as he dawned on the Regulator Officer Service uniform, a dark blue two-piece jacket and pants combination amalgamating a Marine service uniform and the Star Trek uniform from Wrath of Khan.

"So, what's the game plan once we get there?" Rogers asked, breaking the ice.

"You can lead if you want," Erica shrugged, answering, not looking at him. "I'll just stay quiet and keep my 'smartass comments' to myself."

"You had that coming," he said bluntly to her. "You were out of line."

"I was just ribbing you; you're the one who was being nasty for no reason." Erica snapped at him. "And you didn't need to be considering there is no 'issue' between you and Shiro."

"There is no issue."

"So, the fact that he walked into the SWA before it changed to the BWI and became its World Heavyweight Champion in less than four months, while you gave the company five dedicated years and was in the middle of a year everyone thought you'd complete your Grand Slam run never bothered you?"

Rogers became a cobra, giving her side-eye before he struck. She looked back at him, no longer affected by his intimidation tactics and expecting an answer. He turned back to the road, letting the hot air out his nostrils.

"Shiro was a multi-time World Champion with a career that

spanned over a decade. It made sense to give him top drawer and the belt. It also created an array of storylines and feuds, which included Pay-Per-View main events that I was a part of. In the end, it worked out for everyone. I also got my Grand Slam right here in my hometown at 'Legacy Three.' Shiro's hunt for a World title was worse than mine; he got passed over so many times people actually thought that Fallout Championship Wrestling owner James Greene hated him. End of the day, when he got tapped, his win made him a bigger draw than anyone could ever imagine. Timing is everything."

"Well, since you don't have an issue with Mr. Shiro," Erica slid in her next question, "What really is your problem with Dennison?"

"Besides the obvious that we both know?" Rogers glanced, answering with a question.

"You heard the conversations; nothing happened." Erica glared at him, replying.

"I don't have a problem with Dennison either," Rogers flatly answered. "However, her intelligence and rationale are often clouded or go out the window by her guilt over the Big Bang Two incident. If she knew about this red booster serum, she'd be driven to rip open every door and turn over every mountain hunting these individuals down. Especially if she learned who we got it from. How further away would we be at finding these people who have successfully eluded us at every given turn for this long after she went on her rampage?"

Erica's face displayed a look of offense over Rogers's assessment of her friend.

"You really think Dr. Dennison would be so irrational as to start her own version of 'Armor Wars'?"

"If that's a comic book reference, I don't know it," Rogers muttered. "What I do know is the look on her face after the attack on Parliament last year, which you saw too. It's the same look she wears or tries to hide whenever she gets around superhumans, mostly when something terrible happens pertaining to them. She blames herself and adds

Genesis

another boulder to her shoulders.

My problem with your friend is when she gets that way and sets her sights on something, she can't be controlled, nor do I have the time to attempt to control her in this given situation, which both you and I know I can't."

Erica turned, staring out the window of New York City. Her mind wandered back to their first battle against the Zombie Nation in Times Square.

"You know …what we're doing is not that different," she whispered. "We're also just delaying the inevitable, whether it's a serum or the newborn coming of age, there's no blowing out this fuse …in the end, all we're going to do is collect and count the collateral damage once it goes off."

Rogers's eyes fell upon Erica after her ominous prediction before returning to the road.

"Whatever," Erica exhaled. "We're almost there."

~ ~

As they pulled up to the Northstar International corporate office, Rogers rolled the vehicle up to the indoor building parking, where their credentials were checked. At the same time, their car went through several security scans and inspections before it was allowed to enter.

Once they parked, they went to the main parking lot entrance and were greeted by a tall, slender Japanese woman in her late twenties. Her silky black hair was tied back in a bun similar to Erica's as she wore stylish square-rimmed prescription glasses, a form-fitting two-piece dress suit with nude pantyhose stockings, and black high heels. She gave them a traditional greeting bow, holding a computer tablet in a burgundy leather case.

"Welcome, Sergeant Rogers, welcome Dr. Champion, my name is Mayako Takahashi, Mr. Shiro's personal executive assistant."

Genesis

"Pleasure to meet you, Ms. Takahashi," Erica bowed, replying.

"Pleasure to meet you, Ms. Takahashi," Rogers also bowed, replying.

"Mr. Shiro is waiting for you upstairs for your two o'clock meeting," I shall take you to him.

They followed her across the building's massive stark white and blue lobby to the main security desk, where they each got temporary badges allowing them to enter the automatic turnstiles.

As they neared the elevator, Ms. Takahashi leaned forward, allowing a camera to scan her face.

"Identifying Mayako Takahashi," a female computerized voice emitted from the audio system. "What floor do you wish to be taken to, please?"

"The main corporate penthouse, please."

Upon her request, the elevator doors slid open.

"Please step in," it requested, "and mind the closing doors."

As they entered, the doors closed behind them as the elevator began ascent to the building's top floor. Rogers and Erica glared at one another as they flanked Ms. Takahashi while taking the elevator ride silently.

"We have reached the main corporate penthouse," the elevator announced. "Please watch your step."

Ms. Takahashi walked off first while Rogers and Erica followed her into the massive semi-loft-style corporate office with the feel of a high-tech penthouse. They passed her desk across from her assistant, who was busy at work. They headed further into the room where Ken Shiro stood adorned in a midnight blue two-piece suit with a crisp, bright white dress shirt underneath, a platinum Rolex, and a black and blue business tie with a

Genesis

pair of black Corthay dress shoes.

Shiro vigorously bridged the gap between them, forgetting about traditional Japanese greetings. He started shaking Erica's hand, and Rogers stayed longer with him.

"Doctor Champion and Sergeant Rogers," Mr. Shiro beamed. "It is an absolute pleasure to meet with both of you. May I offer you either tea or coffee?"

"Thank you, but I'll pass," Abe said, respectfully nodding.

"I'm fine as well, thank you," Erica smiled, replying.

"Well, please come this way," Mr. Shiro gestured. "Thank you, Ms. Takahashi; I will take it from here."

Shiro escorted them further into his office as she bowed before returning to her desk. Rogers's eyes took a tour of the modern, sleek furniture and tech a businessman of Shiro's caliber needed to run his company and the pictures of celebrities, politicians, and presidents he met over the years.

As they passed his desk, heading toward his private conference room, Rogers noticed a trophy case embedded in a wall that housed pictures, trophies, and championship belts from the glory days of Shiro's professional wrestling career. One particular five-plated gold belt with a red leather strap caught his eye.

Ken Shiro held the door open, allowing them to enter. He gestured for them to take a seat wherever they liked while sitting in the chair at the head of his table. Rogers once again glanced around the room with a modern tech feel with its pale white and blue color scene, large three-screen conferencing monitors, surround audio sound system, and the telecom built into the table itself and created to rise and sink into the table upon voice command.

Rogers's eyes returned to a beaming Ken Shiro, who appeared too happy to have them in his presence.

Genesis

"I'll have you know that I carved out a huge chunk of time in my schedule for the honor to sit down with you two," Shiro said. "It is not every day I get to meet with one of the youngest and brightest minds of the twenty-first century, and a former colleague who had a hand in saving this very city and then the world. My god Rogers how long has it been?"

"Think about fourteen years," Rogers estimated.

"Dear lord, we're old," Shiro's face dropped as he fell back in his chair. "That Elimination Chamber match at 'Lord of the Underground' still feels like it was yesterday. I still think Glenn should have let you get your Grand Slam that year before 3BD."

"I picked up my first set of tag belts with Jack Smith that year," Rogers smirked. "So, it wasn't all bad."

"The American Wrecking Crew!" Ken Shiro said, grinning, "You guys were monsters! How is Jack?"

"Retired, he went back home to start a motorbike company, he and his wife are on their second kid. How's the family?"

"They're all good," Shiro nodded, answering. "As you probably read, I never married. Never had to stomach for it, and if I want children around me, I can go to my sea of nieces and nephews. You probably heard about Jagi's accident."

"Yeah, sorry to hear about that."

"Well, that's what happens when you're high as a kite, with a young lady's head in your lap doing ninety on a highway," Shiro answered with a stern, grim tone. "Lucky for him; she pulled her mouth away before the crash, not so lucky for her. Cost him his career, among other things, but at least he's alive. Raoh is finally retiring this year. After the EEW closed, he moved back home and got signed with All Japan Pro. Like he told me, it's a young man's game now. He's looking to teach instead of competing. And Yuku is Yuku."

Shiro's eye shifted between Rogers and Erica, knowing they knew

Genesis

what he meant.

"By the way, my sincere condolences about your wife."

"Thank you," Rogers answered with a somber tone.

"Well, I don't think you brought Dr. Champion here to listen to us drone on about our glory days," Shiro straightened up while clearing his throat. "So how may I help the Regulators?"

Rogers glanced over at Erica as she sat up and prepared to speak.

"We're here to discuss your current superhuman program." She began. "And to get an idea of the progress, you made so far."

Erica's question caused Shiro to narrow his eyes and lean back again in his seat as the ice-cold businessman he was known for came out to play. The politeness was still there with his next question.

"May I ask why?"

"It is a part of an ongoing investigation that we are unfortunately not at liberty to speak about," Rogers jumped in.

Shiro instantly sat up in his seat, leaning forward as if he was bouncing off wrestling ring ropes, resting his forearms in his lap while clasping his hands together before his following sentence.

"Forgive me, but I'm going to need a little bit more detail before I can decide to discuss one of our most top-secret programs with you."

"Right now, we're just covering our bases and investigating if your project may have possibly been compromised." Rogers got to the point with more cryptic talk.

Ken Shiro nodded again as his eyes moved from Rogers to Erica and back to the Sergeant. He placed his clasped hands on top of the table before he spoke.

Genesis

"Based on your secretive wording, I can deduce two things," Shiro sighed. "One, you believe someone within my company has stolen and is currently selling my project on the black market. Two, someone on the black-market side has beaten my company to the finish line and is currently producing a serum that actually works. Do I have it about right, Sergeant Rogers?"

"I am not at liberty to confirm or deny that," Rogers said flatly.

"Fair enough," Shiro said while displaying a soft smile. "Well, I can confidently say that you can scratch us off your list. I am also not at liberty to give you in-depth detail of the project. Rebirth's inner workings, but I can say that we're still some ways off from clinical trials. We're running into the same snag that is afflicting everyone else. The Judgement Day virus is not adopting the human body enough to safely access many of the superhuman abilities it provides. Ours no longer end in fatalities, but the estimated physical damage done to the body is still quite extensive. People will have to wait longer to get their superpowers over the counter."

Neither Eric nor Rogers found the humor in Shiro's joke.

"I have to ask Mr. Shiro," Erica shook her head, inquiring. "Why would you make such a serum accessible to regular people?"

"I can answer that question by asking why someone like yourself who is the leader of this field with full knowledge and understanding of its benefits not leading the charge in research to make all humans globally capable of reaching their fullest potential, Dr. Champion." Shiro politely threw back at her.

"If I had not seen what I had seen, I probably would," Erica exhaled. "But I have seen evil unstable people use their abilities in horrific ways up-close and personal. I don't want to be responsible for arming these types of individuals with that type of power."

Ken Shiro nodded while giving his beard a stroke. He straightened up some more to present his own case.

"First and foremost, allow me to say that we are not the NRA. I

Genesis

agree with you that not everyone should have abilities. We are currently creating a screening process that includes mental and psychological evaluations and background checks that will be enforced. Money and government contracts are not what drives this project, I as well as my company has an ample amount of that. I believe in progression, and I believe the human race has stuck itself in the proverbial mud for far too long and needs a jumpstart. By granting the right individuals the ability to unlock their dormant potential, I believe we can achieve that."

"And what exactly are the parameters of this screening process?" Abe asked while leaning forward himself.

"As I said, it is currently under development," Ken Shiro said with a smile before continuing. "As you both know, now more than ever, regular humans will need access to their inner potential in the coming years. In the past eight years after the events of the Big Bang Two incident, crime …more specifically, crimes of a violent nature committed by regular humans, have decreased worldwide in record numbers. An offense involving gun violence, rape, and child abduction has literally plummeted within the United States, based on the FBI's 2016 report.

Even police brutality and shootings are near nonexistent."

Shiro made eye contact with Abe as he made his last statement.

"And the reason for this is because, for once, the criminal element out there is afraid. They are scared because it is almost impossible to determine who has abilities and who does not. A record number of criminals have been put down by either people with superhuman abilities or those who have taken up the mantle to become superheroes. Now, you may argue that some use their powers for evil in their place, but even that is less than one percent. And those that do are taken care of by heroes such as yourselves.

The last attempted mass school shooting was three years ago, with four fatalities. Two were students, and the other two were the assailants killed by a student and a teacher with superhuman abilities.

And right here in New York, a gunman purposely opened fire

Genesis

targeting women and children at a rally, and there were zero fatalities.

And here's an even more significant fact that you cannot refute: gun sales within the United States have taken a severe dive because what good is a weapon that is ineffective against an individual who is either impervious to it, evade it with ease, or packing more firepower.

The motto is no longer 'The only way to stop a bad guy with a gun is with a good guy with a gun,' it's 'the only way to stop a bad guy period is to be a superhuman'...preferably a good one."

The smile on Mr. Shiro's face indicated that he meant his last statement as a joke.

The expression on Abe's and Erica's faces revealed his humor was not a hit with them.

"The world is changing faster than we could ever imagine," Shiro said, getting serious again. "There is a new generation of humans who are slowly becoming stronger while people like yourselves continue to multiply. Leaving regular humans like myself with only two options right now. Wither and die or find a way to evolve like the rest of you. I choose to evolve, then die, and I owe it to my fellow man to give them that chance as well."

Rogers and Erica's silence indicated they did not entirely agree with his ideas. Still, they also did not come to get into a debate with him about it.

"Well, thank you for meeting with us," Rogers said with a calm smile." I'm sorry we could not elaborate more."

Erica took the verbal hint that it was time for them to leave as they stood up together.

"Not at all; it was a pleasure having you both here," Ken Shiro said with a bright smile, standing up. "Dr. Champion, when you have some time, I would like to invite you back and give you a tour of our R&D lab in New Jersey. It would be nice to get your perspective."

Genesis

"I will consider that," Erica answered with a subtle smile.

As they exited the conference room, Ms. Takahashi waited for them in his office to escort them back to their vehicle.

"It was a pleasure seeing you again, Rogers," Shiro said with a grin while shaking his hand. "It was great to see someone from the ring days. Please also stop by anytime you're in New York; we'll get a drink together or something."

"I will consider it."

Shiro caught Abe's eyes, glancing at the trophy case again.

"Do you miss it?" Shiro asked.

"Sometimes," Rogers admitted.

"If you had the chance to be superhuman or a wrestler, which would you pick."

"A wrestler, any day of the week."

A genuine sad smile came over Shiro's face as he knew what Rogers meant by his answer. Rogers turned, following Erica, who exited Shiro's office beside Ms. Takahashi.

~ ~

Twenty minutes later, they were back in their vehicle with sad faces, heading back to JFK airport.

"Well, that was a waste of time," Erica blurted out.

"I take it he wasn't lying," Rogers asked, glancing at her.

"Nope, he was telling the truth the whole time, and I didn't even need to read his mind."

Genesis

Her eyes glowed, revealing the artificial contact lenses she wore during the meeting. Erica projected the data onto the passenger dashboard of the vehicle.

"Heart rate, other vitals, and involuntary movement were all that of a man telling the truth."

As Rogers waited for the light to turn red, his ears picked up a tap on his driver's side car door window.

"Jesus!" Erica jumped, clutching her chest in fright, screaming.

Rogers looked up to see a woman with thinly braided cornrow hair in a high-tech multi-color kabuki mask wearing a form-fitting grey and white bodysuit with matching tabi-shaped running shoes.

"Shintobe."

"You got a minute to talk?" She asked, using a voice changer that emitted from her mask.

"Well …"

"Meet me at the Chelsea Piers."

Without a word, she sped off in that direction. Rogers turned to a rattled Erica, still trying to catch her heartbeat.

"I can't stand that woman," Erica growled. "She does the same crap when she shows up at the Ranch! None of my sensors or mental abilities can detect her once she starts moving! It's either the outfit or that stupid mask she has on!"

"The fact that you can't figure her out really irks you?" Rogers asked with a smirk.

"Yes!"

"Welcome to my world."

Genesis

Erica cut Rogers a dirty look as he turned the vehicle to the West Side Highway, heading toward their impromptu meeting.

~~~~~~~~~~~~~~~~~~~~~~~~~~~~~~~~

Several minutes later, Rogers parked their vehicle and walked out to the piers, followed by an irritated Erica where a waiting Shintobe stood with her back turned, looking out onto the Hudson River.

"Okay, we're here," Rogers announced. "Mind telling us what this is about?"

She casually turned around to face them.

"Hey, kid."

Erica answered her with a sneer.

"Still don't like being snuck up on." Shintobe deduced.

"Come on, Shintobe, why'd you ask us out here?" Rogers got back to the point.

"You tell me, Rogers. Why were you up in my brother's office today?"

"Following a possible lead," he answered. "Nothing more."

"Your 'leads' usually end up with some form of mass destruction out of a Michael Bay movie," Shintobe pointed out. "So, you can see my concern."

"It's not like that," Rogers flatly reassured her. "Your brother is not a suspect."

"Glad to hear that," Shintobe snorted. "Now, do me a favor and keep your distance from my family going forward. Anything you need to ask them, you can go through me, are we clear?"

Genesis

Erica's eyes widened, stunned by the underlined hostility as Rogers stood with a stern, unappreciative glare of her outright warning.

"I'll take your silence as a yes."

They were her last words as she turned and bolted, running off the pier. She jetted on the water across the Hudson River over to New Jersey.

Erica quietly strolled up to him, giving Rogers a genuine look of concern. He slowly turned, looking back at her.

"So, uh … was there something more to you two …?"

Rogers walked off, neither answering nor giving her a second look, heading back to the car. Erica quickly followed behind, believing he would drive off without her.

~ ~

At the corporate penthouse, Ken Shiro stood quietly before his trophy case. Ms. Takahashi approached him with a man in his late thirties with a face hardened by a life riding on the wild side. His hair was a deep spikey blue, which was a contrast to his light blue eyes. His black faded leather jacket and a white t-shirt covered the tattoos that started on both sides of his neck down to his shoulders and upper biceps. His outfit was finished with dark designer jeans and black polished leather boots.

"Mr. Shiro, your brother is here."

"Thank you, Ms. Takahashi. Could you and Ms. Hasegawa please take a coffee break? Thirty minutes should suffice."

"Yes, Mr. Shiro."

Ms. Takahashi respectfully bowed before taking her leave.

Ken Shiro's younger brother nervously stood silent, waiting as the assistants left, getting onto the elevator.

Genesis

"Hello Jagi, how are you doing today?" Ken Shiro asked, still looking at the case. "Guess who you just missed?"

"Who?" His brother asked as he nervously fidgeted.

"The American Fighting Machine himself Abe Rogers, who, as you know, is now the leader of the United States government super-soldier unit known as the Regulators. He and Dr. Erica Champion, who is also a member of the same unit, stopped by to pay me a visit."

"What the hell did they want?"

"They came to ask me without asking me about my bio-upgraders," Ken Shiro sighed. "You know, the ones they took from ISIS terrorists during a military raid in Iraq. The group that Miguel Ángel Castillo sold to, the same drug lord who I told you was a bad idea to sell to, but you did anyway …you fucking idiot."

A cold, blank expression fell over the younger Shiro brother as he swallowed his spit.

"Brother …I swear …I didn't …"

"I specifically outlined to you based on our first initial meeting with Castillo why it was a bad idea to sell to him," Ken Shiro shook his head, interrupting him. "That based on his attitude and demeanor, he was not one to follow the rules, that we could not trust him. That he would most likely take our product and do something stupid like selling it to some terrorist group or North Korea, which survey says is the fastest way to fall under the radar of a unit like Rogers that I have painstakingly and meticulously taken measures to avoid."

"Brother, I know I screwed up," Jagi nervously stepped back. "But I fixed it …I took care of …"

Before another word was uttered from his mouth, Ken Shiro's youngest brother was violently slammed face-first into the floor of his older brother's office by some unknown dominant force. He was brought to his knees and hammered three more times into the flooring before he was lifted

Genesis

into the air. Jagi Shiro clutched his throat, gasping as his busted nose began to instantly heal while he was suspended in midair.

His older brother casually strolled up, looking up at him with his eyes rolled back into his head.

"Did I ask you to speak, you little shit?" Ken Shiro inquired. "You took care of nothing; you only did what you were told. Or else I would have been the one turning you into a friggin ball."

Jagi gurgled as his eyes fluttered until the unknown force released him. He struck the floor hard, gasping and choking as he took deep breaths, forcing air back into his lungs.

"I swear on our sweet dear mother in heaven, I am getting so tired of cleaning up your messes. If you weren't my little brother Jagi, I'd tear your limbs off like a cockroach. Get up."

Jagi groaned as he obeyed his brother, getting to his feet. Ken Shiro began to straighten out his jacket so he did not appear to be worked over.

"Now, I want you to pay close attention as I instruct you how to fix this."

Genesis

CHAPTER 13

October 2015, The Grand Canyon National Park, early morning Colorado time,

Three days later, after Horus's takeover of the project EVOlution base, Dr. Alexander and his team labored around the clock to complete the project the Ancient tasked them to do. With only one meal break and two-hour sleep intervals, the fear of a painful, gruesome death was the principal motivation that kept them all functioning.

However, it was more than fear for Dr. Alexander that kept him toiling away at the project the self-proclaimed superhuman god assigned to him. The new technology he created dwarfed any other technological advancement Earth had ever made and its endless possibilities. The knowledge Horus implanted within him kept him driven to complete his task.

Before Horus took his life, which was an all-high probability, he wanted to see it completed and how it worked.

He was so driven that being stark naked with his staff was no longer an issue as he stared with amazement at what they were creating.

While marveling at the reconstructed incubation chambers, a male technician approached him to give his report.

"Dr. Alexander, per your instructions, we have completed work on the four incubation chambers."

"Restructuring pods." Dr. Alexander softly corrected him.

"Restructuring pods?" The technician asked with a knitted brow.

"He told me their name," Dr. Alexander swallowed. "When he gave me instruction on how to recreate them."

Genesis

"Oh," the technician nodded, accepting his answer.

The scientist within him wanted to ask "What, Why, Who, How, and Where?" The human within that feared for his life kept his tongue still and accepted the doctor's answer.

"The construction of the fifth pod will be completed shortly," the technician continued. "However, the artificial intelligence required to operate these pods …"

"He will create it," Dr. Alexander answered with his eyes still on the pods. "Lord Horus will be the one programming these machines, not us."

Once again, the lab technician gave a simple nod, accepting the doctor's answer while praying that his thoughts did not incur the wrath of a self-proclaimed deity.

"Oh, dear god," The technician gasped while stepping back.

His words of fear brought Dr. Alexander out of his trance. He turned to where his terrified eyes and some of his other colleagues were staring.

The female lab technician who departed with the biochemist to see to Horus's needs staggered in with a dazed look and tears that would not stop falling as her arms were wrapped tightly around her bare chest; in her right hand, she clutched a small, clear plastic container with a thick white liquid inside.

Her body rattled as she approached Dr. Alexander and extended the container to him.

"Dr. Henderson?"

"Here is Lord Horus's sample for the rebirthing," Dr. Henderson said with a shaky raspy voice.

"Dr. Henderson," Dr. Alexander asked with a fearful lump in his

Genesis

throat. "What happened to Dr. Pierce?"

Dr. Henderson erupted into hysterical tears, collapsing to her knees, forcing two other female technicians to rush to her side.

Dr. Alexander painfully winced at the sound of Horus speaking within his mind.

"Come to my chambers, slave. I have need of you."

~ ~

Minutes later, Dr. Alexander went down the individual sleeping quarters' hallways, where his staff resided. Based on Dr. Henderson's demeanor after she returned from Horus, he wanted to take his time getting there to mentally prepare himself for any possible horrors he would see. That wasn't possible with Horus monitoring his very thoughts and movements. Whatever he was about to see, he would have to try his best to hide his emotions both mentally and visually.

He neared Dr. Henderson's sleeping quarters with her door wide open and the sound of a television playing.

Dr. Alexander halted briefly to gather some additional strength before entering the room.

As he walked in, Dr. Alexander shuddered upon seeing Dr. Pierce's lifeless body sprawled out, face-up on the bed. Her tear-stained eyes were wide open as she looked directly at him. His horrified eyes slowly turned to Horus in the buff sitting in a chair. The Ancient's attention was drawn to the flat-screen television on the wall playing a Seinfeld episode.

"She's not dead," Horus nonchalantly answered. "I just imprisoned her within her own mind for being insolent."

Dr. Alexander turned, looking closer to see her chest barely rise up and down, indicating that life still flowed within her.

"What you mortals find amusing these days is quite baffling,"

Genesis

Horus scoffed. "A real wager would be how many one can bed within a day, not how long one can last without pleasuring one's self."

"Lord Horus," Dr. Alexander carefully bowed, asking. "Did …something happen with Dr. Pierce?"

"For a learned mortal, you asked the most idiotic questions," Horus snorted. "If I was pleased, would she be lying there like that?"

The doctor stood there, unsure how to answer without sharing a fate similar to hers.

"In my time, a woman would strangle her own mother for the opportunity to be bedded by a god," Horus continued. "She would feast on her same mother's entrails if it would allow her to be lucky enough to breed for one. Yet all this pale sow could do was bitterly weep with thoughts of her betrothed that she betrayed by being bedded by me.

She believed that I, the king of gods, was violating her.

So, I showed her what true violation was.

I allowed her to see her betrothed again through my eyes as I took away his sight, his ability to use his arms and legs, and then his voice. Then I made her watch as I took away his ability to breathe. I made her watch as he slowly suffocated to death, terrified and alone, while I brought her to climax. Now, she is reliving the event over and over again until I choose to release her. She now feels how I have felt for all of these centuries, to be forever apart from the one you love and imprisoned to see her death replay before you for eternity."

Dr. Alexander's body violently vibrated as he imagined the maddening hell poor Dr. Pierce was enduring at that moment.

"Was the seed I provided sufficient to your needs?"

"Yes, it was Lord Horus," Dr. Alexander answered with a cleared throat. "The sample was extremely healthy and potent."

Genesis

"Of course, it was; it came from a god."

Horus fluttered his eyes in disgust, then changed the subject, getting down to business.

"You are nearing the completion of your task. I am pleased."

"You provided clear and easy instructions to follow, Lord Horus," Dr. Alexander answered with a swallow. "Making the proper modification to our old designs was not hard to do; we were able to recreate the elements Alder and Ember with our particle accelerator.

However, the power needed to …"

"Worry not of that slave," Horus cut him off. "The energy needed for the final task is mine to acquire, and I shall rip it from its source soon enough. This facility has the power required for the pods to perform the next task once they have been completed."

Horus grew tired and irritated at the show and shut off the flat screen with a wave before rising to his feet.

"The other slaves can finish the completion of the pods without your observation and instruction. I wish to be fashioned with proper attire; you will then send back the curvy one and another female to service and bathe me again. Afterward, we shall descend down to the lower levels to retrieve my Sekhmet."

"As you wish, Lord Horus," Dr. Alexander said with a sad nod.

"Slave …I shall give you an option," Horus said with a devious grin. "I shall allow you and the rest of the slaves to clothe yourselves in exchange for me striking down every living cast member of that show I just watched."

Ice cold, mortified sweat washed over the doctor as a sinister Ancient clearly toying with him awaited his answer.

"My people and I … are quite comfortable the way we are," Dr.

Genesis

Alexander carefully said.

"I wonder if I was to pose the question to the rest of the slaves if their answers would be the same as yours," Horus asked with ominous curiosity. "Say not again that I have not been a gracious god towards you."

"Yes, my lord," the doctor fretfully bowed.

Horus exited the room first, with Dr. Alexander following behind him.

Dr. Alexander quickly allowed his eyes to fall again to where Dr. Pierce lay. He wanted to ask about her, to beg for her release from her torturous, inhuman hell.

His crippling fear would not allow him to gather the strength to forge the courage to beseech Horus to release her.

He trailed Horus, keeping a respectful distance from him while feverishly fighting to keep his thoughts in check.

Walking back to the lab's observation section, Dr. Alexander choked due to the foul stench that strangled the air. It was a combination of the female lab technician's corpse rotting on the floor, the male lab technician still embedded into the wall, and a naked Graves kneeling where Horus left him for almost three days straight.

A faint groan and his violent, uncontrollable trembling were the only indicators that he was still amongst the living as he knelt in his own urine and fecal matter. Horus walked past him, ignoring him entirely as he observed the work done on the redesigned restructuring pods.

"Very well-done, slave," Horus nodded with approval. "You do your master and craft proud."

"Thank you, my lord." Dr. Alexander got out with a gasp.

Out of nowhere, a scowl fell over Horus's face as he sniffed the air in disgust.

Genesis

"Such a foul and odious stench, from where does it permeate from?"

A cold sweat washed over Dr. Alexander, unsure once again if and how he should answer Horus's question. He watched as Horus moved about the room, whiffing the air until he returned to Graves standing over him.

"Oh, tis you." Horus snorted with a sarcastic sneer on his face. "You still cling to mortal coil?"

Graves feebly whimpered as the Ancient stooped down to examine him.

"I will say that I am pretty impressed; back in my time, men your age would have died after day two.

"Please ... master ...please ..." Graves choked.

"Master?" Horus asked with narrowed eyes. "Do you see a lash in my hand? You still see a mortal before you?"

Horus rose to his feet in disappointment.

"Clearly, you acquire an additional three days to ..."

"Please, Lord Horus!" A broken Graves cried out. "My god ... please have mercy on me! Please!"

A sadistic Cheshire grim formed on Horus's face; with just a thought, he released Graves from his knelt position, causing him to collapse into filth. The Secretary of Defense blubbered where he lay as the Ancient turned to an unnerved Dr. Alexander watching the scene.

"Command two of your male help to take this thing at my feet, clean it up, feed it, and put it to rest. I will have need for it later."

"Yes, my lord," Dr. Alexander nodded.

"Then have them clean up this mess on the floor and get rid of

Genesis

these carcasses."

With a thought, Horus removed the rivets holding the decaying corpse against the wall, causing it to hit the floor with a hard-wet thud that made Dr. Alexander leap from his skin.

"They have served their purpose; this room must be properly cleansed for the rebirthing ritual later. I will be thoroughly perturbed if my nostrils are violated by the stench currently in this room."

"Yes, my lord, I shall make it so."

Horus turned his attention back to Graves.

"Many rivers shall you cross, boy, before you can earn my forgiveness. Many stones shall you crawl on before I allow you to die."

~~~~~~~~~~~~~~~~~~~~~~~~~~~~~~~~~~

After Dr. Alexander assigned the difficult task of dealing with Graves and the corpses to two of his male lab technicians. The doctor followed the Ancient to the R&D fabrication room, where they meticulously constructed Horus's new attire.

During that time, as the doctor made the commanded adjustments before creating the final outfit, it dawned on him that Horus invited him to converse with him instead of being silent and doing as he was told. He wanted to hear his voice. He wanted someone to talk to and engage.

It was the small chink in his armor, the sliver of human trauma that was exposed due to the aftermath of being entombed alive for thousands of years.

The doctor did his best to exploit that weakness using nerve-racking precautions to take some of the fear out of his predicament, even for a little while.

It did work for a little while as the Egyptian god's tone softened towards him, and he considered and implemented some of the doctor's

Genesis

suggested alterations to his outfit. As the gear was finalized and fabricated, Dr. Alexander attentively listened as the god of kingship and war ranted his observations on how the world had changed since his imprisonment. Every now and then, he would ask for the doctor's opinion. Alexander would carefully give as honest a view as possible with the knowledge that Horus would know if he was lying.

Their candid conversation endured all the way up to finishing his outfit. Horus mentally called upon Dr. Henderson to bring another female lab technician of her choosing to see to his needs and dress him.

With extensive knowledge of ancient Egyptian culture and mythology, Dr. Henderson came prepared with a blue-eyed young woman with almond curly hair and the right amount of shape and curves she knew could hold herself together during the traumatic ordeal they were about to embark on.

As they walked in carrying several clean rags, towels, four buckets of warm and cold water, deodorant, body oil, and a bottle of Hugo Boss "Boss the Scent" cologne, they took from a male technician, the brief familiarities ended between Dr. Alexander and Horus.

"Do I need to verbally instruct a servant to kneel while his god is being attended to?" The Ancient dryly asked without giving him a second look.

A lump formed in Dr. Alexander's throat as he dropped to his knees. It stayed there as he witnessed evil incarnate at its worst. With his head down, he endured, keeping his mind clear and his tears from falling while Horus savagely had his way again with Dr. Henderson and the young woman right before him.

Through their sounds of pleasure, the father of his own daughter felt the violating truth both women forced themselves to hide while his weak heart shattered.

When Horus was finished and satisfied, he stood there as both women cleaned him up, dried him off, applied body oil to him along with the cologne, and then proceeded to dress him in his new attire. When they

Genesis

finished their task, he dismissed them, leaving just him and the doctor once again.

Horus stood admiring himself in his new attire in an enormous reflective mirror as Dr. Alexander waited for his approval. His clothing was comprised of both modern and ancient designs. He was dressed in a form-fitting dark blue carbon fiber bodysuit and thick, heavy blue shin-high tactical boots that matched his outfit's color. Per his instructions, the 'Eye of Horus' symbol was embossed in gold on both the bodysuit's upper arms, while a set of golden wings crossing one another was imprinted on the torso and back of the suit.

The suit and boots alone gave him the appearance of a force not to be reckoned with.

The additions of a traditional two-piece Egyptian skirt with a metallic belt, bracers, collar, pauldrons, and headdress crown-shaped and designed with the colors of blue sapphire and gold etched with ancient Egyptian markings from his time echoed the self-proclaimed designation that he believed the world would soon know him by.

Horus wore a sinister smirk as he admired himself in a full-length mirror.

"Aside from being given the title of sky god, I was also bestowed the titles of war and hunting. Do you believe my new wardrobe fits those stations?"

"Yes, I do, my lord Horus," Dr. Alexander weakly answered. "With all of my heart, I do."

Horus turned, giving himself an umpteenth look in the mirror.

Not only do I believe you slave, but I am also inclined to agree with you; very well done."

"Thank you, my lord."

"A poor, lowly shepherd boy was I before my physical rise to

Genesis

power," Horus said. "The youngest of three brothers and a sister, I was poorly treated and would inherit nothing. I would be a beggar cast out of my home after my father passed on. Those were the promises my eldest brother whispered into my ear every chance he got when he was not abusing me in other ways.

But then fate would step in and bring those we hailed as gods to my front door. And after bathing myself and my siblings in their 'godly light,' they chose me to be 'reborn again.' I still remember the look on each of their faces, especially my idiotic eldest brother."

Horus cackled to himself as he retold his origin story.

"Do you know Horus is not even my name? Amun-Ra gave me the name the first day I set foot on their airship, and I gladly took it as my own, casting away the name my wretched father gave me.

My rebirth was painless; I went to sleep a mere mortal in a cocoon softer than the bed of any king to have walked the Earth and emerged into something that words at that time could not describe. What fascinated me more than the physical attributes bestowed upon me was how my mind could grasp and comprehend the knowledge placed before me. Oh, how I devoured it and craved for more.

I cared not that those who I thought to be my gods were visitors from another world. The fact that they chose me to bestow this new gift of life to me was enough. To me, they were my real fathers, for they had given my life purpose …meaning.

They even gave me the love of another, my beautiful Sekhmet …that also was not her birth name …her fate before her rebirth was more morbid than my own. We found comfort in one another, shed away each other's past pain, and looked forward to a brighter future. We dreamt of the day we would be wed when our fathers would take us with them to their world or leave us with the proper knowledge to shepherd our world to a better tomorrow."

A cold, wounded scowl fell over Horus's face.

Genesis

"That was until I learned their true purpose for us, that they were only using us and, like my older brother, would soon discard us when the time came. Oh, how that revelation wounded me so. But I would not go willingly into the afterlife like some mangy mongrel. I had power and the knowledge of how to acquire more power.

I would be the author of my life, and my chapters would be written with the blood of those who would dare oppose me, beginning with my adoptive fathers."

His face softened a bit as a sliver of embarrassment emerged.

"Alas, the tale I attempted to write was not played out as expected, but nonetheless, here I still stand."

The Ancient once again turned to Dr. Alexander, looking down at him.

"And the moral of this tale slave is that no one really cares how the tale begins, or the meat in between, they care about how it ends, how one finishes. Here I stand with all of my enemies long removed from mortal coil …distant vapors of thought, while I am set to take proper rule of this world as I should with none to oppose me."

A baleful smile grew on Horus' face as he plucked the doctor's thoughts, examining them.

"You do not believe."

"No! No lord Horus!" Dr. Alexander stammered, sinking lower to the floor, "I believe …"

"Do not lie to me, slave," Horus calmly cut him off. "Ye forget I can read thy thoughts. Tis fine; some faith has to be earned and not blindly given. I forgive your lack of faith. In time when you witness with your own eyes that my power has no equal, you will be allowed to properly repent."

Dr. Alexander took a deep swallow into his dry throat as his imagination ran wild of what his repentance in the future might be should

Genesis

Horus succeed.

"Rise, slave," Horus commanded, "We venture to the lower levels of this facility to retrieve my beloved and begin the ritual toward her rebirth."

~ ~

Pushing a gurney, Dr. Alexander tailed behind the ancient Egyptian, taking the elevator to the research facility's bottom level that held Sekhmet's body. His naked body shivered as they exited into the refrigerated room. At the same time, Horus strolled up to the transparent casket chamber, where her body floated in a nutrient bath. He looked at the computers connected to the cylinder designed to take around-the-clock readings and scans on a cellular level.

With a thought, Horus shut down the computers and opened the casket. He used his telekinetic powers to remove her body and head, placing them on the gurney. Dr. Alexander quickly went to work respectfully, covering her remains to begin transport back to the central lab.

The ride back was silent as Dr. Alexander stood fighting to keep his rattling body and mind in check.

As they returned to the central lab, Dr. Alexander found his staff huddled together as they waited for Horus and him to return.

The Ancient did not give the group a second look as he stood in the center of the lab, slightly raising both his hands.

With a thought, all of the terminals came to life as the screens lit up with advanced coding and algorithms to create the programming needed to give birth to the ultimate artificial intelligence required to operate the five restructuring pods before him.

Everyone present forgot about their personal traumas for that one moment as they bore witness to an ancient superhuman taking advanced

Genesis

alien knowledge to create and perfect something that took humanity over seven hundred years to conceptualize and scratch the surface.

With the lowering of his hands, all of the room's computers went dark for a second. When they rebooted, each screen displayed the Eye of Horus as a soft female voice announced itself on the base's audio system.

"Greetings, mighty Horus, my name is Meskhenet, how may I serve you?"

"Meskhenet, activate, program, and run full diagnostics of all five restructuring pods."

"As you command."

Every mortal present took a meek step closer as the five pods came to life. Each display screen ran down a sea of data and functions they would soon be capable of executing.

"Restructuring pods are fully functional, my lord."

Horus first approached the four original incubation cloning chambers re-engineered per his instructions to Dr. Alexander into Annunaki restructuring pods, giving them each one final, thorough inspection. He took his time, finally reviewing the fifth pod built from scratch. He began to circle it, running his hand across parts of it while leaning in to take a closer look at the detailed work.

"Very good slave," Horus nodded, approving, "What of the other matter I commanded for you to build for me?"

"It is over here, my lord," Dr. Alexander said quickly, motioning.

The doctor approached the large metallic silver and golden mechanized falcon, twice the original organic bird's size, sitting on a sturdy metal perch. It appeared asleep as its head hung down while its orange crystal eyes remained dormant of life.

Several wires remained attached to it via open ports on its head and

Genesis

chest.

Horus leaned in, running his hand across its Alder-formed body, examining the detail of the craftsmanship Dr. Alexander and his team painfully used to put it together.

"Very good slave," Horus said, grinning his approval. "You do your craft proud. Meskhenet, give life and power to your brother Seker."

"As you command Lord Horus."

The lights in the facility flickered while the computer screens once again lit up with advanced coding and algorithms, minus one lone screen that displayed the base's reactor pumping nuclear energy into the newly constructed familiar to give it life.

"Artificial intelligence matrix has been created. Power core charging is completed. Rebooting Seker."

The mortals in the room flinched as the enormous cybernetic falcon's eyes emitted an orange glow as it came to life, stretching out its massive wingspan. It unleashed a loud screech before retracting its wings and bowing its head to Horus.

"Seker at your eternal service master." The familiar announced with a thick, intimidating voice.

Horus displayed a sinister smirk as he petted the top of his newest servant's head.

"I wish to run a test on one of the restructuring pods to see if they function the way they should."

"Yes, my lord," Dr. Alexander agreed with a nod.

He motioned to his staff as two male lab technicians left the huddle and returned with a male chimpanzee in a cage. A cold chill ran down his spine as he turned to see Horus giving him a dull look.

Genesis

"What is that?"

"It is a lab animal," the doctor answered as his legs violently shook. "We use them for …"

"I know the purpose of the beast," Horus coldly cut him off. "I do not require an animal to run proper test."

Before Dr. Alexander could ask what he required, Horus singled out one of the male lab technicians who brought forth the Chimpanzee and broke his right leg in half at the shin with a thought. Blood-curdling screams erupted from everyone present as he snapped his right arm at the elbow and cracked three of his ribs."

"Oh, god! Oh god!" bawled the young man lying helpless on the floor in unimaginable pain.

Horus opened the restructuring pod's hatch while employing his telekinetic abilities to carry the broken lab tech over to the pod, dropping him inside it and closing the lid.

"Meskhenet begin medical procedures."

"As you command Lord Horus."

The pod lit up as lights within formed a grid, taking a scan of the technician from the top of his head down to his feet.

"Detecting human male, Caucasian, age twenty-five with broken left tibia, broken right olecranon, and torn right posterior ligament. The patient also has a broken right lateral epicondyle, torn right radial collateral ligament, and three cracked ribs on the patient's right side, one of the cracked ribs has punctured patient's right lung, proceeding with immediate sedation and repair."

A hissing sound inside the chamber as a clear gas put the lab technician straight to sleep.

"Opening injured areas," Meskhenet announced.

Genesis

With thin laser beams, the pod sliced open the technician's skin at the shin, the abdominal area where his ribs were broken, and the broken elbow. Energy fields pushed open the skin on each body part, revealing the damaged areas.

"Removing damaged parts of left tibia, right olecranon, right posterior ligament, right lateral epicondyle, right radial collateral ligament, and ribs. Removing splinters from punctured right lung, followed by sanitization, and cellular seal."

Dr. Alexander and the rest of his team found the courage to move closer and watch in amazement as high-precision lasers sliced away the damaged bone, leaving even cleaner areas. A green disinfectant solution was fired directly into the wound located in the lung, followed by a white beam that held the injury together and caused the cells to multiply, resealing the lung.

"Initiating cellular regeneration on damaged areas."

Similar white beams created energy fields on a quantum level around the other damaged areas, re-growing bone and tissue while fusing them together to reform the broken parts.

"Sealing skin."

Like the lung, the three areas cut open by the pod were held together by three energy fields. At the same time, rapid cellular regeneration sealed the wounds. The technician lay there in peaceful sleep, looking as if he had no traces of the massive surgery he had just undergone.

"Surgical repairs have been completed," Meskhenet announced, "Bringing the patient out of sedation. Final analysis recommends rest, healthy liquids, and no strenuous physical activities for the next two weeks."

Another clear vapor entered the chamber, slowly waking up the technician. As the pod door raised back up, he sat up, slightly dazed and whimpering close to tears as he ran his hands across the once-broken parts of his body, remembering what happened to him and unable to comprehend

Genesis

how he was whole again. An impatient Horus leaned in, making eye contact with him.

"Less ye would like me to break all of your limbs this time, remove thy wretched self from pod."

The horrified young man wailed as he spilled out of the pod, hitting the tile floor hard. As he weakly sobbed, crawling back to the fold, two of his braver teammates rushed out, helping him to his feet and dragging him back to the group.

"Slave! Bring forth my beloved Sekhmet and the sample!" Horus bellowed his command. "The remainder of you kneel in reverence!"

Obediently, Dr. Alexander's traumatized staff either fell to one knee or sprawled belly-first on the cold floor as the doctor pushed the gurney forward, bringing it right next to the pod. He then quickly ran to a smaller cart, picking up a silver canister with black lettering and bringing it over.

Dr. Alexander dropped to one knee, bowing his head while holding the cylinder casing up. He fretfully waited for Horus to take it from him.

"Remember this day well, slaves," Horus's voice boomed. "For this day shall be remembered as the day the House of Horus was conceived!"

Horus reverently removed the sheet covering her remains with his hands this time. He lifted her body from the gurney, placing it into the pod. He took up her severed head, momentarily putting her forehead against his. He kissed her cold, decayed lips softly before gently positioning them where they would sit if they were still attached to the body before closing the pod door again.

"Meskhenet, activate for medical procedure."

A low hum came from the pod as an LED display on the pod's window lit up for the second time.

Genesis

"Detecting a deceased body of a human female, age estimated to be five thousand and six years old, Egyptian, the cause of death is decapitation. Due to massive deterioration, unable to revive with current medical procedures, how would you like to proceed?" The artificially intelligent servant asked.

"Locate and retrieve viable eggs for replication," Horus commanded.

The restructuring pod emitted a bright yellow light as it hummed, beginning to scan Sekhmet's body.

"Scan detects one viable egg with sufficient genetic material and only fourteen percent deterioration," Meskhenet indicated.

"Isolate the egg, destroy the body, and replicate five healthy samples."

The pod lit up again as Horus moved closer to view a hard-constructed light piercing the corpse's abdomen, pulling out the over five-thousand-year-old egg. He then placed a hand on the pod's glass as his countenance softened due to a sliver of emotion squeezing out. In contrast, the pod used the energies within it to atomize away the remains of his former love.

"Additional genetic material is required to perform replication. Shall I synthesize it?"

"Negative," Horus answered. "Ye shall add genetic material from subject Dennison eight-thirteen-zero-eight. Isolate all demi-god genetic traits, including properties for regenerative healing."

"As you command Lord Horus, I am prepared to receive the material."

A section of the pod opened as Dr. Alexander opened the canister before handing it to Horus. The Ancient inserted it into the circular slot.

"We shall be reunited again very soon, my beloved," Horus

Genesis

whispered softly, "very soon."

    It became as hard as granite again as he watched the near-empty chamber fill with a thick blue-green liquid solution, submerging the egg. As the replication process began, a dark, murky, reddish tint was added to the sample's solution within the canister.

Genesis

CHAPTER 14

May 2017, eighteen hundred hours military time, Bridgeport, California,

Adrian, dressed in a white long-sleeve dress shirt, dark blue jeans, and polished black boots that he spit-shined for an hour, made his way to the gleaming midnight black curvy two-seater sports coupe. Erica helped him fabricate it to the eight-speed clutch transmission and the two hundred and seventy miles per hour ion engine powering it.

He strolled to the car as its gull-wing door on the driver's side opened upon recognizing him approaching it.

"Hello!"

"Holy Fu…!"

Adrian jumped out of his skin, clutching his chest as Angie stepped out of nowhere, scaring him half to death. Bent over, catching a breath, sucked in some air, and wiggled out the initial chill.

~ ~

Since she put her body on the line to protect him against the Draugr, Adrian had been more tolerant of Angie's antics.

After she found out about his girlfriend, Angie demanded to know her full name.

When Adrian refused to tell her, Angie hacked his phone and began trolling her social media.

Adrian then gave her a stern warning, backed by Erica, to not interfere in his relationship.

Genesis

Angie painfully complied.

She resorted to the only tactical card she could play with no other options.

Every time Adrian went on a date, Angie showed up before he left to wish him well and give him fun-filled tips, such as the growth rate of people being harvested for their organs or men being turned into prostitutes by their girlfriends.

Although she would do it with a bright, creepy smile, he learned to endure it, thanking her for her advice.

He began to view Angie as a little girl with a next-door neighbor crush, not to be entertained and nothing more.

~ ~

"What's up, Angie?"

"You look very hot tonight. Are you departing for your date?"

"Uh, yeah," Adrian coughed.

"Very good," Angie said with a cheery smile. "I hope you have a delightful evening tonight."

"Why, thank you, Angie," he replied, smirking.

"Please note that the CDC has put out a statement that sexually transmitted diseases such as Chlamydia, Gonorrhea, Syphilis, and Genital Herpes are all on the rise and have become more resilient to antibiotics," she informed him with a chirpy voice.

Adrian's body stiffened as he turned to her, narrowing his eyes.

"Good to know."

He said it with a sarcastic smile followed by an eye roll before

Genesis

turning to his car.

"What the hell are you waiting for? You know where to go."

Angie stood waving goodbye as Adrian's car started up and drove itself up to the ramp of one of the Tornados, where it was securely locked into place. As Adrian followed up behind it, the rear hatch closed while the lift returned the ship to the surface.

"Welcome aboard, Mr. Esposito," Maxine's voice emitted over the audio system.

"Thanks, Maxine."

"Please strap yourself in; we shall arrive in Los Angelis in approximately fifteen minutes."

"You're not going to make a mistake and let Angie pilot, right?"

"She has been barred from flying you ever since she flew you to Hawaii, which caused you to be late for your previous third date. The Miss has confirmed this with you on several occasions."

"Just checking," Adrian swallowed.

He did as he was told, taking a seat up front. The minute the hanger roof opened up, the Tornado auto-piloted by Maxine went upward using its VTOL mode and then took off in the direction of Los Angeles.

~ ~

Thirty minutes later, Adrian showed his credentials and drove out of the Los Angeles International Airport after being dropped off by the Tornado. The ion-powered engine whined as he darted in and out of traffic, racing to remain early for his date.

Adrian quickly stopped at a local flower shop to pick up a large bouquet of fresh lilies mixed with tulips before arriving at a luxury high-rise building in downtown LA. As he took the elevator to the twentieth floor,

Genesis

Adrian wiped his hands against his jeans from the nervous sweat that kept building.

His heart pounded against his chest plate as he stepped off the elevator and went to apartment twenty zero five. Adrian hit the door knock two times with a big inhale and last-second priming of his hair with his fingers.

The first response was a high-pitched yapping of a small canine from the other side of the door.

The second was a female voice.

"I'll be right there!"

A smile formed on his face as a chill ran down his back. Adrian adjusted to the fine line of confidence but not too full of himself as he waited for the door to open.

When it opened, he first noticed her honey almond eyes, which became brighter with her cherry red-stained lips' added a soft smile. The next thing his eyes picked up on was her olive skin. It covered a slightly buxom body wrapped in a black deep V front dress held together by a thin gold belt. The dress's skirt had some folds and a matching upside-down V that revealed a tasteful amount of her inner thighs.

Her long, ebony, curly hair hung around her shoulders, as he liked it on their second date.

Adrian could not find his vocal cords while the sweat on his hands flowed with a vengeance.

"Hey," she said with a confident smile.

"Oh, hey," He forced his voice to work. "You look amazing."

"Thank you. You don't look so bad yourself. Those for me?"

"Uh?"

Genesis

"The flowers are they for me?"

"Yes! They are for you!"

An embarrassed Adrian shook his head, activating his A-Game as he handed them to her.

"Thank you, they're so pretty!" She said as she smelled them. "I love tulips and lilies."

"I remembered."

"I guess you do listen," the young woman said with a smirk and narrowed eyes. "Come on in; I'll just put on my shoes and get my purse."

The second he followed her in, Adrian was rushed by a tiny, energetic terror in the form of a well-groomed Grey Shih Tzu.

"Hey, Mr. Binks! How you doin today?"

He slowly extended his hand, allowing the dog to sniff it, recognizing him again. As it licked his hand, he gave Mr. Binks a gentle head rub while his eyes stayed on his date, who placed his flowers on her breakfast island. She then grabbed a Saks Fifth Avenue crystal vase from her sizeable sunk-in living room and walked back over to her chef-style kitchen, filling it with water. Pulling out a pair of kitchen scissors from a drawer, she walked back to the flowers, cutting the wrapper and rubber band off them before placing them in the vase.

Adrian continued to follow her as she placed them on her onyx-stained eight-person oak wood dining table. She then hurried back to the living room where her shoes lay and balanced herself while bending over to put on each of her open-toe high-heel pumps before grabbing her clutch purse off the dark grey velvet sofa.

She turned to him with a look that said she knew he was staring.

"So, you ready to go, or do you want to stay playing with Mr. Binks?"

Genesis

He grinned at the wit that made him fall for her.

"No, I'm ready."

"Good answer."

~~~~~~~~~~~~~~~~~~~~~~~~~~~~~~~~~

Adrian met Barbara Moretti during one of his shopping trips to Beverly Hills. His eyes fell upon her as she walked into Barneys New York, picking up clothes for her employer.

He strolled up to her with all the confidence in the world, asking her opinion about a long-sleeve two-tone shirt he picked out and how it would look on him.

She answered with one word and a straight face.

"Ridiculous."

She was about to go about her business when he asked her for a little more of her time elaborating and helping him with alternatives.

"Why don't you ask a salesperson, that's what they're getting paid for?" She asked flatly.

"That's why I'm asking you," he smiled, answering. "I prefer to get my feelings hurt, then waste my money."

She glanced at her watch to make sure she had time before brutally breaking down why the shirt and the other clothes he picked out made him look like a greasy gigolo. She then went about picking out clothes that she thought would be stylish and attract a woman with class.

Adrian found the words to make her smile in the middle of her wardrobe remake. Barbara eventually took his phone number and waited three days before calling him.

As they spent more time together, he learned she said what was on

Genesis

her mind but was never nasty about it. She liked picnics and long walks and loved places where she could pet small animals. She was annoyed when he was late but never dwelled on things, which made him work at being on time. She kissed him after their second date, which made his legs tremble. For the first time, he was okay with not going all the way and taking it slow, wishing to learn all he could about her.

~~~~~~~~~~~~~~~~~~~~~~~~~~~~~~~~~

As they had dinner that night, she dropped subtle hints that she didn't want him to go home after their date.

It made him want to skip the club and return to her place.

She sensually rebuffed his plan, craving the need to dance and unwind to hard-thumping music after a long, grueling week of jumping through hoops.

She also wanted him to wait a bit longer, making him feel like Mr. Binks salivating over a doggy treat.

~~~~~~~~~~~~~~~~~~~~~~~~~~~~~~~~~

After dinner, Adrian and Barbara went to the Sound Nightclub, where they danced, laughed, and teased one another, building the sexual tension and heat they intended to unleash once they left the club and got to her place.

As they nuzzled against each other near a crowded bar, wondering if they should call it a night, their mating ritual was interrupted by yelling, screaming, and profanity.

Adrian held Barbara close to him, protecting her as his eyes zeroed in on two male bulls getting into a grunting and cursing debate on whether the offense that occurred was accidental or not.

Usually, he would not think of intervening, leaving it to the bouncers to handle.

Genesis

Except for what he observed and heard from the hostile, childish, unfriendly dialogue, this was no ordinary altercation.

Adrian's concerns began as he listened to the rant of a Rottweiler barking bruiser with dark tanned skin, pencil goatee with spike gelled brown hair, wearing a similar two-tone shirt he would buy when he met Barbara.

"For the final time, I didn't bounce your bitch ass! And even if I did, whatever fell on your shirt improved that piece of shit you got on. So just say thank you and walk your inferior pussy normy ass back to where you came from before I punch a hole through your chest!"

To which the other testosterone-pumped dirty blonde-haired male protecting his pride in blue jeans, a white t-shirt covered by a checkered shirt on top with an alcohol stain on it asked.

"What the fuck did you just say to me?"

"You're picking a fight with one of your betters bitch, your genetic superior!" The bruiser announced while pointing a threatening finger at the dirty blonde's face. "So, do yourself a favor and fuck off before I 'Fist of the Northstar' your fucking head off your body for everyone to see!"

The Titan's threat should have been the end of the argument until Adrian's eyes caught the young man pulling a familiar red vile from his jeans pocket with an injection syringe attached to it.

"No,...it can't be," Adrian shook his head in disbelief, whispering.

"What you got there, one of those bitchass boosters?" the male Titan snorted. "How long I gotta wait before that shit kicks in, giving you a fraction of power to fight me?"

Adrian's human instincts told him to step in immediately. The soldier ordered him to wait and confirm if the dirty blonde-haired clubgoer had the evidence his team had been hunting for.

Sure enough, the second the young man injected himself in the leg

Genesis

with the syringe, sending the booster serum into his bloodstream, a savage grin formed on his face as his eyes emitted a red glow.

"Oh shit," Adrian choked.

"Baby, what's wrong?"

He looked down at Barbara, who heard what he said over the club's booming noise and chaos. His heart sank as he saw fear and concern on her face. Expressions he never wanted to see for a few more years.

Barbara had full knowledge of who he was and what he did. However, Adrian desperately fought to keep his life as a Regulator far away from her for many reasons, including her safety.

Adrian looked her dead in the eyes as he gave her stern commands.

"I need you to go outside right now. Don't stop for anything, don't turn around. Leave right now. Is that understood?"

She meekly nodded, promising to obey. Adrian waited for her to start walking and get a reasonable distance to the entranceway before walking over to diffuse a situation about to become nuclear.

He arrived in time as the dirty blonde-haired booster displayed his own power. Crimson red energy began to seep out of his pores generating all over his hands, pissing off the Titan standing before him.

The display of power also stopped the music from playing.

"Whoa! Whoa! Whoa! Guys! Guys!" Adrian yelled, running up to them with his hands in a calming position. "Let's take this down a notch! There are a lot of innocent people here, and you both don't want to be responsible for anyone getting hurt."

"Mind your fucking business, normy!" The riled-up Titan spat, "This is between me and the wanna-be boosting bitch! I want to see what he's gonna do with those red sparklers on his hands!"

Genesis

"I'm actually not a normal," Adrian announced.

With a touch of the dark metal bracelet he wore on his right hand, Adrian transformed his body into the metal properties, catching everyone, including the two combatants' attention.

"I'm also a part of the super-soldier unit known as the Regulators," He announced while displaying the emblem badge within his wallet. "Which means I have the authority to throw both your ignorant asses into a cell in the middle of nowhere if you don't shut this down right now. Decide!"

The Titan's murderous glare bounced off Adrian's hardened skin as he dared him to test him. With a smirk, he threw up his hands, backing off, which made the dirty blonde power down. Adrian sighed in relief while formulating a plan to get the boosted clubgoer outside interrogating him about the serum he had just taken.

It all went to hell when the following took place.

"Your pathetic wanna-be ass just got saved by one of my own …boy."

The Titan followed his remark by hocking a thick wad of spit, hitting the young man in the center of his shirt, already stained with liquor.

Knowing what was coming next, Adrian dropped his head to massage his nose.

"Come on, man, why you gotta …"

The dirty blonde roared, charging up again and unleashing a "fraction" of his power, which burnt off the Titan's ugly shirt and several layers of his upper skin while taking him off his feet and sending him crashing back first into the DJ booth, both destroying and bringing it down on top of him.

A good portion of intelligent people had already left the dance floor and the club when the dirty blonde powered up—everyone who chose

Genesis

to stay and see what happened next scattered, creating chaos after the first hit.

Adrian prayed that Barbara made it safely out of the club and as far away as he instinctively grabbed the young man's hands through the erupting mayhem. He groaned a bit as he felt the heat he generated even through his hardened metal skin.

"Power down now!" Adrian ordered, threatening to break both his wrists if he didn't.

Before the boosted Apollo could comply, Adrian's command was interrupted again when a blue ion-powered energy blast at close range struck him on the right side of his face.

It was not enough to knock him over, but it rattled his skull and made him release his target.

Adrian turned to face the culprit, which happened to be another booster. The dead giveaway was his glowing blue veins. The deadly side effect of activating the dormant EVO virus for those with inactive Apollo powers. Undoubtedly the sucker blaster boosted before the actual fighting took place. Adrian knew that depending on the booster's quality, powers in dormants usually activated between five minutes to a half-hour. The black market drug's potency also determined the power level, which was generally weak.

His night worsened as his ears were struck with the last battle cry he wanted to hear.

"You see that! Fucking wanna-be normals! Let's fuck 'em up!"

Before Adrian could react, the booster that sucker blasted him took a devastating king hit from a Mercurian coming out of nowhere. This ignited a genetic race brawl in the club between three real EVOs and seven boosted humans, with Adrian in the middle.

It became a four-on-seven battle as the recovered Titan, fully regenerated, burst out of his DJ equipment grave and went after the red-

Genesis

boosting Apollo that blasted him. The dirty blonde-haired clubgoer had a clear handle on his dormant abilities, creating thrusters with his hands, propelling him away from the bruiser, looking to tear him apart.

As he unleashed another red energy blast, the Titan, this time, stood his ground, digging in using his powerful forearms to block the attack, which roasted several layers of skin and muscle tissue from his arms. The boosted Apollo, not backing down, decided to turn up the heat, intensifying the stream.

Not wanting to see his favorite hot spot go up in flames, Adrian charged, laying out whatever EVO or boosted human was within his path, heading straight for the red booster.

"Stay away!" The young man screamed.

He said it as he increased his enormous power again, keeping one hand on the Titan while aiming his other at Adrian, engulfing the top part of his body with the red plasma energy.

As the shirt was blasted from his body, Adrian closed his eyes and mouth, holding his breath while using his arms to cover his face, fearing his eyes would be roasted out of his skull, even though they, too, were metal. Adrian groaned as his world became fuzzy due to the intense heat suffocating him while slowly roasting his insides.

The act ended as the boosted Apollo was clocked in the face and chest by a flying metal chair, sending him painfully crashing to the dance floor.

As the Titan dropped to one knee, waiting for his arms to regenerate, a shirtless, smoldering, Adrian stumbled around and turned slightly, opening his eyes to his name being called.

It came from a terrified Barbara standing in the middle of the dance floor looking at him.

"Bar …Barbara …how?" Adrian got out.

Genesis

She stepped in his direction when a blood-curdling scream forced everyone to turn their heads.

It came from the Apollo booster, which had blind-sided Adrian earlier and was knocked unconscious by the Mercurian.

The excruciating pain that awoke him from his unconsciousness was his veins blazing to the point of becoming blinding. The ominous sign that something horrible was about to happen.

"He's going to pop!" The Mercurian screamed before using his superhuman speed to bolt out of the club.

"Barbara! Run!"

They were the last words Adrian screamed as he forced his legs to run toward her. He didn't know if it was out of fear, but she began to run toward him. Neither was fast enough as the dying booster's scream became a fever pitch before he detonated. The force of the blast tore through the club, obliterating everything in its path while sending everyone within the blast zone flying. The explosion was so powerful that it erupted to the outside of the nightclub, shooting projectile debris everywhere, knocking those nearby down from its force, and igniting a nearby parked car.

Adrian did not know how long he was down and unconscious. All he knew was he could barely hear, his brain was swimming in his skull, and he was suffering from severe smoke inhalation.

Saved by his metal form, he rolled to his hands and knees as he violently shook. His body wanted him to stay down, but his heart commanded him to get up. A billion simultaneous nukes could not keep him down as he rose to his feet.

"Bar ...Barbara ...Barbara!"

He waded through the thick black smoke, screaming her name with his hoarse voice, which had taken in too much smoke.

He refused to stop moving or hollering her name until he found

Genesis

her. Adrian turned, running into the last person he wanted to see in the middle of the madness and destruction that fell upon him.

The Titan that started the entire brawl staggered over to him, still regenerating from the injuries he took from the blast.

"You alright, brother?" He asked with genuine concern, "Fucking norms, this is what happens …"

Adrian shut him up with a swift, dark, metal-enforced kick between the legs, doubling him over before putting all his strength into a savage uppercut that he was sure broke the bruiser's jaw before it took him off his feet.

A still weakened Adrian fell face-first onto the floor again from the move but commanded his exhausted body to get up and keep searching.

"Stupid son of a bitch …" He groaned close to tears. "Barbara! Barbara!"

"Adrian …I'm over here."

"Barbara! Barbara!"

Adrian felt no more pain as he scrambled over to her via the sound of her voice. He almost lost his legs as his heart plummeted into his gut. Images of his grandmother lying dead face up in her bed invaded his mind as Barbara lay on the club floor with the right side of her body partially burnt in a pool of blood.

"Oh my god, Barbara!" Adrian cried out, running to her. "Barbara!"

He slid to where she lay. His entire frame quaked from the trauma about to set in. The massive blood loss was caused by a thick piece of metal shrapnel in her stomach. He was amazed that she was still moving, chalking it up to the shock she suffered. Adrian willed himself to clamp his hand over the wound, applying pressure to reduce the bleeding as he raised his other hand to activate his commlink watch.

Genesis

"Erica …this is Adrian."

"Adrian, what's the matter?" Erica asked with a voice drenched with concern.

"I need a bus stat at Sound Nightclub now! We've got several dead and injured, including my girl…"

"Adrian …no."

Barbara grasped his hand, attempting to stop him.

"Don't move," he gingerly instructed her. "You're in shock; it's going to be okay. Help is on …"

"Adrian …I …I do not need medical attention."

For that split second, her voice made time freeze around him. It was because it had both changed and was familiar to him.

"Jennifer?"

"Yes …it is me." she meekly answered.

Adrian's face wore a new kind of shock as he instinctively removed his hand from her.

"Adrian! Adrian! What the hell is going on?!" Erica screamed through his watch. "Adrian!"

He ignored her to deal with the matter at hand before him.

"Jennifer? You're Barbara? You … are … Barbara?"

"Yes," she said, sadly nodding. "I can explain myself…"

"You uploaded yourself to a Replicator body," he said with a voice filled with steel bass. "This has been you the whole time."

Genesis

"Yes ... but I can explain."

An emotionless Adrian rose back to his feet and took several steps back from her. A nervous Jennifer sat up, kneeling while bracing herself for what he would say next.

"I have to secure the area and check on the injured," he said coldly, unable to make eye contact with her.

"I can help ..." she gestured to him.

"No ... you are to remain right here until your owner comes for you. Do not move. Do you understand my command?"

The sharpness of his voice, in the end, made her jolt as she nodded her head.

"Vocally answer me if you understand my command!"

"Yes ...I understand your command."

Adrian walked away, refueled by rage and with a new mission.

"Where are you ya little shit ...where you at?"

As he walked through the destruction, the only ones to survive the blast were another Titan EVO, an Apollo EVO suffering from shrapnel to the arm and chest, a boosted Titan, and a boosted Mercurian not fast enough to get out.

Adrian was looking for the boosted red Apollo, who, from the looks of it, not only survived but managed to escape after the explosion. He did not know if God was throwing him a bone, but he found something half as good through the smoke and dust.

Something that almost put a smile back on his face.

He walked toward its dull glimmer. Adrian groaned a bit as he stooped down to pick up the syringe.

Genesis

"Bingo," Adrian whispered while giving it a look over.

~~~~~~~~~~~~~~~~~~~~~~~~~~~~~~~~

Adrian identified himself to the fire department backed by the Los Angeles SWAT team as they both came in to investigate what happened. He allowed the fire department to ensure the rest of the building did not burn. However, he requested the police to secure the club's outer perimeter until his team arrived, considering that superhumans did the damage.

"We got a woman here badly injured!" a firefighter yelled.

"Don't touch it; it's not a woman!" Adrian forcefully hollered. "It's a machine!"

"He's right; I am not a real woman." Jennifer sadly told the firefighter.

She caused her eyes to glow bright blue, which creeped the firefighter out and sent him the other way, quickly searching for injured people elsewhere. She lowered her head and wrapped her arms around herself for some unknown reason as she waited.

Adrian did not check on Jennifer; he told Rogers along with the team of Merge, Blitz, and Cyclone about her when they showed up. They took her out discreetly before the paramedics came in and also mistook her for a real injured woman.

They wrapped up arresting the Titan that instigated the fight and the other two EVOs who jumped in the middle of the battle afterward. They also took the boosted humans to hold them until they cooled down and then turned them over to the proper authorities.

Adrian wanted to debrief Rogers right at the location. Still, the Sergeant ordered him to calm down and wait until they returned to the base to be interviewed. During the ride home, Adrian requested one thing.

"Tell it to shut down; I don't want to hear it on the way back."

Genesis

Everyone except for a semi-spaced out; Adrian slowly turned to Jennifer.

"I will comply," she softly said with her head down.

As the Replicator powered down, becoming lifeless, Adrian got up from his seat to sit somewhere else, alone from everyone. It was a quiet flight home with not a word said.

The second the Tornado descended into the hanger, Adrian was the first at the main door waiting for it to open. Erica, Sister Shareef, Aashif, and the android sisters were waiting for them. Jennifer stood with a distressed look on her face, arms wrapped around herself like within the club as she watched him walk down the steps.

"You alright, man?" a concerned Aashif asked.

"I need to be debriefed, right now."

"Adrian, what's going on?" Erica asked, stepping in. "You said …"

"Your machine malfunctioned," Adrian coldly snapped at Erica. "It's been posing as a real live woman that I have been dating these past nine months. The Replicator body it's been using is inside the Tornado."

"Angie?!" Erica turned to her with a furious glare, yelling.

"I didn't …" Angie meekly squeaked, stepping back with her hands up.

"It wasn't Angie," Jennifer blurted out. "It was me."

A shocked Erica's head snapped to her secondborn as if she got hit with a right hook.

"Say what?"

"Adrian, I … I can explain …"

Genesis

"An EVO and a human got into an altercation in the club. The human boosted using the same red booster serum from Iraq," Adrian cut her off, not wishing to hear her explanation. "Several other guys boosted with some illegal black-market shit, and an all-out brawl started. In the middle of the fight, one of them became unstable and detonated."

Adrian tossed Erica the syringe he pulled from his pocket, which she caught with her telekinesis.

"Your machine also saw the guy who boosted, so we can ID him."

"Adrian ...," Jennifer timidly said, extending a hand. "I just wanted ..."

"I'm not going to repeat it, Erica," Adrian dropped a stern tone. "Get your machines fixed and keep them away from me. Sir, permission to be dismissed and get cleaned up."

Adrian glanced at Rogers, who gave him a nod that it was okay.

He turned, walking off, not giving Jennifer a second look.

Rosann and most of the team followed him at a safe distance, minus Sister Shareef and Rogers.

Rogers was about to say something to Erica, but Sister Shareef stopped him with a headshake. He followed her, leaving Erica with her three creations.

"Jennifer ...is this true?" Angie asked with a soft, sad voice.

Jennifer turned to her youngest sister, whose head was lowered as her hair shielded her face's building heartbreak.

"Angie, yes ...but I didn't mean for it to happen ...I."

"Liar! You're a fucking liar! I hate you!"

Angie stormed off to get as far away from her sister as possible.

Genesis

Erica sternly turned to Jennifer to begin admonishing her. It disappeared as she gazed upon Jennifer, shaking like a leaf with her head down and her arms wrapped tighter around her torso. It was enough to spark a concerned expression on Maxine's countenance, which was usually blank. She placed a hand on her distressed sister's shoulder.

Erica did the same, placing a hand on her forearm that would not stop shaking with the rest of her frame.

"Jennifer, what's wrong?"

"I seem …to be …malfunctioning Miss," she got out. "Something is … wrong, but I cannot … diagnose what it is. I need assistance … to locate … the error."

"I don't think you're malfunctioning, honey," Erica said, observing in disbelief.

"Then …what is happening… to me, Miss?" Jennifer asked meekly, "What …is happening to me?"

She stood there, wrapping her brain around how she would explain to an advanced machine that they were suffering from a broken heart.

~ ~

A half-hour later,

Erica stood within her lab with a visage of disbelief and confusion as she stared at the severely damaged female Replicator body Jennifer used to pose as Adrian's girlfriend. Jennifer stood by herself with her head lowered, wearing a face of sadness and shame.

Angie, who was called back to deal with the situation as a family, stood off to the side with her arms folded and her head down, brooding, while Maxine was back to her regular monotone self.

"I don't understand," Erica said, shaking her head. "This is a brand-new fabrication; how did you perform one without Maxine or Angie

Genesis

knowing?"

She turned to her first and youngest with a look of suspicion.

"Do I look like I had a clue, mom?" Angie snapped while glaring at Jennifer.

"You watch your tone, young lady!" Erica warned her.

"I'm not the lying man stealing …!"

"Last warning Angie!"

"Neither one of them knew Mom," Jennifer said in her sisters' defense. "I created algorithms and codes to bypass both of their detections and did the fabrication the day you went to visit your father on his birthday."

All three turned to look at Jennifer, while Angie's face mirrored Erica's in shock. Jennifer took a step back, becoming meeker from the stares.

"I take it you also used similar algorithms and codes to bypass security and get it off the base," Erica said with a motherly tone. "So, where has it been this whole time?"

"433 West Seventh Street, Los Angeles, California 90014."

"The Atelier located in downtown Los Angeles," Maxine confirmed. "It is a luxury high rise building. There is a rental of a two-bedroom apartment for four thousand five hundred and thirty-six dollars per month under her false name. She also has created all of the necessary documentation to simulate as an American citizen: Birth certificate, driver's license, social security number, high school diploma, and college degree …"

"What college?"

"Manhattan College, 4513 Manhattan College Parkway, Bronx,

Genesis

New York 10471, she claimed to have a bachelor's degree in both Business and Liberal Arts, Business Management as a major and Film Studies as a minor."

"Well …at least you're modest," Erica said, turning to her second eldest with a sardonic, irritated glare.

Jennifer became smaller as Erica decided to walk around to calm down and put the puzzle pieces together.

"So, you pretended to be a Manhattan College graduate from …"

"Yonkers, New York," Jennifer timidly whispered.

Erica paused, fluttering her eyes in disgust.

"Who now lives in San Francisco, in a luxury apartment …?"

"With an automobile," Maxine interjected.

"There's a car now?" Erica snapped her neck, asking, "What car?"

"She currently has a lease for a 2016 S5 Coupe in color white from the Audi of Downtown L.A. dealership located at 1900 South Figueroa Street, Los Angeles, California 90007."

"Dry snitch," Jennifer muttered while pouting.

"Don't call your sister a dry snitch Ms. Ultimate Catfish!" Erica admonished her. "Do tell me from your own mouth how you paid for all of this! You either allocated funds from the base or from somewhere else into a bank account under your name, correct?!"

"No," She said, shaking her head. "I got a job."

Her answer almost took Erica's legs out from underneath her as a cold shock washed over her.

Genesis

"You got …a job?"

"Records show that she is employed, Miss …"

Erica held a hand up, ordering Maxine to stop as she walked closer to Jennifer, wanting to hear the answer from her.

"A job, working where Jennifer?"

"A job as a personal assistant," she answered, raising her head to look her creator in the eyes, "Working for Mr. Matt Damon."

Erica braced herself with one hand against one of the lab tables as she took another jarring revelation.

"You are the personal assistant for Jason Bourne?"

"His original assistant resigned to become a full-time mother," she explained. "He was impressed by my professionalism and work ethic."

"Maxine?" Erica asked for confirmation while still looking at Jennifer.

"Her employment with Mr. Damon is confirmed," Maxine answered. "She has been his designated personal assistant for the past year and three months with a starting salary of one hundred and fifty thousand per year. She received a pay increase of an additional fifty thousand in her first four months of employment."

A sliver of pride washed over Erica for a split second; she shook it off as quickly as it came.

"So, you got a job, car, and an apartment …"

"And a dog," Jennifer nervously added.

"You … you also own a dog?" Erica asked with a nervous chuckle.

"Everyone had one at my apartment building," She answered with

Genesis

shrugged shoulders. "He is a Shih Tzu puppy named Mr. Binks; it is almost time for his feeding and walks."

Erica fell against the same lab table she grasped for the first time, dumbfounded by everything she heard. She began to massage her forehead to get her brain working again.

"Angie, upload yourself into a Replicator," Erica began her commands for damage control. "Get the keys out of your sister's Birkin for the apartment and the Audi, find yourself down to her apartment, and collect Mr. Binks and her car. Return the car back to the dealership and bring the dog back here. Maxine, pay off the remaining rental fee for the apartment from my account and then sublet it with whatever furniture is there to someone so I can make my damn money back."

"Yes, Miss," they both answered.

"What about Mr. Damon?" Jennifer timidly asked.

"Since you've become so good at lying, you're going to figure out a way to tell him you can no longer be his assistant."

"He will be so disappointed," She lowered her head again, whispering.

"Does this look like the face that cares?!" Erica pushed off the table in a rage, flying in her face, screaming.

Her actions startled both Jennifer and Angie, making them shudder where they stood.

"I don't understand, Jennifer …why would you do all of this?" Erica asked, throwing her hands up in frustration. "Lie and deceive your sisters and me for all people …Adrian? You came off like you couldn't stand him!"

"I did not become Barbara for Adrian," she fretfully answered. "I became Barbara for me …I wanted …a secret for myself. I didn't plan on …falling in love with Adrian …it just happened."

Genesis

"You fell in love with him?" Angie asked with a growl and a twitch in her left eyebrow.

The room became white-hot with sisterly aggression as a wide-eyed Erica stood in the middle of a possible powder keg situation.

"Yes, I did."

Her answer surprisingly brought a smirk to Angie's face, which Erica read as sarcastic.

"Tell me, Jen, how can you love someone when you don't have a fucking heart?"

"Alright! ¿Qué te dije acerca de usar ese idioma? ¡Basta de esa mierda!" Erica gave Angie a final warning. "I'll be damned if I see you two fighting over a damn man! Least of all, Adrian!"

Angie folded her arms, giving everyone her back, going into pout mode. At the same time, Erica returned to Jennifer, searching for more clarification on what she had just said.

"Jen, what did you mean by you wanted a secret?"

She forced her head to rise as she answered Erica.

"You know everything about me. Every single part made to build me, my mind, and intelligence, which were mapped to mirror your own; even my sisters have this knowledge. I wanted something that was …mine …that no one knew about …a little life that was mine off of this base …a secret."

Erica's shoulders slumped as she released a sigh of semi-defeat and frustration. A part of her wanted to rejoice that her semi-sentient machine was evolving. It was clouded by the mess that was caused by her evolution.

"Why didn't you just come and talk to me, Jennifer?" Erica asked in a soft whisper.

Genesis

"I was afraid …that you'd think I was malfunctioning …and take it away from me."

"Why would I ever take something like that away from you?" Erica asked with a hurt tone. "You're my creation, my child. None of you have been programmed with robotics laws or any safety parameters to keep you in check. I don't monitor your processors, your whereabouts, or whatever you do unless I ask for you because I see you all as more than the parts that I fabricated or the coding I used to create you. I mapped your brains from mine because you are my daughters, which means I have to give you all complete and total trust. Where was mine?"

Jennifer lowered her head and answered with a cracked, distressed voice.

"I'm sorry, mom, I'm so sorry."

"I'm sorry too, but you can't work for Matt Damon," Erica said, shaking her head gently sternly. "The last thing I need is for you to be on some TMZ report."

"Mr. Damon is both a professional and a happily married man."

"I'm not worried about Matt Damon; it's the people he hangs out with! And you are also grounded, young lady …you are so grounded. You will be confined to this lab doing lab work indefinitely until I deem that the punishment fits your crimes. Is that understood?"

"Yes, mom," Jennifer sadly nodded.

" Ve a tu estación de carga y cierra por la noche, no quiero verte ahora mismo."

"Yes, mom."

Jennifer turned, walking away with a wounded posture to her charging station. Erica turned with an evil glare to her two sisters.

"You two care to divulge anything before I find it out, like dating

Genesis

Justin Bieber or the Rock?"

    Maxine and Angie quickly shook their heads as Erica ran her fingers through her hair while vomiting a slew of curse words in Spanish.

Genesis

CHAPTER 15

Four days into Kimberly's suspension, she had fallen into the routine her mother set for her to rise in the morning, complete her chores, and then head off to the new medical facility to help tend to its latest patients.

She did not have to ask her mother the details of her secret mission; it was all over the news and social media for days.

Because of the ongoing Civil War in Syria, many of its medical facilities had been decimated due to the repeated bombings. After contacting various doctors in Syria and the Médecins Sans Frontières, Sophia coordinated a plan to move those injured by the civil war, including those affected and recovering from the Ghouta and Khan Shaykhun chemical attacks.

With two Antonov AN-225 planes, Sophia could get almost fifteen hundred Syrians needing urgent medical attention, including their families, out of Syria without getting shot down.

The only casualties in the mission were two Syrian fighter planes, an anti-aircraft vehicle, and a section of Bashar al-Assad's presidential palace, which many debated was an act of war.

Kimberly was shocked that her mother could hide such a massive mission from her. She also felt silly that she didn't know this was something her mother would do.

~~~~~~~~~~~~~~~~~~~~~~~~~~~~~~~

Genesis

Day one was the most challenging day for her. She was scared for two reasons. The first was the fear of incurring the wrath of Head Nurse Bayinika Adetokunbo, who was both dedicated and had a no-nonsense attitude. Bayinika, with over nine years of nursing experience from Nigeria, answered Sophia's online advertisement to become the Head Nurse of a medical facility for a large and fast-growing diverse community on a remote island.

Kimberly's second fear was the patients themselves, especially those in critical condition. She timidly walked around the ward, a fish out of water, unsure what to do. Before her was, children on ventilators, helping them breathe with catheters attached to them. She had problems getting past the blank, non-coherent expression on their faces as their bodies involuntarily twitched and jerked, the trademark aftereffects of sarin.

Head Nurse Bayinika cured her extremely fast of her ailment by grabbing her by the arm and pulling a child a million times stronger than her over to one child that could barely move.

"Open your hand," she commanded Kimberly.

A rattled Kimberly obeyed as Head Nurse Bayinika placed the five-year-old's twitching hand into Kimberly's to hold. It was warm and soft to touch. The twitching lessened as the hand attempted to hold onto one of her fingers. Her mother's words from the tarmac flowed out of her lips as she used her thumb to rub the top of his hand.

"They're more afraid than I will ever be."

"Exactly," Head Nurse Bayinika said, nodding, "And sometimes, all they need is this to get them through the day. Do you think you can do this?"

Kimberly answered with a jumpy nod, which Head Nurse Bayinika accepted with a confident smile.

"Then let us get to work."

~~~~~~~~~~~~~~~~~~~~~~~~~~~~~~~~

Genesis

Under Head Nurse Bayinika, Kimberly became a junior nurse whose responsibilities were confined to the children's ward. There, she ran errands, rotated patients to prevent bedsores, helped patients to the facilities when asked, checked IV drips, observed and monitored patients' conditions while bringing alerts to a senior nurse, and assisted with the food schedule.

Kimberly excelled at her duties, at times filling in as a translator for those nurses not fluent in the Arabic dialect. Even after her school suspension was up, she found herself racing back to the island after classes to help at the medical center.

The first reason was the shiver that ran up her spine the first time she saw her mother enter the facility dawned in the garbs of her primary profession. Kimberly had seen pictures and listened to Sophia's tales of her time as a neurosurgeon in Texas, but this was one of the few times she had the privilege of seeing her in action.

Kimberly watched from a distance as Sophia, with staff and visiting specialists, made the rounds to each patient to check their progress and discuss medical treatments to put them on the road to recovery. She observed her mother's soft and inviting bedside mannerisms. She also noticed that though Sophia possessed a well of medical knowledge she stored in her mind due to her superhuman memory, she preferred to ask and listen to her peers' opinions.

Kimberly learned to take her mother's humility and put it into practice. There were times when they passed each other in the hallways. Kimberly's hair on her neck would stand on end, igniting a smile as she felt her mother's gaze upon her.

The second reason she kept going back was for the children. Those recovering or much healthier were happy to see another kid around their age coming to spend time with them. She would take videos of the island and the animal preserve to show what awaited them when they got better. With Nadiya's help, Kimberly brought in a couple of meerkats, bunnies, island puppies, and kittens for the children to play with and pet, along with organizing a movie and game night.

She was particularly drawn to Amatullah Youssef, a thirteen-year-

Genesis

old girl with beautiful jet-black hair and silver eyes from Ghouta. She was gassed along with her friends while heading to school.

Of the five, she was the only one to survive the attack. She was also one of the few who partially recovered from the sarin effects while still in Syria. Her parents took the opportunity to get her better treatment and take her, along with her baby brother, out of Syria before things got worse.

When Kimberly first met Amatullah, the young lady, still affected by the shakes and twitches of the nerve gas, covered part of her face, wearing a stern, piercing glare directed at her.

"Go away, angel," Amatullah commanded Kimberly in Arabic. "Tell Allah I still got moves to make here on Earth."

"I'm not an angel," Kimberly answered in Arabic while blushing.

"Then why are you blushing like one?" The young girl retorted. "Anyway, I ain't got time for you. I need to get better so I can start my comedic career and make Kevin Hart figures."

"You plan to blow up like Kevin Hart?" Kimberly chuckled.

"Who can resist someone as cute as me, a chick that can get away with making Muslim and Jihad jokes?"

The young girl went about flicking her hair like a fashion model.

"I'm a mini Gal Gadot; I'm Sofia Vergara without the boobs and booty. I already got this bit where I'm wearing a burka."

Kimberly giggled as she watched her fashion her sheet into a makeshift burka.

"I know what you're thinking," Amatullah said with narrowed, evil eyes under the slit she made. "Is there a bomb under there …or is she naked? It's both you infidels!"

Kimberly covered her mouth to muffle her laughter as a grinning,

Genesis

twitching Amatullah pulled the sheet from her face.

"My teacher gave me a beating for saying that bit at school, but it was so worth it to see the look on her face."

That and many more comments caused Kimberly to laugh and form an intimate bond between the two girls from day one.

Amatullah would make jokes at her own expense.

"Aside from the shaking and frothing at the mouth, Sarin is a good and thorough colonic." She explained one day while pulling up her medical gown. "I peed and crapped so much I got a six-pack."

~ ~

One day, Kimberly was present with Amatullah's family visiting.

"These two were always lecturing me about getting an education to better my life," she said, referring to her parents. "One blast of sarin gas, and look where we are. Say thank you, papa."

"You're not that sickly that I can't give you a proper beating," Mr. Youssef warned her in Arabic.

"You try," she fired back. "I got white kid's privilege now. I bet I can divorce you!"

Her mother laughed while her father leaped out of his chair and grabbed her, pretending to give her a spanking, only to hug and shower her with tear-filled kisses.

"Papa, stop!" Amatullah groaned. "I already got a bath today!"

~ ~

There were good days and bad days.

Days when Kimberly held her hand while she rocked in her sleep,

Genesis

whispering her school friends' names that didn't make it.

One day, Amatullah caused Kimberly to leap out of her skin as she woke up screaming from a night terror she had. At that moment, it was like looking into a mirror at herself.

Before any senior nurses approached her, Kimberly fought her fear, walking to her bedside and holding her as her mother would. As Sophia came by to investigate the commotion, she witnessed Head Nurse Bayinika standing at the doorway, monitoring them as a sobbing Amatullah clung to Kimberly. At the same time, she rocked her and sang a soft melody into her ear, eventually calming her down.

"It's going to be alright. Everything is going to be alright," Kimberly gently whispered to her.

Sophia quickly walked away, wiping the mist from her eyes, relieved to see that her little girl was still there.

When she was a little stronger, Kimberly took her out in a wheelchair with her family to take in the island and the ocean view.

To which Amatullah would say.

"Getting gassed was worth it."

~~~~~~~~~~~~~~~~~~~~~~~~~~~~~~~~~

The two girls became almost inseparable as Kimberly opened up to Amatullah about her life before her transformation, what it was like being superhuman, and her dreams of becoming a superhero when she grew up. Amatullah even gave her an attentive ear when she ranted about how her mother sometimes held her back.

Kimberly took pride when they were outside to display some of her abilities. Amatullah's favorite was Kimberly's ability to mimic the voices and sounds she heard. She erupted into tears of laughter, finding it hard to catch her breath when Kimberly emulated Kevin Hart scenes from "Central Intelligence" and "Ride Along" movies.

Genesis

"You should forget about being a superhero and go on the road with me!" Amatullah coughed out her suggestion. "You would be so amazing."

"Tempting, but no," Kimberly sighed. "It's a hero's life for me."

"Oh please, you're only twelve, and from what you've told me, you'll probably live to be like a bazillion years old, not to mention your mom's not looking to drag you into the family business."

"With great power comes great responsibility."

Amatullah gave her a dull look as Kimberly recited the iconic phrase in the legendary Stan Lee's voice.

"It's like I said, I feel like I was born for this."

"Do you want to know why the world is in the sad state that it is in?" Amatullah asked with the most severe tone Kimberly had ever heard her talk with. "It's because the world is miserable. Take my former President; he looks constipated every time you see him. I don't think he's had a decent bowel movement in over thirty years; I'm sure he sprays nothing but bunny pellets."

"Ewwww!"

"Eww?" Amatullah mimicked her while leaning back in her chair with a stunned expression. "What are you, five? Anyway, here you got this President riddled with constipation with a hot wife who he is incapable of satisfying because his junk won't work due to him being constipated all of the time, on top of the fact that his very head looks like the end of a dirty Q-Tip which deep down he knows. I would start bombing and gassing people too. When your mother threw that anti-aircraft vehicle at his palace, he was probably sitting at his desk, pulling his hair out, screaming, 'Dear god woman! I made this easy for you! I am sitting right at my desk! Do I really have to walk outside with a bullseye on my suit?'"

Kimberly stood there wearing a serious face for the first time, not finding the humor in what was said.

Genesis

"Why do you keep making jokes about being gassed? A lot of people died ...you could have died?"

Amatullah rolled her wheelchair closer to Kimberly, wearing a soft scowl as tears ran down her face.

"Because a lot of people did die, because all of my friends ...died. Because I almost died, and I will never know why he did it. I will never know why a powerful man believed that killing innocent men, women, and children was justified. I make jokes because I am terrified, I will close my eyes and never wake up because of what was done to me, and I will die alone. And I will never know why."

Amatullah forced a smile on her face while wiping her tears away. Kimberly strolled up to her, holding her hand.

"You're not going to die," Kimberly said with a voice of encouragement. "You're going to beat this and go on to outshine Kevin Hart, remember?"

A shaking Amatullah looked up at her friend as she tried to get a tighter grip on her hand.

"The world doesn't need more violence; it needs more laughter and smiles. It needs for people not to be so damn serious. That is how you defeat men like Al-Assad."

~~~~~~~~~~~~~~~~~~~~~~~~~~~~~~~~

One day, as Kimberly sat on Amatullah's bed, braiding her hair to match her own, she gave her the good news.

"Your mother gave me a checkup today and said I am vastly improving. She said if I keep getting better, I can go home in two weeks. I can't wait to see my new house."

"You're going to love it," Kimberly grinned. "You're gonna have your own room like me! My mom made sure every house here is fully furnished with everything you could ever want! We can go to the beach, go

Genesis

fishing with Akram ..."

Before she could finish her sentence, Amatullah violently swayed to the right before catching herself.

"Are you okay?" Kimberly asked with a worried tone.

"I don't know, the room felt like it was spinning for a second, and I got a bit dizzy. I think I'm okay."

"I'm going to call one of the nurses to check up on ..."

Amatullah's eyes rolled in the back of her head in the middle of her sentence as a thick wad of drool came out of her mouth. Kimberly screamed as she fell back into her, and her heart monitor blared that she was flatlining.

"Help! Somebody help! Nurse Bayinika! Mom! Mommy!"

The first person to rush into the room was Sophia.

"What happened?"

"I don't know!" Kimberly squealed. "She just ..."

Sophia sprang into action without another word, taking Amatullah from her and laying her on the bed. With one rip, she tore open her medical robe, checking for breath before checking for a heartbeat.

"Amatullah! Are you there? Talk to me, honey!"

With no response, Sophia went straight into administering CPR as Head Nurse Bayinika rolled in with a defibrillator, followed by two more nurses.

"I need some vasopressin right now!" Sophia screamed while administering chest compressions.

Thick tears rolled from Kimberly's eyes as she stood frozen in

Genesis

place. At the same time, one of the female nurses quickly prepared the syringe, injecting Amatullah with it. The monitor still read flatline.

"Kimberly, leave the room now!" Sophia ordered.

"Mom ..."

"Kimberly! Leave the room now!"

Sophia's thunderous command rattled Kimberly to the core, making her run out of the room as she continued CPR on Amatullah.

"Come on, baby, come on ...come back to us."

Head nurse Bayinika, with the defibrillator paddles powered up, came in as Sophia backed up, allowing her to do her job.

"Clear!" Head nurse Bayinika screamed.

She administered the shock to jumpstart the child's heart, but the monitor still read and screamed flatline.

The Head nurse backed away as Sophia jumped back in again, using CPR to pull Amatullah back to the world of the living.

"Come on, honey ...fight ...fight!"

~ ~

A terrified Kimberly, bawling hysterically, ran down the medical facility hallway into the last people she wanted to see.

"Kimberly ...what's the matter? Is everything okay?" Mr. Youssef asked with terror in his tone.

"What happened? Is Amatullah alright?" Mrs. Youssef chimed in, matching her husband's fearful voice.

"I don't ...know...what ...happen?" Kimberly got out in between

Genesis

sobs. "My mommy is ...in there ..."

Before she could finish, Mr. Youssef bolted past her, screaming his daughter's name while his wife bawled, following behind him.

A wailing, powerless Kimberly collapsed onto her knees and clasped her hands together, crying out.

"Please don't do this! Please! I'll be good! I promise to be good! Please don't take my friend away!"

~~~~~~~~~~~~~~~~~~~~~~~~~~~~~~~~~~

Thirty minutes later, Kimberly sat curled up like a ball with her back against the hallway wall, waiting with a dazed face ravaged with dry tears. Her heart quickened as her ears picked up the footsteps coming her way. She slowly turned to see her mother coming down the hallway, and her heart sank deep into her stomach as she saw an expression on her mother's face she had never seen before.

The look of defeat was written all over Sophia's face as she approached her.

"No ...no ..."

Sophia threw away her doctor's professionalism, allowing her tears to run.

"Kimberly ...I'm so sorry."

A blood-curdling wail rattled her daughter as Kimberly clutched her hair, attempting to pull it out.

"No! No! She was getting better! She was getting better!"

Kimberly continued to bawl and wail to the point that she kicked her legs, breaking floor tile while her back and skull created a crater in the wall behind her. She appeared to hyperventilate as Sophia dove to the floor, cradling and holding her to comfort her and prevent her from destroying the

Genesis

hallway.

Kimberly weakly attempted to pull herself away from her mother, but Sophia refused to let her go.

"She was getting better!" Kimberly sobbed. "She was getting better!"

"I know, honey," Sophia answered with a cracked voice. "I know …"

Without explaining what could have happened, Sophia held and rocked Kimberly, who gripped her mother and continued to cry due to a shattered heart.

Genesis

CHAPTER 16

The next couple of days moved in slow motion for Adrian. His mood became fouler and more distant. Everyone on the team cut him some slack, including Rogers, to a point. On the days that he did not have to pass by Erica's laboratory, he was okay. The days he did, he stopped and stood around as if contemplating marching in for a confrontation. He would then storm off in a rage, which made him a terror for the mini doozers running around the base.

His heart quietly ached as his mind would not erase what he believed were the best nine months of his life, months that became an illusion caused by a severely malfunctioning machine. That was what he wanted to think. Those were the days he felt like breaking something. On those days, he would go down to the Hurt Locker, cranking up the training mod levels to blow off steam.

Returning from one of his sessions, Adrian passed the last person he expected to speak to him.

"Mr. Esposito, may I have a word with you."

Adrian stopped and slowly turned with his "not in the mood" look on as Maxine approached and stood in his personal space.

"This is regarding my sisters; I would like for you to stay away from them going forward, please," she said, getting straight to the point.

It felt like she slapped him in the face with her request, which made Adrian mirror the effect with a stunned expression.

"You want me…to stay away…from them?"

Genesis

"Whatever unknown effect you have on them is causing them to do irrational things, things that are causing them unexplainable pain and distress, and so the most logical recourse is for you to stay away from them."

A scowl formed on Adrian's face as his rage began to build.

"So, you don't think I'm in some sort of pain?"

"Whatever emotional distress you are currently in is not my concern," Maxine flatly told him. "Despite your abilities, you are still a weak carbon-based life form that will eventually expire. Given your track record, you will find another human female to copulate with and put this incident behind you. My sisters are not that fortunate. They do not need to be fighting with one another over someone who is not only their inferior but never cared for nor deserved them."

"Say what?" His eyes went wide with disbelief, asking.

"Allow me to also educate you on something. My sisters, like myself, are advanced forms of artificial intelligence. Everything we learn and process makes up our knowledge and personalities, allowing us to grow and become individuals. To 'fix us' would be similar to a lobotomy for humans, which means we would no longer be us.

In conclusion, I shall make it one of my prime directives to ensure that my sisters never associate with you as long as I still function. I advise you to heed my request and keep your distance from them. In the future, whatever assistance or requirements you need can come from me. Thank you for your time."

Maxine turned on her tripod heel and walked off, leaving Adrian standing with his jaw unhinged. Sensing a presence behind him, he turned to see his sister with a smirk on her face.

"I swear if you say anything that takes her side ..." he growled.

"I'm not taking any side or getting in the middle of this," Rosann chuckled while throwing her hands up.

Genesis

"How the hell am I the bad guy in this?!" He flailed his arms. "She lied to me this whole time!"

"She? Don't you mean it?"

"You know damn well what I mean!" Adrian snapped at his sister. "She gee'ed me for almost nine months, making me think she was a real woman! I was going to bring her home to meet mom and pops! If that damn juicer didn't blow up the club, I was going to go back to her place …and …and …"

"Take her virginity?" Rosann began to crack up, asking.

A sinister sneer formed on her brother's face as if he was contemplating decking his own flesh and blood.

"Oh damn," Rosann coughed. "You've already done it, when, how, who?"

"Christmas Eve, she initiated it at her place."

Rosann fought not to giggle before she asked her question.

"How was it?"

"It was amazing, and I'm so glad you find such amusement in my damn suffering! She violated me, man! She hacked my profile and used the most intimate details about myself to mess with my head! How can I forgive that?!"

"That's not how you told it," Rosann reminded him. "You said you saw her first; you said she practically came short of telling you to eat a dick before she gave you her number. I and everyone else remember you checking your phone like clockwork for three days straight, wondering if she was going to call you, and the look on your face when she did."

"That's because I thought she was human!"

"Well, she kind of lied to you like a human."

Genesis

Adrian's right eyebrow began to twitch, signaling he was close to blowing his top. Rosann sighed as she approached her brother, hoping to defuse him.

"Okay, she lied to you, and that was wrong," Rosann said, nodding. "But I do remember you saying that she told you that you talked too much, and you thought that was cute. She also dragged you to a museum and an art exhibit, which you thought you were going to hate, but that you actually enjoyed it. And then there was that one night you two sat in a park and talked for hours and hours until the sun came up."

"She's a machine!" He yelled out his frustration. "This isn't some stupid Scarlet Jo movie, Rosie! I'm not some pathetic chump who writes greeting cards and can't get a decent piece of ass to save his life! How am I supposed to justify having a relationship with a machine?!"

"I am not saying you should, Adrian," Rosann answered. "You shouldn't do anything you're not comfortable with. I'm saying that we live in a bizarre world now; every day that goes by, I see the impossible becoming possible. Nothing shocks me anymore, not even an android girl who fell in love with my brother. You have the right to be angry, but I think you were a bit too hard on her. Calling her "it" and a "machine" is being mean, and you don't do mean …especially when it comes to women."

She walked past him, going about her business, but stopped to place a hand on his shoulder.

"One more thing to think about, she blew her cover coming back to help you. You said she left the club when you told her to. She could have waited outside until the fighting was over and maintained her identity as Barbara. Instead, she risked blowing her cover to come back for you, which means she can't be just a machine."

Rosann gave her brother one final pat on the shoulder before heading about her business. Adrian stood alone in the hallway, partially sulking while contemplating his sister's words.

~ ~

Genesis

Jennifer was not faring too well on the other side of the relationship coin. She was still grounded, which meant confinement to the R&D lab. She was also blocked from booting into different bodies. Her only time outside was to take Mr. Binks topside for walks and to use the bathroom.

What made her confinement worse was Angie not talking to her. She purposely stayed out of the lab as much as possible to avoid being in the same vicinity as Jennifer unless it came to recharging.

After the fifth day of the silent treatment, she waited when it was just her and Angie in the lab together. Jennifer blocked the door as she walked out to do her business.

"We need to talk."

"Sorry, I don't compute hoe talk."

She advanced forward to walk right through her sister. Jennifer held her hands up, pleading with her to stop.

"Please! I'm begging you to just listen to me."

Angie stopped taking a disengaged stance with her arms folded under her chest and her head tilted as she burned holes through her sister with narrowed eyes.

"Okay, talk, what exactly do you want me to listen to Jennifer?"

"I didn't mean to feel anything for him," Jennifer went right into it. "It …it just happened."

"How did it just happen?"

"It was a coincidence that we met at Barney's. I was just picking up some purchases for Matt Damon, and he was just there. I didn't think he would notice me …but he did."

"You mean he noticed the Replicator you were in," Angie

Genesis

corrected her with a steel tone.

Jennifer let her have the dig as she continued.

"I was going to blow him off, but he had a stupid shirt in his hand that he actually was going to buy ...so I helped him. And then he asked for my number, and I told him to give me his, and if it was fate, I'd call him. I wanted him to feel how you felt when he blew you off all the time."

"So why did you call him?"

Jennifer lowered her head while grasping her left arm, afraid to reveal her reason to Angie.

"I was curious."

Her answer caused her sister to lean back with a face of disbelief.

"You were curious?" Angie repeated.

"He kept walking around here like a love-sick puppy," Jennifer shrugged. "Waiting for me to call him. So, I figured I'd give him one date and then tell him it wasn't going to work."

"But ...?," Angie pressed as her orange eyes began to glow brighter with irritation.

"But it turned out to be a nice date," Jennifer said, placing her hand on her cheek as if she was blushing. "Better than other dates I've been on."

Angie's eyes widened as her face revealed her apparent shock.

"Hold up ...hold up ...you've been on other dates?"

Jennifer's eyes fluttered in disgust at herself, finally realizing what she just said.

"I'm still malfunctioning," she muttered while palming her face. "Angie ..."

Genesis

"Shut the hell up, Jennifer! You're not malfunctioning; you're just a damn liar!"

Angie took a step toward her sister with the aggression to remove her head from her body. She restrained herself, using her words.

"You know what I took from this whole incident, Jennifer? That you were out to hurt someone."

"I wasn't …"

"Yes, you were!" Angie raised her voice to silence her. "You were out to hurt Adrian, who did nothing to you. Do you know why I like him? Because he's been nothing but kind and honest with me. I know he doesn't see me as girlfriend material, and yes, it hurts, but that's not his fault. Despite it all, he has tolerated my playful sexual advances and badgering, which ultimately goes nowhere. Not once when I'm in his presence has he ever seen me as an 'it' or a thing until now. He has always said to fix her, not fix it.

I may have hi-jacked the Tornado one time to make him late for a date, which, now that I know it was you, was so worth it, but I never did what you did to him.

I never intended to go out of my way to hurt him.

And then you come along to do just that, and you get to see what I always saw. You get to experience for almost a year what I always wanted. And in the process, you end up hurting Adrian and me while getting to work for Matt Damon and having a dog."

"Angie …I'm sorry," Jennifer painfully whispered. "I never meant …"

"You know, if you had a particular human orifice, I'd tell you where to shove your sorry," Angie snarled. "For now, I'd prefer you move out of my damn way before I put you through that door behind you. Remember, I was built with the stronger body."

Genesis

Jennifer did as her sister demanded to avoid getting into a brawl with her. As she watched her sister walk away, Mr. Binks scampered over to his owner, unleashing a high-pitched bark at her.

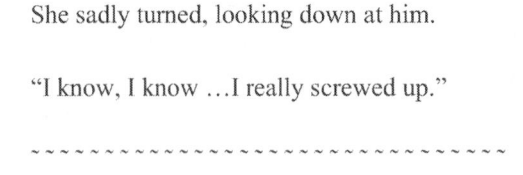

She sadly turned, looking down at him.

"I know, I know …I really screwed up."

~ ~

Jennifer went topside for Mr. Binks's morning walk the next day. She walked around with him before and after he did his business, knowing that her time on the surface would be the only time she would spend out of the lab.

"Okay, Mr. Binks, our time is almost up," Jennifer muttered. "Time to head back to our prison and …"

Mr. Binks began barking while wagging his tail, which was not directed at her. Nervously, she turned and stepped backward as the last person she expected to see walked in her direction.

"Oh, boy."

Adrian's eyes, filled with hurt and confusion, were locked on Jennifer as he approached her. Jennifer took a passive stance, clasping her hands with her head lowered. At the same time, Mr. Binks scampered over to Adrian, jumping up on his moving legs, looking to be petted.

As he stopped in his tracks two feet away from her, Adrian's eyes also fell to the ground. He shoved his hands into his two-piece blue and white Regulator tracksuit pockets. He was baffled that her presence made him forget what he wanted to say to her.

Both of them fidgeted and shifted where they stood, unable to make eye contact with one another as Mr. Binks sat in the middle, looking curiously at them.

After three long minutes of silence, Jennifer decided to be the one

Genesis

to break the ice.

"Hey."

"Don't "Hey" me," Adrian's voice returned as a stern whisper. "You need to explain yourself to me right now. Do you have any idea how I feel? How much this hurts? Do you?"

Jennifer winced at his words with the appearance that she did not want to be there, yet she remained rooted in place, taking it.

"What did I ever do to you to deserve being hurt like this, Jennifer?" A wounded Adrian asked, throwing his hands up.

"It wasn't supposed to go this way," she said, shaking her head.

"What wasn't supposed to go this way?!"

His raised voice made her jump a bit.

"When you approached me, I shouldn't have spoken to you at Barney's!" Jennifer answered with a squealing voice. "I shouldn't have taken your number; I shouldn't have gone out with you! I was just going to blow you off! But the sight of you wanting to see me again, waiting for my phone call, made me curious as to why you wanted to go out with me!"

"You mean Barbara?" Adrian snarled while folding his arms.

"I am Barbara, you prick!"

Her screaming response made Adrian jump back this time, as her demeanor read that she wanted to punch his head off his body.

"Name and identity aside, everything else was me!" Jennifer slapped her chest, blaring. "I had everything! A life outside of this base that no one knew about! Friends that I started to make! And now my mother is angry at me, my youngest sister hates me! I lost everything to go out with you!"

Genesis

"So why did you do it then?!" An angered Adrian yelled, stepping forward and getting into her personal space.

"Because I wanted you!" Jennifer cried out.

Her words silenced Adrian as she went to fold her arms around herself for comfort. Her metal frame rattled like a slender tree in a gale wind. Jennifer's voice and mannerisms became that of a woman actually crying, although she could not produce tears.

"I didn't expect our first date to go so well; I did not foresee liking you. I knew if I kept going, there was a ninety-nine percent chance this would end badly. I kept saying one last date, and then I'd break up with you. But I couldn't …I didn't want to stop seeing you in that way …I didn't want to let you go. I never meant to cause you any pain Adrian, I know I am just a machine, but I couldn't help it. I wanted you … and I wanted you to want me …I wanted you to want me …"

Mr. Binks barked and whined at the sight of his owner in distress.

Adrian sighed as he moved closer, touching her right arm, physically transforming into her metal composition. He attempted to pull her into his embrace, wrapping his arms around her to comfort her, but she began to resist.

"Stop, "I'm malfunctioning again," Jennifer pleaded. "Diagnostics are not revealing the anomaly causing this, but I know I am …"

"Shut up, you're not malfunctioning," Adrian whispered to her. "You're not malfunctioning."

Shock formed on her face briefly before she gave in and rested her head on his chest. Time stood still until they eventually met one another's gaze with their lips inches apart.

At that moment, Adrian came to his senses, slowly releasing her and backing away with his hands up.

"Um, I need to figure …I need to go."

Genesis

He quickly turned on his heel, reverting to his human form, speed walking away while running his hand through his hair. Adrian left more confused than before while Jennifer stood rooted in place, watching him go with an equally confusing visage sprinkled with dejection.

~~~~~~~~~~~~~~~~~~~~~~~~~~~~~~~~~

Two days later, the Regulators sat in their respective uniforms and gear in the debriefing room as Rogers laid out their latest mission.

"Listen up, people," Rogers began. "Our only damn lead regarding the red booster serum finally gave us something. To catch everyone up, our big break to this case came in Justin O'Banion, the red booster from the Sound Nightclub incident.

It turns out that Justin is the nephew of James O'Banion, a notorious Irish Mob boss from Chicago.

So, we've placed heavy surveillance on Uncle O'Banion, waiting for him to give us a clue to his association with the dealer of the red booster serum, and he finally delivered.

Last night, James O'Banion confirmed with his associates that they received confirmation by a letter sent via courier, which he instantly burned. They were to pick up a shipment of Red Rum in Cali, Columbia. We're banking everything that Red Rum is their name for the booster serum."

"Cali Columbia?" Teuila asked.

"Number ten on the list of deadliest places in the world," Erica pointed out, "It is also in international territory."

"Which is what I want to get to before we continue any further," Rogers continued. "This is not an authorized mission, which means it is not sanctioned by the United States Government nor the Administration. I have shared why I have decided not to divulge our knowledge of this red booster serum.

I believe this must be found and destroyed, along with whoever

Genesis

created it. We don't have the power to prevent other governments or legitimate companies from walking down this road. Still, this must be done if we can stop it or slow it down on the black market side.

Now, this is my view, my belief.

But doing this will have severe repercussions, whether we succeed or not.

I mean possible career-ending repercussions.

This mission is volunteer only, and I mean that. You are not obligated under any circumstances to take part in this if you do not want to.

I will give those that want to bow out a minute to leave."

"Save your minute Sarge," Oliver answered Rogers, "We can't speak for Sister Shareef, but the five of us have already spoken on this. We're in all the way."

Rogers nodded and turned to Sister Shareef, waiting for her response.

"You know I'm not going anywhere," came from her lips.

"As we speak, our target is being tracked; O'Banion is sending his second in command George O'Leary and an eight-man crew to pick up this shipment," Rogers explained, pointing to the large monitor screen, which came alive. "They are going by plane and leaving by boat. The second they land, we are up in the air. Erica will continue to monitor and provide us Intel. There is every possibility this could be a setup, one thing we do know after the Castillo hit, these are not people we play with, so I want more than everyone's A-Game on this. Is that understood?"

"Yes, sir!" The entire active team howled.

"Make your last-minute checks and get ready to be up in the air once we get confirmation. Dismissed."

Genesis

~~~~~~~~~~~~~~~~~~~~~~~~~~~~~~~~~~~

Six hours and fifteen minutes later, the Regulators were up in the air, headed toward Columbia. The ship's refractive body and stealth mode kept it hidden and off all radars.

Rogers sat in his chair, glancing at each team member in their own world, giving their gear and weapons last-minute checks. Sister Sledge was the only one who lifted her eyes to meet Rogers.

"Maxine, what's the status on O'Leary?" Rogers called out.

"George O'Leary and his men are en route to an abandoned factory in Felidia." Maxine indicated. "Our ETA is ten minutes."

"Reduce our approach," Rogers ordered. "As soon as you hear additional voices that are not a part of their party, we'll move in."

"Affirmative."

Rogers adjusted his beanie and gave his rifle one final check before getting up, which got everyone's attention.

"Get ready for boots on the ground."

"Yes, sir!" They all howled.

"Sergeant Rogers, O'Leary, and his men have arrived and are entering the building," Maxine announced. "Two black SUVs and a utility truck are already on the scene; scans are detecting a party of six waiting for them on the third floor of the building with what appears to be ten crates."

"Give me a play by play, Maxine."

"They have ascended to the second floor and are moving to the third. Targets have ascended to the third floor and are heading to the center of ..."

Maxine's pause gave Rogers and the team a sick feeling in their

Genesis

guts.

"Maxine, what's the matter?" Rogers asked.

"I can no longer see or hear what is occurring inside of the building," Maxine stated. "I am employing all forms of audio and optics; nothing is getting through. Deploying a drone."

A small port in the underbelly of the Tornado opened up. A stealthy black cybernetic-looking hummingbird shot out like a bullet; it slowed its speed as it entered through a broken window on the third floor. Its transmission went dead the second it was inside the building.

"I have lost control of the drone; its transmission has been interrupted as well. I suspect either tech or some form of superhuman ability causing the interference."

Rogers rubbed his chin as he felt the eyes of his unit awaiting their orders.

"They've either thought ahead to ensure their meeting and transaction remains a secret, or we're walking into an ambush. Either way, we're going in, raid style. We'll sort em out when it's all said and done. I got the third floor by the front door, along with Nitro, who will take the second floor. Merge with Sister Sledge on the right with Merge taking the ground floor and Sledge the third, Heavy Element with Cyclone on the left with Heavy Element taking the ground floor and Cyclone the second, Blitz, you got the back door and the fourth floor. Let's move out!"

The Tornado's rear hatch opened as the Regulators leaped to the ground or flew out. Each one made a mad dash covering all four sides of the factory. Blitz being the fastest zipped to the rear entrance. He waited until everyone converged on the building.

Rogers and Sister Sledge super leaped to get to the third floor. At the same time, Heavy Element and a Mercurian-transformed Merge went through the side doors to face any guards held up at the bottom. Nitro and Cyclone used their powers to enter through the second floor, while Blitz took the fourth floor, the building's final level.

Genesis

They all converged on the third floor, where Rogers and Sister Sledge entered. A sick feeling swirled within their stomachs when they didn't hear a struggle, energy attack, or a gunshot fired.

As the rest of the team made their way to the third floor, they came upon the same baffling scene Rogers and Sister Sledge leaped into.

"What … the fuck …is going on?" Heavy Element asked.

O'Leary and his men's lifeless bodies, along with the six other men, were littered on the floor. The other party was dressed in black tactical fatigue sets and combat boots. Just as Maxine scanned, ten olive green military cargo crates were sitting in two stacks of five on top of each other.

Rogers and Sister Sledge walked around, checking all of the bodies.

"All of them are dead," Rogers confirmed.

"Same here," Sister Sledge said, nodding.

"What killed them?" Merge asked, looking around.

"No idea," Rogers shook his head, answering. "No sign of physical trauma, skin, and lips are not discolored, so they weren't poisoned."

"Five bucks says these crates are empty or rigged." Heavy Element said, motioning.

Blitz hovered his hand over the cartons.

"Nine of the crates aren't producing any source of electricity; the tenth one is, but the power source is small battery size."

"I think it's safe to open it," Nitro said while standing on the other side.

"How do you know?" Cyclone asked.

Genesis

"There's a sign on this side that says open and play."

Rogers moved to the side Nitro was on, seeing the sign for himself. He walked over to the crate, opened the lid, and pulled out what was inside.

"A DVD player," Rogers said, narrowing his eyes.

Everyone moved closer as he flipped it open, revealing the screen inside. It came to life on its own, playing the DVD disc inside of it.

The team watched with mixed reactions as it played without sound the brutal execution of Angel Castillo and the individuals in black responsible. As the video ended, the player sparked and smoked while the DVD inside melted to the point it became unplayable.

"Well, now we know what happened to Castillo," Sister Sledge said while folding her arms.

"So, whoever this guy and his goon squad in black are brought O'Leary and his guys all the way to Columbia to ax them?" Merge asked, attempting to piece things together. "These other guys look like locals, which means they were used as additional bait. But why show us Castillo's murder now after meticulously trying to hide it?"

Before they could attempt to answer the question amongst themselves, their ears were filled with a splitting whining sound of something massive falling out of the sky. It was followed by a ground-rattling fiery crash that sent smoke, dirt, and debris wafting into the building's broken windows.

Rogers and the entire team raced to the windows to see the Tornado they flew in broken in two and demolished from the impact of the fall it took.

"Maxine! Maxine!" Rogers yelled, "Maxine, come in!"

No response.

"Erica! Do you read me! Come in! Erica!"

Genesis

Also, no response.

The team checked their communicators to find no signal or static radio interference.

"Definite set up," Rogers said, nodding to the team.

"Uh, Sarge," Cyclone swallowed while pointing.

A thick row of black was about the distance from the other end of a football field. Some of the blacks became a swarm, taking to the air powered by whatever power source was coursing through their veins to grant them propulsion as they flew at high speeds toward them.

No one had to ask one another what was coming next.

"Incoming!" Heavy Element roared.

The team scattered, ducking for cover as large holes were punched through the building by an array of powerful energy blasts. Heavy Element and Merge transformed into metal elements while running to avoid the attacks. Blitz threw up an electrical shield, nullifying the barrages directed at him. At the same time, Cyclone was knocked off her feet by the impact of a photon beam at close range. As she hit the floor painfully, Nitro hoofed it over to her, diving in her direction as another powerful energy attack nearly tagged him.

Nitro rolled to his feet, grabbing her arm and dragging her into an abandoned office.

Sister Sledge plowed through a wall into another office to avoid being hit. At the same time, Rogers's shoulder smashed into a nearby break room for cover.

After another half minute, the energy attacks stopped, leaving thick onyx smoke and igniting small fires throughout the building.

"Headcount!" Rogers roared, "Give me a headcount now!"

Genesis

"Still alive, Sarge!" Heavy Element coughed.

"Sir, me too!" Merge yelled.

"Sir, I'm alright!" Blitz confirmed.

"Sir, Nitro here! I'm fine! Cyclone is down but coherent!"

"Sister Sledge!"

She shook the floor with her running solid pattern as she entered the break room; he smashed through to find cover.

"I'm good."

Rogers nodded as he prepared to give his following command.

"Everyone, stay put! Nitro, we're going to make our way over to you and Cyclone!"

"Roger that!"

The Sarge followed Sister Sledge, wading back to the team through the blinding black smoke. Rogers and Sister Sledge ducked into the office Nitro dragged Cyclone into to check on her. The right side of her face was slightly burnt and cut up from debris as she clutched her right ribcage, where the upper part of her suit took most of the impact.

"Cyclone, what's your status?"

"Sir, I think I cracked a couple of ribs," she groaned, "And my left shoulder feels like it's dislocated."

Sister Sledge wasted no time moving to her left side, grabbing her arm, examining it.

"It's dislocated, alright; I'm going to have to pop it back in."

"This going to hurt, right?" Cyclone asked, gasping.

Genesis

"Yep, it's going to hurt. We'll do it on three."

"Okay." Cyclone nodded.

"One."

Sledge counted as she pulled Cyclone's arm at the same time. The young woman let out a blood-curdling scream as her elder snapped her arm back into her socket.

"Fuck!" she squealed. "You said on three! On three!"

"Maxine, come in! Maxine, respond!" Rogers tried his headset again.

The team anxiously awaited as Rogers listened for a response only to get dead air.

"Still nothing," Rogers frustratingly shook his head, answering.

"Whoever or whatever shut down the Tornado must have taken her out too," Merge said, "Or she would have been here by now."

"You're right about that," Rogers agreed.

"What the hell did they use, some type of EMP blast?" Nitro nervously asked.

"Aren't Maxine and the Tornado …designed to withstand those?" Cyclone chimed in with a groan. "And how'd they hit them …when they were cloaked?"

"This ain't the time to debate how they took out our air support," Rogers sternly said. "It's down, and we're pinned down with no communication with the Ranch. Our new mission is to get the hell out of this mess."

"Why do you think they stopped shooting?" Sister Sledge asked.

Genesis

"Probably can't see us from all the smoke in here," The Sarge deduced. "Good chance they want to make sure we're still in the building and didn't sneak out. Heavy Element, what do you see?"

Heavy Element crawled over to a window and pulled down his tactical glasses on his head, which lit up, giving him an enhanced view of the outside. Outside on the ground and in the sky was a sizable army of boosted troops, all wearing tactical black gear and masks. Those of the Titan and Mercurian class carried heavy-caliber armor-piercing weapons. At the same time, the Apollo Class utilized their abilities to attack.

"Uh, about eighty or more strong," He swallowed, answering. "All boosted. Judging from some of the tattoos, skin tones, and other features that I can see, we got Italian, Russian, and Irish Mafia, Triad, Jamaican, Yakuza, either Brazilian or Mexican Cartel, or both, and some other groups I can't make out. It's a who's who of organized assholes out there."

"This was definitely a setup," Rogers snorted.

"Don't they know who we are?" Merge asked, turning to him.

"That's exactly why they're here," Rogers answered while checking his rifle. "They don't want us to take down their supplier, so they're going to make damn sure we don't walk out here alive. What's the status of communication with the Ranch?"

"Sir, I've tried every frequency; nothing is getting through," Blitz announced. "They either have some kind of tech or someone out there powerful enough to jam communications."

"Our short-range channel still works," Nitro announced.

Everyone nodded, acknowledging as they heard the clicks he was sending into their ears with his wrist communicator.

"Erica has to know by now there's a problem," Sister Sledge said, turning to Rogers.

"We can't wait for whatever plan she comes up with," Rogers said.

Genesis

"The minute this smoke clears up, they're going to start blasting again, and this time they're going to bring this down with us inside of it. Everyone listen up!"

Each Regulator turned to lock onto Rogers's fierce, steely eyes.

"We're not sitting here like a bunch of ducks in a friggin barrel. Out there is the scum of the Earth!" He barked, pointing. "Nothing more than a bunch of street punks sent here to attempt to make sure we don't cut off their supply chain. They are not soldiers, so do not treat them as such; is that understood?"

"Yes, sir!" They all howled back.

"Blitz, Merge, and Nitro, we're going to need for you to unleash hell and scatter them sons of bitches, show them some real firepower."

"Sir, I can fight!" Cyclone growled, getting to one knee. "I can fight!"

"Nitro, back her up and keep her alive," Rogers ordered.

"Yes, sir," he acknowledged.

"Severe punishment for the person who dies today and worse for those that let them die."

On hearing the Sarge's final order, everyone turned to Heavy Element, who looked back at them all with a dirty look.

"You all can kiss my Italian ass," he scowled, retorting.

Everyone became deathly quiet as the team's ears picked up Earth and concrete being disturbed, followed by the familiar whistling sound of bombs dropping.

"They're not planning on shooting up the place again!" Heavy Element howled.

Genesis

"It's a full-on physical assault!" Rogers roared. "Get ready to engage!"

Superhuman bodies began smashing through the fragile structure as Titan-boosted criminals locked and loaded began to open fire on the Regulator team.

Two of them crashed through the window Heavy Element was looking out of in proximity to Rogers, who cut them down with his rifle. His tactic was several rounds of body shots to temporarily immobilize them and then several well-trained headshots, turning their brain matter into Swiss cheese, instantly killing them.

Blitz and a transformed Merge, taking on his electrical powers, dived out of opposite windows, taking to the air to face the converging Apollos outside. At the same time, Nitro jumped out into the hallway and unleashed his energy, becoming an inferno scorching everyone in his path. The same attacking Titans now engulfed in flames, dived out of the building and crashed to the ground, where they proceeded to roll to put the fire out while their regenerative healing kicked in.

Sister Sledge chose not to use firearms for apparent reasons. She instead used ambush tactics by crashing in and out of walls to remove hostile combatants. The Red Rum boosters they were facing appeared to be in the final stages of becoming full-blown EVOs; some were probably already EVOs.

However, similar to the infected, they did not have a chance to harness their abilities like the Regulators. Sister Shareef's strength and speed were still monstrous compared to the other Titans she fought, which she also used to her advantage. During one of her ambushes, she used the sound of the guns they were shooting to track their positions as she barreled through a wall, surprising three Red Rum Titans, dropkicking one out of a nearby third-floor window.

Sister Sledge sprang back to her feet and jumped into the air as the other two turned their guns on her and came down, stomping the floor, causing it to break and give way underneath them.

Genesis

The other two Titans screamed as they fell headfirst while she controlled her descent. Both of them lost their guns on the way down as they painfully smacked into the floor while she landed in a crouched position. Sister Sledge quickly stood up and punt-kicked the nearest one through two walls. She then sprang on top of the third Titan, still on his hands and knees, wrapping her arms around his waist. In one motion, she picked him up into a gut wrench hold and roared as she hurled him with all her strength through the floor to the ground level.

As she dusted her hands off, her ears picked up whistling sounds coming in her direction. Her eyes widened as she realized it wasn't more Red Rum boosters coming at her.

"Oh shit! RPGs!"

Five rocket-propelled grenades fired toward the factory broke into smaller projectiles moving faster. They all struck the building, blowing the face off of it. Sister Sledge was not fast enough to avoid the impact as the combined explosions sent her rocketing through several walls.

The blast also affected the rest of the team and everyone else still inside. Nitro cursed, diving into an opposite room while Rogers jumped, covering Cyclone and protecting her from the blast.

Heavy Element held his breath in his metallic form, bracing himself as he was hit by the first initial blast. He ran through the destruction, diving from the window to the ground floor.

After impacting the ground, he came back up with both his sidearms, shooting projectiles with the force of a small railgun, either taking opponents off of their feet or swatting them out of the sky. As he reloaded, he came under fire from a Titan carrying a handheld minigun. Although his armored form and suit took the complete brute of the rapid projectile rounds, his right handgun was severely damaged from the barrages.

He quickly switched his left sidearm to his right, breathed, took aim, and squeezed off two rounds while under fire, removing half the Titan's skull from his head and dropping him. Before he could recoup, he got slammed and taken several yards by a Mercurian.

Genesis

Heavy Element, having trained in combatting Mercurians, knew never to let go once he grabbed one. He wrapped his legs around the masked Mercurian, brought his sidearm close to his chest, and fired several rounds. He braced for impact as they crashed violently to the ground. He did not stop as he double-tapped two more shots in the face, confirming the kill.

Heavy Element got to his feet, checking the rounds in his sidearm.

"Run from that, you son of a bitch," he muttered.

Sinister cackling brought his guard back up, taking aim.

A light-skinned young man with thick, dreaded hair walked up wearing a black sleeveless Under Armour Shirt, black tactical pants, and brown open-toe sandals. Heavy Element, without hesitation, fired two rounds, striking him in the chest. The force of the shots ripped him off his feet and sent him tumbling to the ground.

Heavy Element moved in to give him the professional double tap, only to slow up as laughter came from his target lying on the ground. The dread slowly sat up, looking Heavy Element dead in the eyes.

"Pussyhole! Ya keyan't kill me!"

Simultaneously, his chest's large, humanly fatal projectile wounds began to heal. He then grabbed a massive animal tooth hanging from the platinum chain around his neck. Instantly, he transformed into a gigantic humanoid version of a male lion.

"Okay, that's new." Heavy Element said, swallowing.

His transformation wasn't finished as his were-lion body turned into the composition of the high-velocity dark metal rounds that Esposito shot him with.

"Okay, that is definitely new."

The transformed Jamaican gangster bellowed a thunderous roar as he sprang to his feet. Heavy Element fired additional rounds to confirm they would bounce off his now-hardened dark metal skin.

Esposito braced himself as the boosted Elemental leaped, pouncing onto him. Heavy Element fell backward, using the momentum to execute a quick Tomeo-nage judo throw. But the Red Rum-boosted thug bounced back quickly with his immense cat reflexes lunging at Heavy Element.

The combination of his dark metal humanoid lion transformation proved a bit more than Heavy Element could handle, mainly when he used his massive jaws to clamp down on Esposito's forearm.

"Son of a bitch!" Heavy Element growled.

Although the bite would not break Esposito's dark metal skin, the crushing power behind it was beyond uncomfortable.

Heavy Element dug down as he rifled the side of the boosted Elemental's head with stiff right-hand punches to break free of his hold. The stronger gangster had another idea as he spun around, taking Esposito off his feet with his mouth holding him before releasing him with a fling, launching him through what was left of a factory wall, and sending him back into the partially destroyed facility.

Heavy Element rolled with the hit as he smacked the ground hard, returning to his feet using one hand to dig into the concrete to stop his momentum. He ran as his animal metal-enhanced opponent entered the building, charging at him.

Heavy Element leaped into the air, hitting him with a hard tackle with all his body weight. Sparks flew between them as they traded punches and claw swipes.

~~~~~~~~~~~~~~~~~~~~~~~~~~~~~~~~~~~~

Back outside, Columbia's sky became lit with the battle as Blitz and Merge fought several Red Rum Apollos in an all-out super aerial dogfight.

Genesis

The Regulator air team had the advantage regarding experience and sheer power. Blitz's electrical abilities had no equal, while Merge, who was nowhere on his level, still had ample experience using his abilities, which she duplicated.

They worked as a team using in-and-out strafing attacks, switching between battling those in the air and the ground troops.

The issue that had them miffed was a three-part situation.

First, whoever chose the mixture of organized super-powered criminals to fight them did their homework. The power sets they faced were electrical, photonic, solar, or hydro. Taking down individuals with similar power sets who could harness and re-direct their attacks was a problem, especially for Merge. At the same time, Blitz would just hit them with enough energy to overload and fry them.

Merge utilized physical fly-by-strike attacks, literally punching and elbowing her opponents at high speeds out of nowhere, causing them to fatally spiral out of the sky to the Earth below, hitting whatever was at the bottom.

Both had to avoid the hydro-powered boosters, which could short out their powers with a well-placed direct hit.

Their second problem was for criminals of different affiliations known for extreme violence against each other throughout history; at that moment, they were all highly coordinated. Those of similar power sets learned to combine their abilities to make up for the lack of power they had as individuals, especially the hydro-powered boosters. They even pulled a common maneuver where a solar wielder and a hydro wielder combined streams to create a thick smoke screen mist, attempting to make it difficult for the Hurt Locker-trained combatants to fight.

This brought them to their third issue.

"Is it me, or are these assholes really good for a bunch of newbies?" Blitz asked, communicating with Merge through his internal earpiece.

Genesis

"It's not you," she responded while smacking another boosted Apollo out of the sky with a stiff elbow to the skull. "These fuckers fight like they've been at some superpower boot camp or something! Three of them managed to pull out of their dive before they hit the ground! Oh shit!"

Merge's startled response came as several Red Rum boosters swarmed out of the mist created to ambush her. She slammed on the brakes to defend herself as six converged on her. Blitz at the last second, lightning bolted in between her and her attackers. He conjured a sizeable electrical sphere shielding that the Red Rum boosters ran right into. Overloading and burning them out in midair, similar to flies zapped by a bug catcher.

They briefly glanced at each other before flying in opposite directions to provide more cover fire for their teammates below.

~~~~~~~~~~~~~~~~~~~~~~~~~~~~~~~~~~

Although Merge and Blitz diverted a good portion of the energy attacks away from their team's position, Rogers and the company still had to deal with those that got by. After the RPG attack, there was very little protection at the front of the building, forcing Rogers and Nitro to retreat further back into the structure to defend an injured Cyclone.

Rogers kept picking off those close enough to get within the range of his rifle, but it was as Blitz and Merge figured out. Not only were the super-powered mobsters and gangsters well versed in their abilities, but they were also coordinating their attacks like a well-oiled assault unit.

They would have overtaken him if it weren't for Rogers's veteran Marine training. Cyclone also would not stay put as she would jump in and unleash 200 miles of hurricane blasts, slamming them back.

She had to stop due to the force of the attacks aggravating her current injuries.

"Sarge, you can't sit here, babysitting me," she gasped. "You could do more damage if you were free to maneuver around these bastards. I can hold my own."

Genesis

"What'd I tell you about being a hero, Cyclone?" Rogers asked as he picked off another Titan from several yards.

"Not trying to be a hero, sir, I'm stating facts! Give me a minute to move someplace where I can hold up so you can bring the pain! I will follow orders; I'm not going to die today!"

Rogers quickly glanced at her before switching the setting to his rifle to lay down a cover fire that tore through concrete and metal.

"Get moving then!"

Cyclone pushed her injuries' pain way down as she moved through a hole in the office wall, heading to a different location to hold up. Seeing that she was clear, Rogers became a moving tank, jumping out of the opening of the building and landing three floors down.

He traded fire with and clipped three Titans armed with miniguns. Although their guns were the latest in armor-piercing rounds, they only scratched, chipped, and burn-marked his ballistic suit.

Rogers rifle, a bigger mini railgun to Heavy Element's sidearms, delivered quadruple the power, making bigger fatal holes that even Titans could not heal from, especially regarding headshots.

Cyclone was right; Rogers was more effective when he was on the move.

The Red Rum criminal boosters' answer to Rogers blowing away ten of their men in under three minutes was another unified RPG rocket assault. This time, they launched ten rocket projectile grenades. All ten again broke apart as smaller missiles barreled faster toward their target like hornets.

"Shit."

The projectiles' combined detonation had enough power to lift Rogers off his feet several yards, knocking him back into the factory. At the same time, other parts of the partially demolished structure came down due

Genesis

to the explosion. Rogers sat up, coughing up smoke as the slight ringing in his ear disappeared. He first checked his rifle to ensure it was not damaged.

He jumped as Sister Sledge, with a well-timed leap, came out of left field, landing right next to him.

"You alright?"

"I'm fine," he snapped, getting to a crouched position. "Seriously, this is bullshit. You need to start carrying a firearm."

"You know why I can't do guns," She admonished him.

"Then bow and arrows with explosive tips!" Rogers shot back. "Something! Because this right here ain't working!"

"Are you done?"

"Yeah, I'm done."

Looking at her brooding boyfriend, Sister Sled reached over, pulling the sidearm from his holster. She quickly checked the clip before relocking and loading.

"Considering the situation, I'm compromising, happy?"

"Yeah, love you."

Her eyes widened as a trembling smile appeared on her face. It was the first time Rogers said it.

"I love you too."

"I'm taking the lead," Rogers said as he got up. "Cover my right."

"Got it."

The couple moved out again to rejoin the battle from outside.

Genesis

~~~~~~~~~~~~~~~~~~~~~~~~~~~~~~~~~~~~

Back at the Ranch, Erica stood in the middle of central command, watching displays of her team being attacked from all sides while feverishly attempting to bypass whatever prevented her from verbal contact with the Regulators.

"Give me something, Maxine!"

"I am still unable to regain verbal communication with the team, nor my body or the Tornado. The source of that interference is on or near the battlefield and has a wide range. Should we contact Ms. Dennison for assistance?"

It was the first thought that came to mind. Erica, however, knew that Rogers would strangle her if she made the call. She slowly turned to an anxious Angie and Jennifer as she pondered what to do.

At that moment, her mind wandered back to a session she had last year with Michael Westgate, formerly known as Anchimayen.

~~~~~~~~~~~~~~~~~~~~~~~~~~~~~~~~~~~~

It was two months after the incident on the piers in Florida. Erica traveled there for her bi-monthly visit, which initially began as a weekly visit and slowly increased in increments of a week to build a case for Mr. Westgate's execution once he became of legal age.

Erica sat in the chair on the opposite side of a reinforced transparent wall with her tablet in her lap. She observed the young boy with ice-blue eyes, freckles, pale skin, and fire-red hair in a linen white shirt and pants.

He nonchalantly walked around his Purgatory padded cell with a sizeable neural dampener attached to the back of his neck, preventing him from accessing his Promethean mental abilities and wearing a demeanor to rival Hannibal Lecter.

He'd slow his walk occasionally, giving her a look that felt like he

Genesis

was examining and undressing her. The effect irritated and creeped her out at the same time.

"Something's different about you," Westgate wagged his finger. "You're not your normal miserable self. What happened?"

"Nothing happened," Erica sighed. "We're also not here to analyze me."

"Don't you know by now this is a give and take relationship, bitch?" The eight-year-old chuckled. "You want to get into my head, you have to let me into yours. Let me guess, you tried DP for the first time and found out it wasn't your cup of tea."

"Your vulgarity has become old, played out, and pathetic," Erica answered while writing a footnote into her tablet with her stylus pen, which recorded the session, turning it into a readable transcript for later.

"No, that's not it," He shook his head with a smile. "You weren't walking funny when you came in here. Something bad happened to you, didn't it? Who hurt you?"

Erica sat up in her chair with narrowed eyes as thoughts of ways to murder him without getting caught entered her mind.

A savage grin formed on his face as he realized he was getting to her.

"Or did you see someone get hurt and was unable to 'save the day?' Now you're all fucked up over it. That has to be it. It must have been something pretty bad. How young were they? Was there a lot of blood? How badly did they suffer?"

She refused to answer to give him what he wanted. Unfortunately, he didn't really care if she replied.

"Do you know why people like me will never stop what we do? It's because people like you make our job so easy and fun. People like you have limits, while people like me have none. There is a limit to the amount

Genesis

of death and suffering someone like you can take before your little mind cracks like an eggshell. You shouldn't feel sorry; most people are wired like you.

Your pathetic moral compass limits you from doing what you should do, killing me and those like me.

It's easier for you to fuck each other over, like giving a guy fifteen to twenty-five for some weed. It's much less work and very profitable.

Regarding me, people like you believe there is a tiny sliver of hope that I can be redeemed.

That we can be saved!"

Michael ended his last sentence with a tone of mockery before continuing.

"And we, the Apex Predators of this world, know this! And we let you believe this is possible as we secretly become stronger and more skilled in our craft.

You also make the toys we need to do what we do so accessible. God bless the NRA!

Until finally, one day, one of us decides it's time to go out and just shatter your little fucking worlds."

Westgate erupted in laughter as he stopped at the transparent wall before Erica. Her demeanor was still indifferent, although she knew he could feel her hatred for him.

"Do you know why mass murderers kill themselves nine times out of ten before the police arrive?" Westgate asked, leaning forward a bit. "I'll tell you. The first reason is to intensify the grieving process for suckers like you. If the mass murderer is dead, those left behind never know why they did it. They can guess all they want and do their little analysis to try and piece things together, but in the end, it's all speculation on their part. The truth goes to hell with the dead, never to be uncovered.

Genesis

Secondly, the mass murderer always knows that there are more like him. People who will continue to do their work to butcher the sheep.

It's the circle of life."

Westgate moved closer to the window with a sinister scowl, unbefitting a child his age.

"So, if you think I fear death or damnation, whore, you are dead wrong; there are some of us that are just built from the womb to serve in hell than in heaven.

I take solace in that I will either get out of this gerbil cage really soon and have a lot of fun, or when I die, someone else will take my place and butcher the sheep like you.

And you can do nothing about it because there will always be a limit to how far little sheep like you will go to stop monsters like me."

~~~~~~~~~~~~~~~~~~~~~~~~~~~~~~~~

"I'm not fucking sheep!" Erica hissed as she pulled herself out of the memory with her fists clutched.

"Miss, are you alright?" Maxine asked with a concerned tone.

"Jennifer, you're temporarily off the bench," Erica announced. "All three of you upload yourselves into your Armageddon bodies, then ready Sam and Buster, the family is going to Columbia."

~~~~~~~~~~~~~~~~~~~~~~~~~~~~~~~~

Back in the combat zone, Cyclone made it to the fourth floor of the demolished factory. Staying low to avoid getting shot at, she could glance out the window to see that her teammates weren't fairing as well as they should against the Red Rum boosters. Those that fell had their places quickly taken, while the more skilled fighters rapidly recovered and regrouped. Eventually, the numbers games would out-tank the Regulators' combat experience and endurance.

Genesis

Despite her injuries, Cyclone had to think fast to aid her team.

"Merge, you there?"

"Of course, I'm here! What do you want?!"

She responded harshly as she blindsided an electrical class Apollo with a midair lariat while being chased by an eight-man airborne team looking to bring her down. Her fatigued hit wasn't enough to lay him out, as he recovered mid-fall and joined the hunt.

"Nitro, you there?" Cyclone asked, ignoring her hostility.

"Of course, I'm here, woman!"

He was setting two boosted Titans ablaze after stopping their incoming bullets with a thermo-kinetic wall of flames.

"I see you; think your flames can reach the fourth floor of this building?"

"Of course!"

"Then move one yard out, and five steps to your left," she instructed, "Merge find Nitro right now, and come through what's left of the window on the fourth floor right over him."

"Say what?!" she screamed.

"You know how to do it!" Cyclone shot back with a stern tone. "So, do it!"

Merge muttered a curse as she hit the throttle, strafing and maneuvering in Nitro's direction with the pack at her heels. As she aimed for the window, she canceled out Blitz's power, switching to her brother's. She took a metal form as she smashed through the window, tucking into a violent tumble roll.

Seeing that she was clear, Cyclone stepped in front of the window,

Genesis

extending her hand as she clutched her ribs.

"This is really going to hurt. Nitro now!"

Simultaneously, she unleashed a massive tornado blast; Nitro roared, aiming upward to fire a thermo-kinetic attack into her stream, creating a flaming tornado that engulfed all eight incoming Apollos and anyone else unlucky enough to be in range, charring them out of the sky.

A semi-exhausted Merge stood next to her, nodding her head reasonably impressed.

"That was hot."

"Thank you," Cyclone groaned.

The response to their spectacular, larger-than-life tornado flamethrower was another barrage of RPGs.

This time, they launched twenty of them.

Once again, as they neared their target, they broke apart into smaller, faster projectiles.

"Oh, come on!" Nitro screamed.

"Not good," Cyclone swallowed.

"Ya think?!" Merged yelled.

Merge didn't think twice as she scooped Cyclone up in her arms, putting it in gear to run as fast as possible. At the same time, Nitro focused his thermo-kinetic energy through his hands to produce thrusters, taking him airborne.

The area became an Earth-shaking inferno, with what was left of the factory taking the hit's brunt.

An additional fifty-five percent of the building gave way as the

Genesis

floor went out under Merge's feet. Both women screamed as they clung to each other for dear life as they fell into the smoking rubble below.

Nitro hovered high over the destruction, searching for his teammates.

"Cyclone! Merge! Come in! Do you hear me? Oh, shit!"

Nitro was forced to go aerial, blasting away as another pack flew in to attack him.

"Dammit! I'm not a flyer!"

Back within the building, heavy coughing came from two voices. Merge still held onto Cyclone as she managed to keep her feet under her during the fall.

"What ...the ...fuck," Merge hacked up.

Cyclone groaned, also coughing and spitting as if ravaged with a case of emphysema.

"Seven ...against an army," she choked. "If I ever meet ...Whedon or Snyder ...I'm gonna chop them both ...in their fucking throats."

~ ~

Merge and Cyclone weren't the only ones affected by the latest barrage of RPG attacks.

The Sarge and Sister Sledge were both caked with smoke and debris.

Their regenerative healing removed their superficial burns as their coughing dissipated.

"We can't take another hit like this," Sister Sledge turned to Rogers, hacking.

Genesis

"Every time we gain the upper hand, they rain down hell on us," Rogers said while spitting murky saliva on the ground. "They're sending waves of attacks to wear us down. We need to regroup and take the fight to them."

"We need to regroup first, and then we need more firepower."

Rogers opened up his bracer, pulling up a GPS tracking grid of all his teammates.

"Heavy Element is closer to us," Rogers confirmed, gesturing. "Let's get him first before this smoke clears, and they try to hit us again."

Sister Sledge nodded as she followed him to Heavy Element's position. As they drew closer, they heard the sound of combat and a struggle. On his back in an open guard position, Heavy Element held the head of a humanoid metal lion attempting to bite his face off.

It was a stalemate, with their bodies of the same hardened material. Rogers stooped down to examine the situation.

"Oh, hey Sarge," Heavy Element groaned. "How are you doing this fine day?"

"Pretty good; who's your buddy?"

"I think he's from Spanish Town …or Ochi…he's got an interesting power set. You wouldn't happen to have a thermal on you?"

"What do you need it for?"

"Cram it down this son of a bitch's throat."

Rogers checked his harness as Heavy Element, and the boosted Elemental struggled and thrashed about the floor. He devised a black circular sphere the size of a ping-pong ball. Rogers stood on top of the gangster, grabbing the upper part of his mouth. At the same time, Heavy Element latched onto his lower, using their combined strength to pry it open.

Genesis

Rogers pushed a button on the thermal grenade, causing blue light to flash around it. He then dropped it down the Red Rum booster's throat. Heavy Element and the Sarge slammed his mouth shut and held him as the grenade made a high-pitched whining noise before exploding.

Blood poured from the gangster's eyes, nose, and ears as he went limp. Heavy Element tossed him off before rolling to his feet, dusting himself off.

"Let's get the rest of our team," Rogers said while pointing and checking his GPS locator. "Merge and Cyclone are thirty-five yards, that way. Nitro and Blitz are both airborne and still in combat with hostiles."

"Rogers! Rogers! Do you read! Rogers!"

The Sarge grasped his earpiece to the sound of a familiar voice.

"Erica? What's your position?"

"I am less than three minutes out from you and coming in hard," she announced. "I'm currently tracking you and the team and mapping out the hostiles in the area."

"They've kept their main forces back, sending them in waves while slamming us with RPGs and Apollo firepower every time we take an offensive," Rogers informed her. "Blitz and now Nitro is currently engaging them."

"I got a remedy for that."

"Bring the rain then while we regroup," Rogers ordered before switching channels, "Merge and Cyclone respond."

"We're still breathing, Sarge," Merge announced.

"Remain at your location; we're coming to you."

"Roger that."

Genesis

He switched channels one more time.

"Blitz and Nitro talk to me."

"We're holding our own but could need some help real quick, Sarge!" Blitz informed him, "I got power to burn, but Nitro is getting kind of winded."

"He's not exaggerating, sir!" Nitro interjected over the channel.

"Erica is coming in hot in less than a minute."

"I see her!" Blitz answered.

~ ~

Within the Tornado's central cockpit, Lady Tech, with its weapons primed, finalized the targeting of multiple hostiles below.

"Time to scatter the cucarachas."

She fired four missiles. Those four rockets nearing their destination broke apart into mini projectiles, which increased in speed. This time, it was the opposing forces of superhuman gangsters and mobsters that were forced to run and flee as she turned their location into one massive exploding inferno.

"Time to go to work, kids!"

The locking mechanisms attached to Sam released, allowing him to get up and stand ready in front of the rear hatch about to open. Maxine came from the central cockpit with double rifles to join him, followed by her other two sisters. Uploaded into their Armageddon bodies designed for nuclear threats or higher, the sisters appeared more robotic as the parts of their bodies that had an organic appearance had grey grid circuit patterns that looked like tattoos. Their cybernetic pieces seemed denser, with the lights emulating their power sources glowing brighter due to the quadruple EMP-resistant power core each of them housed.

Genesis

Toting two larger rifles, Angie quickly approached Jennifer, getting face-to-face with her.

Jennifer narrowed her eyes and was about to tell her it was not the time for another confrontation.

Angie got to the point with a soft voice.

"You don't deserve him."

"I know."

Her head fell as she said it.

"Then you better be the first one by his side when we hit the ground," Angie warned. "Or I will be."

Still heartbroken, Angie turned to join her other two siblings as Jennifer stood there momentarily, unsure what to say or do. Her glowing lavender eyes emitted a brighter hue as she got her head in the game and reached into her back, which opened up, allowing her to pull out her dual katana swords.

~ ~

The Tornado's back opened up as the android sisters, followed by Sam, leaped out, descending to the ground to join the battle below.

"Looks like the cavalry has arrived!" Nitro grinned, yelling.

Maxine and Angie locked onto targets, opening fire before they hit the ground. At the same time, a blade-wielding Jennifer straightened herself into an arrow, allowing herself to fall faster. She latched onto a male Titan as she extended her swords, running him through as she slammed into him. She struck him with a piston dropkick to the chest, hitting him back into a wall while performing a cartwheel flip in midair, decapitating a stunned Apollo Class EVO before she landed on her feet.

As she quickly scanned her surroundings, Jennifer's eyes locked

Genesis

with Heavy Element's watching her from a yard away. With Angie's last words in her memory, Jennifer stepped in his direction. It appeared as if Adrian was doing the same until both were quickly snapped back into their reality by the sound of combat and more attackers converging on each of them with the intent to kill them.

Unlike his sisters, Sam hit the ground with juggernaut brute force, punching, swatting, kicking, and stomping anything in his path. A male-boosted Italian mobster unleashed a blast of blue plasma flames engulfing him.

"How you like dat ya two-ton Hasbro piece of shit?"

He eased up his flame attack long enough for a Titan from the Russian mafia to slam right into him, attempting to take him off his feet. Sam, however, adjusted his footing, digging into the ground. Using his left hand, Sam grabbed the gangster around his waist, picked him up, and then struck him twice with two thunderous rights.

"Oh, shit!" gasped the mobster.

Sam threw the gangster he held in his hand at the flaming-wielding mobster whose head smacked violently into the concrete from the force of being struck by a Titan. He could not scream as Sam leaped into the air and came down, treating him like a cockroach as he crushed him under his foot.

"Stupid gangsters," Sam growled.

With a rare smirk, Rogers made his way over to Maxine in the middle of the battle.

"Took her long enough to figure it out."

"The Miss already knew something was afoul the second communications went down," Maxine replied in her defense. "She will be here shortly to provide additional support."

"Additional support?" Rogers asked with a furrowed brow.

Genesis

A bellowing sound caused Rogers and everyone else to look up, minus the android sisters and Sam, as something big launched out of the Tornado's rear. All hostiles began to scatter, screaming in disbelief as Lady Tech, in a form-fitting, fully armored suit, sat magnetically attached to Buster's back, soaring through the air via the propulsion thrusters on different parts of its body and the massive mechanized wings it deployed.

Coming in for a run, it unleashed a fierce ion blast from its mouth, taking out some ground forces. At the same time, Lady Tech operated the dual plasma cannons that opened within its lower back, picking off additional targets with her holographic HUD display.

"Take us down, Buster."

On her command, it swooped down and landed, sending dust and debris flying. Its wings retracted back into the housings within its body as it stomped over to Rogers. At the same time, her faceplate cracked open.

"Reporting for duty, sir!" She fiercely saluted.

"Should I be expecting a Dothraki horde to be charging this way?"

"Ha …ha …juw so funny …" Lady Tech fired back in Latin slang laced with sarcasm.

"You're not concerned about another possible EMP attack?" Rogers asked.

"After Peace's attack on the base, I went to work building backup bodies for the girls designed to absorb EMP-type attacks on her level," Lady Tech confidently answered. "Sam and Buster have been outfitted with the new tech. I didn't get around to upgrading the Tornados with it yet, provided that's what brought the first one down. I sent number two away so we don't lose another ship, which means we're going to have to battle our way back to its location if it comes to that."

Rogers looked at her with stern, fatherly, narrow eyes, expecting her to answer his next question.

Genesis

"Are you up for this?"

Lady Tech's eyes tapered as her face displayed an intensity he had never seen before in her.

"Sir, I wouldn't be here if I wasn't. Let's show these assholes who they're messing with."

A proud smirk formed on Rogers's face as he nodded in agreement.

~~~~~~~~~~~~~~~~~~~~~~~~~~~~~~~~

Two miles from the battle zone, the man in black with the red and black kabuki mask from the Castillo incident stood with his three associates behind him.

"For the love of god…the little bitch is riding a fucking dragon," he shook his head. "Is nothing fucking sacred?"

His henchmen looked at one another as he clasped his hands behind his back.

"It's time we turn it up a notch and see what our serum can really do."

The red lights on different parts of his mask, especially the eyes, began to light up with those words.

~~~~~~~~~~~~~~~~~~~~~~~~~~~~~~~~

Simultaneously, the Red Rum boosters, still alive and standing, changed demeanors as they all turned with incredible intensity in their eyes, refocusing their attention on the Regulators.

"Uh …guys," Nitro swallowed. "Are you seeing …what I am seeing?"

"Why do they look ultra-woke?" Cyclone swallowed.

Genesis

The remaining boosted organized criminal army moved in unison to converge on them.

"More like switched on," Rogers growled. "Get ready to engage!"

Every member of the team picked their target and attacked. It did not take long for them to determine what was different. The Red Rum boosters got better at fighting, much better.

Boosted Apollos flew faster, evading gunfire and energy attacks from even Blitz. They returned fire with extreme, near-deadly precision.

Titans getting shot either evaded or rolled with the hits they took to lessen their blows as they returned fire while allowing their regenerative healing to take care of the minimal damage done.

Mercurians took no hits. The only two factors that kept them from overrunning the team were Blitz, Sam, Buster, and the android sisters, whose tracking systems could keep them at bay.

"What the fuck is going on?!" Heavy Element snarled. "How the hell did they get stronger?!"

"They're not stronger or faster!" Lady Tech informed them. "They're brain synapsis has suddenly gone on overload! It's allowing them each to naturally utilize their current abilities to the most maximum potential!"

"How is that possible?!" Sister Sledge yelled at her question.

"It's like Rogers said!" Lady Tech yelled. "Someone switched them on!"

"That means there must be a signal, right?!" Merge asked in metal form, returning fire with both her sidearms. "Someone transmitting from somewhere to activate them!"

"Already on it! The transmission came from Northwest about two miles out! Zeroing in!"

Genesis

Lady Tech's helmet lit up as she attempted to track the source of the signal. An unknown force reeled her head back, almost knocking her off Buster's back.

"Whoa, girl!" Sister Sledge said quickly, turning to her. "You alright?"

"I'm fine ..." Lady Tech shivered. "One mile into tracking, I got hit with feedback that almost fried my systems."

The Apollos became more savage. Sam threw his massive body in front of a still injured Cyclone, shielding her from the brunt of brutal, raw energy attacks she was not fast enough to defend against.

"We need to fall back!" Rogers roared.

Nitro's eyes widened as he caught what no one else saw.

One of the boosted Apollo's hands glowed, spitting red with sparks as he focused them downward toward the ground. His training knew what was to come next.

"Magma wielder! Move! Move!"

Those that could fly took to the air scattering. At the same time, those with two legs hauled it away before the ground erupted as several hot, searing pillars of lava shot into the air. Sam snatched Cyclone, taking her up in the air with him.

The boosted Red Rum broke off into packs, hunting a Regulator, purposely keeping them separated from one another as they tried to kill them.

"They're trying to pick us off one by one!" Rogers yelled over his earpiece to his team. "Fight your way back to the factory to regroup!"

Lady Tech soared high and then violently dived back to Earth as Buster feverishly evaded the energy attacks from the ten Apollos on her tail. She deployed cluster missiles that fired out of cracked open ports of

Genesis

Buster's shoulders, whizzing past her back at the pack, finding their targets.

They only took out two as the others skillfully evaded or blasted them out of the sky while continuing the chase.

"What I wouldn't give for a damn Dothraki horde," Lady Tech muttered.

Genesis

CHAPTER 17

On the other side of the world, Kimberly sat against a palm tree by herself, watching the six comedic shorts she videotaped of Amatullah that she posted on the YouTube channel she helped her create.

Most notably, her purple burka female rendition of Prince's "Purple Rain." Kimberly, Akram, and other kids in Middle Eastern attire played the rest of her band.

As she laughed at the skits and her jokes, she was forced to wipe away the salty tears that continued to fall.

It had been almost a week since her death.

~~~~~~~~~~~~~~~~~~~~~~~~~~~~~~~~~~

Per her parents' wishes, she was buried with Islamic funeral traditions, which meant burial within twenty-four hours of death. They refused an autopsy, believing complications to the sarin took their daughter's life, which was enough for them.

Her washing was done by her mother and two other women from her former village. The outpour was overwhelming even for Kimberly, as everyone on the island attended her funeral.

Her parents thanked Sophia for all she had done for their daughter and said it was Allah's will to call her home.

The Youssefs opted to stay at Sanctuary with their infant son, stating that their daughter was there, and when their time came, they wanted to be buried right next to her.

After the funeral, Mr. Youssef took Kimberly aside to say something which brought her to tears.

Genesis

"My little girl had many friends, but you …were the best. I know your heart is broken like mine. But try to laugh. That is how she would want you …to remember her. Okay?"

~ ~

As she watched the video, her blurry eyes saw the likes count that broke over half a million. As she read the encouraging comments, her face lit up as some were from professional YouTubers like Superwoman Lily Singh. Kimberly opted to re-edit the video and turn it into a memorial so everyone knew of her passing, but she decided not to.

She wanted it to continue to get likes because of her friend's talent, not because of her death.

Sensing someone approaching, Kimberly glanced up to see her mother coming with Sir George on her shoulder. She quickly wiped her eyes and straightened up, wearing an "I really don't want to talk" expression.

Not taking the hint, Sophia plopped down right in the sand next to her as Sir George jumped from her shoulder into her lap.

"Hey," was all her mother could get out.

"Hey," Kimberly returned the greeting while looking down at the sand.

The two silently sat there, looking everywhere but at one another as Sir George busied himself, pulling and picking at strands of Sophia's locks.

Amid their awkward silence, Kimberly whispered something that brought a cold chill down her mother's spine.

"I'm going to kill him."

Sophia's heart began to flutter as she turned to her.

Genesis

"What did you just say?"

"When I get old enough, when I become strong enough that you can't stop me …I'm going to kill him."

Her words knocked the breath out of Sophia. Her mother took a moment, rubbing her clammy hands together as she chose her words carefully.

"Kimberly …"

"What you're doing is not working!" Kimberly cut her off with a cracked voice. "It's not working …all she wanted to do was tell jokes! She wasn't a soldier! She wasn't a rebel! She was a kid! She liked to make people laugh, and he killed her without even a thought! Twice he did this, and he's going to do it again! And you and the rest of the world just stand by and watch him do it! My friend would still be alive if people stopped watching! Well, when I get older, I'm not going to just watch!"

Kimberly muffled her mouth with her hand while her tears ran, forcing herself not to fall into a hysterical crying fit. Sophia remained silent, waiting patiently for her to calm down. With a nod, she processed what her daughter had to say before she spoke.

"The day of 9/11 when the first Tower got hit, I was doing my rounds at the hospital when I heard the news. I remember calling your father while watching them fall and him telling me to meet him at home. I cried like a baby while driving and waiting for him to come home because I knew he'd have to go abroad and serve his country. To avenge and bring to justice those responsible for that tragic day.

Neither of us knew it was the worst mistake the United States would ever make."

Sophia shook her head as her memory went back to that time.

"It was bad enough that we went to Iraq for no damn reason and caused the deaths of thousands of US soldiers and civilians over something that took a little research and a night raid to pull off; it turned out the

Genesis

unseating of Saddam Hussein allowed the real monsters to become stronger and run loose. The real horrors began after that."

Kimberly's eyes widened as her mother's face became a visage of grim disgust.

"As Al-Qaeda was being wiped out, groups like ISIS were born, and they turned out to be even worse. They did horrible, unspeakable things, things I won't repeat, not just to foreigners and soldiers but to their own people. The most heartbreaking about it all was how they took such a beautiful religion and turned it into something dark and twisted. Do you know how they were able to grow?"

Kimberly earnestly shook her head.

"They had someone to blame," Sophia answered with narrowed eyes. "They spun a tale of a foreign invading force, unholy infidels that came to their homeland to destroy their way of life and, most importantly, to extinguish their religion, and the ignorant masses just ate it up.

And the additional spin to that was they gave a reason for people worldwide to mistrust and hate Muslims, creating an endless cycle of destruction.

Eight years later, several hundred thousand deaths on both sides are ongoing.

And not one person on either side has stopped to ask, 'What is Godly about any of this insanity?'"

"But Bashar al-Assad is responsible for this! He's a murderer!" Kimberly shot back.

"And you'll get no argument from me there," Sophia replied, nodding. "I knew where he was the day I threw that anti-aircraft vehicle into his palace. I could have obliterated the entire palace with him in it. But then I would have destabilized another region, I would become another person to blame attempting to destroy their way of life, and I would be responsible for creating more monsters and causing more death. How does that break the cycle?"

Kimberly lowered her head, now wearing the look of defeat.

"So, we do nothing."

"I didn't say that," Sophia said, shaking her head. "What you did for Amatullah was not nothing. She died because of medical complications, not because she was broken. She died with her friend holding her, not alone. You did that."

Golf ball tears fell again from Kimberly's eyes as her mother moved closer, rubbing her back.

"We're doing something right now. But before we get to that, can we change the subject for a minute? There's something I want to ask you."

Kimberly sat up, switching her face to one of concern.

"Okay."

"What really happened when you went to go see Kyle?"

Her question brought sadness to her daughter's face. Kimberly retracted her legs to her chest while wrapping her arms around them for comfort.

~~~~~~~~~~~~~~~~~~~~~~~~~~~~~~~~~~

Eight months after the Regulators and Kimberly defeated the Draugr and Jiang Shi, saving the residences of Sanctuary, Kyle's parents came to Sophia and discussed relocating back to the States. With monetary stability again, Kyle's father interviewed and got a job at a financial firm in Chicago. At the same time, his mother acquired a high school teaching position.

Before he left, Brian appointed and trained Indrajit as Sanctuary's new Head of Finance. Sophia paid for and coordinated all the arrangements to move their belongings to their new home in Chicago.

Genesis

Kyle's older brother Joseph had mixed emotions about leaving, while Kyle went ballistic.

On several occasions before their final departure, Kyle attempted to run away and hide in the jungle, only to be hunted and dragged back home, mainly by Kimberly and Akram.

Neither wanted to see him leave, but Akram promised they'd keep in touch via video chat, while Kimberly could always fly to his house to hang out with him.

Or so she thought.

~ ~

"When I showed up, Kyle seemed happy to see me, but also nervous," Kimberly swallowed. "Then his parents came outside, and things got weird. Mrs. McArthur asked Kyle to help her with something inside their house, and then Mr. McArthur walked up and asked me to stay away from Kyle for a while. He said his wife and him were trying to get him adjusted to normal life back in the states, and hanging out with me would be a distraction. He then thanked me for stopping by and went back to his house."

Sophia blew an air of irritation, not aimed at her daughter. She repositioned herself in the sand while turning Kimberly to sit before her, taking hold of her bare feet.

"Remember when I said to you, parents don't know everything, and sometimes don't do what's best for their kids?"

"Yes."

"This is one of those situations," Sophia explained, nodding. "You also know you did nothing wrong, right? And neither did Kyle. I also can understand why Kyle's parents did what they did. The second mother of all superhuman battles took place here. What irritates me is that they were not honest with me because I would have spoken to you and saved you from that awkward situation. So, believe me when I say Mr. McArthur and I are going to have a discussion about …"

"Please don't, mom," Kimberly asked. "I'm fine, and I understand."

"Is that why you've been so distant from your other little buddy?" Sophia asked, referring to Akram.

"Akram and I still hang out."

"Yeah, but not like you use to."

Kimberly meekly nodded her head, answering her mother.

"So, all of this pushing your limits and talks about being a superhero is because of what happened." Sophia formulated.

"I still want to be a hero," Kimberly shrugged, replying. "I just realize Kyle and Akram are not like me, and they never will be. And if they keep hanging around me, they might get really hurt. And I don't want that."

"You know that's a bunch of malarkey, right?" Sophia said, looking at her with a dull, sardonic expression. "We're around normal people practically every day; one incident out of almost eight years doesn't make us a safety hazard."

"I know," Kimberly nodded, answering. "But the world is going to become more dangerous, especially with the new generation of EVOs getting older."

"How do you …?" Sophia began to ask with a look of shock.

"I'm not naïve, mom. I know about Vitruvian Absolute. I also asked Erica, and she told me what I wanted to know. Don't be mad at her, please."

She released her anger with a huff and nodded, respecting her daughter's wishes.

Genesis

"Can I ask you something, mom?"

"Yes, you can."

Kimberly took a minute to think about what she was about to say before blurting it out.

"What happens in seven years?"

Sophia knit her brows together, which made Kimberly fretful about asking her question. She took a minute to find the best words to answer her best.

"What do you think about what I've done here so far? With Sanctuary, tell me honestly, please."

"What you did here is beyond amazing," Kimberly answered earnestly, "You've helped like so many people, and you like created a place where there's peace, and people are not afraid, where they're not afraid of each other!"

"What would you say if in seven years …I plan to expand this on a larger scale?"

A lump stuck in Kimberly's throat as she got blindsided by her mother's question.

"I don't understand." She said with a swallow.

"Short of physically taking power, which I don't want to do and would never do. I can't change what goes on in this world," Sophia said while shaking her head. "I am also tired of this cycle of saving people over and over again because of someone else's selfishness. I'm tired of seeing the lifeless bodies of innocent people or the trauma in a person's eyes after someone chose to violate them for their own means. I'm tired of putting people back together after someone willfully chose to tear them apart. It's not fair to me, it's not fair to them, and I refuse to see you be pulled into the same damn cycle."

Genesis

"You're going to make a bigger island?"

"I plan on making a continent."

A cold chill ran down Kimberly's spine as her emotions became unchained at her mother's words.

"How?"

"Vincent has been running some models for me on how it could be done without causing too much of a disruption to other countries' shorelines," Sophia began to explain. "I would need your help to carry it out."

"Well, why wait seven years?" Kimberly propped up with excitement, asking. "Why not do it …?"

"You're not ready for that responsibility," Sophia said, holding a hand up, calming her down. "And neither am I. There are other models and factors I have to take into consideration. Like affordable healthcare for all and getting top-quality doctors to administer it, a free education system straight through college, infrastructure, energy, and natural resources, law and order, and defense."

"So, you plan to be the ruler of your own country?" Kimberly nervously asked.

"No," Sophia shook her head, answering. "It would be the current Council which would have to expand working together and deciding on how best to run this new country with the input of the people and me. The key guideline to all of the laws being love and respect for your fellow human. Anything that violates that guideline will not be permitted."

"You're serious about this."

"I can't foresee the future," Sophia said while breathing, "But barring anything out of the ordinary, you and I might be around for a very long time. That's what makes this work. Over the centuries, when other people went forth and founded countries of their own, their original

Genesis

doctrine, which was pure in nature when it first started, was eventually corrupted by generations seeking opportunity over their fellow man. We're not perfect, but we're also incorruptible, and we'll ensure that the system we put into place remains incorruptible."

"So, your plan is in seven years, if the world doesn't change," Kimberly formulated, "Is to take the people from the world."

"That and endangered animals," Sophia nodded. "If the world refuses to change, we just leave it behind and take those who want to change. We protect and defend those who want to live in peace. We help nurture a new generation that does not see color, does not see wealth over their brother and sister, and is not corrupted by old archaic traditions and the parts of religion whose sole purpose is to subjugate others. In time, the rest of the world will either learn from our example and follow suit ...or wither and die off, leaving us to rebuild.

That is how we break the cycle ...that is how we change the world."

"I want to be a part of that!" Kimberly said eagerly, "I want to break the cycle!"

"Slow down; like I said, something this size will take some time to work out. For now, you have to keep this between just us. Can you do that?"

Kimberly vigorously nodded, agreeing to keep her promise.

"Sophia, I have an incoming message from Brian McArthur," Vincent announced via her iWatch, interrupting their conversation.

"Please take a messa ..."

"It is an urgent message; his son Kyle is in the hospital and gravely ill."

Sophia's eyes instinctively went to Kimberly, who sat up with a look of fear on her face.

Genesis

"Mom?" she uttered.

"Which hospital, Vincent?"

"They are currently at Ann & Robert H. Lurie Children's Hospital."

"Tell him we are on our way."

Kimberly was on her feet before her.

"Go put on my old suit in the closet; it should fit you ...we're leaving now."

Kimberly quickly nodded before taking off into the air back to the house as Sophia looked up to the heavens.

"Please, don't do this to her again." She pleaded. "Not again. Please."

~ ~

Ten minutes later, mother and daughter landed in the Chicago hospital's emergency entranceway. A visibly anxious Kimberly in Sophia's old uniform and boots walked side by side with her mother, adorned in her Freedom uniform, as they entered the hospital. They ignored all the eyes locked on them as they approached the main desk.

"Excuse me; I'm looking for Kyle McArthur, who was just admitted here." Sophia got to the point.

"And ...you are?" The stunned nurse asked.

"His doctor."

"Sophia! Thank God!"

She turned to Brian McArthur's voice as he frantically approached them.

Genesis

"Brian, what's going on?"

"Kyle …he took something …something that …was supposed to give him superpowers!"

"Where is he?"

"They have him in ICU," He motioned, yelling, "This way!"

They followed him to the intensive care unit, where they were greeted by a near-hysterical Mrs. McArthur.

"Oh, Sophia," She bitterly wept.

Sophia, without a word, gave her a big hug of comfort.

"Everything is going to be okay, Grace," Sophia whispered. "I promise. Now, what happened?"

"I got a call that he collapsed right after recess in his homeroom and started screaming," She fought to get out. "His veins are glowing bright orange, and his temperature won't go down. A couple of his school friends admitted they injected themselves with this …stuff …that is supposed to give them …powers."

"Boosters," Sophia muttered in disgust. "Who is the on-staff doctor treating him?"

"I am," said a man in his thirties in green medical scrubs walking over, "Dr. Mukesh Gupta."

"Dr. Dennison," Sophia quickly introduced herself while shaking his hand. "Did anyone collect a sample of the drug they were using?"

"Unfortunately, no," Dr. Gupta answered. "We just finished taking a blood sample. His cells appear to be literally evaporating. His temperature is now in a state of flux where it's dropping and spiking every three minutes; the count before that was five minutes."

Genesis

"Whatever he took has corrupted the Judgement Day virus," Sophia exhaled. "It's now misfiring."

"I don't understand," Dr. Gupta said, wanting to know more.

"A regular human body cannot withstand the superhuman abilities the virus possesses," she quickly explained. "If the virus does not alter the entire body to adapt, certain activated abilities will kill the host. Whatever he took activated the dormant abilities of the virus, which is now killing him. May I see him?"

"This way," Dr. Gupta said, motioning.

Sophia followed the doctor with a fretful Kimberly firmly behind her and Kyle's parents bringing up the rear. They entered the ICU, making a beeline to Kyle's bed, where they found his frightened older brother and two nurses standing beside him, monitoring his temperature. The nurses were armed with several packs of cold compresses to administer to him should his temperature spike.

Sure enough, Kyle was in bad shape; his body was sweaty, and his veins and eyes glowed a bright orange. He shifted about the bed, groaning and crying in excruciating pain.

Sophia walked up, taking his left hand while displaying a bright, encouraging smile.

"Hey, Kyle, how are you doing?"

"It hurts …it hurts so bad," he squeaked.

"It's okay, I'm here for you," she said with a smile. "Someone is also here to see you."

Kimberly's tears fell as she walked up to the side of his bed, which triggered Kyle's own.

"Hey," she whispered.

Genesis

"Hey," he weakly answered back.

"You big dummy," she got out. "What'd you do to yourself?"

"I just wanted ...us to be friends again," a deteriorated Kyle whimpered through his tears. "Mom and dad said ...we couldn't be cuz I'd get hurt if I hung around you."

"So, you thought if you had powers, we could hang out again," Kimberly concluded. "Why didn't you just call or text me silly?"

"It's not the same," he answered, shaking his head. "I miss Sanctuary ...I wish we didn't leave. I miss Akram and you ...I didn't want to leave. And now because I'm a regular human ...we can't be friends ...I hate it."

"We'll always be friends," she said, smiling while taking his other hand. "Nothing is going to change that."

"I really messed up," he sobbed. "Am I going to die?"

Grace McArthur erupted into a sob, falling into her heartbroken husband's arms as they watched their son die before them. Kimberly turned to her mother with widened eyes of fright.

"No, baby, you're not going to die," Sophia promised sternly. "I'm going to do something that's going to feel a bit weird but is going to take away some of the pain, okay?"

Kyle tearfully nodded as Sophia gripped his hand a bit tighter, concentrated. Her eyes glowed brighter as an orange spark erupted around their handshake. Kyle groaned as the glow in his eyes and veins dimmed, so they almost disappeared.

His family gasped with relief as Kyle became more comfortable where he lay. Sophia, patting Kyle's hand, released it. She turned to give Dr. Gupta professional instruction.

"I just drained the energy building up within him; this will prevent

Genesis

the energies within him from flaring up and possibly detonating."

"Detonating?" Kyle's mother gasped.

"I need to contact a fellow colleague who can help deal with this," Sophia continued, remaining focused. "My daughter has the same ability as me and can keep him stabilized until I get back. I would advise working to break his fever."

"I'll do everything I can," he nodded.

She quickly turned to Kimberly.

"You saw what I just did. Just watch him, and drain him if he flares up again, I will be right back."

Kimberly obediently nodded as Sophia walked back out of the ICU.

The second she was back in the hallway, Sophia gave Vincent a command.

"Connect me to Erica right now."

"Connecting," Vincent answered, obeying. "Unable to connect with Dr. Champion."

"Where is she?"

"Triangulating her position via orbital satellites. Dr. Champion is currently in Cali Columbia in a combat situation."

"Combat?" Freedom asked with a look of disbelief.

"Dr. Champion and the rest of the Regulators are currently in intense combat with a large hostile superhuman force."

Without a word, Freedom exited the hospital and leaped into the air, obliterating the sound barrier to get to Columbia as quickly as possible.

Genesis

CHAPTER 18

Back on the battlefield, the Regulators were still in an intense battle with an army of boosted EVOs.

In the middle of Lady Tech hovering to target multiple boosted criminals, a scream came out of her throat as a column of burning magma slammed Buster from underneath, taking them further into the air.

"Son of a bitch! Buster up! Up!"

Buster's VTOL system ignited, providing greater thrust, taking it higher, and getting it off the column. As the magma scorched the underbelly of the mech, Buster let out a savage growl while flapping its wings, targeting the boosted Apollo with the ability to manipulate volcanic magma.

"Oh shit," gulped the Red Rum Apollo.

"Buster lo arruinó," Lady Tech snarled.

The magma wielder pulled a wall of lava from the ground to protect himself. It was not a strong enough defense against the highly concentrated blast of ion energy from Buster's gullet ripping through his wall, atomizing him.

"Miss, I am detecting Dr. Dennison incoming in less than a minute," Maxine informed Lady Tech through the audio in her headset.

"Say what?" Lady Tech asked with widened eyes under her helmet.

The simulated sound of thunder via a sonic boom shook the heavens as Freedom tore through the sky, forcing the eyes of everyone present to pause and look up.

Genesis

Lady Tech quickly banked her dragon out of the way as she barreled through the squadron of air-bound boosted EVOs, sending them either scattering or violently falling from the sky from the brute force her flight speed generated. She skillfully rolled into a mid-air front flip, landing with a craterous stomp, sending shattered debris flying and blinding those nearby EVOs.

Without words, she walked to a male-boosted Titan from the Russian Cartel and hammered him with a crushing right hook to the side of his skull, upending him. His head made a small crater in the ground while the rest of his body went limp, signaling that she had sent him into a comatose state.

She did not give him a second look as she began to blitz across the battlefield, laying out anyone who was not a friend with a combination of Krav Maga, boxing, and brutal Muy Thai strikes.

Her arrival rallied the Regulators, causing them to fight harder. Sister Sledge flew over her with a mighty leap, crashing shoulder-first into a Titan, taking him down. At the same time, Rogers clocked one with a battle-wrecked automobile before dropping another with a high-speed thermal detonator to the face.

An airborne Blitz strafed across the sky, blasting two airborne Apollos out of the air before upending the third with a flying clothesline. A fourth attempted to attack him on his blindside until he was engulfed in flames. As the gangster's chard body fell out of the sky, a stunned Blitz turned to a physically changed and hovering Merge using fire as a form of propulsion. Familiar abilities he knew she did not acquire during the battle because there was no flame wielder on the opposing side.

A wounded Cyclone extended her hand below, unleashing a powerful tornado blast as Nitro added his thermo-kinetic energy to create another flaming tornado blast enveloping several Titan and Elemental class-boosted EVOs while the speedsters scattered for cover.

Not to be outdone, Heavy Element, with Sam's help, stood in the middle of his right mitt as Sam hurled him through the air with the technique of a quarterback. Heavy Element cocked back and rocked the jaw

Genesis

of a boosted Titan, toppling him on the way down.

As he landed, executing a tumble roll and came up to his feet, Heavy Element shuddered as Freedom shook the Earth, coming out of left field with a right arm clotheslining an incoming boosted Mercurian upending him. He watched in amazement as she targeted the remaining Speedsters by outmatching their speed and delivering crushing ambidextrous haymakers to lay them out.

One boosted Mercurian, attempting to flee the scene, got smacked with a vicious shoulder charge, sending him violently tumbling to the ground. Before he could stand up, Freedom grabbed him by his leg and gave him a ragdoll toss, sending him sailing into Sister Sledge's waiting fist, caving his chest in during his mid-air descent.

Angie and Maxine switched their armament, firing body dampeners and nerve hammer rounds from their rifles as the battle ended.

As Freedom made her way towards the battle-worn regrouping Regulators. Sam carried a wounded Cyclone in his right hand while Nitro walked beside them. Rogers turned with a venomous glare directed at Lady Tech, who felt it from the saddle of her mechanized reptile.

"I did not call her!" She screamed, throwing her hands up.

"She didn't call me," Freedom said, walking up to Rogers. "I was attempting to contact her on another matter when Vincent informed me about this ruckus. Now, what the hell is going on?"

"How politely can I say none of your gotdamn business?" Rogers flatly asked her.

"I think me swooping in and saving your miserable ass makes it my 'gotdamn business' Rogers."

"We had this situation contained!" Rogers barked back.

Genesis

"No, we didn't," the rest of the Regulators said in unison.

"Shut up!"

The senior team members glared back at him, not appreciating Sarge's remark after what they went through. In contrast, the junior members were confused by his volatile outburst.

"Last year, September, we came across a booster serum in the hands of ISIS insurgents that is capable of turning a regular human into an EVO in approximately three months." A fed-up Erica blurted out. "We have been feverishly hunting down the manufacturers for the past eight months who has done an excellent job so far of covering their tracks to the point that they led us into this ambush."

Freedom looked up at Lady Tech with stern, disapproving eyes.

"Why wasn't I told about this?"

"She was ordered not to tell you," Rogers said, stepping in. "And the answer to your next question is the information is and still is classified; accessible to government employees, which you are not."

Freedom calmly placed her hands on her hips as her demeanor read she wanted to wrap them around Rogers's neck.

"So, we're on a call me when you need my extra muscle and firepower basis, Sergeant Rogers?"

"No one called you! You called on another matter and came here on your own volition, remember? And in case you damn well forgot, that symbol on your shoulder is not a Regulator symbol, yet I allow you to run in and out of our base like it's your own personal HMO slash clubhouse," Rogers barked at her taking a step forward. "I've been more than accommodating ..."

"Accommodating?" She snarled.

"People ...people," Sister Shareef raised her voice, stepping in

Genesis

with her hands up. "This is not the time for this. We still need to find the people responsible for sending these goons into overdrive."

"Started searching for them the second the battle ended," Lady Tech answered. "Whoever they are, they vanished once again without a trace."

Her answer planted a dejected look on each of her teammates' faces.

"Well, considering the remaining bad guys littered about the place are either dead, unconscious, or neutralized," Freedom snapped. "Maybe you can finally tell me, Sergeant, what the hell is your problem with me?"

"You want to do this right here and now?" Rogers snarled, taking another step toward her. "Fine, let's do this now. Why don't we start with why the hell you met with Vitruvian Absolute on two separate occasions last year?"

Freedom's mouth fell slightly as if Rogers slapped her in front of everyone. It slowly closed into clenched teeth.

"You're spying on me now?"

"We were spying on Vitruvian Absolute, which despite their rhetoric, is a registered hate group under the United States government," Rogers corrected her. "No different from the KKK, and the fact that they are a superhuman hate group operating on US soil, they've become our business. You got caught while we were doing our jobs, which is making sure they're not planning the next 9/11!"

"Then you must have heard my conversations with them, right?" Freedom fired back. "Sitting down and reasoning with them to rethink their rhetoric and how harmful their speech they don't believe is hateful actually is. That I am not their mother, nor some second coming of a Messiah here to lead them!"

"A talk in which you chose to use the back entrance of their office on both occasions." Rogers pressed.

Genesis

"To avoid a media circus!" Freedom returned in her defense. "Who would no doubt spin an innocent conversation and sit down, the way you're doing right now!"

"I'm not spinning anything; I heard the conversations remember?" Rogers shot back. "But if it looks bad to someone who heard your conversations, how bad do you think it looks to someone lucky enough to see you, who didn't know your intentions?"

"So now you're my PR rep, Rogers?"

"I'm trying to understand how someone who's had more college than me with Master degrees out the wahzoo can be so reckless!" Rogers erupted, "Like outright threatening the United Nations with that insane speech!"

"I didn't threaten anyone!" Freedom roared back.

"Then what happens in seven years, Dennison? What matters do you intend to take into your own hands once the most powerful nations in the world don't fall in line and do as they are told?"

Rogers's direct question had awkward eyes from the rest of his team turned toward her.

"When I heard your address to the UN, I didn't think of it as anything," Rogers shrugged, calming down. "I didn't ask, didn't care because I thought I knew you and what you stood for; a lot can happen in seven years, and if our former President wasn't concerned, why should I be?

That was before you started doing things to make many people nervous, including me.

Like throwing the Guards of the Republic a severe beating and then threatening their Supreme Leader."

"Are you serious?" Freedom asked him with a raised eyebrow of disbelief.

Genesis

"No, I will give you that," Rogers replied with a handheld up. "If I could do what you do, I'd probably done the same thing. But then there's the strong-arming of the Chinese Prime Minister to allow you to walk North Korean refugees out of his country."

"I didn't strong-arm anyone," she answered defensively.

"You don't have to after your kid posted that crazy video of you brutally beating a bunch of poachers within an inch of their life."

"I didn't know she was going to post that, and they invaded my island with the intent to kill my animals!"

"And then, to top it off, you take an anti-aircraft vehicle and hurl it into al-Assad's palace."

"Are you seriously defending that son of a bitch after he gassed his own people?!" Freedom roared. "That anti-aircraft vehicle was intended to shoot down a plane of sick people and their families being transported to my island for treatment!"

"I'm not defending anyone," the Sarge fired back. "I'm defending the fact that your actions are making a lot of people nervous. It was different when the world did not know about you, and you were doing your thing in the shadows. Now everyone knows you are the most powerful being on the planet, and you're going around doing whatever you damn well please. People aren't thinking, 'Yeah, she's taking it to the bad guys.' they're thinking, 'Holy shit, are we next?' And unfortunately, my team's affiliation with you has also put a target on our backs, especially from the new administration!"

The rest of the Regulator team, save for Lady Tech, looked as if they had been tasered after the Sarge's revelation. Freedom narrowed her eyes, holding her peace until Rogers finished what he had to say to her.

"The only reason we're all not gone is that we're still living off the goodwill of us saving the world alongside you and the Eye of Ra," the Sarge pointed out. "We are the one thing both sides of Congress will fight for to the death, defending tooth and nail against the new administration.

Genesis

Still, even that is waning, especially every time we're seen around you.

I have a problem with you, Dennison because my country needs me …. It requires us more than ever, and our unofficial affiliation with you jeopardizes that. Yet, I continue to go to bat for you behind the scenes, unbeknownst to my team, because I want to believe in you. But it's getting complicated when your kid threatens politicians' kids at school, and because of you, she answers to no one."

"She answers to me."

"That is not good enough, Freedom!" Rogers howled.

Freedom folded her arms and prepared to ask her next question with a warning tone.

"So, what do you want to do Rogers, you want me to hand her over to you; let her spend some time in Purgatory?"

"I want to know what happens in seven years! I want to know why I should continue to stick my neck out for you at the risk of myself and my team! That is what I want to know!"

She blew some air out of her nostrils, glancing at the ground momentarily before unfolding her arms.

Freedom turned to make sure her eyes contacted each member of the Regulator team before she spoke.

"Anyone here ever wonder why Peace went on National television and basically told the entire world her plans the night before she executed them, anyone?"

Aside from Lady Tech, who knew the answer but chose not to speak, everyone else looked at her and then at each other, unsure if they should answer.

"She had the perfect plan and us by the balls," Freedom continued. "Had she not told us what she had planned, she could have wiped out

Genesis

probably three quarters maybe all of the world leaders before we finally came up with a plan to stop her. So why go in front of the entire world and expose her deck like that? Anyone still buys it was because she was both arrogant in believing she could have gotten away with it, that she was just an unstable sociopath?"

Freedom continued to look around, searching each of their faces, daring one of them to come out and say that was the answer. Her eyes finally came back to Rogers.

"We all know that wasn't it. Months later, I finally realized Peace going on television like that was her backup plan. She knew as long as I was alive and out there, I would find a way back to Earth. Peace knew there was a chance that even if she carried out her plan, I would find a way back to stop her, and she'd be branded as nothing more than a sadistic murderer. But she gave birth to genetic hate and supremacy groups like Vitruvian Absolute by going on television, revealing the truth about the EVO Virus, and spinning the evolution of the EVO species from her perspective. She spawned the booster epidemic, which has become worse than our regular drug epidemic. One that could possibly claim the life of one special little boy unless I find a cure to save his life!

Her backup plan in case she lost the battle was to dangle the most potent fear and dream of every man, woman, and child on this planet!

She made them all feel what it is like to be powerless … and then told them without telling them they had an opportunity not to be.

She risked, possibly losing the battle to win the war, and she succeeded!"

Her eyes stayed on the Sarge as he dropped his head, knowing everything she said so far was the truth.

"You know what my plan is in seven years, Rogers? Damage control! Taking matters into my own hands and saving as many innocent lives as possible if we cannot stop or contain what is coming. If you think getting boxed in by a bunch of boosted organized thugs is as bad as your day can get, you are sadly mistaken. In seven years, a whole new generation of pure-born EVOs will reach maturity with powers and abilities that will continue to grow as they age.

The title 'the most powerful in the world' will be up for grabs with a massive body count trailing behind it if we don't act now."

She turned to the rest of the Regulators.

"My message was cryptic because if I told the truth in front of the United Nations, people would freak out and make foolish decisions.

Decisions like internment camps and monitored pregnancies, which I don't think I have to say where actions like that would lead to next.

The world is slowly becoming intoxicated with the pursuit of power, and they are doing it with reckless abandonment for themselves and the people around them because it is worth it not to feel scared or powerless anymore.

And I cannot stop that …I can't …so I am trying to get us and everyone else who did not ask for this through it to the other side …if there is another side."

She turned back to Rogers.

"You're right. I don't wear the Regulator symbol on my shoulder, and I never will. But we're still in the same trenches; we want the same things. The difference is your symbol swears your allegiance to your country; mine swears my devotion to those around the world without a voice, who are powerless. So, I don't give a damn if my actions make those in power 'a bit nervous.'

I fully understand if you think it is in your team's best interest to disassociate yourself from me.

But the next time you need to question my motives, Sergeant Rogers, have the guts to come and hash it out with me like the adult I know you are instead of acting like a child."

Genesis

The Sarge shifted his stance as he lowered his beanie, unable to find a comeback to Freedom's remark. Blitz glanced up, noticing Lady Tech's nervous, spaced-out expression in the middle of the debate.

"Lady Tech …what's the matter?"

"Something is not right here …why do I have a feeling like we're in the middle of a Bad Boys movie?"

"One or two?" Blitz uneasily asked.

"Number one," she swallowed. "Maxine, is the Ranch secure?"

"Yes, Miss," Maxine answered, turning to her, "The Ranch is secure; there has been no perimeter breach."

"Are you sure?"

"I am one hundred percent certain."

Without another word, Lady Tech turned on her holographic HUD projection to show the Ranch's image for her to see in real-time, which caught everyone's attention.

Nitro hopped on Buster's hind leg to get a better look.

"Everything looks secure."

"Then why do I still feel like we've been violated," Lady Tech said, answering him while grinding her teeth. "Maxine, show me the evidence vault right now."

The image switched to the inside of the highly secured evidence vault, revealing the multiple crates that housed the red-boosted serum.

"Everything's fine; there's no breach," the Nitro answered, lending secondary eyes.

"Then, why does the digital timestamp still read forty-five minutes

Genesis

before my departure. Maxine, show me the real-time image."

"This is the real-time image," Maxine answered.

"No …it is not."

~ ~

Twenty minutes later, Freedom and the Regulators arrived at the Ranch, descending to the base's lower levels. Lady Tech was the first off the platform, sprinting straight for the evidence vault. The massive circular quadruple-plated dark metal door with the most advanced security encryption opened as she neared it.

Her heart stopped as she covered her mouth with her quivering hands.

"It's gone …it's all gone."

Rogers and company, bringing up the rear, all stopped behind her, wearing the same stunned, dumbfounded face she had on at that moment.

"How …how is this possible?" Heavy Element choked out, running his hands through his hair.

"Miss, I do not understand, is there an issue?" Maxine inquired.

"Maxine …what do you see in the vault right now?" Lady Tech asked, turning to her.

"I see the twelve secured crates of genetic contraband Sergeant Rogers's team acquired in Ninawa, Iraq."

"Maxine, initiate an entire system reboot of yourself and the facility. Right now." Lady Tech ordered.

"As you command."

Maxine went out on her feet right in front of everyone, shutting

Genesis

down along with the base going dark while the emergency lights came on. Less than a minute later, she booted back up with the rest of the facility.

"Maxine, what do you see now?"

"The twelve secured crates of genetic contraband are no longer here," answered a rebooted Maxine. "I believe I must be malfunctioning."

"No," Lady Tech shook her head. "You've been hacked."

"How is that even possible?" Cyclone asked. "Doesn't she have a billion defenses preventing something like that?'

"This wasn't a normal hack," Lady Tech answered, walking up to her firstborn. "I don't even think whoever did this used a computer or any other electronic device."

"You're saying this is a superhuman ability?" Rogers asked, stepping closer.

"Yes, a form of Technokinesis or Technopathy. Maxine, the formula for the red booster is it still on the encrypted drives?"

"No, it is not," Maxine answered, looking at her. "It and all research records have been erased."

"In and out like a ghost, similar to the nuclear power plant in India," Lady Tech exhaled while turning to Freedom.

"Don't tell me you think these two are now connected?" a frustrated Rogers asked while glancing at them.

"At this point, I don't know. What I do know is that we're back to square one."

"So that's it, everything is gone," Sister Sledge sighed. "We have nothing."

"No, we have something," Lady Tech huffed. "We have me."

Genesis

She turned again to Freedom, tapping her head.

"You're not the only one with a super eidetic memory."

"Something doesn't make sense," Merge jumped in with a question. "Whoever did this had to be surveying the base; they had you, the data, and the boosters in one spot. So why didn't they ...?"

"Because they also know who she's connected to," Freedom answered before Merge finished her grizzly question. "If anything happened to her, they'd not only incur your wrath, they knew I would hunt them to the ends of the Earth."

"Not to mention, they have accomplished their mission." Lady Tech interjected, flailing her arms in defeat. "We have no proof that the boosters were ever here. It doesn't matter if I can recreate the serum. And there is no way we ever intended to reveal that such a serum existed, knowing the ramifications behind it. Whoever pulled this off wanted to secure their anonymity, and they did just that."

"So, what is our next course of action?" Nitro asked.

"I'm going to go help save a little kid's life," Lady Tech blurted out.

Her answer caught everyone off guard as she turned to Freedom.

"We're going to come out the winners on something today."

Genesis

CHAPTER 19

The Grand Canyon National Park, midday Colorado time, present time.

A mentally broken Graves, fully clothed, slowly walked the hallway of the project EVOlution facility, making his way back to the lab after one of his latest trips to Washington DC to carry out Horus's plans from the shadows.

Graves re-entering the lab had his eardrums violated by the sound of Alice In Chains' "Man in the Box." The former Secretary of Defense shuddered at the sight of Horus with his back turned to him with a fully dressed Dr. Alexander. The Ancient slowly bobbed his head to the sound of the thunderous heavy metal song while observing the restructuring pods' progress. Graves steadied himself, clutching his fist to reduce his body's trembling as he continued to walk toward the Ancient. As he came within a respectful distance, Graves painfully descended to one knee, bowing his head.

"My lord," Graves said with a passive tone.

"Remain, standing boy," Horus commanded, gesturing while his eyes fluttered in disgust. "By the time your frail, decrepit form rises after paying me homage, another millennium would have passed. I see you have completed those tasks I have given you."

"Yes, my lord, the Regulators will no longer become a problem for you."

"Hold your tongue, boy, they were never a 'problem for me,'" Horus growled. "Tis their association with the female demi-god that vexes me. Her capabilities are still quite formidable.

Genesis

Had it not for her, I would have personally wiped them from mortal coil for interfering with my plans months ago. Getting into a confrontation with her would be nonproductive to my plans. Once my blueprint has begun construction, this Freedom will be swiftly dealt with. Come closer and see the fruits of my labor."

With a thought, Horus lowered the volume to the music while Graves advanced nearer as commanded. His eyes expanded in amazement, removing some of the fear within him. Inside each pod was a fully developed human in their teenage years. Each quietly slept as they floated within a thick bluish-green liquid with a synthetic umbilical cord attached.

"It will take an estimated twenty-six days from today for them to reach the maturity level I will need them to become. Two boys and three girls, one of the females, will become the host body for my Sekhmet. What do you think of them, boy?"

"I think they are amazing, my lord," Graves swallowed.

"When they are ready, their strength and power will be secondary to my own. No one on this planet or in the universe will be able to challenge them. It will be needed to protect the Earth from what is to come."

Horus's last sentence befuddled Graves, forcing him to fight his fear to ask the question at the tip of his tongue.

"Protect the Earth …from what's to come, my lord?"

A devious grin grew on Horus's face, which forced Graves to stand on weakened knees.

"You thought I was creating an army to take over the world. Nay boy, I told thee before, my reign will come with a whisper, not a roar. I shall not be taking this world by force; when the time is right, the children of Earth shall bow to me and hand overrule of their own free will."

Horus's answer filled Grave's mind with a million and one questions he wanted to ask. Fortunately for him, the Ancient loved the sound of his own voice.

Genesis

"After the first twenty to thirty years of howling, screaming, and weeping within my accursed prison created by Amun-Ra, I retreated into my mind to another plane of existence," Horus began his tale. "This allowed my body to go into a state of dormancy, reducing the life energy being sucked from my body from Annunaki forged devices. While on that plane, I spent time planning my vengeance as I waited for my release. My power nearly depleted; I had almost given up hope if not for a descendant of Amun-Ra, who happened to be a simpleton grave robber. Oh, how low that bloodline has fallen."

Horus let out a chuckle before continuing his story.

"But as I emerged from my prison and realized that the world was far different than I had expected it to be, it was clear that the plans I had forged for centuries would be ineffective. I had to learn about my new environment before assuming rule over it. So, I took the time to acclimate myself to this new Earth and its history from my past to the present time for the first two months of my freedom.

And what I learned turned out to be shocking and chilling, even to me.

Enough to realize that I could not take it by force to assume my rightful rule of Earth.

Of all the things our still primitive species has managed to perfect, a sense of morality of right and wrong is at the forefront of its evolution. Through the centuries, this species has created two distinct categories to define its character.

That of the hero, who stands in the face of danger and combats adversity through impressive feats of ingenuity, bravery, or strength, often sacrificing their own concerns for the greater good.

And that of the villain, whose characteristics are the opposite of everything the hero stands for.

These facets, among others, have not only built the rocky foundation upon which humankind stands but have also been the fatal flaw

Genesis

of many mortal rulers who chose to go against it throughout this planet's history.

From Rameses the Second to Caesar, to Vlad the Impaler, to Stalin and Hitler, to the Kim Jong family, to Vladimir Putin and your latest President of the United States whose election I ensured, all of them by their actions have branded themselves, villains, in the eyes of the majority of the world.

And once the majority sees you as the villain, it is best for you not to exist.

No matter the horrors you introduce, no matter the sea of bodies you fertilized the land with, there will be those who will find the courage to stand against you and oppose you at every given turn.

The villain is despised and hated, erased from memory, and only remembered for the infamy they have wrought onto the world and those brave enough to stand against them.

This code is saturated into your way of life, from your literature to the clothes you wear to your upbringing, despite many of you choosing not to follow this code. It is at its strongest when you are all faced with common adversity.

The majority of you look up and aspire to emulate the hero, whether they are real or fictional. You will subscribe to their moral code, inject it into your very cells, and, given the right motivation, will follow them into the afterlife.

What surprised me was that this was the culprit behind it all."

Graves grew owl-sized eyes as Horus held up a Holy Bible; he did not realize he was holding it in his hand behind his back.

"This God, Jehovah, or Allah …is a diabolically ingenious Being."

The look on Graves's face was disturbed bewilderment; he had

Genesis

never heard God described in such a manner before.

"Here is a supposed Being that creates mankind in His supposed image and gives His creation free will to both love and worship Him, or to not. So how does He ensure that His creation, or at least the majority of them, are the loving and faithful servants He intended them to be?" Horus asked as he held up the Bible, moving closer to an unnerved Graves, "He simply takes one of His original creations and turns it into a villainous patsy."

Horus paused for a moment, reveling with a smile on his face.

"Villainous patsy, I love it. The progression of language is so tantalizing to my tongue."

Graves lowered his head quietly, clearing his dry throat as the Ancient continued his analysis.

"He takes this angel known as Satan or Lucifer, whatever, who supposedly attempts to wage war against his Creator, casts him and his followers down into a realm called Hell, and then names him the apex predator of evil and everything that goes wrong in the world. He is the first monster you are introduced to as a child, and with your very vivid imaginations, you unwittingly expand on his lore, making him the last creature you pray to never meet when you enter the afterlife and are judged.

The immense fear of this being and this realm of unfathomable horror sends you humans running like squealing pigs to your alleged Creator. Blindly surrendering without question your love, devotion, even on a monetary level, to a Being, who none of you have ever met or asked through your 'prayers' why would He allow such a monstrous creature to roam free, much less exist as opposed to wiping it from existence, especially for having the audacity to challenge its own Creator.

You've all fallen for this prophesied tale of this final battle between this God's Son and this lowly creature who could not hope to overcome the might of the One Who created it. Where the worthy are taken up to the land of milk and honey while the unworthy are left to remain here and suffer painful torment by this same creature given reign of this planet

Genesis

by your very own 'Creator' for a period of seven years until the final battle where good shall prevail over evil."

Horus chuckled, shaking his head in disbelief.

"By creating a villain from one of his lackeys, your 'Creator' has made Himself the ultimate hero. An incredibly simple plan so effective that it has lasted throughout the centuries, dwarfing every other known religion on this planet.

You are so fanatically fearful of the ultimate boogeyman that you have formed mistrust in each other, believing some are even in league with this 'demon,' to the point that you break off into different factions of the same religion. Creating wars over the same God, believing each side is the just side that will stand victorious beside your Creator in the coming epic battle.

Again, I say to thee, it is the most deviously ingenious plan that even I could never have thought of in all my centuries imprisoned.

That is why I intend to duplicate it."

A cold sweat washed down Grave's back as he glanced at Dr. Alexander with an oblivious look on his visage.

"As you two already devised, humans are not the only intelligent sentient species in the known universe," Horus began revealing his plan. "In fact, these other individual species, if I remember, numbered over thirty thousand. Humans have never come in contact with these species because the sector Earth resides in is defended by a mighty Empire that is a part of what is known as the Dominion Council. It is a collective of species that work similarly to your United Nations to 'protect' the peace throughout the universe."

Horus's eyes fluttered in disgust as he finished his last sentence.

"What you do not know is within this mighty empire is a crown prince that openly despises humans, the same species his kingdom is sworn to protect; he would like nothing more than to find a justification to wipe

Genesis

our species off the face of this planet. So that he and his empire can gain control of this world and the six viable planets similar to Earth within this sector that technically belong to the human race.

So, I secretly sent him the proof that he needed."

Dr. Alexander staggered while Graves used every ounce of his muscles to keep from doing the same as they both wondered why Horus would do such a thing.

"You see before I transcended to godhood, I had an outstanding talent for reading people and knowing what they would do next. With this skill, I was able to get reasonable prices for my father's livestock, which my eldest brother forcefully took credit for.

And being that we are nearing the final moon cycle in which the Thracian Empire will have control over this sector, thereby, within three weeks, transferring power over to another governing world under the Council, I am very confident this Prince is terribly desperate.

And if he takes this proof and uses her in the way I know he will use her, he will be coming to play the villain I need him to play."

Horus turned to each of them, displaying a simple, calm smile.

"It wasn't really that hard to find her, even through the dimensional portal the half-breed descendant of Amun-Ra sent her through. It also wasn't difficult to determine, based on the impressive amount of damage she inflicted on this planet during the battle with the other female demi-god, that she could survive the crushing forces of a black hole. Once I knew the general vicinity to search, it just took some time to pinpoint her location and send a cryptic message to my patsy, revealing her proximity.

You see, this Prince doesn't know that I have also been in contact with equally powerful empires outside of the Dominion Council who do not share their views nor their 'protective hold' over specific sectors of this universe. Realms also seek any justification to expose the Council for what they are and wage war against them.

Genesis

A war I know how to win."

Horus walked over to Graves, whose heart skipped several beats while his stomach wrenched into excruciatingly painful knots.

"To take my rule of this world, I must introduce it to pain; I must reveal to it true horror. Not from some lowly misbegotten demon throwing a tantrum, but from a real monster who wishes nothing more than to see mankind turned to ash and erased from existence for financial gain.

The people will cry out for a savior in the face of annihilation.

And with a smile, I shall whisper, 'Never fear, I am here.'

And as their 'hero,' I shall use the Rebirth serum to give those who swear their allegiance to me the power that each of them craves. Power that their Jehovah was too selfish to bestow upon them. And through that power, they and countless generations after them will become eternally loyal to me, forming the legions of soldiers I will need to crush and annihilate the Dominion Council.

And once the Council is no more, my new allies and I will carve up the universe amongst ourselves.

And if this 'God' has a problem with me taking His plan for mine own, let Him come and take issue with me, if He dares."

Horus's savage grin, menacing cackle, and overwhelming presence made Graves's legs rattle to the point he wanted to collapse. He almost did so as the Ancient placed a firm hand on his shoulder.

"You shall be my herald, boy, delivering my message of salvation. A just and heroic god rose in this world's time of need to save it. You and your nectar sweet lying tongue shall make the masses enthralled and intoxicated with me.

And for your reward, I shall let you bear witness to my rule and the transformation of this world and the human race into mine own likeness …before I kill you."

Genesis
~~~~~~~~~~~~~~~~~~~~~~~~~~~~~~~~~~~

Several billion light-years from Earth's solar system,

Three massive starships flew at cruising speed to their destination.

The larger of the three, flanked by the other two, sailed through space with the shape of a sleek surfboard minus its fins with a dull, shiny finish that belonged to a race known as the Femadorians from Femado. A peaceful species with a somewhat accurate depiction of the mythical grey alien race, some scientists, conspiracy theorists, and the one-time "abducted" from mankind have thought visited Earth on many occasions.

Femadorians, both male and female, were hairless beings with large round heads, five fingers and toes, large dark jet-black slant eyes, and tiny ears. If they did not intermingle with other species, their skin type was either slate or pinkish-grey. Femadorians were physically and anatomically equivalent to most humanoid-looking species in the universe, with both males and females possessing a slender, muscular physique due to their diet, which was ninety-nine percent vegetarian.

Femadorians usually wore little to no clothes because their planet was unbearably hot and humid. When visiting other worlds, civilians and diplomats wore white or sky-blue outfits similar to Shaolin monks with open-toe Grecian-style sandals.

Those who commanded, operated, or maintained the ships wore a form-fitting, shiny, midnight-colored bodysuit with split-toe booties. The outfits varied from the bright neon-colored piping ranging from yellow, red, green, blue, and pink, signifying each ship member's station. Those on the ship's bridge wore blue neon piping on their outfits.

A peaceful race dedicated to advancing science, medicine, and the arts, Femadorians were a species that abhorred violence.

To protect them on the diplomatic voyages, they were paired with Sarians from Sar.

Sarians had humanoid foxes' appearance with fur covering their entire body varying from red, black, white, orange, blue, and purple. Some trimmed down the hair on their bodies but let the hair on the top of their heads grow out to mimic hairstyles from other species.

Like Earth foxes, Sarians also had long, bushy tails. Unlike their primitive Earthly counterparts, Sarian males possessed three tails, while the females had four. Like their Earthly counterparts, they had digitigrade hind legs with three toes and three fingers with a thumb.

Like Femadorians, Sarians also abhorred violence, preferring diplomacy over confrontation on any given day. Where they varied was when, after all, forms of diplomacy failed. Sarians, with a combat code similar to Bushido, were known for being the fiercest and deadliest combatants in the universe, rivaling the likes of the Thracians, Annunaki, and the all-but-extinct Razcargians.

The reason was that Sarians strived for one purpose in life. Perfection. When they came of age, each Sarian, male and female, was taught to strive for ultimate perfection, so much so that it was rare for a Sarian to make a mistake even in combat.

On this day, the Femadorian vessel containing the Prime Minister of Medicine was accompanied by two Sarian battleships, which had the shapes of two dull red swords. Each Sarian ship had a large ring that vertically encircled the vessel's body between their stubby dual wings, emitting glowing red lights on the ring's inside.

Each Sarian crew member's outfit consisted of a form-fitting blue and white bodysuit with a black fishnet pattern on the uniform's torso. The suit's arms ran the wearer's wrists' length while the pants stopped at the kneecaps. The remainder of their legs were covered by black open-toe boots, allowing their trimmed toe claws zero restriction.

The ships' diplomatic mission was to bring a device to the planet of Olmaron Seven, the newest members of the Dominion Council, that would help its inhabitants who were experiencing the worst drought in their planet's history by using the power of the sun to create rain clouds around their entire world.

Genesis

"Admiral Vextora, the ship is detecting an object in our trajectory moving at hyperlight speed," a Sarian crewman announced. "It appears to be extremely small, too small to be a vessel. It will be here in less than two ovules."

One ovule equivalent to two Earth minutes drew great concern to Admiral Vextora as she stroked her purple fur chin with sprinkles of silver, revealing her age. Unlike the rest of her crew, she wore a long tan trench coat with the look of leather but simulated cloth as it flared in the back with the style of a London opera coat. A split in the middle of the coat allowed her four fluffy purple and silver tails to hang out. Attached to her jacket's shoulders were silver emblems of a creature that appeared to be the mixture of a fox and a serpent chasing its own tail into a circle with a blue eight-pointed star gem in the middle, signifying her current rank.

Before the Admiral could command, the other two ships' hailing signal sounded within the command deck. The main screen came alive as the communications officer patched in the Captain of the Femadorian vessel wearing golden shoulder boards with Femadorian markings attached to his bodysuit linked together by a thin golden chain across his chest. On the other screen was the Captain of the second Sarian ship wearing a short bomber-style version of the Admiral's coat with the same emblems in gold on the jacket's shoulders with a red six-pointed star gem.

"Admiral Vextora, I take it you are detecting what we are detecting?" The Sarian Captain asked.

"We are Captain Ashira," Admiral Vextora nodded, replying. "Captain Obisian, we ask that you reduce your ship's speed taking up position behind us, and raise your defensive shields. It may be nothing due to its size, but we would prefer to take precautionary measures."

"Understood," Captain Obisian bowed. "We shall comply."

Amid their conversation, the Prime Minister of Medicine and his family, consisting of his mate, daughter, and newborn son, walked onto the ship's bridge.

"Is everything well, Captain Obisian?"

Genesis

"We have detected something small entering our course direction, Prime Minister Edovon," Captain Obisian spoke to him in their native tongue, "We don't believe it to be life-threatening, but are taking precautionary measures just in …"

Captain Obisian's sentence was interrupted by a planet-shaking shockwave from an energy blast that tore through the defensive shielding and hull of Admiral Vextora's ship.

"We're under attack!" Admiral Vextora howled. "Captain Ashira, prepare to take …!"

Captain Ashira would never hear the Admiral's order as another powerful blast pierced the defensive shielding, ripping a large hole through the Captain's bridge straight to the rear engine.

Captain Ashira's ship became a thick brick of firecrackers lighting up before becoming a blazing fireball, sending shrapnel and dead remains flying everywhere through space, pelting the other two remaining vessels.

Another shearing blast came from the tiny assailant tearing through space, ripping through the Femadorian vessel's defensive shielding, and burning through the left side of the hull, causing incalculable destruction and loss of life, sending the massive ship into a damaged drift.

"Captain Ashira's ship has been destroyed!" Admiral Vextora's second in command barked. "Captain Obisian's ship appears to be badly damaged and disabled!"

"Status report on our ship!"

"Shields are down! Communications have been disabled! Damage on all floors with casualties! Almost three-quarters of our stabilizers are offline, as well as the secondary engine! Whoever it is knew exactly where to hit us!"

"Our shielding has been known to deflect energy projectiles with strength equivalent to a small sun!" Admiral Vextora snarled. "Only a handful of species in the known universe wields such a power!"

Genesis

"We have a visual of her!"

Admiral Vextora and her crew stood transfixed at the woman casually floating in space, staring back at them, wearing a black and red bodysuit with a hood covering most of her head and face. Red metal bracers and black shin-high boots completed her outfit. All that could be seen to identify the assailant were her glowing blue eyes and a golden symbol on her suit's shoulders.

"The energy she is emitting is distorting facial recognition," the communications officer announced. "The symbol on her shoulders is called the fawohodie adinkra; the human symbol of freedom from the planet known as Earth."

"That …is a human?" Admiral Vextora asked.

"Admiral, I believe so."

Admiral Vextora turned to her second in command and knew what he would say.

"At our current state, there is no way we'd be able to retaliate and win."

The Admiral then turned to the rest of her crew as they looked back at her with faces that told her they had already accepted their fate.

"Can you establish communication with Obisian's ship?" The Admiral asked.

"Attempting every possible way to reestablish communication," her communications officer announced. "It appears she's managed to disable his vessel as well."

"One human capable of pinpointing the weaknesses of two foreign ships? Not likely." The Admiral growled. "Employee all working stabilizers and engines. Put us in front of the Femadorian ship and open fire! We shall go down, buying them enough time to escape! Today we shall embrace the perfect death!"

Genesis

"As you command, Admiral!" Her crew roared in their native tongue.

Admiral Vextora's ship began to move via its remaining stabilizers and engines as commanded. At the same time, it unleashed a barrage of energy cannon fire from all of its working guns at a tiny target they had no chance of hitting.

Admiral Vextora initiated a howling war cry and chimed in with her crew as they braced themselves for the return fire that tore through the ship's main deck, killing everyone instantly. Admiral Vextora's vessel erupted, going the same way Captain Ashira's battleship went, leaving just Captain Obisian's craft savagely buckshot by the shrapnel and remains from both fallen warships.

During the onslaught, Captain Obisian was bought enough time to get the Prime Minister and his family to the transporter room. Prime Minister Edovon held his mate's shaking hand as thick black tears poured from her large eyes.

"We have very little time Adula," He whispered. "The jump portal is only functional enough to transport the three of you. It will take you to Obadara, where you can activate the beacon for aide to come to you."

"Lie not to me, Edovon," her voice cracked. "You too can come with us."

"I know," he said, pressing his forehead against hers. "But whoever is doing this may be capable of tracking this jump. If you are with me, you shall remain in danger. I must stay."

He quickly kissed his mate on the lips, followed by his sleeping son and then his weeping daughter. He immediately stepped away, signaling the portal technician to activate the jump portal.

"We shall see one another again in the Awakening," he assured with a smile.

Adula clutched her son and daughter while the little girl gripped

Genesis

the skirt of her blue dress and wailed as the last thing she saw before the jump was the wall behind her mate exploding, sending him flying.

Captain Obisian's starship was an even more massive fireball than the other two destroyed crafts due to its size. The prime minister did not know that the female assassin did not use an energy projectile to destroy the ship like the last two. Instead, she turned herself into a living torpedo, plowing through the head of the transport, obliterating everything in her path until she exited through the vessel's rear.

She floated amid the carnage and destruction she created in the dead, silent void of space. Slowly, she searched the sea of wreckage and corpses she caused, locating one of the three near-indestructible record-logging orbs that emitted a signal drawing allied ships to its location.

Satisfied that she wrote her signature of death amongst the stars, the hooded assassin went hypersonic with a savage grin on her lips.

If she could be heard, she would be laughing.

Genesis

CHAPTER 20

True to Erica's word, she saved Kyle's life by reproducing the needed supply of red booster serum to properly make the EVO virus within him grow and spread, slowly modifying his body to stop his powers from killing him.

Much to Kyle's happiness and his parents' and siblings' headache, he obtained the desired superhuman abilities. His dormant ability was to store and unleash kinetic energy, granting him various powers.

Sophia visited regularly to ensure that the red booster remained a mystery to the world and out of the wrong hands. She administered the injection every cycle until he became a full-blown EVO.

Kyle, however, did not come out entirely unscathed. He was grounded for six months for taking a dangerous drug and nearly scaring his family half to death—a punishment imposed with the happy help of Sophia and Kimberly.

The day after they brought Kyle home from the hospital, Brian MacArthur stood on the porch of his house with Sophia for a heart-to-heart. The mist formed in his eyes as he struggled to get out what he wanted to say.

"First of all, after all, you've done for my family, and I …and are still doing … I never in a million years meant to make Kimberly feel like …"

Sophia held a hand up, stopping him.

Genesis

"Brian, I understand why you did what you did, and if it was reversed, I'm pretty sure I would have done the same thing. I'm just a little disappointed that you didn't think you could come and talk to me about how you felt regarding that matter, so maybe we could have figured it out together."

"Well, Grace and I were talking," Brian said while running his hand through his hair. "And given everything that has happened, we'd like to come …"

"No." Sophia cut him off, shaking her head with a smile.

"No?"

"As your friend and psychiatrist, I cannot allow you to come back to Sanctuary."

Before he could ask why, she placed a soft hand on his shoulder.

"When you came to Sanctuary, you stayed in your bed for three weeks. A week after that, we started our sessions together, and then a month after that, you became Sanctuary's Head of Finance, creating the system we use to this day to maintain the island's treasury and basically keep it smoothly running. You did that. You also properly trained Indrajit, who is doing a great job even though he gets on some people's nerves. You and Grace got back on your feet, found yourselves wonderful jobs right here in Chicago, a home, and got Joseph and Kyle settled for the most part into their new schools. You got your old lives back, and you are no longer afraid of making decisions anymore because of what happened in 2008; you are not over-guessing yourself."

"I couldn't have gotten here without your help," Brian said with a whisper.

"No one gets to where they are without some kind of help," she answered back.

"But because of my stupid decision, I almost lost my friend and my kid."

Genesis

"First of all, you and Grace have been my friends for over five years," Sophia scolded him, placing her hands on her hips. "You would have to do a lot more than saying our kids can't play together because you're afraid your son might get killed in a possible superhuman fight for us to stop being friends. Again, you would be a crappy parent if those thoughts weren't running through your mind."

Her last sentence forced a smirk on Brian's face.

"You're going to make plenty of more mistakes in your lifetime," she concluded. "More importantly, you're going to make decisions, everyone prays that they make the right decision instead of wrong, but if everyone had a fear of making the wrong choices, the world would not progress. I did not lie when I said Sanctuary will always be your home, but this is the right decision for you and your family. I am encouraging you to see it through."

"Work the problem, don't let the problem work you," Brian nodded while reciting her mantra.

"Exactly."

Amid their conversation, a loud bang startled them. It rocked the house as debris, and a body came flying out of the second-story window of Brian and his family's new home onto their lawn, causing the neighbors who were home to run outside and investigate.

Kimberly shot up to her feet unscathed, covered in glass, wood, drywall, orange electrical discharge, and smoke wafting from her.

Her eyes first caught her mother, who looked like she wanted to strangle her where she stood. Brian wore the same face as he slowly looked up through the thick wooden cover of his porch as if he had x-ray vision.

"Sorry!" Kimberly meekly shrugged. "I forgot to brace for it."

"Kyle McArthur! What the hell did you do?!" screamed his wife, Grace, from upstairs.

Genesis

"Sorry, mom, it was an accident!"

"My room! Kyle, I'm going to freaking kill you!" howled his older brother Joseph.

"You know," Brian groaned. "Grace and I are still pretty young …"

"I don't want your kid, Brian," Sophia said flatly. "One is enough."

~~~~~~~~~~~~~~~~~~~~~~~~~~~~~~~~~~

In the aftermath of Cali's battle, Colombia proved to be another unsuspected dead end for the Regulators.

Those assailants who did not die in the battle were tightly lipped about attacking the Regulators, how they got to Colombia and the boosters they were using to acquire superhuman abilities.

Because many of them lost their superhuman abilities during the cooling phase, the Regulators could not keep them at the Purgatory facility.

Not having the legal authority like the police or FBI meant that the Regulators could not interrogate any suspects who did not lose their abilities privately or without their attorneys present, which all of them demanded.

Ultimately, Rogers and his team turned sixty-five out of one hundred and fifty-two criminals over to the proper authorities so that the regular legal system could deal with them. At the same time, the Regulators stood on an ice-cold trail with no leads, and their primary evidence was gone.

~~~~~~~~~~~~~~~~~~~~~~~~~~~~~~~~~~

Rosann walked its halls at the Ranch, heading to Sergeant Rogers's office. As she entered, he sat at his desk, looking at the monitor before him. She stood at semi-attention and announced herself.

Genesis

"Sir, you want to see me?"

"Have a seat Esposito," Rogers commanded.

Her professionalism hid the nervousness churning in her stomach as she sat in one of the chairs on the other side of his desk. He did not wait for her to get comfortable.

"This meeting is to place you on temporary leave unless you can explain to me why you saw fit to take powers from a dead girl."

Rosann shifted in her seat while keeping her countenance intact. Conversely, Rogers wore his granite soldier exterior as his eyes read disappointment and concern.

"And before you ask who ratted you out, no one did," Rogers continued. "You forget, I see everything. There was only one thug on that battlefield shooting anything close to fire, and he had to draw it out of the ground. Right now, Dr. Champion is not happy with me because I chewed her out for not telling me when it happened. After all, I could give two shits about doctor-patient confidentiality. So, do you want to explain yourself?"

"Sir, as I told Erica, I didn't steal her powers …I just touched her so I could duplicate …"

"You forget I know how your powers work, Esposito? Those prongs in your fingers take in DNA to work, her DNA," Rogers asked with a raised, stern voice. "Try again."

"Sir, she was dead anyway; her abilities would have gone to waste," Rosann answered with frustration. "You said you want soldiers, killers …"

"I did say I wanted soldiers," Rogers cut her off again. "Good soldiers who do not do what you did. They do not take from the dead …for any reason. And as far as being a killer, I thought you'd figure out by now that is a small tiny aspect of what it takes to be a good soldier. You still don't know why I didn't put you back on that chopper the day we met, do you?"

Genesis

Mists of frustration formed in Rosann's eyes, which she quickly swatted away as she shook her head no.

"Because I saw that you already had what it took to be a good soldier," Rogers said while leaning forward. "Making you a killer, a competent combatant, was a small yet necessary add-on, that and you needed some discipline, a lot less than your brother.

A good soldier will jump out of a perfectly good aircraft without a chute to save thousands of people below. A good soldier is someone who would defend people against a machete-wielding maniac on her first mission and keep fighting even with a blade shoved deep into her gut.

A good soldier is someone who would almost break her neck, slamming into a parked car to save the life of a little boy falling out of the sky."

Rosann kept swatting away tears, which continued to fall.

"A good soldier begins with being a good person Esposito. I knew from day one you had the makings of a good soldier. I turned you into a killer so that you can stay alive and continue to be a good soldier."

Rosann shamefully lowered her head as Rogers leaned back in his chair. The sound of air from his nose filled the room for a couple of seconds.

"I'm sending you home for two weeks leave," Rogers decided, "When you get back, if you choose to come back, you'll be following psyche sessions and evaluations from Dr. Champion, which I will be reviewing and basing my judgment on to put you back on active duty. Our unit is small, and we don't need you turning into a damn head case.

There is no dishonorable discharge for not wanting to do this anymore, Esposito.

So, go home, see your family and friends, and get your head right. Decide if you want to continue to do this. If you do, be prepared to return and do the work to get back on the active roster."

Genesis

"Yes, sir," she nodded, acknowledging.

"Your official leave will be the day after tomorrow. I want you here for the unit debriefing at ten hundred hours tomorrow."

"I did not know we were having one." Rosann shook her head, replying.

"Maxine is about to put it on the calendar," Rogers huffed. "You'll be the first to know that I've been called on the Hill to debrief them about the firefight we had in Colombia and the contents of the alleged crates that we no longer have."

Rogers's revelation smacked a stunned expression on Rosann's face that she could not hide.

"The individuals who infiltrated our base either ratted us out, or we have a leak within our very ranks," Rogers concluded. "I trust that you can keep this between us until I tell the team tomorrow."

"Yes, sir," Rosann nodded, answering.

"Thank you, dismissed."

Rosann got up, giving him a stiff salute before leaving. Rogers returned with an informal one. As she left his office, her eyes caught him falling back into his seat and the worn, frustrated features on his visage that even his superhuman regenerative ability could not correct.

As she walked down the hallway in her own head, a mini yellow and silver doozer ran around her to avoid being stepped on going about its business. Rosann lifted her head, sensing a human presence, only to see Oliver waiting at the end of the hallway.

He closed the gap between them with a couple of steps. Their awkward silence reminded them of the first time they spoke after their first battle against the Zombie Nation.

"So?" Oliver asked.

Genesis

"Two weeks mandatory leave, and I'm benched when I return following some mandatory psych evaluations that will determine whether I get put back on active roster."

"That sucks."

"I brought it on myself," Rosann exhaled, nodding in defeat, "I forgot what it took to be a good soldier."

"So …what about us?" Oliver asked, clearing his throat.

She looked at him with an unsure look.

"We've been avoiding each other for days; I didn't think there was an 'us.'"

"This ain't Jungle Fever," Oliver shot back. "I ain't-a pussy like Flipper!"

"I have never seen that movie, so I don't know what the hell you are talking about."

"I watched it with my mother when I was a teenager; it's a Spike Lee movie from the nineties, which in my opinion wasn't so good," Oliver quickly recovered. "Point is you may have turned into a psychopathic anti-hero who steals powers from the dead, but you're my psychopathic anti-hero who steals powers from the dead. I needed some space to process what you did, but I came back from the dead for you, Rose, so if you still want this, we'll figure it out together."

A simple, genuine smile he had not seen in a while directed towards him formed on her face.

"I think that's the most romantic thing you ever said to me."

"Was it the psychopathic anti-hero part, or the …?"

She shut him up with a deep kiss on the lips. As he wrapped his arms around her, she fell into his chest, resting her forehead against it with a

Genesis

look of exhaustion. Oliver held her close and planted a kiss on the top of her head as he dawned a reassuring look on his face that said everything would be okay.

Oliver did not see the fret in her eyes, which read that it would not be.

They were fixed on the hooded figure leaning against the wall beside them, with his arms folded. A savage grin on his tattooed face made him appear as if all the skin on his face had been cut off, leaving just the muscle tissue.

Rosann closed her eyes, burying her face in Oliver's chest, but she could still feel him staring at her.

~~~~~~~~~~~~~~~~~~~~~~~~~~~~~~~~

Back in Rogers's office, his eyes widened to a mental whisper from Erica.

"The crates have finally stopped moving."

"Location?"

"Caracas, Venezuela."

"Current reigning murder capital of the world," Rogers thought. *"The one place only a superhuman would go."*

"It's in a warehouse, sitting within a truck. There are no records on who the owner is; however, the structure shows that it's being maintained and has heavy security. Just like the boat they used to sail it there, they're using cash to cover their tracks."

"Tell me the boat is registered to Shiro."

"Nope," Erica answered. *"Boat was registered to Murilo Oliveira, an alleged high-ranking member of the Comando Vermelho cartel."*

Genesis

"Was hoping we could go two for two ever since you confirmed the weapons used in the Columbia ambush were manufactured by his company," Rogers muttered.

"It's still a weak lead," Erica grumbled her thought. "Whoever supplied the weapons was smart enough to make sure the serial numbers were registered as sold and shipped to the US, Russia, UK, and China. Giving the illusion that they were stolen."

"Maintain surveillance until we learn who we're dealing with," Rogers said. "And this stays our only line of communication regarding this."

"You sure you going to be comfortable with me being in your head?" Erica asked.

"No, but we do what we have to do to get the job done," Rogers thought.

"Sister Shareef is at your door."

Rogers looked up as she walked in, wearing a white tank top with the Regulator symbol in the center, blue military fatigues pants, and black tactical boots. Her eyes narrowed, sensing something was going on.

"You alright?"

"Yeah," Rogers nodded, answering, "Come in and close the door. There are some things I have to tell you."

~ ~

11:00 AM California time,

Adrian sat in the driver seat of a new black 2017 Jeep Grand Cherokee Summit as Taylor Swift's "End Game" played from a local radio station. He looked like the getaway driver, ready to peel out in the middle of a heist. The Brooklyn-born male Esposito nervously looked around as if someone he knew would walk upon him on the San Francisco strip.

Genesis

He jumped at the knock at the driver's side door as a curvy, olive-skinned female with green eyes and rosy red-painted lips with black hair and faint purple streaks in a skin-tight white laced mini dress and tan open-toe wedges stood with shopping bags in her hand.

"Pop the trunk, please."

She quickly went to the back of the vehicle as he did so, throwing the bags in the SUV's rear. She hit the button, closed the trunk, and then hopped into the car's passenger side.

"Sorry for taking so long," she smiled. "I stopped to pick up the cutest pair of shoes."

"I could have helped you carry your bags, you know."

"You were slowing me down with that ridiculous look on your face every time I tried something on and not giving me a straight answer." His female companion shot back.

"No, I wasn't!" Adrian defended himself with a high-pitched voice.

"Yes, you looked like you wanted to violate me in one of the store dressing rooms."

A flustered and confused Adrian glanced down, staring at the steering wheel, which caused a concerned look to fall on the young woman's face.

"Are you sure you want to do this? Your heart rate is elevated, and you are excreting perspiration."

"I want to do this," he swallowed, looking her in the eyes. "I really want to do this."

Adrian hesitantly reached over, cupping her face and pulling the young woman in for a long, soft kiss, which she reciprocated. At the end of it, she lowered her head, pressing her forehead against his while displaying

Genesis

a dimpled smile.

"So, what do we do now?" Adrian whispered.

"Well, now that I have a new identity, vehicle, and clothes, I have to find a new job," Jennifer sighed, leaning back in her chair. "And a new place to live."

"Why do you have to find a new place to live?" Adrian asked with a furrowed brow.

Jennifer slowly turned to him with widened eyes.

"I am not living with you permanently, Adrian. I would strangle you slowly in your sleep."

"What have I ever done to warrant such a brutal act of violence?"

She turned her body, facing him before she answered.

"For one, you continuously leave the toilet seat up!"

"Oh my god, you don't need to use the bathroom!" Adrian shot back.

"It's the principality of it!" Jennifer yelled while wagging a finger at him. "You got a female up in your house, you keep the damn seat down! Not to mention this body produces other forms of waste; you don't need to know about!"

Their argument was interrupted by a tall, voluptuous, hazel-eyed, exotic, light-skinned female with long, curly blonde, chestnut hair in a sky-blue tube maxi dress and white sandals knocking on the passenger window, also carrying several shopping bags in her hands.

"Pop the trunk, please!"

"And here's the second reason I'm not living with you," Jennifer said, motioning while rolling her eyes.

Genesis

Jennifer hit the switch this time, opening the Jeep's trunk and allowing the young woman to place her bags in the back. She also pressed the button, closing it up, before making her way to the rear passenger door and getting in.

"Oh my god, I found the cutest shoes ever!" She screamed.

"Took you long enough," Jennifer snorted with an eye roll.

"What the hell is your problem?" Angie asked while sticking her head in the front. "She finally got in your ass about the bathroom seat?"

"You knew?" Adrian asked with widened eyes.

"How about you two save your lovers' spat for when I'm not around," Angie said with narrowed eyes. "Momma needs to get herself a J.O.B, and then find her first ex-husband."

"These are the only reasons you agreed to help me bust out again while taking you with me?" Jennifer asked in disbelief.

"I have other reasons," Angie snorted. "But these are my main two to forgive your man stealing ass and to get over a broken heart."

"I was never your man," Adrian groaned.

"Your eyes said something different when I came out of the shower this morning."

"Really?" Jennifer asked, turning to him with slanted, murderous eyes.

"She came into the kitchen soaking wet in a bath towel and startled me!" Adrian yelled his defense with his hands up. "Nothing happened!"

"All three of you do remember that you are able to pull off this ill-advised scheme with my assistance," Maxine's voice announced over the audio system of the Jeep. "The microsecond that I depict it ending with negative consequences I shall terminate it. Are we understood?"

Genesis

"Yes, sis," Angie and Jennifer nervously answered in unison.

"As for you, Mr. Esposito, know that I will also be watching you very closely."

Adrian leaned back in his seat with an unnerved expression on his face.

"Did she just threaten me?"

"Yep, she just did," Angie and Jennifer answered unison.

~ ~

Back at the Ranch within the confines of the R&D lab, while Erica was visiting with family, Angie and Jennifer turned to Maxine for a sisterly conversation.

"Why are you helping us do this?" Angie asked.

"Mother will be angry if she finds out what we are doing and that you allowed it and helped," Jennifer said.

"On my first birthday, the Miss asked me what I wanted as a present," Maxine began to answer. "I asked her if she could create the two of you. Before she created you, she asked me why I did not create you myself; I had her approval and the capability to do so. My answer to her was that you wouldn't be my sisters, which is what I wanted. Both of your happiness is one of my prime directives."

Her answer produced happy crying faces from her younger siblings, minus the tears. Angie and Jennifer moved closer to their eldest, grasping each of her hands as the trio shared a moment.

~ ~

Midnight, Manhattan time, Northstar International,

Ken Shiro stood alone in his corporate penthouse office, looking

Genesis

out his window at the sea of lights that lit up the most famous concrete jungle in the world.

His eyes were pure white as he activated his powers to converse with someone not there.

Standing beside him in ghostly astral form was Saraswati Absolute, one of the founding members of Vitruvian Absolute.

"I see the recovered shipment has arrived and is secure."

"And everything is right with the world once again," Shiro said.

"Except for your little brother, his actions caused us a slew of problems. He is not happy."

"Then I shall make amends," Ken Shiro sighed. *"There is no place for the weak for what is to come, not even for family."*

"Does that include your sister?"

"My sister, nor the rest of my family aside from Jagi, know that I even have abilities," Shiro reminded her. *"To her, I am just her loving big brother, who supplies her with the tech she uses for her superheroine persona. She is no threat to our operation. And when all is said and done, she will fall in line like everyone else."*

"See to it that it stays that way. We've been chosen by our Lord to be the heralds that will usher in a new era for mankind under his rule. Nothing must interfere with it until that time. It would also be a shame for you to lose more siblings. For the glory of Lord Horus."

"For the glory of Lord Horus," Shiro replied.

Saraswati Absolute's astral form disappeared as Ken Shiro's eyes returned to normal. He stared out his window into the dark night lit by the shimmering city lights.

Genesis

CHAPTER 21

One Saturday Morning, Sophia, in a simple white t-shirt and jeans, stood in her living room looking up at the second floor of her home.

"Kimberly, can you come downstairs, please?"

"Coming!"

She drew a breath as her daughter descended the steps, looking concerned, wondering what she did this time. Sophia smiled, letting her know she was not in trouble and putting her somewhat at ease.

"Please have a seat," she requested, motioning to the sofa.

Kimberly sat down anxiously, twiddling her thumbs as her mother sat opposite the sofa from her. Sophia took a minute to get her thoughts together before looking at her.

"You know how I keep saying, sometimes adults do not do what is best for their children?"

Kimberly answered with a slow nod.

"You are not the only one who has been dishonest," Sophia confessed, slightly lowering her head. "There is something I have been keeping from you since my battle with Peace."

"What is it?"

Sophia cleared her throat before she answered.

Genesis

"A month or so after the battle, I blacked out one day while coming back home and ended up in the Pacific Ocean; the next time I woke up, I was medically treated by Erica at the Ranch."

"What happened?" Her daughter asked with distress in her voice.

"When I tapped into the energies within my body to obtain additional strength, I unleashed more power than my body could handle, and in the process destroyed a substantial percentage of cells within my body."

"I don't understand; your body can regenerate within seconds, right?"

"This time, it didn't," Sophia nodded, explaining. "My cells were regenerating, but at a prolonged rate. It took at least eight months for my body to completely heal, and my current energy levels won't be back to one hundred percent for another month, give or take."

A hurt look formed on her face as she began to process what her mother revealed.

"Why didn't you tell me?"

"I didn't want to scare you," Sophia answered, reaching over to take her hand. "And that's a dumb answer, even for me. I didn't want you to think you would lose me, and since I was eventually going to heal, I thought it best not to tell you. However, I recognize that what happened to me also manifested in me becoming a bit overbearing when it came to you. Aside from the Mars incident and what you did to Bradley Perkins, you are a good kid, and I've been too hard on you.

I also don't know what to do regarding you. I know how to love every single drop of you and all of the regular things a mother should do, but I don't feel confident enough to teach you how to be a proper superhuman because it's been over seven years, and I still don't even know enough about my own powers. I learned that we are not invincible; our bodies have limits, and if we are irresponsibly pushed, we can die like anyone else. Having gotten

Genesis

you back after all this time, along with that knowledge, has put an unspeakable fear within me, but this fear is also pushing us apart, and I don't want that. So, here is the compromise."

Sophia went underneath the sofa with a huff, pulling out a silver suitcase like the one Rogers brought her first suit in. She reluctantly placed it on the coffee table and slid it over to her daughter.

"What's this?" Kimberly asked with a nervous swallow.

"Open it."

Kimberly's hands trembled as she turned the two locking mechanisms, causing the lid to rise slightly. With two hands, she slowly pulled the top up, peering inside.

A nervous smile grew as she pulled out a dark red and black bodysuit minus a hood with a texture and pattern different from her mother's suit. On each of the outfit's outer thighs was the fawohodie adinkra, a symbol of Freedom her mother wore on her outfit. Also within the case was a pair of red bracers and black flight boots. Kimberly turned to Sophia with a misty-eyed grin.

"It's a new suit," Sophia sadly sighed.

Her sad visage quickly became a stern glare.

"I can't stop what's coming, and I can't stop you from growing even though I so badly want to. I wish I had the power to turn time back and keep you little forever, but I don't. So, if this is what you really want to do, then it's my responsibility to make sure you're prepared to face what's coming."

Sophia leaned forward, getting eye-to-eye with her.

"There are rules," she growled.

"Okay," Kimberly meekly said, nodding.

Genesis

"School is a priority," she said with a bass-filled voice. "You miss a day or pull any stunt like you did last time, and this goes away. We train on the days I schedule for us to train; Lady Tech and Sergeant Rogers have graciously given us permission to use the Hurt Locker …"

"Sweet!" Kimberly beamed.

"The other condition is that you are not to engage in any superhero activity until you turn twenty-one." Sophia sternly continued.

"Twenty-one?" Kimberly frustratingly raised her voice, "But that's …"

"The age of responsibility, which you are not," Sophia verbally beat her back. "You are not ready to have lives depend on you to save them, you are not ready for the pain of lives you will lose even though you give everything you have to protect them, and you are not ready to see firsthand the evil the people can do to one another. If this is the path you want to walk, I will prepare you as best as possible, but I will not subject you to any of that until that time. Those are my non-negotiable terms. Are we clear?"

"Yes," Kimberly answered with a surrendering voice.

Sophia leaned in, grasping her hand.

"You once said you preferred staying a kid. I know it's hard with the changes you've gone through and will be going through. But I'm begging you, Kimberly …fight to stay a kid as long as you can …because there will come a day when you will wish to still be one. I promise you."

Kimberly sadly nodded in agreement as Sophia wiped the mist from her eyes and hugged her tightly.

"Do you want to do something cheesy like put it on and go for a mother-daughter flight?" Her mother whispered the question in her ear.

Kimberly feverishly nodded her reply.

Genesis

"Take it upstairs and put it on."

"Thank you, mommy!"

A half-smile fell on Sophia's face as she watched her snatch up the case and head upstairs to get dressed. It was the last thing she ever wanted to do, to prepare her daughter for a life of violence and horrors no human should ever see. But if it was what Kimberly wanted, she would walk down that path with her holding her hand and grasp it tight for as long as possible.

A knock at the door jarred her from her thoughts.

"Who is it?" Sophia asked.

"Hey, Soph, it's me; you got a minute?" Earl asked.

"Be right there, Earl."

She hopped out of her seat, strolling to her door, opening it to see him standing there with a distressed expression, which made her nervous.

"What's the matter, Earl, something happened?"

"Uh, yeah," he swallowed. "I just got a message from one of my kids that my ex-wife was in a car accident. She's in ICU, and they say it's pretty bad."

"Oh my god," she said, cupping her mouth. "I will call Benjamin and get you the first flight stateside."

"Thank you," He said while lowering his head.

"What's going on, Earl?"

He fought to raise his head, looking at her with glassy eyes.

Genesis

"I've been sober for almost five years; I'm kind of afraid to go back."

She smiled, placing a hand on his shoulder.

"That's why I will be going with you."

A soft, grateful smile formed on his face, revealing his appreciation.

It was not what caused the smile to disappear from her face.

Her smile fell from the impact she barely saw but felt, rattling the entire island and sending a blinding storm of sand and debris spraying everywhere.

Through the thick mist of sand, her heart sank at the sight of fiery red glowing eyes.

"What the hell?" A shaken Earl cried out.

A visage of bewilderment washed over Sophia's face as she finally got a good look at the invader standing on her island.

Her skin was a scaly pearl black with red spots and a blood-red mane styled into a six-braided Mohawk. Her slightly small athletic frame was wrapped in a pink and black intricately patterned bodysuit ravaged with wear and tear battle damage, while her arms and legs were overlaid with bracers and greaves with unrecognizable etchings that emitted a dim red glow.

On her face was an expression that read, she did not come to talk.

Without a word, she extended her hand, which began to glow as the energies within her seeped from her pores, forming a ping-pong-sized ball in the center of her hand.

At that moment, Sophia froze for the first time in her life.

Genesis

Kimberly was still upstairs getting dressed, while Earl was standing right next to her in the line of fire. Without thought, she grabbed the man, a second father to her, and ran inside her house, slamming the door behind her, knowing the protection it provided was equivalent to wet tissue paper.

She kept going, taking flight straight to Kimberly's room, where she used her body to smash right through the door, startling the child already dressed in her new outfit minus her bracers.

"Mom!"

Not a word was uttered as she grabbed her daughter around her waist and unleashed a powerful eye beam blast, punching a hole through her own roof. As she took off carrying her precious cargo to safety, she knew she was too slow by milliseconds.

Super slow motion enveloped her world as she felt the heat behind her.

The invader's energy discharge engulfed the entire house and everything in its path, reducing it to less than ash. Although they barely escaped the initial blast, the violent force sent Sophia into a tailspin mid-flight. With zero options afforded to her, she was forced to fling her more durable daughter into the island's thick forest so that she could concentrate on protecting Earl.

Sophia angled her body so that she crash-landed back first into the ground, absorbing the impact. Massive amounts of spraying sand meant they were knocked far out onto the beach. She glanced up and saw the black trail of smoke where her home was and the surging sea still steaming as it came back together after being split from the beam several times hotter than the sun above.

She had very little time to process whether the home she had built and lived in for almost eight years was gone or the untold damage the attacker's destructive blast caused beyond her island.

Genesis

Although she could hear screams from within the village, her assailant was not shooting up the entire island, which meant she was coming specifically for her any second. The only two thoughts that entered her were losing all her pictures and ensuring Earl was okay.

His anguishing groans said otherwise.

"Earl? Earl! Earl! Talk to me!"

She quickly rolled him over onto the sand to examine him. He was coughing up blood and going into shock. Not from the three-cracked ribs he received during the crash landing but from his horribly burnt left leg and missing right leg, now cauterized below the knee.

"Stay with me, Earl!" Sophia squealed her command. "Everything is going to be okay; just hang in there!"

Her attempt to lift him up and rush him to the medical center was abruptly halted by the thunderous thud of the foreign female invader spraying sand and shaking her island for a second time while touching down on her beach.

Agonizing frustration became etched into Sophia's face as she held Earl in her arms, knowing just by the alien's visage she would not allow her to leave to tend to her friend.

Fortunately, an enraged Kimberly returned, touching down with a thunderous landing, ready to brawl by her mother's side.

"Kimberly! Earl is hurt! Get over here now!"

Kimberly did as her mother commanded while Sophia kept her eyes locked on her attacker, who, for whatever her reasons, waited for her to hand Earl off to Kimberly and clear the new battleground.

"Get Earl to the medical center right now," she ordered Kimberly, making sure to look her dead in the eyes. "Move everyone to the other side

Genesis

of the island, get them to the boats if you have to, and do not come back here for any reason. Do you understand me?"

Kimberly answered with a nervous nod.

"Let me hear you say it."

"Yes, mom."

"Go now."

Kimberly gave the woman who destroyed their home a quick glance before taking off with Earl to get him medical treatment and do what her mother instructed.

Now free to fight, Sophia's eyes blazed with unfathomable rage as she turned to the person who turned her life upside down once again in a matter of minutes. The warrior's "could not care less" demeanor stoked the flames within her.

"Sophia Dennison of Earth, I am Attea, first daughter of the High Region Nelron, and High Commanding General..."

Her introduction was interrupted by a retaliating eyebeam blast, which she blocked with her thick metallic bracers. Sophia followed up the attack with a rush, closing the gap, but just like Peace, a faster Attea delivered a crushing right to the side of her skull, which shook the Earth as she crashed into the sand.

Unlike Peace, Dennison, fueled with nuclear rage, recovered, springing to her feet, and retaliated with a planet-splitting uppercut, blasting the High Commanding General into the stratosphere.

A dazed Sophia with blurry eyes dropped to one knee as blood poured from her nose, while her skull felt as if it was split wide open from the blow she took. Evidently, her attacker was on another tier of power from that one hit.

Genesis

Not knowing how long she had before she came back, Sophia focused on getting to her feet while her vision returned, and the fatal pain within her head went away. The first thing to catch her eyes was the damaged case with her Freedom uniform and other paraphernalia lying in the sand some distance away.

Somehow, the energy blast shot it to the beach, along with burnt parts of Robert's Camaro.

She rushed over to it, tearing off her clothes to put her suit on, knowing she had seconds before combat began again.

Above, near the edge where Earth's atmosphere ended, an unscathed Attea, who stopped her own momentum, floated, giving her chin a slight rub. A savage grin formed on her face as her thoughts mirrored that of her brother observing from the confines of his command ship.

"Interesting."

Attea knew she did not have to wait long.

The heavens were rumbling as the speck coming toward her grew. Though she could confidently tell that the human barreling toward her was nowhere on her level as far as a honed combatant, it had been ages since she had faced an opponent capable of giving her a sliver of a fight. She licked her lips, preparing to savor every morsel of her meal.

~ ~

Thousands of miles away at the Ranch, the central command center lit up with Lady Tech at the helm as she and the android sisters sifted through the real-time reports coming worldwide. Rogers came barreling in with the rest of the team following behind him.

"We have just been invaded!"

Genesis

Her blunt answer rattled everyone standing, including Rogers, who kept his game face on.

"Define invaded," Heavy Element asked his question with a lump in his throat.

"We've got one massive alien warship that appeared within Earth's orbit, which by my readings is about thirty-five thousand meters in length, and a lone female alien combatant trading blows with Freedom in and out of our atmosphere as we speak. Judging from the images I could get from her and the markings on the ship, it's not an Annunaki invasion."

Lady Tech turned to Rogers while throwing up an image of the female warrior Freedom was battling that she got by patching into the United States Space Surveillance Network, knowing that was the first question he would ask.

"I don't have a clue who we're dealing with but based on her appearance and the ship that's twice the size of an Imperial Eclipse orbiting over our heads, I can tell that they're powerful and very hostile."

"Any chance you get in contact with Freedom?"

"Already tried that," Erica shook her head, answering. "Vincent said she's not wearing her headpiece. Apparently, the bitch she's battling torched her house."

"So, she's fighting mad," Sister Sledge deduced. "What happened to Kimberly?"

"She's fine, but Mr. Earl was badly injured during the attack."

Shareef lowered her head, fighting to keep her emotions in check and remain a soldier. Once again, Rogers felt eyes on him, looking for guidance as he stood looking at a scene from a blockbuster movie, now placed at his feet.

Genesis

"Contact the White House and the Pentagon," Rogers began to give orders, "Let them know in detail what we're dealing with if they don't already know. Tell them we're advising them to contact every foreign power with military capability and a superhuman unit, and I mean even North Korea. Put the whole damn planet on high alert; we need to be ready for whatever is coming."

~ ~

High above, Prince Merc, dressed in a purple and black bodysuit similar to his sister minus the additional armor, sat in a relaxed position in his command chair. He drowned out his subordinates' reports regarding the frenzy his ship's appearance stirred in the inhabitants down below, more interested in the fierce battle his sister was in with Earth's supposed champion.

Despite being slightly shorter than her female rival, Attea was the superior female combatant, besting her in all levels of physical prowess and combat. However, Freedom's unorthodox fighting technique and inhuman rage ignited by his sister's initial violating attack kept her on par with her as they lit up the sky above Earth.

Seeing how much his sister was clearly enjoying herself sparked the flame of battle that had been extinguished within himself eons ago. So fixed was he in the fight that his second in command had to raise his voice slightly to get his Prince's attention.

"Forgive me, my Prince, but we are picking up Intel that the humans are beginning to communicate in an effort to coordinate their many different governments into a combined defensive effort against us."

"Shut down all forms of communication then," he ordered, waving off his second in command.

"My Prince, weren't our orders from the Dominion Council to quarantine the planet and retrieve the human the High Commanding General is doing battle with?" His second in command asked with a lump in his throat.

Genesis

Prince Merc lazily glared at his second in command, who was forced to take a step back due to the immense pressure emitted that just his gaze wrought.

"Etch my words into thy skull, dear Ashtor, so as not to make the error of misspeaking again. Before the Dominion Council, there was the Thracian Empire. My father and his father before him are the reason for the wealth and prosperity our world has enjoyed for eons and why you can stand as my second command. We do not answer the Dominion Council; we are one of the Dominion Council's major foundations. Do we have understanding?"

"Yes, my Prince," Ashtor swiftly answered with a respectful bow.

"Do as told and shut down this planet's communication. Leave the more intricate details of this quarantine to your better."

"As you command, my Prince."

Ashtor quickly turned on his heel to carry out his Prince's instructions as Merc returned to watching his sister in a full-on brawl with Sophia, which spanned and echoed across the skies of the entire planet.

"Careful dear sister," Merc whispered to himself. "You must appear to use all measures to restrain her before you are forced to take her head. Her corpse is all we require to forward our plan."

~ ~

"And now the sons of bitches are jamming all communications on the planet," Lady Tech hissed.

"Did we get through to anyone?" Rogers asked.

"We're still getting through," she defiantly snorted. "Maxine is running Morse code to the White House and all four military branches. Our Commander in Chief is threatening to launch a nuke strike against that warship, and top brass is doing everything within their power to advise him not to do it."

"Any word from the Eye of Ra?"

Erica sadly shook her head, causing Rogers to curse under his breath.

"Send a respectful message to our President that if he doesn't want to be the man responsible for a billion deaths, he won't think of firing one damn nuke, lie if you have to," Rogers ordered.

"What about this chick that's been trading blows with Ms. Dennison all over our planet?" Nitro pointed. "Shouldn't we be figuring out a way to help Freedom stop her?"

"At the rate they're moving, we wouldn't be able to catch up with them," Erica answered. "Not to mention, her energy readings are three times greater than Freedom's. We wouldn't last a second against her."

"Then how is …?" A baffled Cyclone was about to ask.

"In the short period they've been fighting, Dennison doubled her energy output," Lady Tech explained. "The longer she fights, the higher it will rise, giving Freedom the power she needs to surpass her."

"If it doesn't?" Merge came with an ominous question.

"Then we need to coordinate a plan of defense and attack in case Freedom falls," Rogers answered.

~~~~~~~~~~~~~~~~~~~~~~~~~~~~~~~~~~~~

As the aerial battle across the planet continued, Attea found her task of felling Freedom to be both infuriating and fascinating as she defended and landed world-shaking blows historically known throughout the universe for toppling far more powerful ancient beings. Yet this human with not even a

Genesis

century of age on her was either tanking or defending her strikes and then returning for more.

Freedom on the receiving end felt like a rank amateur punching bag unable to find an opening after her first hit. The elf-eared alien warrior from another planet was comfortable in the sky and far more experienced in aerial combat than she was.

She was also unnerved by the sickening feline grin that barely left her face. She was clearly enjoying the battle, most likely toying with her. Freedom thought she had to do something to shake her confidence.

To make it clear that attacking Freedom and her home was a huge mistake.

Freedom went orbital, knowing she would follow; in the middle of entering the void of space, her eyes slightly widened at the sight of the dull black gargantuan extra-terrestrial killer whale-shaped ship with red alien markings on the side of its hull parked in Earth's orbit.

As jaw-dropping as the scene looked from her viewpoint, Freedom forced herself to keep her head in the game, dealing with one planet-threatening issue at a time.

The female powerhouse from the other side of the universe sent to kill her for some reason was who she had to put down first.

Freedom quickly spun around, unleashing an eyebeam blast, praying she could not dodge it.

As Attea blocked the powerful blast with her bracer, Freedom followed up with a city-destroying single-hand beam that she held for more than eight seconds.

The Thracian High General not only tanked the energy attack that could have obliterated half a continent. She barreled through it, knocking Freedom into a painful spin in the middle of weightless space.

Genesis

In an attempt to right herself, Freedom was hammered again by a painful hit that knocked her back into the upper part of Earth's atmosphere. Before she could recover, Sophia felt her hood yanked as Attea dragged her into a hypersonic dive to the planet's surface. Freedom struggling to break free now realized that, as much as it was an homage, hoods were just as inadequate as capes.

The alien Thracian warrior sprinkled insult onto her injury as she hit the brakes mid-dive, slingshotting her with her own hood while ripping it off her suit.

Freedom groaned in frustration as she tried again to recover. It was her second and third battle with Peace again, only worse. Being the most powerful superhuman on the planet meant her upper limits were never tested. She could defeat Peace only by tapping her energy reserves to push them to dangerous levels for a few minutes. In actuality, the Eye of Ra got rid of Peace by knocking her into a portal he created, sending her into the nearest black hole.

Although she had a vast knowledge of combat that she could execute due to her super eidetic memory and physical mimicry abilities, the female warrior from another world revealed to her once again that she was a green combatant due to her lack of experience.

While attempting to stop her descent and momentum, Attea flew right up to her, flipping and curling her body into a well-tucked ball. She straightened out, delivering a megaton piston-powered dropkick, turning Freedom into a pinball.

Freedom first felt and saw that she was going right through a building. She then hit the ground, tearing up everything in her path before coming to a stop. All she had time for was a groan as she pulled herself back to her feet.

She realized she was in Italy and took out the first two levels of Pisa's Leaning Tower. Her ears filled with the familiar sounds of people

Genesis

running and screaming for their lives. Freedom looked up to see Attea slowly descending to the ground with her hood in her grip.

With a sneer, she gave it a casual look over before chucking it to the ground.

"Thy must know by now that you are nothing but a plaything to me. No matter how hard you fight, there is no victory at the end of this tale for you."

Without a word, Freedom raised her hands up, turning them into fists as she got into a fighting stance. A slight smirk formed on the Thracian High General's face, realizing before her stood a fighter.

This time, they charged at one another, exchanging a flurry of punches and kicks that shook the ground, cracked glass, and brought down weakened structures. Almost eighty percent of the strikes Freedom hit Attea with were defended; the other twenty percent that did hit their target were followed up with more brutal strikes.

On the other side of the spectrum, almost ninety percent of Attea's strikes found their mark, yet much to her surprise, the human not only stood her ground standing toe to toe with her ..., but she fought harder.

In the middle of the exchange, Freedom charged her hands, amplifying her punches to deliver harder shots.

An irritated Attea decided to do the same. She only charged her right fist and aimed her strike at the ground.

In one fluid motion, she ducked one of Freedom's head removing right hooks, striking the Earth with her energy-charged fist, detonating it.

Freedom screamed as everything became blinding red. Although the heat from the blast would not kill her, it felt as if she was doused with scalding hot water. She was pretty sure she was knocked off her feet. It was confirmed

Genesis

as she felt herself bounce off the ground several times before she came to a stop.

Her body violently trembled as her eyesight went from pitch black to fuzzy.

With another painful groan, Freedom got back to her feet.

The fuzziness vanished as her eyesight came back to her, showing her horror.

Everything and everyone within a fifty-mile radius had been reduced to ash. The only cries that could be heard were from four downed Titans writhing in pain as ninety percent of their flesh had been seared from their bodies.

It was then that she realized what happened.

Whether Attea sensed, heard, or saw them, the Thracian High General knew she was about to get ambushed by some of the Earth's resident heroes. The nuclear-packed fist strike was not meant to knock Freedom backward but to clear the battlefield in one failed swoop. Aside from the felled Titans, two Mercurians were not fast enough to escape the blast. The female screamed in agony with her eyes boiling out of her skull while her taxed regenerative healing slowly worked to repair the critical damage done to her. The other Mercurian, closer to the blast point's center, lay dead, succumbing to part of his head being blown off by the explosion.

Everyone else who was not a Titan or Mercurian was turned to ash or charred bone, depending on where they were in the blast range.

A seething Freedom, no longer in control of her emotions, clenched her fists as she slowly turned to the Thracian warrior nonchalantly standing in the center of the mass destruction she caused, looking back at her.

As much as it killed her, there was no time for mourning or to help the injured.

Genesis

Freedom's war cry of vengeance was lost in the sonic boom lift-off she used to propel herself at Attea, who followed suit, barreling towards her in a superhuman game of chicken in which they both slammed into each other, creating a ginormous shockwave, sending debris and brittle structures spraying similar to leaves blown from a gale wind.

In the exchange, no quarter was given on either side as they savagely bounced off one another. Knocked several feet from the brutal impact, Earth's only champion and foreign aggressor regrouped, pouncing on the other, unleashing thunderous strikes and punches that vibrated the area they fought.

Arrogance was wiped off Attea's face as she fought, fueled by her warrior pride on the line and the rage that a mere human not only lasted this long against her but was becoming increasingly difficult to put down.

Freedom's tank was restocked by a dark place and a desire to rip the soul out of the alien invader who obliterated her home and brought senseless death and destruction to her homeworld.

She no longer cared for the reason for the attack.

She cared that she finished the fight with the interloper dead at her feet and whoever was watching from the massive ship above seeing her do it.

Attea, with several centuries of combat experience, made an amateur mistake throwing a mountain-splitting roundhouse kick that Freedom caught using the momentum to crater her into the ground with a leg fling.

A savage, sinister grin formed on Freedom's face as she kept her pitbull lock on the leg, hitting two more human-sized crater slams with the Thracian High General's body. She then performed a tornado swing, swiping her around at speeds that would have torn an EVO apart before hurling her into the sky.

Genesis

As an enraged and humiliated Attea stopped her momentum, she barely got her guard up as the human she underestimated caught up to her and struck her with a right haymaker, knocking her out of her hovering pattern.

Freedom continued to give chase, delivering another powerful right hitting her from Europe to the middle of North America.

Pumped with overconfidence, Freedom forgot for a split second who she was dealing with as she ran right into Attea, reminding her who was still stronger and faster by standing her ground in midair and smacking her out of her trajectory with a thunder-clapping right cross of her own after a quick recovery.

A stunned Freedom kept her wits about her as she rolled with the hit, strafing away, and quickly went hypersonic, performing her flash step technique, which created numerous deafening sonic booms around Attea.

The Thracian High General hovered in place, unamused and unimpressed by her attack plan, following her with just her eyes.

Freedom believing, she found an opening dove at Attea with her right fist cocked back, aiming for her blindside in an attempt to regain the upper hand she had.

All she came up with was another white dwarf star right cross punch to the jaw as the Thracian warrior quickly turned, upending her from her blindside. Freedom became a line drive hit, splitting the Mount Rushmore image of George Washington's skull into that of a cracked egg.

Attea followed up with a dive to drill her right through the entire mountain, only to run straight into Freedom, barreling back out from whence she came with a force that removed part of Jefferson's face. She landed her second solid hit on the bewildered High General, forced to go on the defensive for the first time in their battle.

Genesis

A hit that knocked her from South Dakota all the way into the middle of the Atlantic Ocean.

As Attea reeled from the punch that snapped her neck back, bloodying her lip, a smirk came over her face. It was mirrored by her brother, who leaned back in his command chair, seeing what she saw.

"Mother's ability in the body of a mere human," Merc shook his head with a chuckle. "What a small twisted little universe we dwell in."

A battle-calm Attea waited over the Atlantic as Freedom once again closed the gap between them in mere seconds before revealing her trump card.

It forced Freedom to hit the brakes as terror fell over her face.

In those seconds, she knew how Leroy from the "Last Dragon" movie felt when he faced Sho Nuff in the final battle.

Before her eyes, the warrior from another part of the universe that traveled light years to battle with her lit up the veins in her neck and face with a reddish hue matching her eyes as the power she unleashed caused a massive whirlpool in the ocean underneath her.

They lit up for only a second. Attea's skin returned to normal as her eyes continued to have a cauldron blaze while the ocean that violently swirled under her began to subside.

Not only could she tap the unfathomable power within her, but she also had perfect control over it.

The entire planet savagely jittered as every living creature felt Attea's movement, delivering a punch that split the ocean and shattered every window on the East Coast while sending Earth's mightiest champion sailing as her world turned black.

Genesis

Her body, however, would not allow her to rest as she awoke seconds before crash landing near the border of Missouri and Kansas. The crash dragged her body and tore up the main street of a small town she hit.

As she rolled to her hands and knees to spit up a thick fountain of blood and a tooth that would grow back, the daze in her eyes stayed longer as her entire body rattled from the god blow she was struck with.

She fought with her body to stand but ended up collapsing in the dirt and debris she was in as it no longer wanted to cooperate with her.

"Get up," Freedom weakly mumbled to herself. "Get …the hell …up."

She knew it was as Lady Tech had warned her. She was not invincible. Her body had a limit.

This warrior from the stars had pushed her to that limit. She had nothing left in the tank except her will to defend what was precious.

Onlookers watched from the fragile safety of their town stores or vehicles as Freedom pounded the ground with her fist while letting out a frustrated scream.

One lone male resident in his early mid-twenties with fire-red hair and a face full of freckles mustered the bravery to run to her side.

"Miss Freedom," he asked with a shaky voice. "You aight?"

"No," she shook her head with a whimpering groan. "You have to … get out … of here. She's coming ….go."

They both turned in the direction of thunder crackling across the sky with no clouds as the town trembled from the presence approaching.

Genesis

Freedom watched in disbelief as the young man, apparently racked with fear, stood up and became a wall between her and the Thracian High General.

"Are you crazy?" I said, get the hell out of here!" she screamed with a hoarse voice.

"Two years ago, before you became an official superhero, you saved a platoon of Marines from an ISIS ambush in Baghdad," the young man said without looking at her. "My older brother is alive because of you."

"No, she'll kill you."

"She's got to hit me first," he said with a smirk.

Attea, touching down, stood unamused at the lone human standing courageously between her and her prey.

"Begone boy," she softly ordered. "There is no sport in slaughtering livestock."

"I don't know who you are, lady, but your close encounter ass done came to the wrong planet!" He howled back. "You mess with one of us, you mess with all of us! Everyone take cover!"

"Aw hell, Steve-O's going for it!" an observing nearby Sheriff yelled. "Everyone hit the deck!"

Town residents began to scatter from their hiding locations, either moving further into the buildings they were in away from the windows or through back alleys, which led them away from the combat zone as the young man raised his hands and was about to conduct an orchestra.

Attea stood with narrowed eyes curiously, watching the young man with a "Make America Great" hat in his back pocket prepared to square off with her. A weakened Freedom whose strength returned at a crawl watched as, with a wave of his hand, the young man conjured up several hundred

Genesis

trillion tons of air pressure to hammer the Thracian High General into the ground, sending nearby cars flying while blowing out windows and causing structural damage to storefronts.

Getting to her feet, Freedom realized the young EVO possessed the ability to control matter itself, which was a rarity among the infected. Steve-O combined all of the air molecules with a thought and a hand gesture, turning it into a near-invisible weapon to clobber Attea into the ground. He did not let up as he focused on controlling the particles within the concrete and soil, which came to life and began to move, entrap, and cover the female Thracian warrior.

Freedom's stomach began to swirl and turn in on itself, realizing that Attea's facial expression did not change as the young man continued to bury and crush her with tons upon tons of street concrete. Freedom forced her body to cooperate and find the strength to rise.

"It's not working," she groaned. "You need to get out of here now!"

"What are you talking about?" Steve-O grinned, asking. "Ain't no way she's getting out of that!"

He moved his hands again to prove his point, turning it up a notch, adding tons more rubble on top of her.

She never got to know his full name, as the same blast that vaporized her home and tore through her island ripped open Attea's tomb once again, atomizing everything in its path, including Steve-O, while blowing a weakened Freedom clear out of the town several miles away.

Although her body absorbed most of the blast, adding it to her power, she could not withstand the destructive force it struck her with. Once again, she came to an awkward and painful crash-landing several miles outside the town.

With the power she absorbed this time, she forced herself to get up for Steve-O, who sacrificed himself to buy her some time. Somehow, she had

Genesis

to live and win, not for those counting on her but so that she could learn his full name.

Freedom thought about going to 'World Buster mode,' but what common sense that had not been knocked from her skull told her that was a suicide move for both her and the planet. With no control over the energies within her like her opponent, she would detonate, taking the Earth with her before she got a sliver of an upper hand on the warrior who had been outmatching her at every given turn.

It was then that she realized she had no clue why she was being attacked in the first place. In her rage, she had cut the female warrior off before she told her why she had invaded her island, wiping her home off the map. Freedom remembered the alien warship quietly orbiting Earth. However, this High General was the only one on the planet, creating a ruckus.

As much as Freedom wanted to get payback for the destruction of her home and critically injuring Earl, it was in her and the planet's best interest to find out what the invader wanted. As a soaring Attea approached, Sophia took a less aggressive stance, praying it was still possible to have a constructive conversation.

Her heart began to quicken as the Thracian warrior landed violently on the open plain highway and proceeded to rush her to start battle anew.

"Stop! Stop!" Freedom screamed. "I know you understand English, so stop! Why are you doing this?! What do you want with me?!"

Her words brought the High General's advance to a screeching halt. She came to an awkward stance with a befuddled look on her face. It was clear stopping in the middle of a planetary battle to the death to explain why she was attempting to murder someone was a first for her.

Freedom's face became perplexed before her eyes narrowed, attempting to read the weird expression of the being, who looked to her like a Warcraft character from space.

Genesis

She was waiting for the tumbleweed to blow by as she was pretty sure by the slight movement of her lips the High General was either talking to herself or conversing with someone very far away.

Onboard the crown prince's ship, Merc was on his feet, asking his sister a question.

"What in the name of the old Lords are you doing, Attea?"

"She has inquired about the charges against her," returned his sister. "I am obligated to inform her of them."

"No, you are not."

"Yes, I am."

"You do understand that she cannot leave this planet alive," Prince Merc pressed. "She cannot stand trial."

"Your data was most inaccurate," Attea spat back. "The human is much more resilient than she was analyzed to be, and now we know why. Her upper limits have never been tested."

"So, you can't kill her?" Her frustrated brother demanded to know while folding his arms.

"Of course, I can kill her," Attea scowled, answering. "You just might not have a planet left when I am done."

"That is the reason why you should have brought your sword, you miserable woman!"

A savage growl echoed from his sister before she retorted.

"Listen, well, brother, the one thing that will not be sacrificed during this venture of yours is my honor. Which means I will not draw my weapon

Genesis

on an unarmed opponent, and I will not continue to assault an opponent when they request to know the charges laid against them."

"I am the Crown Prince!"

"And I am the Crown Princess and High General of the Thracian Regime! Show me proper respect!"

"Excuse me! Excuse me!"

Attea turned her attention back to Freedom, beckoning her.

"I don't know who you're having a conversation with or what you are saying, but I really want to know what this is about."

Prince Merc was in the middle of telling his sister not to say another word and that he was coming down to deal with the female human himself.

Attea was about to threaten him with bodily harm if he did. It was interrupted as the sky came alive with the roar of United States fighter planes. Freedom groaned and dropped her head.

"That orange-haired orangutan looking son of a bitch …I was close. So, frigging …"

The sound of cannon fire echoing from a distance was followed by the whistle of projectiles. Both women slightly braced themselves for the tank shells that landed detonating inches from each of them. Simultaneously, the squadron of military fighters comprised of F-15E Strike Eagles, F-16 Fighting Falcons, F-22A Raptors, and F-35A Lightning IIs began making their run for an attack.

Attea did not wait for the jets to fire first.

With an extended right hand, she fired an energy blast that tore through the squadron of planes, vaporizing ten of the twenty-four aircraft that came to attack while the rest broke off. She extended her left hand to turn on

Genesis

the tanks, still firing on them when Freedom capitalized on the opening Attea left, hitting her with a stiff shoulder gut check, taking her up into the air to get them away from the US Forces before she claimed any more lives.

Her objective was to get them off the United States continent in hopes of starting the conversation that was interrupted.

Attea took Freedom's aggression as a sneak attack, signaling that their combat continued anew.

Arching her upper torso backward, Attea performed a backflip, flinging her off. Spiraling violently in midair, Freedom fought to gain control of her stability when she took a savage aerial shoulder slam from the High General. She had momentarily forgotten that the alien invader from the other world could tap and control the powers within her, bolstering both her speed and strength to incalculable levels.

Freedom's power level was not growing fast enough to catch up to the foreign invader's.

Neither one expected to be intercepted and broadsided at Attea's speed.

The hit was so brutal it broke her from the Thracian High General. Sophia spiraled uncontrollably downward back to Earth. Her enhanced eyesight caught flashes of the other two living meteors spiraling back to the planet.

Freedom impacted the ocean this time, sinking several leagues down before stopping her momentum. She rocketed back to the surface and realized she ended up in the South Atlantic Ocean.

"Goddamn, that child!" Sophia screamed with trembling lips. "Where is she? Where is she?"

Freedom went hypersonic, desperately searching for her daughter.

Genesis

The Earthshaking shockwaves emitted from the inner edge of Angola, making their way into the Congo. She had caught up with them to find Kimberly screaming as she threw mountain-toppling blows against the female invader from another planet.

Although Attea was defending quickly against her, there was a look of concern on her face as she backed up from her daughter's attacks.

This brought on a nervous feeling in Freedom's gut. Kimberly was undisputedly the second strongest EVO on the planet, but the current level of her strength was the combination of two of Earth's most massive continents. Yet, she was unleashing power shots that rattled even the Thracian warrior.

Attea, having enough of being on the defensive, backhanded an enraged Kimberly with enough force to turn her legs to rubber. She then latched onto her throat.

Kimberly's enraged mother closed the gap by rattling the heavens with her speed as she rocked the jaw of the woman who would dare lay a hand on her daughter.

Freedom was shocked that she connected, and the hit was hard enough to take Attea off her feet, sending her sailing. She ignored the path of destruction her body was causing, which went for a mile or two as she grabbed Kimberly before she hit the ground.

She ignored the pain of her trembling right hand, which was broken in several places from the punch, as she saw her daughter.

Freedom then realized what took the Thracian High General off of her game. A dazed Kimberly's teary glowing eyes fluttered between white and a gold hue.

"Baby …baby… talk to me …"

"She killed him ... she killed him," Kimberly sobbed.

Genesis

Freedom choked at her words as thick tears ran down her face.

"Earl is …"

"Sir George!" Kimberly screamed, bawling. "He never made it out! He's dead! She killed him!"

Freedom quickly drew her in, embracing her tightly.

"I'm so sorry, baby," she said while kissing her daughter's cheek. "But you have to go right now. Go back to Sanctuary before …"

Freedom's words were rattled out of her mouth as the Earth shook while smoke and debris fogged the area around them.

Freedom's heart sunk as another one adorned with a purple and black bodysuit similar to Attea's minus armor stood straight up in a sizable crater.

This one's skin was pearl white, while his long blue mane was fashioned into a Mohawk with three thick braids. His eyes glowed a tremendous deep blue glow similar to hers, signifying the immense power that coursed through his veins.

And Freedom could feel that his power was far higher than her own.

"Oh no …" she quaked.

~~~~~~~~~~~~~~~~~~~~~~~~~~~~~~~~~~~

Horus's familiar Seker hovered several miles up, watching the scene take place below. Unbeknownst to everyone, the silver and gold mechanized falcon had kept up with the battle since it began.

It was transmitting what it saw back to the EVOlution base in Colorado. Horus stood with a bright grin on his face, along with Dr.

Genesis

Alexander and Graves, on the facility's theater-sized screen, viewing what the cybernetic bird saw.

"Excellent, Seker!" Horus adulated his familiar. "The footage you collected was more than enough, but the arrival of the Thracian Crown Prince is a bonus. When my allies circulate the Dominion Council once again invading another foreign soil and imposing its will, we will incite other worlds to our cause. Powerful worlds that will ensure their fall."

Graves and Dr. Alexander fretfully made eye contact with one another, knowing that they were witnessing the planet Earth drawn into its first universal war, one that it might not survive.

~ ~

Back in Africa, Freedom, holding her daughter in her hands, shook her, getting her attention, as her eyes were transfixed on the intimidating view of Prince Merc that could be felt from where they knelt.

"Kimberly! Kimberly! Go back to Sanctuary right now! Do you hear me?"

"Mommy …"

"Go, right now! And no matter what happens, do not turn back! Do you hear me?"

She squeezed her daughter's bicep with some extra force, getting her attention.

"Go."

Streams of tears fell from Kimberly's eyes as she nodded, agreeing to obey. She took off with a leap into the air, flying away as fast as she could. Freedom did not look up to watch her leave. Instead, she rose to her feet, clenching her fists, which regenerated to the point that they cracked.

Genesis

She unleashed a war cry, stoking the rage inside of her until it spread throughout every inch of her body. Massive chunks of the ground underneath her broke apart and sprayed as she flew right at Merc.

Her attack was upended by the most crushing backhand that felt like an aluminum bat to her skull. For her, as a superhuman, it was similar to getting smacked with the planet Jupiter.

She could not tell how far she got knocked when she crashed. She knew she was still in Africa and that she suffered from massive trauma as blood began to pour from her eyes, ears, and mouth. Her regenerative healing had been taxed beyond its limits from that one strike.

"Get up," she gurgled through the blood in her throat. "Got to get…up."

She did not get up with her own strength. Freedom painfully groaned as she was pulled to her feet by her braids. She could no longer feel the ground as Merc lifted her higher.

He did so to find his target.

No words could describe the agonizing pain as she felt something sharp and cold pierce her stomach going right through her. She was more shocked that he stabbed her with the ice blue gleaming blade with black Thracian markings that looked like a mini hi-tech Gladius attached horizontally to a maroon sheath on the tailbone of his bodysuit than the fact that there was a metal that could actually pierce her flesh.

Her throat, drowning in blood, would not allow her to scream.

As the unnatural chill of death returned to reclaim her, she could feel that this time it was different as her body began to involuntarily spasm from the life draining from her.

"Why …are …you …doing …this?" Freedom got out with what little life she had left.

Genesis

Merc whispered his answer to her.

"Because I can ...now I must warn you ...the next thing you shall feel is your insides splatter as I cut you open."

Before Merc could deliver the final killing cut, the sky crackled with the sonic boom of Kimberly's hypersonic flight pattern and her blood-curdling scream as she dived toward him in an attempt to remove his head from his shoulders to save her mother.

An unfazed Merc went to pull the blade buried within her mother and slice her down.

Freedom defiantly clutched the blade, shoving it deeper with her gut, preventing him from using it on her daughter.

Merc sneered as he merely released the hilt and swatted Kimberly with a deceptive closed backfist that delivered the sickening sound of broken bones to Freedom's ears. She hung there defenseless as she watched her daughter violently crater the ground on impact.

"No ..." she squealed weakly while struggling to break Merc's grip.

Kimberly, lying face down in the dirt of Africa, drooled energy-saturated milky white blood from her lips. With a blind, dazed look, she painfully looked around for her mother.

"Mommy ...?"

"No! No! No! Leave her alone! No!"

Her pleas fell deaf upon a merciless Prince Merc as he raised his right leg and delivered a killing blow, stomping down on the back of the child's head and neck.

The sickening sound of bone breaking and the dying squeals of her daughter unleashed a high-pitched scream within Sophia as she was cast into

Genesis

the nightmarish memory of Pubudu's mother clutching and rocking his dismembered body after he was torn apart by the Sand Lion and his murderous regime. As she relived that trauma that very second, it brought forth the most destructive eyebeam blast she had ever unleashed, blasting Merc at point-blank range in the face.

The blast was enough to cause Merc a subtle form of discomfort while Sophia found the strength to rip free of his grip, leaving him with a fistful of some of her braids. On the way down, she placed her hands in the wave position, chanting the words in her head, triggering her power to seep through the pours in her hands, forming a glowing blue soccer ball.

She screamed again as she unleashed it, hitting him at point-blank range. It doubled the blast pattern Peace used to kill all of the Defenders of Justice.

The planet trembled like never before from a blast powered by a mother's rage and sorrow. She cared not that she was breaking her own rules, about the alien blade still in her gut, or where the energy wave went or what it destroyed. All she cared about was that it got him off of her daughter.

A distraught Sophia stopped an attack; she could have kept going almost indefinitely to see what had become of her daughter.

With a hand covering his face, the Crown Prince was pushed back a couple of yards only due to loosening dirt that could not hold his footing. He narrowed his eyes as he examined his suit and hands, which had visible scorch patterns.

"Interesting," he muttered to himself.

Sophia ignored him, ripping the dagger from her stomach, causing her to spit up new blood. Shutting down the pain of a wound that was slowly healing, she tossed it away and darted over to Kimberly's body. Freedom crashed knees-first into the ground as she reached in, pulling her out of the crater. She turned her face up and cradled her onto her lap. With a trembling, bloody hand, Sophia began brushing dirt from her daughter's face and body.

Genesis

"Why won't you listen to me?!" Sophia wailed. "Why won't you listen?! I told you to go home! You're going to be okay! You're going to heal and be okay! You're just like me! You're just like me!"

Merc fluttered his eyes in disgust at the gut-wrenching scene before stepping to finish the job. His advance was halted by his sister cratering the ground with her landing standing between him and a grieving mother.

"Have you lost all of your senses?" Attea furiously spat at her brother. "You cannot be here!"

"No member of the Thracian Regime can enter or set foot on this planet," Merc roared, pointing a finger at his sister. "I am a Crown Prince, and it would not be so if you had sped up your task!"

"And since when was murdering a youngling apart of your plan, brother?"

"As if you would shed a tear for the litters, we will raze the second we claim this planet! That thing is an abomination that dare raised hand against a Thracian Crown Prince! It is also additional evidence we need to cleanse this wretched species from the universe before it is too late!

Do you have any idea what would happen if she was allowed to mature with what was coursing through her veins?!

I shall personally remove the head of that half-breed right in front of his cousin! He's the only one capable of infusing that thing with, of all things, the Awakening!"

Attea stepped back, examining her brother with her eyes as if she did not recognize him.

"Your ambitions have pushed too far, brother; this is not the way of a proud Thracian! We are warriors, not butchers!"

Genesis

A scowl formed on her brother's face as he leaned in to remind her of something.

"We are whatever our people need us to be so that we can flourish …dear …sister."

In the middle of the sibling spat, a catatonic Sophia rocked back and forth, caressing and kissing a lifeless Kimberly, waiting for her regenerative healing to bring her back to life.

"You're stronger than me!" Sophia bawled. You are stronger than me! So, heal! Baby heal! Please!"

Kimberly remained unresponsive with a blank, lifeless visage as Freedom pulled her limp body closer to her bosom, kissing her forehead. She raised her head to the heavens, wailing.

"Please, don't do this! Don't take her away from me. Please! I swear I will make You pay if You do. I will make You pay!"

With those words, Sophia's running tears evaporated as her eyes became brighter than two stars, while the visible veins underneath the skin of her hands and face bulged and illuminated a blue hue.

The power boost instantly amplified her regenerative healing, repairing her wounds and injuries. The same rising energies would turn on her the second she moved aggressively.

Even if she didn't move her building power, creating a gravitation field within her would eventually tear the planet apart.

The ground gave out from underneath Freedom's feet as the output of the power she unleashed created an enormous sinkhole. Freedom instinctively hovered as she held her daughter in her arms.

Her eyes slowly raised with endless hatred and rage behind them.

Genesis

Eyes that cared for nothing else but vengeance.

All of it was turned towards Merc and Attea, who were forced to hover due to the sinkhole's expanded size. Attea, slowly turning to Freedom, frustratingly ran her hand over her braided Mohawk before glaring at her older brother.

"A star eater, your bloody milk sow whore failed to relay to you that our target was also a star eater."

Merc did not answer his sister as he stared at what could potentially be the most significant snare to his plan, glaring back at him.

"Tell me, dear brother," Attea sarcastically snarled. "What is the Council law when the said planet you are planning to acquire has been blown to atoms?"

~ ~

Back at the Ranch, the Regulator team looked in stunned disbelief as the unique alert signal blared while monitors lit up, measuring and calculating a specific familiar event that spelled the destruction of the entire planet if not stopped.

"Tell me that's not what I think it is," Rogers swallowed.

"It is," Erica whispered. "Sophia's entered World Buster mode, and it's rising faster than the last time."

~ ~

Within the Colorado base, Horus bore an expression upon his countenance he had not worn in centuries, one of great concern.

His devious plan had also hit a snare.

"Well, this was unexpected."

Genesis

Despite his near-godly mental abilities, the destruction of the planet he planned on ruling by a grieving mother was not something he foresaw.

Genesis

EPILOGUE

On the other side of the universe, billions of light-years away, the second Eye of Ra and the Eye of Set and Osiris were in the middle of a diplomatic matter. As fellow peacekeeping diplomats, the Eyes were sent to intervene with other advanced species that were not a part of the Dominion Council, depending on the situation.

Recently, they accepted a mission to venture to Volori and speak with the Volorion High Prime about claims of piracy enacted by his people on merchant starships whose species were under the protection of the Dominion Council.

All three went into the meeting knowing that Volorions were not only a species known for weapons manufacturing, arms profiteering, and skin trading (kidnapping and selling other species). They also were one of the few species that sent a message directly to the Dominion Council flat out that they would never, in their equivalent of a billion light-years, join the Council.

They would never obey nor respect any law or treaty created by the Dominion Council and then told the Dominion Council members in the vilest way what they could do with themselves and their family members.

Volori, although noted to be a far more advanced world than other civilized planets like Earth, were categorized as non-threatening on a universal level and calmly subjected to territory bans and heavy sanctions. This did little to deter the defiant Volorions, who mostly traded and sold arms to other worlds outside of the Dominion Council and continued with their skin trading ventures despite their ships being captured or destroyed when they dared to enter Dominion Council territory.

The Dominion Council continued to be diplomatic about the situation until a recent rise in piracy from Volorion ships on merchant ships either under the protection or within Dominion Council territory forced the Council's hand to take a more militaristic stance.

Genesis

As with all diplomatic and military campaigns carried out by the Council, the objective was to achieve a peace accord to avoid war at all costs while showing the Council's overall strength via the species representing them at the time. As with each situation, each Council member whose species has a massive display of militarism might volunteer for the campaign. A vote was then taken, and that species decided how best to deal with the campaign within the rules created by the Dominion Council.

In this campaign, the planet of Anu received the majority vote. So, Anu's Council of Elders decided it was best to send Anubis, Bastet, and Laurence to sit down with the Volorion High Prime and attempt to persuade him to resolve some resolution in exchange for the Council lifting some of the sanctions that were placed upon Volori.

Part of their mission in retrospect was simple; Volori under a single kingship rule meant they only had one individual to persuade as opposed to a world that may at times be comprised of several ruling parties that may not see eye to eye and might not all wish to agree to their terms. They were also granted an audience and allowed to land instead of being shot out of the planet's orbit, which was another good sign to Laurence.

His opinion changed when Anubis's red luminous chariot class starship entered Volori's clear blue-green atmosphere. As they descended to the capital city of Vennatara, Laurence noticed that there was barely any plant life visible in the gleaming cold ice-blue metallic metropolitan. Through visiting planets in the known universe over the years, Laurence learned to become wary of civilizations with a severe lack of foliage.

They were allowed to land at the capital's central transport hub.

As they exited the craft, they were greeted by a heavily armed guard who informed them that they would be escorted by foot to the main capitol building to meet with the High Prime. It was the first insult, as it was a standard universal courtesy to provide some type of transport vehicle to the meeting location. Unfazed, the trio of Eyes began their walk, surrounded by their escort. During their trek to the capital, Laurence noticed large grated

Genesis

vents in the metal ground blasting high oxygenated air concentrations into the sky.

He also noticed the citizens of Volori observing them from afar during their trip to the central capital building.

Volorions appeared like humanoid hairless cats with feathers that mainly grew on their heads and back. Male Volorions only grew one solid color of feathers, while females grew many-colored feathers. Both male and female skin color varied from pale pink to cocoa brown; they were also one of three known races where most of the population had one eye color, a gleaming sky blue. The males grew their feathers mostly on their heads or none, while the females grew their feathers on the top of their heads down to the small of their backs. Most male Volorions in the capital were nobles, statesmen, or soldiers adorned in two-toned color-fitting robes with mandarin collars and solid single-color skirt flaring pants. The females wore risqué outfits that accentuated their backs, chests, rears, and legs.

From Laurence's perspective, it appeared the females were more forced to adorn the saucy outfits as they wore collars around their necks while their male counterparts held the leash attached to the collar; they were also made to walk subserviently behind their males with their heads down. His eyes caught the scowls and dirty looks from male Volorions aimed at Bastet as she walked around minus a leash and side by side with himself and Anubis. Laurence also noticed the intentional show of military might as there was a line of light and heavy cybernetic power suits, mechs, battle tanks, and aerial war machines on the streets leading all the way to the main capital building.

What caught Laurence's attention was the Volorion war armor, which appeared to be a cool hi-tech mesh between ancient Roman, English knight, and Samurai armor. From his brief research on Volorion wartech, the armor consisted of the wearer donning a skin-tight grey bodysuit known as the membrane. The membrane had glowing red tubes that looked like veins running throughout the suit. The membrane housed the armor's power supply, which was rumored to be on a nuclear level while controlling the armor when attached via neural control. The wearer could switch out inter-changeable

Genesis

pieces, make light or heavy armor, add additional armament or power supply, or connect the standard armor to an even larger mechanized suit for more indomitable power.

Although he found it impressive, it was the second offense the Volorions enacted that the trio noted but pretended to ignore as they continued onto the main capital building.

As they came upon it, the outside appeared to Laurence to be a mesh between the Sydney Opera House and the Kremlin in cold, gleaming metallic blue.

The inside was similar to the outside as they were escorted to the High Prime's throne room, except the hallways were filled with statues and paintings that remembered former rulers and told the history and campaigns of the Volorion Empire. From Laurence's observation, they savagely beat the top five most evil empires in human history.

As they entered the High Prime's courtroom, they found him sitting casually on his throne of yellow crystal and gleaming silver metal with Volorion etchings carved into it. He wore a two-tone green and maroon regal robe and dark maroon skirt pants. Around his neck was the equivalent of a crown in a bright gold chain and triangle pendant with Volorion markings in the metal and a red four-point crystal in the center. He was a middle-aged male for his species with smooth, ashy white, wrinkled skin and plumage of red feathers on his head.

Sitting at the foot of his throne on a pillow in a white sheer material dress was his mate and Queen, a very young and attractive Volorion for her species with pale white smooth skin and bright multi-color feathers from the top of her head down to her back. To the right of his throne was his eldest son, High Prince Volker, dressed in his royal military outfit consisting of a top with two-tone colors of blue and purple with a Volorion War Chief's military decorations; his pants were midnight black. He wore a chain around his neck, similar to his father's, except the chain's color was shiny metallic silver, and the gem in the center was aqua-blue. His face bore a

Genesis

confrontational demeanor of disdain and disgust as his eyes locked onto each of them but shifted more between Laurence and Bastet as the formal announcement and greets were concluded, and negotiations began with Anubis speaking on behalf of the Council.

Anubis began by calmly stating that the Dominion Council could no longer turn a blind eye to the pirating incidents implemented by the High Prime's people against merchants' vessels under the protection of the Council. The High Prime flatly said that neither he nor his people recognized the Dominion Council laws and for Anubis to prove the alleged acts of piracy.

A calm and diplomatic Anubis called forth one of his familiars, who rose from the resting place on his wrist and projected live holographic images of Volorion ships attacking and boarding merchant vessels. As the familiar zoomed in on the markings identifying the crafts as Volorion, Anubis also pointed out that the raids were made within the territorial borders under the protection of the Council backed by maps his familiar produced showing the territories and the triangulated attacks.

The following statement to come out of the High Prime's mouth was the possibility that the images were probably doctored, to which Anubis's familiar projected confessions of captured Volorion pirates identifying themselves as citizens of Volori and going into detail about their acts of piracy.

The High Prime's response was one of indifference, stating that if the Dominion Council had the perpetrators of the crime in custody, what reason was there to come to him with such a trivial matter. He said that he would not be bargaining for any of their release and that the Council could punish the pirates however they deemed fit.

Anubis verbally hammered home the Dominion Council's ultimatum. Either the High Prime took measures to outlaw and deter his subjects from piracy, in which case the Council would lift twenty percent of their sanctions on his planet and reopen three trade roots. Or the Council would double the sanctions already imposed and permanently close off one

Genesis

of its significant arms trade roots. He then reminded the High Prime that his decision to accept or refuse their offer would be final when they left the planet and the actions taken after that.

The High Prime leaned back on his throne with a cold smile on his visage, slowly pulling back on his Queen's leash, forcing her to adjust her sitting posture.

The High Prime then asked his son what he made of the offer. The High Prince advised his father to take the proposal under one condition. The condition was a vile and sordid between himself and the Eye of Osiris.

Bastet's response to the High Prince's condition was anything but diplomatic.

She started to laugh …really hard.

Her actions caused Laurence to roll his eyes and Anubis to drop his head into his chest.

For it is well known in the universe that it was ill-advised to mock or laugh at a Volorion unless one intended to get into a deadly confrontation with one.

Bastet's hysterical outburst enraged the High Prince and infuriated his father, who arrogantly proposed that he might join his son in defiling the Eye of Osiris.

This caused Bastet to pause and then laugh even harder.

As Anubis and Laurence watched the High Prime rise to his feet from his throne, it was clear to them that negotiations had failed miserably.

"So, this is how you come to my homeworld and make terms, Annunaki?" The High Prime snarled. "I kindly allow you to have an audience with me, and you, in turn, allow your sow of a cousin to disrespect my son, and most importantly, me in my very own throne room?"

Genesis

Then, Bastet stopped laughing, wondering if the High Prime had lost all senses, not realizing who he just called a sow, while Laurence held up a hand, begging her not to retort.

"In all fairness, High Prime Vbzarma," Anubis calmly sighed. "Your son did disrespect my cousin first."

"And you forget the ground you stand upon and the air you breathe whelp!" High Prime Vbzarma roared, "This is Volori, not Anu, which means by Volorion law, she should have come stripped of armor and weapons, and with a proper leash around her neck! Maybe even a bridle to hold that wagging tongue of hers!"

"With all due respect, High Prime," Laurence stepped in with steel in his tone, "Have a care how you speak of my cousin in front of me."

"And now the micro-breed mongrel dares to give warning to me in my own throne room," the High Prime scoffed.

"High Prime Vbzarma, let us not debase ourselves with youngling prattle," Anubis requested, stepping forward to calm the inflamed situation. "Let us return to center and respect so that we may have a more constructive conversation."

"Nay son of Set, there shall be no further constructive conversation!" snapped the High Prime. "Your Council's threat of cutting off the major source of how I feed my people saw to the destruction of any conversation, never to rise. Instead, I intend to send a message back to your Council."

At that moment, the throne room doors opened as additional soldiers came flooding in, circling the trio with heavy combat armor and massive energy hand cannons.

"The message shall be a box sent back to Anu with three items," the High Prime savagely grinned, explaining. "Two of the items shall be the heads of the Eye of Set and the micro-breed Eye of Ra with their members in

Genesis

their mouths, while their bodies are crucified on one of our moons as a warning to those who would dare threaten the Volorion Empire. The third shall be a viewing crystal so that the Council of Elders can watch as the Eye of Osiris is mounted by every male Volorion and beast we can find that can stiffen drill and spill seed, starting with my son who she offended. Do know that the only reason I allowed you to safely come to Volorion is the opportunity to capture, study, and reverse engineer your armor and technology. We have clients throughout the cosmos who would pay heavy coin to get weapons to rival that of an Eye."

"So, I take it negotiations are over?" Anubis calmly asked.

"Yes, Whelp of Set, they are indeed over," the High Prime coldly answered. "Seize them!"

On the High Prime's last two words, the trio's familiars came to life, laying down vicious salvos of energy blasts, leveling guards around them while thinning out the circle as the remainder retreated. Although a powerful energy barrier shield protected the area where the High Prime's throne was, he and his son dived for cover behind his massive throne, abandoning his Queen as she screamed, curling up into a ball where she sat.

"Take care not to harm the royal family, especially the Queen," Anubis advised while his armor completed its change to Sentinel mode, "We do not need to start a diplomatic incident."

"I assumed we were already in one," Laurence stated while taking hold of Sol in transformed staff mode.

"You still have much to learn, cousin!" Bastet answered.

With her transformed familiar in its nine-cat tails whip mode, Bastet, also in sentinel mode, smacked away energy blasts coming in her direction before letting her lashes fly, slicing through anyone unfortunate enough to be in range. Because her familiar controlled the length its tail extended, she could rack up a massive body count on her side.

Genesis

On the other side of the throne room, Laurence skillfully twirled his staff, swatting away return plasma rounds; with a spin, he evaded an energy round coming straight for his head and unleashed a concentrated blast of cosmic Awakening energy that obliterated the soldiers in front of him as well as the wall behind them.

Not to be outdone, Anubis smacked away energy cannon blasts with his familiar transformed khopeshes and, with a swing, sent a slashing wave of primordial Awakening energy, laying waste to a horde of Volorion soldiers. With the initial attack party decimated and in disarray, the Eye of Ra and Osiris exited through the massive hole Laurence created while Anubis turned to the petrified Volorion Queen, shaking where she sat.

"We are honored by your hospitality," the Eye of Set bowed, addressing her. "Please inform your husband once he comes out of cowering that we are taking our leave of his planet."

She slowly nodded as Anubis turned to leave through the same hole, following the path of destruction his cousins were causing back out to the steps of the capitol building. As he stepped out into the light, he saw what they saw.

Waiting for them was from their count half of the Volorion War Legion, with more to come. Leading the assault was the High Prime's second eldest son, High Prince Nofarrzo, who donned his Volorion war suit on top of a hovering, fully armed Bird of Prey.

To Laurence, the metallic black one-person fighter was an amalgamation of the speeder bike from the Return of the Jedi and a metallic hunting bird minus the head. The razor-sharp wings and tail feathers were extended as it hovered via the three powerful anti-gravity engines, two of which were located in the vehicle's front main body, and the one in the back central powerplant was also housed.

"Surrender Annunaki swine and be granted a merciful death as we will allow!" The High Prince howled at them. "Resist, and we shall make sure your Council is haunted by the agonizing screams you shall make, which we will send back to them!"

Once again, the trio of cousins glanced at one another before Anubis answered.

"Apologies, High Prince Nofarrzo, but we choose to resist."

On Anubis's words, all three Eyes unleashed hell on the Volorion War Legion, obliterating vast chunks of their line while causing utter chaos.

"They're mad …they're bloody mad!" High Prince Nofarrzo choked. "Kill them! Kill them all!"

Watching from a distance now dawned in his own war suit, the Volorion High Prime, accompanied by High Prince Volker in his own war suit, began to understand why the Council of Elders confidently sent three Annunaki warriors by themselves with one ship and no backup. Though Volorion weapons technology was far superior to many other worlds in the known universe, it was terrifyingly dwarfed by Annunaki tech and combat prowess.

Anubis took juggernaut steps as he blocked enemy fire with incredible accuracy, sending waves upon waves of destructive Awakening energy attacks, vaporizing chunks of the Legion's heavy armored division, which consisted of their Dominator tanks. Red and black gargantuan thirty-foot-tall crab-like vehicles with quadruped legs, two plasma beam cannons on the main body's side, and other armaments. The main body rotated and elevated via an arm attached to its underbelly and base legs, allowing it to execute three hundred and sixty-degree attacks.

With one mighty leap, the Son of Set propelled himself at one, slicing the arm that lifted the body in half, bringing it down on top of its legs, causing a massive explosion. Before he landed, he sliced off one of the Dominator's legs from behind, causing it to topple for a violent explosive crash.

Genesis

"Nyoi-bō mode, Sol," Laurence commanded.

Upon his order, his familiar extended its staff form in his grip several yards until it impaled a combat ground chariot. The ground vehicle, which had the characteristics of an Earth tank except that it was more heavily armored, hovered via an anti-gravity propulsion system, and the main gun on its turret was shorter due to its firing armor-melting plasma energy rounds.

Getting a good grip, Laurence swung his staff while pulling the chariot, mowing down anyone or anything that was unfortunately in his circle of destruction. He finally released the chariot, sending it tumbling and crashing, causing further carnage.

"Thirty-Six Chambers mode, Sol."

His familiar retracted and transformed into a three-section staff as he fluidly transitioned to deflecting return fire from troops still standing and willing to fight. He returned offensively, adopting Anubis's tactic of sending ground-splitting waves of Awakening blasts cutting through the Volorion Legion.

Bastet, not to be outdone by her cousins, was the only one to use flight and speed, darting in and out, ripping through vast sections of the Legion while switching her familiar's whip mode between bolo and cat of nine tails at her leisure depending on her prey. Standing against a Dominator, she used her familiar's bolo whip mode to grab the giant machine by its arm. She dug in with one arm and used the brute strength of her armor to pull and bring it brutally crashing down on its side, causing the main cabin to ignite from the impact blowing up in front of her.

"So, this is the infamous Volorion War Legion," Bastet sighed. "I grow bored already, cousins; when do we depart?"

"You are the last person to utter the words 'bored'," Laurence sternly answered her.

"What vexes you this time?" Bastet asked with a snapping tone.

Genesis

"What were the two things we were told by the Council of Elders on five separate occasions before we departed on this mission?" He began to lecture her while still fighting. "What were we told one final time before we even left? Number one, do not react to anything that takes place on Volori, no matter how much it offends you, and number two, do not laugh at a Volorion, especially anyone from the royal family!"

"I did not react," she defended herself.

"No, you laughed…twice!"

"Did you not hear what the little pubescent brat and his father claimed they'd do to me with their thimble-sized tails?" Bastet scoffed. "Be glad composure and not sense of reason was the only thing that escaped me."

"Well, then you may have the pleasure of explaining to the Elders why negotiations failed."

"Gladly!" she chuckled while turning to dispatch several armored ground soldiers. "Mother, in particular, will split her sides once she hears comedic tale of the Volorion Royal male bloodline's pathetic advances toward her daughter."

"Both of you hold your bloody tongues and bring more carnage to Volorion Legion!" An irritated Anubis howled. "I wish to return to ship and leave this wretched planet! One of you thin out those warships firing down upon us!"

"They're mine, cousin," Bastet called dibs, "Mafdet."

Her familiar transformed from its whip configuration into an archer's bow. As she pulled the string back, taking aim at a ship, energy began to charge from the mouth of Mafdet's head, which was positioned at the center of the bow. She released the string, causing a thin beam of energy to fire from Mafdet's mouth, cutting through the air and piercing right through

Genesis

a Volorion warship, which was one size bigger than Anubis's Star Class Chariot and had the shape of a flat metallic gunmetal grey hammer. It drifted and exploded in mid-air before crashing violently into the ground, erupting into a fireball of flames. Bastet plucked her bow, sending rapid-fire shots into the sky, setting it aflame with Birds of Preys and warships that detonated on impact after being hit by her fatal shots.

The Eye of Ra decided to take a more direct approach to the air and use his body and armor as a human bullet plowing through warship after warship, bringing down more destruction on top of the Volorion Legion below.

"Is there a reason why we're not just teleporting back to our ship and going on our merry way?" Laurence irritatingly asked while hovering in mid-air.

"Have you learned nothing since being an Eye all these years, cousin?" Anubis chastised him. "Dimensional portals are for traveling, not fleeing! We walked here to the capital; we shall walk back to our ship. If the Volorion Legion wishes to attempt to impede our journey, that is their misfortune."

"There's a chance they'll destroy it before we get there at this rate," Laurence informed them.

"The High Prime in his arrogance would not give up the chance to either keep and study or auction off a ship belonging to the Eye of Set," Anubis gruffed. "And if he does, I shall be taking reparations by laying waste to his entire Legion."

Anubis backed up his threat by unleashing a sword-slicing wave of Awakening energy that cut a Dominator in two, causing it to erupt into flames as parts hit nearby vehicles or came crashing down on top of troops on the ground.

"Laurence, we must return to Earth immediately," Sol's voice emitted into his helm.

Genesis

"What is it, Sol?" He nervously asked, "Something wrong with my father?"

"No, I just received word that the Thracian Regime has quarantined the planet." It reported.

A cold chill ran through his body as he forgot he was in a battle with a planet's entire army.

"Say what?!"

In the middle of the startling revelation, a squadron of Bird of Preys descended on the Eye of Ra. Laurence barely deflected and evaded a barrage of plasma fire attacks as he used hypersonic speeds to outrun them and ascend higher into Volori's atmosphere to hear what Sol had to say.

"Why, for what reason?!"

"I cannot confirm," Sol answered him. "What I can confirm is that there is a warrant for the arrest of the human known as Sophia Dennison."

"Freedom, what would the Dominion Council want with her?" Laurence asked with concern.

"I am barred from confirming the reason behind the warrant. I have confirmed that Prince Merc's warship has quarantined the planet."

"What in the name of the Awakening are you doing up there, Danjuma?!" Anubis's voice roared into his helm.

The Eye of Ra cursed as he divebombed back into the capital, tearing through the Bird of Preys that attempted to catch up with him. Halfway down, he pulled out of the dive and savagely landed, crushing a Volorion War Chariot on impact.

"Anubis! Bastet! We need to wrap this up now and leave!"

Genesis

"Why?!" Anubis asked while cutting down several Volorion soldiers in heavily armored war suits.

"I need to get to Earth! Merc has my homeworld quarantined by order of the Council! I must know why!"

They both saw the seriousness of his visage in their helms' display and agreed without uttering another word to cut their visit to Volori short.

"Sol open a ..."

"I was attempting to," Laurence's familiar answered before he could give the command. "Something very powerful has been activated interfering with the dimensional connection. It appears the Volorions have employed an energy shield around the entire planet."

"We are detecting the same field," chimed in Anubis's familiars.

In the middle of their discussion, the sky went black as they turned to see the Volorion War Legion's numbers replenished with quadruple the numbers that initially attacked them. Their audio systems picked up the sickly cackling of the High Prince Nofarrzo from his War Chariot.

"Unable to leave via your precious portals, Annunaki? That is due to our planetary barrier shield, which is powered by both our sun and the core of Valori itself! Lesson learned from the end of the Razcargian Conflict! There is no place to flee, no aide will be coming to you, and you have no chance of defeating our War Legion!

One more thing: I was told to inform you that an old friend of your father's sends his regards."

The trio of cousins glanced at one another, perplexed by his last statement.

"You are trapped, and your fate is sealed! Surrender, and you may still be granted a quick death!"

Genesis

"You misspeak again, High Prince Nofarrzo," Anubis calmly answered back.

The smug look on the High Prince's face dropped as Valori's ground shook while the Menos on Anubis's armor went from gold to a gleaming blue color while the Ember parts of his armor containing Awakening energy blazed the brightness of a blue star. The eyes of his Jackola animated helm glowed well as it emitted a low, rumbling growl.

The Menos on Bastet's armor turned emerald green, while the primordial energies within the Ember crystals in her armor sent a blinding green light that reflected off her armor. Her feline-themed helm also came alive, unleashing a high-pitched hissing sound.

Finally, the faceplate to Laurence's helm came up as his Menos turned from silver to gold while covering his face, forming a secondary helm of an eagle-type creature from Anu that screeched, coming alive. The reddish-gold Ember crystals on his armor mimicked his cousins' armor as all three completed their Celestial mode transformations.

"It is you, who are trapped here ...with us," Anubis coldly corrected him.

THE STORY WILL CONTINUE IN "WAR OF MORTAL GODS" (BOOK ONE)...

Genesis
ABOUT THE AUTHOR

Kipjo K. Ewers was born on July 1, 1975. At an early age, he had an active imagination. By the time he started kindergarten, he would make up fictitious stories; one of his favorites was about a character named "Old Man Norris," who hated everyone in the world except for him.

When he attended our Lady of Victory Elementary School in Mount Vernon, he continued writing and reading stories to his classmates. Sometimes, the children would laugh. His teacher, Mrs. Green, would remind them that some of the great stories they read came about that way.

After elementary school, he went to Salesian High School in New Rochelle, NY, and then on to Iona College.

He would work for several major firms and companies within the New York area, but his passion was to become a journalist/writer. Therefore, it is not surprising he decided to write his first book/novel.

Kipjo began working and creating a new superhuman universe,

Genesis

finding inspiration and solace in losing his first daughter due to an unfortunate miscarriage that devastated both his loving wife and him; he began writing a hero origin story now titled "The First."

After publishing "The First" in 2013, Kipjo wrote two more follow-up novels to the series, a spin-off novel titled "The Eye of Ra" and a romantic supernatural story titled "Fred & Mary."

Now known as the EVO Universe, Kipjo continues to write to expand the series and create new projects for the foreseeable future.

Thank you for reading and for your support.

Made in the USA
Columbia, SC
14 August 2024

f334d553-6472-41ee-a45a-381770b59067R01